Nowhere to Hide

Stephen Puleston

ABOUT THE AUTHOR

Stephen Puleston was born and educated in Anglesey, North Wales. He graduated in theology before training as a lawyer. Nowhere to Hide is his seventh novel in the Inspector Drake series

www.stephenpuleston.co.uk
Facebook:stephenpulestoncrimewriter

OTHER NOVELS

Inspector Drake Mysteries

Brass in Pocket
Worse than Dead
Against the Tide
Dead on your Feet
A Time to Kill
Written in Blood
Prequel Novella– Ebook only - Devil's Kitchen

Inspector Marco Novels

Speechless
Another Good Killing
Somebody Told Me
Prequel Novella– Ebook only -Dead Smart

ISBN: 9781082207235

In memory of my mother
Gwenno Puleston

Chapter 1

Panic gripped Dawn Piper's thumping heart. She let out a long slow breath as she pressed her body tight against the wooden door that creaked a complaint. Her pulse spiked when a light came on in the small bedroom window at the top of the stone-built end-of-terrace property in front of her.

She leaned out as slowly as the fear pumping through her body would allow. A yellow streetlight cast a dull, soft glow along the narrow lane in her direction. She half expected to see the black Audi, graphite alloys and tinted glass parked on the street under the light, waiting for her. A red car filled with youngsters, music blaring. drove past and she enjoyed a moment of temporary relief.

Turning her gaze, she peered down the lane. It led into one of the other terraced streets and a sense of panic returned. Maybe he had parked where the lane emerged onto the street. Perhaps he was leaning on his car. Waiting for her.

Going home was out of the question – he knew where she lived. Only one person could help her now and negotiating the maze of side alleys and narrow lanes would be the only way she could make it unscathed.

She drew the zip of her fleece tight against her chin and started walking. It wasn't cold, but she felt alone and frightened and it comforted her to feel wrapped up.

She slowed as she neared the junction and pressed herself against one wall until she could cast a surreptitious glance along the street. Her breathing returned almost to normal. A couple walking caught her attention. She watched them as they chatted amiably before their conversation died as they opened their front door. A few cars had mounted the pavement but there was no Audi in sight. Reassured by its absence she gazed at the houses. Lights burned in downstairs rooms, television screens flickered across net curtains.

She darted over the road and into another alley where tall walls bounded rear yards. The gloom enveloped her, matching her mood. It was easy now looking back, regretting past decisions, foolishly believing she was invincible, immune. She paced on.

Cats scrambled over bins with insecure lids. The stink of rubbish and urine grew stronger as she neared a property where music thumped. Oddly it gave her a sense of safety. Here, she was amongst people with ordinary lives untainted by the drugs that fuelled the desperation in the town. She jogged down to the end of the lane and another junction with a row of terraced properties. She stopped abruptly checking that he wasn't there. And that it was safe.

The headlights of a car turned into the street and she crept back into the shadows drawing her face away from the light. The vehicle passed her and slowed before parking. She read the time. None to spare.

He couldn't possibly know where her friend lived. Confidence built that he had abandoned his search when she reached the end of the lane and his Audi was nowhere in sight. She dismissed as paranoia a nagging doubt in her mind that he could have changed his car or, even worse, that he might have an accomplice with a different vehicle.

There was no time for self-doubt now: she had to get on.

She had to reach her friend's place. She had to be safe.

At the next junction she glanced swiftly to either side and dashed across the road in the direction of the lane near the rugby club. There could be danger there she knew. She drew the collar of the fleece tighter against her face.

Her breathing became heavy and sweat pricked her brow as she walked purposefully towards the flat-roofed building by the goal posts. She kept her head low, but her eyes darted around. The smell of a barbecue lingered in the air. A man passed on the opposite side with a greyhound panting at a leash. She gave the customers of the club the briefest glance as they disgorged from the building and headed for the waiting taxis.

She darted into the lane and then ran to the bridge crossing a stream in a few quick strides. Ahead of her a tarmac path, badly in need of repair, stretched out over a field.

In the distance was her friend's house; it reassured her that safety was in sight.

Moonlight was her only guide, but she had strolled along the path so many times she knew her way. She paused and glanced over her shoulder – nothing. Then she looked ahead – there was no movement, nobody waited in the street at the top of the field.

Clambering over a stile, she lost her footing and stumbled onto a grassed area. Only a few more feet, she was nearly at safety. She scrambled upright and then she noticed ahead of her the sidelights of a car. A vehicle she recognised. A black Audi.

A bead of sweat formed on her forehead and her right leg shook as she stood rooted to the spot. From the shadows a person emerged.

'Hello, Dawn.'

She frowned away her recognition as her blood turned icy-cold when she sensed the presence behind her. A gloved hand smothered her face and mouth drowning out the gathering scream. Then a voice whispered.

'You do realise there's nowhere to hide.'

Then she saw the brief flash as he raised the knife and she knew he was right.

Chapter 2

Ian Drake had time to spare before the meeting at the Deeside community centre was due to start so he found a café where he hoped he wouldn't look too conspicuous. But the carefully knotted navy striped tie, the white shirt under the dark grey suit, together with the file of papers tucked under his arm would probably give him away as a police officer to anyone interested in paying him attention. He should have read the briefing memoranda the evening before, but Annie had insisted that the final arrangements for their trip to Disneyland Paris at the end of the school holidays was his priority. Completing the details with his ex-wife Sian had been protracted and since everything had been finalised his daughters Helen and Megan had talked of little else.

An extended television documentary and recent high-profile press coverage had resulted in Superintendent Price insisting that Drake attend the Deeside Community Action Group as a senior member of the major crime team. Price's comments about the effectiveness of the officers dealing with tackling the so-called 'county lines' drug activity couldn't be repeated, and Drake wondered if his impending retirement was contributing to a certain exaggerated indiscretion. Price had muttered darkly at their last meeting that the appointment of his successor was imminent.

Drake sat at a window seat and the waitress who appeared by his table took his order for an Americano. She looked irritated when he insisted it have two shots of espresso. He laid out the file in front of him and began reading the paperwork. Working on a complex cross border drug investigation was difficult and the details of the three deaths from overdoses in the previous six months were harrowing. Drug dealers from the inner cities of England took advantage of children and vulnerable adults to sell drugs in their home areas using burner phones that called only one number: another untraceable mobile. The cynical activity of the city centre drug dealers using impressionable youngsters in the Deeside towns of Queensferry, Shotton, Connah's Quay and north along the coast to Flint, sickened Drake.

The waitress returned with a coffee its surface a respectable cream colour. An Italian type biscuit in colourful plastic packaging nestled in the saucer. Drake stirred the drink needlessly – he never added sugar. It was mid-morning and the café was full of elderly women and young mothers with toddlers and pushchairs. Despite feeling out of place, nobody gave him a second glance, so he turned back to his papers.

The county lines suppliers from Birmingham or Liverpool had been staking a claim to the drugs trade in the north-east Wales towns straddling the Dee estuary. Drake read briefing notes from the detective sergeant in charge of the investigation. Progress was painfully slow, witnesses reluctant to come forward, Drake guessed that lives had been threatened, silence was safer than cooperating with the police.

The sergeant hadn't established yet in which of the conurbations of England the gang directing the drug trade was actually based. The report referenced some second-hand intelligence that pointed to the users being in the Liverpool area and at other times Birmingham. No conclusion had been made about whether this meant a gang moving from one city to another or two separate organised crime groups. Frustration seeped from every sentence. Drake sympathised with the task the team faced.

Superintendent Price had included copies of correspondence from various stakeholders including the social services department of the local authority and belligerently-toned letters from a charity complaining at the inactivity from the police inquiry leading to the possibility of more deaths. More chillingly was the tone of reports from other police forces about the use of knives in county lines related violence and murders.

The absence of intelligence contributed to the impression things weren't going well. Without evidence there wasn't a great deal they could do and gathering that evidence could be painstaking and laborious.

The strength of the coffee pleased Drake and discarding the packaging on the saucer rim he crunched on the biscuit. He turned his attention to the minutes of the last meeting: recording no more than the briefest summary and at its end an agreed course of action. His role was to support the sergeant in charge of the county lines investigation, add gravitas, look important. Satisfied he was as prepared as he could be, he left enough change for the coffee and walked back to his car.

After a short drive he parked outside the community centre. A room on the first floor had been set aside with tables forming a square in the middle and eight chairs neatly arranged around them.

Drake recognised Sergeant Jim Finch standing by a table from an inter-departmental meeting. The officer had struck him as thorough if a little intense. He pushed out a hand towards Drake, whispering. 'I'm really glad you could attend.'

'Is it going to take long?'

Finch made certain no one else could hear his reply. 'You know what these do-gooders are like. Depends how long they talk. We could be here for hours.'

Drake hoped that that wasn't an accurate prediction. A tall man with an ill-fitting suit came over. A tie knotted clumsily hung below the collar of his shirt.

'George Beedham – county councillor.' He thrust out a hand.

Drake offered his own and Beedham yanked Drake's hand towards him giving it a violent shake at the same time. 'I hope you've got something constructive to tell us.'

The accent was typical of north-east Wales, a watered-down version of the harsh Scouse tones from Liverpool, but he had a politician's inflated sense of his own importance. He made the statement sound as though Drake were single-handedly responsible for the area's drug problem.

'Good morning, Councillor Beedham.'

Activity at the other end of the room drew Drake's attention and he glanced over Beedham's shoulder as three women sat down, one of whom announced it was time to start.

As Drake pulled up a chair, Finch whispered, 'The chair of the meeting is Toni Walker who works for social services; next to her is Olivia Knox, an outreach worker for a drugs charity. Watch the sparks fly between her and Beedham. Everybody else is here to make up the numbers.'

'Sounds exciting,' Drake whispered back.

Finch rolled his eyes.

'I'm sure that everyone has read the minutes of our last meeting.' Walker raised her voice just enough to silence the murmurs. Drake counted six other people around the square-shaped collection of desks. Beedham had his smartphone on a file in front of him alongside two ballpoint pens.

Walker continued. 'I'm delighted to welcome Detective Inspector Ian Drake of the Wales Police Service to his first meeting of the Deeside Community Action Group.'

Drake silently dreaded the implication his attendance at more meetings was expected. He gave Walker a courteous nod.

'Perhaps everyone could introduce themselves.' Walker gave Drake an inclusive sort of glance.

Drake followed the various voices as the attendees announced who they were. Drake recognised most of the participants from the minutes of the previous meetings.

Walker turned to Olivia Knox sitting by her side once everyone had identified themselves. 'Olivia, perhaps you can bring us up to date with the latest developments in the programme you're pursuing.'

'Thank you, chair,' Knox said.

As Knox outlined various outreach work she and a body of volunteers were doing with vulnerable adults and youngsters deemed to be at risk, Drake glanced around the room. Beedham was paying little attention and fiddled with his mobile before adjusting the ballpoints needlessly. He struck Drake as a sort of cardboard cut-out figure of a councillor who had his own agenda and wasn't going to listen to common sense from anybody.

Knox's intense tone suggested that to disagree with her would be the height of stupidity. Occasionally she paused for dramatic effect after making a serious point which was met with equally serious nods and encouragement from some of the other participants. Drake struggled to remember their names, but he knew they were social workers or probation officers.

Knox lost the sympathy of the meeting as she droned on. It was about time Walker cut across her and invited comments, Drake thought. But she gazed over at Knox with a thoughtful sympathetic look on her face.

'Isn't it time we heard from some of the other stakeholders?' Beedham announced.

Knox gave him an angry glare.

Walker looked perplexed, almost surprised, by his untimely interruption. 'Well… I suppose… Olivia, have you finished?'

Knox shrugged, the irritation clear on her face.

A social worker sitting to the left of Drake made complimentary comments about the programme Knox had outlined referring to statistics compiled by the local authority suggesting drug usage was declining. From the surprised faces of the others present, Drake could see no one shared her optimism.

'Come off it.' Beedham raised his voice. 'We all know that the county council's statistics aren't worth the paper they're written on.'

Even from across the table Beedham had been able to intimidate the social worker, who visibly cowered. He continued undaunted. 'What I want to know is what the police are doing about it. Our streets are awash with drugs. We all know there are suppliers on every street corner practically. So why aren't they being picked up, arrested, interrogated and locked up?'

'I'm not sure it's that easy, Councillor Beedham,' Walker announced formally whilst glancing over at Finch and Drake.

'It's always very difficult to give specifics about operational matters,' Finch began.

'Don't give me that crap,' Beedham said.

Finch continued undeterred. 'We are working on several lines of enquiry involving valuable intelligence. It would be improper to discuss the details of what's involved.'

'That's really not good enough. We've had three deaths. Are they being investigated as possible murders?'

'It's—'

'Isn't it about time you did something? How seriously is the Wales Police Service taking all this, Detective Inspector Drake?'

Drake moved in his chair, taking a moment to gather his thoughts. 'Investigations like these are never easy. The last thing we would want is for a prosecution to fail because the evidence hadn't been correctly assembled.'

'That's not an answer. It's throwing sand in my face.'

Walker butted in. 'We have to respect the formalities the police have to follow as part of their investigation.'

'And we've got a right to expect the police to do everything they can to catch the people flooding drugs into Deeside.'

'It can be a slow process,' Drake said. 'These drug dealers can be clever and resourceful.'

'That sounds like an excuse to me.'

Drake took another few seconds. Beedham was getting under his skin. He was the most self-important little man and intensely annoying.

'The practicalities of day-to-day policing make it difficult for us to provide you with specific information.'

'Let's move on,' Walker said, to the obvious relief on the faces of the others around the table.

Beedham glared at Walker.

A youth outreach worker raised a hand to gain attention. The young man studiously avoided looking over at Beedham or at Drake and Finch and kept his comments directed at Walker. Beedham chortled but Walker ignored him.

Drake could see that Walker was doing her best, managing a disparate collection of people with different agendas. It struck Drake they were losing sight of their shared goal of minimising the impact of illegal drugs on the community. Beedham's belligerence did nothing to help the common cause, Drake thought.

Walker moved on to other items on the agenda and within a few minutes, after various contributions, she brought the meeting to a close. Beedham ignored Drake and Finch and spoke loudly into his mobile as he left. Walker came over to Drake.

'Thank you for attending, Detective Inspector. I hope it won't put you off from coming again. We all appreciate how difficult it is for the Wales Police Service.'

Drake nodded. 'Thank you.'

Walker rejoined Knox and gathered her papers together, ready to leave.

Drake looked over for Finch, mobile pinned to his ear, his brow wrinkled. When he finished he joined Drake. 'I've been trying to reach someone I thought you might like to talk to. She's given us some useful intelligence in the past. Have you got time for a detour?'

Drake read the time on his watch. 'I've got an hour to spare.'

'Okay, let's go. I'll try and contact some of her friends.'

Outside Finch made several brief and inconclusive phone calls while dragging on a cigarette.

Drake followed Finch's car through the streets of Connah's Quay. A dilapidated, worn out feel permeated the centre of the town populated by betting shops and charity outlets. Drake couldn't recall when he had last visited a town centre to shop and he felt vaguely guilty that his Internet shopping had contributed to the dwindling fortunes of town centres.

Finch took a route through the back streets, passing building sites, rough ground overgrown with weeds and takeaway restaurants with garish signs advertising cheap food.

He indicated left and at the end of the terrace he parked. Drake did the same.

Finch still had his mobile pinned to his ear when he emerged from the car. Drake heard the snippets of conversation as he joined him outside the end property. He finished the call and knocked on the door. No response. He glanced at the upstairs windows.

'Round the back,' Finch said.

They walked till they got to a lane at the rear of the terraces. Finch pushed open the gate to the backyard of the house. They reached the rear door, which stood ajar. Finch frowned at Drake.

'I hope she's okay,' Finch said as he nudged the door with his foot and called out. 'Dawn?'

There was no answer and Finch led Drake into the kitchen.

Tins of baked beans, soup and packs of takeaway food littered a table. Bottles of cheap cider stood on a worktop near a sink stacked high with dirty plates. And a putrid smell assaulted Drake's nostrils.

Finch moved through into the rest of the house, speaking to Drake over his shoulder.

'She's had a history of drug abuse, but she's been trying to get clean recently.'

The downstairs sitting room was just as chaotic as the kitchen and Drake screwed up his face at the stink that intensified. Nobody had cleaned the place for weeks, maybe months. Cheap carpets covered the staircase and at the top Finch shouldered open the door to a bedroom overlooking the street outside and took two paces inside. Drake followed him, but seconds later Finch grasped his hand to his mouth. 'Jesus H. Christ.' Then he barged past Drake and kicked open the door to the bathroom at the end of the small landing.

Drake looked over the body slumped against the bed. He heard Finch puking.

It wasn't a drug overdose that had killed her. A gaping wound in Dawn's stomach and blood all over her clothes made that very clear.

Chapter 3

Dr Lee Kings stepped out of Dawn Piper's property into the small rear yard. He took a deep breath.

'It stinks in there.'

Drake nodded at the pathologist. Behind him, crime scene investigators bustled inside.

'What can you tell me about the time of death?'

Kings tilted his head skyward. He closed his eyes for a second allowing the early afternoon sunshine to warm his face. 'I'll get a better idea once I've done the post-mortem but the body is beginning to lose its stiffness. So at a rough guess I'd say within thirty-six hours.'

Kings followed Drake to the street outside the front of the house and leaned on one of the marked police cars as he took a long sip from a bottle of water. 'Is this part of the county lines drugs activity I've heard so much about lately?'

'It's too early to tell.'

Beyond the fluttering yellow crime scene tape Drake saw Sara Morgan parking her car. She hurried over and flashed her warrant card at the uniformed officer standing by the perimeter. She ducked her head under the tape and her auburn hair fell over her shoulder. She moved with the nimbleness of a regular runner and Drake wondered how she motivated herself to tramp the streets at all hours.

'Good morning, Detective Sergeant,' Kings said formally.

Sara gave Kings a brief smile. Even with flat heels she managed to look Kings, who was a good four inches shorter than Drake at about five feet seven inches, directly in the eyes.

She turned to Drake. 'What's the story, boss?'

'Sergeant Jim Finch and I found the body of Dawn Piper in the first-floor bedroom.' Drake tipped his hand towards the property. 'She'd been stabbed and there was blood all over her clothes.'

'But not a great deal around the corpse,' Kings added.

'Are you suggesting she wasn't killed in the house?' Drake said.

'You'll have to wait and see what the CSIs tell you. But if she was killed in that bedroom, I would have expected more blood on the floor and on the wall.'

Sara looked around. 'Where's Finch?'

'He puked over the bathroom and himself after we found the body. He went to clean up.'

Kings took a slurp of water and straightened. 'I've got to get back to the mortuary. I'll see you tomorrow morning for the post-mortem.'

Drake turned to Sara. 'Let's go inside.'

Mike Foulds stood in the kitchen, the sound of activity from investigators upstairs drifted down the staircase. The crime scene manager shared a glance with Drake and Sara. 'I've seen some shit-holes but this place is one of the worst.'

'Anything you can tell us?'

Foulds blew out a mouthful of air. 'We'll be a couple of days before finishing. I've requisitioned some additional manpower. Superintendent Price offered me extra investigators from Western Division. He complained like hell about some local councillor whingeing on about inadequate police resourcing.'

'Did he mention a name?' It intrigued Drake whether Beedham had got involved so quickly.

Foulds shook his head. 'It will be odd without Wyndham Price. Have you heard about his retirement party?'

'Everyone has,' Drake said.

'Apparently it's a Superintendent Hobbs from Cardiff taking over. Have you met him?'

Facing the possibility of having to answer to a new superintendent unsettled Drake. Although part of him felt reassured that Hobbs wouldn't know about his background and the difficult case a few years ago when two officers had been killed that had meant a period of counselling for Drake. He wanted to believe Superintendent Price wouldn't share with his successor all the intimate details he knew about Drake's obsessions and how they could drive the rituals that could dominate his mind.

'Not yet,' Drake replied.

'One of the crime scene managers I know from Cardiff has worked with him. He reckons Hobbs is a right pain in the arse.'

Drake made no reply. He'd make his own mind up about Superintendent Hobbs.

Foulds made for the staircase. 'We haven't started downstairs yet so be careful.'

Drake snapped on a pair of latex gloves. Sara followed suit.

Now he paid more attention to the detritus on the table. Half eaten tins of baked beans accompanied a loaf of bread, the top slice dotted with green fungus. Stacks of dirty crockery filled the sink. The draining rack alongside it heaving with grease-smeared dishes. Sara opened the fridge. 'Not much here to suggest a healthy lifestyle.'

Drake gazed over – two shelves were stacked with more plastic bottles of cheap cider. No sign of a vegetable or piece of fruit. The dried up remains of a microwave meal looked wholly uninviting.

Pot noodles, packets of instant soup and tins of rice pudding were the only contents of the cupboards. Drake forced open a drawer of the floor units and as he did so unopened mail cascaded over the grubby lino. He spotted envelopes from utility providers with 'urgent priority' stamped on the outside.

Once satisfied there was nothing the kitchen could tell him about the life of Dawn Piper, Drake walked through into the sitting room at the front of the property. He stood for a moment taking in the battered furniture, the worn, almost transparent, curtain hanging limply to one side of the window. He barely noticed the smell now. Drake stepped around the mulberry-coloured sofa towards the television – behind it were shelves neatly constructed in an alcove lined with DVDs and computer games.

Drake ran a finger along the plastic jewel cases.

'Anything interesting, boss?' Sara said.

'She was into computer games in a big way. It looks like her favourites were zombie games.' He tilted his head and read the titles on the spines. 'And she loved zombie films and videos.'

Drake pulled out a couple of the cases – 'Pride and Prejudice and Zombies' caught his attention as did the words 'living' and 'dead' that appeared frequently.

Drake and Sara turned when they heard activity from the kitchen and saw Sergeant Finch standing in the door to the sitting room.

He looked pale, drawn. When Drake had first seen a dead body, he'd almost vomited on the spot but he had choked back the nausea, determined that the inspector in charge of the investigating team wouldn't see his weakness.

'How are you feeling?' Drake said.

'I've been better.'

Drake nodded at Sara. 'This is Detective Sergeant Sara Morgan.'

Finch gave her a nod of acknowledgement.

'I need you to tell me what intelligence Dawn Piper gave you.'

Finch ran a hand over his mouth and kept his voice flat and quiet. 'She was convinced the Beltrami family were muscling in on the drugs scene in Deeside.'

Drake paused. He had dealt with the Beltrami family years ago in another drug-related case. He had never been able to get close to John Beltrami, the 'godfather' of the clan, but his daughter was serving a ten-year sentence for conspiracy to supply drugs.

'Is that the Beltrami family from Rhyl?' Sara said.

Drake nodded his head slowly. 'The one and only Beltrami family.'

Sara turned towards Drake. 'Sounds like you know them, boss.'

'They are a regular bunch of gangsters. There isn't much that goes on in Rhyl that doesn't involve the Beltrami family. They own pubs, amusement arcades and dozens of properties in multiple occupation.'

'Dawn Piper reckoned that Jack Beltrami wanted to expand the family business into the day-to-day supplying of drugs into the Deeside area.'

'Jack is John Beltrami's son?' Drake recalled the meetings he'd had with John Beltrami, the frustration still raw that he had been unable to gather the evidence to successfully prosecute. Every officer Drake knew in the economic crime department of Northern Division would have given up a substantial chunk of their pension for the pleasure of seeing John Beltrami before a judge, being sentenced to a decent stint behind bars. Drake warmed to the possibility he had unfinished business with the Beltramis.

'Did Dawn Piper have any family?' Sara asked.

'There was a sister. And Dawn had an on-off relationship with a man called Cameron Toft. I'll get you his contact details.'

'We'll talk to her sister first.'

Drake steeled himself for another difficult conversation.

Chapter 4

Jane Piper burst into tears once Drake had broken the news of Dawn's death. She darted her gaze between Drake and Sara as she sobbed uncontrollably.

'I know this must be a difficult time,' Drake said, 'but when did you see Dawn last?'

Jane slumped back onto the leather sofa. The starter home she shared with her two children was a world away from the dingy terrace her sister lived in.

'It was last week sometime,' Jane gasped, struggling to take a breath.

Sara leant towards Jane, keeping her voice soft and caring. 'It really would help if you could be more specific.'

'Wednesday,' Jane spluttered. 'I think I saw her when I was in the supermarket. It might have been Tuesday. I can't believe she's dead.'

'How did she seem to you that day? Did she seem frightened?' Drake said. 'Did she ever tell you she felt her life had been threatened?'

More loud sobbing followed.

Sara added, 'We can arrange for a family liaison officer to be with you during this difficult period.'

Jane blew her nose noisily and nodded. Sara continued. 'Do you and Jane have any other relatives – parents?'

Jane shook her head. 'What will happen to Jamie?'

'Jamie?'

'Dawn's son. He's in care. The social services are looking after him. Dawn wanted to get her life cleaned up and get him back living with her.'

An image of Dawn's home came to Drake's mind and he dismissed the idea that might have ever been a possibility.

'We'd like to know as much as possible about her past. Where she worked and her friends.'

Jane took a deep breath and Drake listened as she summarised Dawn's life story. A period working in the amusement arcades of the Beltrami family in Rhyl after leaving school had given her a taste for wasting her money on slot machines that in turn led her to an addiction to cannabis and then cocaine. Their parents had despaired when they realised the depths to which Dawn had sunk as her life spiralled out of control.

'They took advantage of her.' Jane spat out the comment.

'Who exactly?' Drake asked.

'The Beltrami clan. She tried to get clean and she even left the arcades and found a job in a launderette back in town, but I was sure she was dealing small-scale and using too.'

'Can you be a bit more specific with the dates?' Drake nodded at Sara who readied a ballpoint above her open notebook.

Sara had to interrupt regularly to get a clear picture of the exact dates in Dawn's history as Jane summarised her sister's background. Occasionally Drake interjected, seeking clarification, and almost an hour had passed when Drake surreptitiously glanced at his watch. Jane paused and it gave Sara an opportunity to ask, 'What can you tell us about her boyfriend, Cameron?'

'He didn't help. He was involved in drugs too. He could be all nice to your face, but he was as hard as nails. He'd been in the army, kept bragging that he'd been a sniper and that he'd killed dozens of terrorists in Afghanistan.'

Sara asked, 'Do you know any of her friends?'

A vacant look enveloped Jane's face and her body seemed to collapse in on itself. She had aged in front of their eyes.

'I know Dawn had been involved with some crazy stuff. But she was desperate and recently she been trying to get clean of the drugs. She talked about a support group she went to. I met her once in a café with a woman called Olivia Knox who was some sort of charity worker.'

Drake recognised Knox's name from the meeting that morning. He might even have her phone number and address somewhere.

Jane continued. 'And then she played all those stupid zombie games. I tried to tell her. I really did.' She grabbed another handful of tissues and blew her nose vigorously. 'It was such a waste of a life.'

'We'll need the names of all her friends please,' Drake said.

Jane left them, returning from the kitchen with her mobile. She dictated several names and numbers that Sara jotted into her notebook. Drake got up, indicating to Sara that they should leave.

They left Jane standing at the doorway of her neat property, peering at them with a bewildered look on her face.

Sara punched the post code Drake had given her into the satnav and the journey took them back into the centre of the Deeside area where the towns of Connah's Quay and Queensferry merged into each other. The small towns that lined the estuary of the River Dee had given its name to the Deeside industrial estate on the opposite bank, still in Wales – just. Drake scarcely noticed the sign for Shotton as he drove to an address at the southern end of the estuary, before the dual carriageway leading off the A55 made its way towards the M56 and the motorway network of England.

The disembodied voice of the satnav directed Drake to take a right junction into an industrial estate. Small units with workshops and car repair firms mixed with a company selling double glazing and another manufacturing signs and livery for cars and vans. At the end was a small office block and Drake parked after the satnav had announced they had reached their destination.

Drake pressed the buzzer for the entry system, introduced himself and the door bleeped open. A woman stood behind a Perspex screen, the left side of her head had been shaved carefully whilst the hair on the other side had been grown into long folds that draped over her shoulder. It had the effect of pulling her head to one side.

Their warrant cards did little to change her lifeless look. 'We'd like to see Olivia Knox.'

'Hang on a minute.'

The woman picked up a handset from the desk in front of her announcing that two policemen were in reception. Moments later a woman appeared from the door at the end of the hallway and gesticulated at them to follow her into an office.

'I'm Olivia Knox. I've heard about Dawn.' She looked over at Drake, recognition evident on her face. 'You were in the meeting this morning.'

Drake nodded. 'I was there with Sergeant Finch.'

Knox frowned and pointed to visitor chairs that Drake and Sara dragged over to her desk. Knox wore a T-shirt blotched in florid colours that complemented the red and burgundy shades of her spiky hairstyle. She had clear eyes but a pasty complexion.

'It's terrible. Shocking. Dawn had been clean for a couple of months. She was doing her best to get back on the straight and narrow. She was trying to straighten her life out. She was even talking about getting back with her boyfriend and being a proper mother to Jamie.'

'How well did you know her?' Drake said.

'We do outreach work here. We try and help addicts and their families. Dawn was bright and intelligent, but she got in with the wrong crowd years ago.'

Drake raised an eyebrow – she hadn't answered the question. 'Did you know her well?'

Knox nodded. 'She had one of those personalities that couldn't help herself. And recently she got into believing she could influence these drug dealers and get them to back off. I told her... warned her to be careful.' Knox displayed the palms of both hands in exasperation. 'But she wouldn't listen. She was very determined.'

'What did she do?'

Knox pointed her index finger at Drake. 'She was pissed off with you lot – the Wales Police Service – useless. And now she's dead and it's clear—'

'What do you mean by that exactly?'

'Nothing, nothing at all.' She looked away avoiding Drake's stare.

'When did you see her last?' Sara asked, attempting to defuse the tension.

Knox looked puzzled. 'I didn't always make a record of when I saw her. She could pop in unannounced. Sometimes she'd meet me in a café and take up half an hour of my lunch break.'

'What did you talk about?' Sara sounded intrigued.

Knox shrugged and paused before replying. 'All sorts. Nothing much. Recently she'd become focused on the dealers coming in from Liverpool.'

'The county lines activity?'

Knox nodded at Sara. She spat out the next words. 'Evil bastards.'

'We're going to talk to her former boyfriend, Cameron Toft.'

'Don't rely on anything he tells you. He's been involved in cannabis cultivation and supply in the past.'

'Is he linked to the county lines activity?' Drake said.

Knox shook her head. 'He's small-scale compared to them.' She leaned over the desk and opened her eyes wide. 'I've recently heard about youngsters from Liverpool being brought into Deeside – teenagers from broken homes used to traffic drugs to kids of their own age.'

'Have you got any evidence of this?' Drake said.

Knox guffawed. 'Isn't that your job? I've told Finch a thousand times to organise surveillance around every school and every playground at critical periods of the day. Surely he could find out where they live?'

Drake knew exactly how Finch would react. How any police officer would react. Resources were scarce, the demands limitless. The Wales Police Service could only do so much. It would never be enough for Olivia Knox, Drake thought.

Knox continued. 'I've given Finch the name of Ritchie O'Brien, a pernicious individual in this area. He's up to his neck in everything that is wrong about Deeside. You should lock him up.'

'We can't just—'

'Of course, of course I know. I get so angry.'

Drake made to leave. Sara did the same before turning to Knox. 'Did Dawn ever mention the Beltrami family from Rhyl as being involved in the drugs scene here?'

Knox frowned. 'No, I don't recall her ever mentioning that name.'

Drake's mobile bleeped with a message and he read the address of Cameron Toft that Finch had promised to send him. He turned to Knox. 'If there's anything else you think might be of relevance then contact us.'

Knox nodded and Drake and Sara left.

Drake's mentally prioritised the tasks in hand as he drove out of Shotton. Establishing the precise movements of Dawn Piper in the last few days of her life would be crucial. Everyone left a digital footprint, texts on mobiles made and received, debit cards used. Somehow it never made investigating a murder any easier though.

'Do you think the Beltrami family are involved?' Sara said.

'Oh yes,' Drake said with feeling. 'I know a sergeant in the economic crime department who pinned a picture of old man Beltrami on the wall in his room. It rankled him until the day he retired that he hadn't put Beltrami senior behind bars.'

'Is it realistic they would murder someone like Dawn

Piper?'

'For now, we treat Jack Beltrami as a person of interest. And we need to dig into the background of Ritchie O'Brien.'

The main road towards Flint hugged the Dee estuary and to the right the Flintshire Bridge, which crossed the estuary, loomed large. Immediately after a junction, Connah's Quay power station dominated the skyline. The towns along the Dee estuary had a proud industrial history that had left a legacy of poverty and low-skilled employment although the Deeside Industrial Park on the opposite side of the estuary promised high-paid jobs and future opportunity. Drake doubted that Dawn Piper had shared in any economic prosperity.

The remains of the thirteenth century castle built by Edward 1 as part of his campaign to subdue the Welsh stood between the town and the estuary as a reminder that the place really did have some history. After making his way through the back streets, Drake pulled into a car park near the block of flats where Cameron Toft lived.

The main entrance door creaked open and paint peeled off in chunks around the frame. Drake avoided the lift and made for the stairs. A sharp tacky smell hung in the air which made Drake ignore the handrail. On the third floor music and the sound of human activity drifted through the thin walls of the building. Drake stopped outside a door that had 312 screwed to the surface in plastic numbers. He hammered on the door.

Inside the volume was turned down a notch or two. Drake sensed movement behind the door and guessed that someone was looking out through the spy hole. A security chain fell against the doorjamb.

'Who are you?' Toft asked as he opened the door and glared at Drake and Sara.

Drake held up his warrant card. 'I'm Detective Inspector Ian Drake and this is Detective Sergeant Sara Morgan. We'd like to come in.'

A moment's hesitation crossed Toft's face. 'What's this about?'

'It would be better to discuss this in private.'

Drake had seen hostility from people suspicious of the police many times so Toft's attitude was no surprise. He probably distrusted everyone in authority – council officials, probation officers, anyone who might want to suggest how he should live his life.

Wordlessly he motioned an invitation and Drake and Sara followed him into the flat.

The stink of day-old cannabis hung in the air. Drake gave the contents of the kitchen a surreptitious glance as he passed the door. It was barely tidier than Dawn's but at least the sink didn't heave with dirty dishes.

Toft fell into a worn-out wing chair. Drake and Sara opted for an old sofa. Three people made the room feel cluttered.

'Cameron,' Drake used a warm mellow tone. 'I'm afraid we have some bad news. We found Dawn's body this morning. I'm sorry to tell you that she was killed last night.'

Toft flinched, and he blinked repeatedly. 'What the fuck are you talking about?'

Drake didn't reply.

'Jesus,' Toft continued. He wiped a tear away from his face. 'It's all your fault. She was convinced she could help clear the drugs away from this town. And from the Quay and every fucking place.'

'Can you tell us about her whereabouts in the past few days?' Drake said.

'I saw her last week.' His eyes watered as he took a moment. 'On Tuesday we took Jamie for a pizza. The place where she lived was a shit-hole so social services don't like me taking him back there. She never took enough care of herself. You need to speak to her mate, Cynthia Holland; Dawn was in a group with her and they sat around wasting their time playing zombie games.'

'We'll need Cynthia's contact details.'

Toft nodded.

Drake added, 'When was the last time you saw Dawn?'

There was a purposefulness to the way Toft shook his head this time. 'I followed her on Thursday. She went to Liverpool. She kept talking about these county lines operators who are bringing in a lot of shit and because she was so fucking naïve, she thought she'd go and talk to them.'

'Do you have a name for who she was planning to meet?' Drake said hiding the excitement in his voice.

'I can do better than that.' Toft reached for his mobile. He thumbed through it before passing it over to Drake. There on the screen was the image of a man clearly angry at Dawn Piper. Despite the poor lighting, Drake could see that the man towered over Dawn, was clean shaven, not only his face but his entire head, and he carried himself like a man who lifted weights regularly. It wasn't a face Drake recognised, but it was a face that Drake guessed would be familiar to the police in Liverpool.

Once they had a list of Dawn's friends and their contact numbers, and the address where Dawn had met the man Toft had photographed, they made to leave. By the threshold Toft turned to Drake and Sara.

For the first time he looked and sounded vulnerable.

'What do I tell Jamie?'

Chapter 5

A little over an hour later they pulled into headquarters. Before leaving the car, Drake quickly texted Annie a message telling her he'd be late home. That morning he'd hoped to be back in time for a barbecue on the garden overlooking the Menai Strait, enjoying a glass of cold beer and watching the glorious sunset over Anglesey. But it would have to wait. Annie's acceptance of the demands of his job had made life easier. After his divorce from Sian he had often thought a normal relationship would elude him and that no woman would tolerate the irregular hours and demanding lifestyle of a detective.

Sara followed Drake as he took the stairs for the Incident Room. Luned Thomas, the least experienced of the two detective constables on Drake's team was on the phone. From the conversation Drake guessed she was organising house-to-house inquiries. Luned frowned a lot, it matched her serious personality, but she was dedicated and professional.

Drake draped his jacket over a wooden hanger on the coat stand in his room, brushing away some imaginary flecks of dust. He hung it carefully on the coat stand and gave the desk and its surroundings a quick visual check. He had to be certain that things had been undisturbed. Pictures of Helen and Megan were still in the same position, the columns of Post-it notes demanding his attention.

He called Jim Finch, arranging for the sergeant to brief the team the following morning and then he dialled Mike Foulds.

'Any progress to report?' Drake said.

'We recovered two thousand pounds in cash and some cannabis and coke. More than enough for a supply charge.'

Drake nodded. It meant Dawn was still involved in the drug trade, no matter what Olivia Knox believed.

Foulds continued. 'And we found an old laptop in a

cupboard and dozens of DVDs of zombie films. I'd no idea they made so many of them.'

'When are you likely to be finished?'

'We finish when we finish.'

Foulds abruptly ended the call.

Drake headed back into the Incident Room as Gareth Winder bustled in. He seemed slighter than Drake recalled; perhaps the recent Spanish holiday with his girlfriend had encouraged him to lose weight. Or perhaps it was a change of clothes.

'Afternoon, boss.' Winder put a tray of coffees on the table.

'Did you get my email with the image of Dawn meeting that man in Liverpool?'

Winder reached over to a photograph on his desk. 'I sent a copy to the Merseyside Police. They promised to get back to me.'

Luned joined Drake holding the printed image from the police national computer's records for Dawn Piper. 'She was convicted of petty shoplifting a few years ago,' she said as she pinned the photo to the middle of the board. Drake picked up the image from Winder's desk of the man Toft had photographed and stuck it alongside Dawn's.

'We need a photograph of Jack Beltrami too,' Drake said.

Winder whistled under his breath. 'Not *the* Beltramis?'

Sara filled in the details for Winder and Luned. 'We have intelligence that Dawn was in contact with Jack Beltrami who was muscling in on the drug scene in the Deeside area.'

'So he's not satisfied with just robbing people with his fruit machines and watered-down lager in Rhyl,' Winder commented, sounding sceptical.

'I've never heard of the Beltrami family.' Luned took the first sip of her coffee.

'Scum bags and toe rags,' Winder added.

Drake took a second to gather his thoughts. 'We should have the result of the post-mortem tomorrow. The pathologist speculated there might be a possibility she hadn't been killed in the house. So, in the morning,' Drake nodded at Winder and Luned, 'organise house-to-house inquiries. I want a full team calling at every house in the neighbourhood next to Dawn's property. We need to establish her movements for the last few days of her life and how someone transported her into that house – dead or alive. And do all the usual background searches, mobiles, financials, et cetera et cetera.'

'Is her death linked to the county lines inquiry?' Luned said. 'I watched a documentary on the television last week about the overdoses in the Deeside area. There are some politicians who want to stir things up, particularly as there's a by-election looming.'

'By-election?' Drake said.

'One of the members of the Welsh Assembly died after a long illness. All the main parties are standing as well as an independent local councillor.'

'Not Beedham?' Drake groaned.

Luned nodded. 'He was on the news earlier.'

Drake groaned again. Another layer of interference. Councillor Beedham was one thing, but the attention of the national press in a by-election campaign could mean demands for more police activity. It was early summer and not the time for politics.

'We need a list of all the CCTV cameras that could possibly have recorded Dawn Piper's movements. Garage forecourts, shops – all the usual.' Drake cast a glance at Sara clicking on her mouse and then he heard the purr of a printer coming to life. Sara got up and collected a piece of paper the machine had spewed out.

'It's a picture of Ritchie O'Brien,' Sara said walking over to Drake. She pinned it to the side of Dawn Piper's image.

'Olivia Knox reckons O'Brien is heavily involved in drug dealing in Deeside. So if she's right, we need to know everything about him.'

Drake scanned the three images – Dawn in the middle and O'Brien and the mysterious man from Liverpool either side. Were either of the men involved in her death?

'Sergeant Finch of the county lines team will give us a briefing first thing in the morning.' He turned to face the others. 'In the meantime, let's get to work.'

It was after nine pm by the time Drake parked outside the house he shared with Annie. Classical music drifted down the stairwell from the second-floor sitting room. He shouted out a greeting as he made his way upstairs. She met him at the top and kissed him warmly. 'You must be exhausted.'

'It's been a long day.'

'There hasn't been anything on the news.'

The brutal death of a drug addict probably didn't warrant valuable air time, Drake thought.

'I'll organise something for you to eat.'

Driving from Colwyn Bay to Felinheli gave him time to purge the day's images from his mind. Annie didn't want to hear the details, Drake didn't want to share them. It was a part of his life he had to leave locked away in the Incident Room at headquarters.

He strolled over to the fridge, found a bottle of lager and walked over to the balcony. At least he could enjoy the sunset as it created a glorious scorched red band across the skyline over the island of Anglesey. After two mouthfuls of beer his mind relaxed.

Annie called over as the microwave pinged.

She smiled at him as he reached the kitchen table.

'Are we going to be okay for the holiday?'

Drake sat down. He had a month to solve the murder of Dawn Piper. He'd tell Superintendent Price in the morning that, come what may, he was going on holiday with his daughters.

'Of course we will.'

Chapter 6

Drake sat in his car mulling over two squares in a moderate sudoku puzzle in the morning's newspaper. Recently he had found himself dwelling on solving at least five squares before allowing his mind to focus on the day's work. Annoyingly, a lot depended on the severity of the sudoku puzzle – a variable outside his control. Five had become a magic number for him. And he didn't feel able to vary the challenge he posed for himself each morning.

A siren screeched and he noticed an ambulance heading from the hospital emergency department, its lights flashing as it hurtled towards the A55. He turned his attention back to the sudoku puzzle and it pleased him when he solved the fifth square. The brief moment of distraction had been enough – now he could face the day.

He left the car and strode over to the mortuary. The usual truculent assistant hadn't arrived, so Drake ignored the signing-in procedures and followed the sound of an orchestra from further down the corridor. The volume increased once Drake opened the door where Dr Lee Kings busied himself organising the well-used stainless-steel instruments for the post-mortem. He hummed along to the crashing cymbals and strings of the orchestra. Drake called over, 'Morning, Lee.'

The pathologist smiled and waved him over.

'Where is your friendly assistant?' Drake said.

'He called in sick. So, I shall need to organise everything myself.'

It puzzled Drake how Kings always appeared cheerful. How could any doctor want to spend their entire career carving up dead people? Interviewing criminals, being spat at and assaulted wasn't the ideal component for a job description but at least he could lock up the bad guys.

'Let's get started. Apparently, there was another drug overdose victim from Deeside last night. Getting to be the wild west out there.'

Councillor Beedham would be the first to agree.

Drake watched as Kings examined the corpse in front of him.

Kings paused announcing for the recording, 'This is the body of a malnourished female. Present on both limbs are signs potentially consistent with long-term intravenous drug use.'

He turned to Drake. 'It doesn't look as though she's had a proper meal for weeks, months even. How old is she again?'

'Thirty-four.'

'Christ, she looks more like fifty-four.'

Kings continued the macabre work: taking scrapings from Dawn's fingernails – labelling and recording everything in turn.

'The evidence of intravenous drug use is patchy – some are recent but others older. I'll send for toxicology tests for the usual spectrum.' Kings sounded stoic.

He carefully examined her head, neck and shoulders, pulling at the skin to examine each blemish. He tilted his head and ran a hand down the left side of her body. Then he repeated the same ritual of inspecting the right side of the body running his hand over the dead woman's flesh. Drake averted his eyes from staring at the gaping wound where the knife had sliced open her abdomen leaving a lump of bright yellow fat hanging out surrounded by dark red, rusty bloodstains.

Kings turned and faced Drake. 'It confirms what I suspected from the crime scene.'

'What?'

'I don't think she was killed in the house. Her body was moved. She has been lying on her right side for at least six hours. Livor mortis, Ian. Take a look at where the blood has settled down on the right side after death, discolouring the skin. The blood starts to settle half an hour or so after death. It becomes fixed after a few hours.'

'What does that tell us about the time of death, Lee?'

Kings frowned. 'When I examined the body yesterday rigor mortis was still visible, but it was beginning to fade so it was getting to the end of the period when rigor leaves the body which is no more than forty-eight hours after death.'

It meant Piper's body had been moved.

'And there would be a lot of blood. And you know how difficult it can be to remove traces of blood from a crime scene these days.'

Drake folded his arms together. All they had to do was find the location of the murder and bring in a full team of crime scene investigators, recover the killer's DNA from the scene, make an arrest, and a conviction would soon follow. It sounded so easy.

Kings continued. 'Make certain the CSIs send everything for a full forensic examination. There could be fibres, soil samples, hair. Something, anything, which links the scene to your killer.'

After examining the wound, photographing and measuring it, Kings reached over for the scalpel. He began the gruesome task of opening the chest and abdomen with one large deep and deliberate Y-shaped incision extending from both shoulders to the navel. After making his way down to bone came the task of splitting the ribcage. Kings dropped his scalpel into a stainless-steel kidney dish before reaching for what looked like a pair of stainless-steel garden shears. Kings then opened the chest like a clamshell to reveal the heart and lungs. Drake put a fist to his mouth and took half a step backwards. Getting accustomed to the smell was difficult. And there was something defiling about the process even though common sense told him Piper was dead and that the purpose of what they were doing was to establish a cause of death. Kings next turned to the abdomen, investigating the path of the murder weapon and commenting on the devastation it caused.

Once he'd finished, he moved away from the trolley, a

contented expression on his face on a job well done. 'It's very sad, Ian, seeing a young woman like this having her life destroyed. I hope you catch whoever did this.'

'So do I.'

Sara felt tired and irritable when she woke. She hated sleeping badly. She had tried reading her Kindle twice in the middle of the night but each time she had drifted off into an unsatisfying shallow sleep.

She checked the time on the alarm clock on the cupboard by the side of her bed and decided to don her running kit, believing that if she did three or four miles, she'd feel better and ready to face the day. It was a warm summer's morning; hedgerows of hawthorn and field maple lined the roads and oaks in the fields were heavy with leaf. Drake hadn't asked her to be present at the post-mortem and a worry he was excluding her from important stages of the inquiry wormed its way into her thoughts. She dismissed them – she was being oversensitive. He was the senior investigating officer and it was his decision whether to invite her or not.

Usually when she ran, she could focus on missing potholes, avoiding cars and tractors on the roads around her home, but that morning images of Dawn Piper filled her mind. She was about her age, but their lives had taken a very different route, with Dawn's being cut short prematurely. Sara wondered what would happen to Dawn's young son, Jamie, and how her death might affect him. Dawn's sister had mentioned the involvement of the social services department of the county council and Sara resolved to discover exactly what was happening with Dawn's child.

After returning home, she stood for a moment looking out over the countryside that stretched away behind the bungalow she rented. Running was her only pastime – she had little time for anything else after the demands of her job. She needed to get out more, meet new people. A couple of attempts using online dating agencies had proved unsuccessful. The loneliness of Dawn Piper's death and her empty existence made Sara contemplate that there was more to life than police work. Sara envied how Drake had changed once he had a girlfriend. He was friendlier even if he still had some annoying habits.

The long weekend with friends to Dublin she had been forced to cancel at Easter still rankled. She had lost several hundred pounds, money she could never recover. The Wales Police Service would never pay for a cancelled vacation. The same group of friends had booked a house in the Peak District of Derbyshire over the August bank holiday, only a few short weeks away. Sara knew that Drake was taking his daughters, and Annie, to Disneyland Paris at the end of August, so if Dawn's killer hadn't been caught by then it might mean another aborted holiday. She shook off her disappointment.

Within half an hour she was parking at Northern Division headquarters before making her way up to the Incident Room where Gareth Winder was holding forth about the latest signing for his beloved Liverpool Football Club. She listened to him telling Luned that the forthcoming season would see them crowned champions.

'Shut up about the bloody football, Gareth.' Sara immediately chided herself for sounding too impatient.

Winder pouted.

'Any sign of the boss?' Sara continued.

'He's on his way back. The pathologist carried out the post-mortem very early.'

Sara had barely sat down and booted up her computer when she heard conversation in the corridor outside the door. It creaked open and Drake walked in with Sergeant Finch. Sara struggled to remember his first name.

'Good morning.' Drake made for the board, before he turned to face the team. 'This is Sergeant Jim Finch. He is leading the day-to-day inquiry into the county lines activity in the Deeside area. I've asked him to give us a briefing. But before we hear from Jim, I've just been to the post-mortem. The pathologist confirmed that Dawn Piper wasn't killed in her home. She had been lying somewhere on her side for at least six hours, which means she was killed somewhere else and then moved before she was dumped in her own home.'

'Why didn't they leave her where she was killed?' Winder said.

'Once we find the killer, we can ask him… or her,' Luned said. Winder wouldn't tune into Luned's sarcasm, Sara thought.

Drake continued. 'So, establishing the exact spot Dawn was killed is our priority. Forensics might give us links from Dawn's clothes and personal belongings to a possible crime scene.'

All the officers nodded their understanding.

Drake again. 'We all know about the recent spate of deaths from drug overdoses in the Deeside area. It's been in all the press recently. Dawn Piper had been involved in some small-scale dealing, but Olivia Knox suggested she thought Dawn was trying to get clean. She also suggested that Dawn wanted to tackle the dealers flooding the area with drugs. Whatever she was up to cost her her life.' Drake nodded an encouragement to Finch.

Finch approached the board and kept his voice serious and business-like. 'The county lines activity is organised strictly as a business by these dealers from the big cities. They target youngsters, teenagers or vulnerable adults in the community, promising them vast sums of money in return for the sale of drugs. It's cannabis to start with, then it moves on to the harder stuff and once the users are addicted to heroin, the dealers have a guaranteed regular income and customer base.

'I'll send you details of everything we know about the activity so far, but it's been difficult building a case, gathering evidence we can use. These dealers are clever.

They take advantage of naïve youngsters brought up in small towns who want money and excitement. And sometimes they'll use the homes of vulnerable individuals to house people they've trafficked into the area – it's called cuckooing.'

Nobody said anything, and Sara realised how focused everyone had become listening to Finch.

'There was another overdose death last night,' Drake announced.

It stunned everyone into silence.

Drake turned to the board and the face of Dawn Piper. 'The pathologist reckons Dawn's time of death could be thirty-six to forty-eight hours. That means she was killed sometime on Saturday.'

He tapped a finger on the image of Ritchie O'Brien. 'Olivia Knox reckons O'Brien is heavily involved in the drug scene.' He looked over at Finch who gave a tired nod.

'It's always the same, sir,' Finch said. 'O'Brien keeps himself clean. He's clever like Beltrami – although we have put some of his runners away. But they never talk, always too frightened of what Beltrami might do to them or their families.'

Drake returned his gaze to the grainy photograph of the mystery-man from Liverpool. 'And we need to know who this is and why Dawn Piper was with him.'

Nobody replied before Drake nodded at Winder and Luned. 'Top priority is building a detailed analysis of where she was in the hours before her death, where she had been and who she saw.'

Drake glanced at Sara. 'And we need to go and talk to Dawn's friends about her love of zombies.'

Chapter 7

Gareth Winder still enjoyed the memory of his two-week holiday in Alicante with his girlfriend. A fortnight of relaxing, drinking cocktails by the swimming pool and sangria late into the evening before retiring to bed and making every effort to wear himself out had been well overdue. He felt energised and refreshed and ready to face the challenges of the new investigation.

He looked over at Luned sitting in the passenger seat of the unmarked police car and guessed she was more a museum and art gallery person. He had never heard her mention a boyfriend, or a girlfriend either come to that. Winder's initial reservations about Luned's value to the team had been replaced by a grudging acceptance. It didn't mean that he had to like her of course.

Investigating drug crime was a matter of priorities, at least that's what the senior management of the Wales Police Service always said. Cannabis had become so commonplace there seemed little point in wasting resources locking up the small-time dealers. Several former high-ranking police officers had recently announced their decision to support the decriminalisation of cannabis. Resources, or the lack of them, were everything.

Winder indicated off the A55 and drove down into Connah's Quay. He had hated every moment of the year spent in one of the police stations in Deeside at the start of his career. At the time he hadn't realised how little real policing was actually undertaken at the sharp end and that many officers were simply glorified social workers preventing people from self-harming, protecting women from abusive husbands and health workers from aggressive patients. Little had changed in the time since he had left.

Winder pulled into the car park of a pub – the Hope and Anchor – and slotted the vehicle into a gap near two marked police cars. They joined various uniformed officers inside the nearby mobile incident room. Once the preliminary introductions were over, Winder listened to the sergeant relishing his role in the house-to-house inquiries. A large-scale map had been pinned to a board alongside colour-coordinated sheets linked to various sections of the map.

'I've divided the town into several sections. I've called the centre portion section C and we've got four officers doing house-to-house. The middle section I've called section B where I have allocated four more officers.'

Winder guessed the final section would be A and if he continued in this vein the officer was going to earn maximum points for being anal. Winder cut across him. 'We'll do the street where Dawn Piper lived.'

If the officer was disappointed with Winder's interruption, he barely showed it.

'Have you had much of a response from the public?' Luned piped up.

The sergeant shook his head. 'No, but a local councillor visited – enquiring who was in charge and asking for regular updates.'

'What did you tell him?' Winder asked.

'I told him to contact Inspector Drake at headquarters. And I'm expecting the candidates in the by-election to make an appearance and stick their nose in. You know what politicians are like.'

Winder and Sara nodded their understanding and implicitly their sympathy.

'Let's get started,' Winder said.

It was a short drive from the Hope and Anchor to the terraced street where Dawn Piper had lived. A yellow crime scene tape still fluttered across her front door.

If Dawn had been killed somewhere else and her body returned to her house, the killer had taken a risk. Which suggested a confident individual, brazen, but it also meant there was a chance somebody had noticed something out of place, somebody's memory might provide a vital clue.

Winder parked behind a Ford Fiesta, at least ten years old. He glanced out of the windscreen and wondered how many of the householders would be at home. He opened the car door as Luned joined him and counted eight houses on the right-hand side and the same number on the left. It shouldn't take them long.

'Ready?' Winder watched Luned organising her notepad.

'Yes, of course.'

No one was home in the first two properties.

The door of the third was opened by a woman holding a toddler in her arms. Another child called out from behind her and she shushed him before squinting at Winder's warrant card.

'We are investigating the murder of Dawn Piper who lived at the end terrace,' Winder said, unable to remember the number of Dawn's property.

'I didn't know her.' The woman made it sound final, and that she wasn't interested in cooperating with the police.

'As you're one of her nearest neighbours I hope you can assist us with building a picture of her whereabouts.'

'Like I said,' she moved the child nearer her shoulder, 'I didn't know her. I saw her a couple of times in the street. But I didn't have anything to do with her.'

'Can you recall when you saw her last?'

'Sorry.' She shook her head.

Winder did his best to conceal his irritation. 'Was it last week or the week before?'

'I don't pay any attention. She was a druggie after all.'

'Is there anyone else who lives here with you?' Luned made her enquiry sound genuine.

The woman started to close the door. 'Just me and the kids.'

Winder thrust a card from his pocket at the woman who gave it a disinterested look. 'If you remember anything please contact me.' His words died as the latch slotted back into place.

At the next property an elderly man welcomed them into his neat sitting room asking if they'd like tea or coffee. They declined. He shared with them that his wife had died several years previously and that now he lived on his own. He'd never been blessed with children, although a nephew and a niece lived in Manchester, but they rarely visited. Winder struggled to deflect the conversation from the man's family background and the loneliness of old age. When he mentioned that he rarely ventured out of the house, Winder realised his value as an eyewitness was limited. 'When did you see Dawn Piper last?'

A serious look crossed his face. 'I always smiled at her when I saw her in the street. She always looked so thin.'

At least he had noticed her, Winder thought recalling the earlier disinterest from the young mother.

'I've seen her sometimes in that newsagent on the High Street. I go there to do the lottery on a Wednesday, and she was in there last week.'

Winder moved forward slightly in his chair. It was the first part of the jigsaw building a picture as to where Dawn Piper had been in the hours and days before she died. 'Where exactly is that?'

Luned jotted down the details.

'You've been most helpful, thank you very much.'

A glimmer of excitement crossed the old man's face. As he saw Winder and Luned to the door he asked, 'Did she have any family?'

Luned replied, 'She had a son, but he didn't live with her.'

The man gave a thoughtful turn of his head as though the circumstances appeared quite normal. 'It's tragic.'

Winder turned to Luned as they stood by the next-door property. 'That newsagent shop could have CCTV.'

Luned nodded. 'I was thinking the same, but it's only taking us back as far as last Wednesday.'

Winder pressed the doorbell and waited: no response. 'We'll call again on the way back.'

Two more of the properties were empty and Winder crossed over to the opposite side hoping that Dawn's near neighbours might be more forthcoming. At the first house a man in his middle fifties answered. He had thin hair, bags under his eyes and a heavy double chin. He cast a glance over Winder's shoulder. 'Are you doing house-to-house inquiries?' He sounded excited by the prospect. Before Winder could reply he opened the door wider. 'Come in, come in. I thought someone might call.'

Winder and Luned followed him into a sitting room with leather sofas surrounding a small carpeted square in the middle of the floor. An enormous television clung to a bracket, screwed to a wall in the corner.

'We need to build a picture of Dawn Piper's whereabouts over the last few days. We're asking every one of her neighbours if they can recall seeing her recently.'

'You'll be wasting your time at number six and ten, both of the houses are empty. The owners died a couple of months ago and they haven't been put onto the market yet. And next door has been refurbished by one of those buy to let landlords.'

Luned scribbled down the details. They would need to be checked of course – something for the uniformed lads to complete.

'We rarely saw her,' the man said un-prompted. 'She didn't exactly do much for the neighbourhood.'

'Do you recall anybody visiting her?'

He shook his head. 'I saw her in the back lane sometimes. She was very thin as though she hadn't eaten for days. I didn't see anybody going into the house. A few months ago, there was a lot of arguing and shouting but I couldn't tell who was involved.'

The sound of the back door closing drew their attention. 'The missus is back.'

Moments later a woman about the same age as the man came into the sitting room, surprised when she saw Winder and Luned. 'These are police officers about Dawn Piper.'

She sat next to her husband who continued. 'I've told them we rarely saw her and apart from that party a while back she kept herself to herself.'

The woman nodded. 'She didn't look healthy. And from what I heard she mixed with the wrong crowd.'

Luned asked, 'Did you ever talk to your neighbours about her?' The man and woman frowned in unison. 'There's been a lot of publicity recently about the deaths from drug overdoses and I was wondering if it was something you spoke about with your friends or neighbours?'

'They should lock them up,' the man said. 'All these drug dealers, I mean. They're evil, preying on youngsters.'

'Do you know anything about Dawn Piper?'

The man shook his head. His wife cleared her throat. 'I've seen her in town – in some of the cafés. And I saw her once sitting in a flash car.'

'When exactly was that?' Winder said, relieved that finally they might have something to go on.

The woman searched her memory. 'I can't be certain but—'

'Was it last week or last month?' Winder realised he'd been a little bit too abrupt, so he softened his tone. 'It really will help if you could be a bit more specific.'

'It was about the time of Jim's birthday, two weeks ago.' She tilted her head at her husband. 'I was looking for a birthday card and I couldn't find one where I usually buy them. I remember passing this car and noticed that it looked out of place – too flashy for Connah's Quay.'

'What sort of car was it?' Luned said.

'A big Audi.'

Winder butted in. 'Do you know the model?'

She shrugged. 'No, sorry, but it was black.'

Chapter 8

'What do you know about zombies?' Drake accelerated down the entrance slip to the A55.

'They don't exist.' Sara managed an exasperated tone.

Drake ignored her. 'I never knew there were so many zombie games.'

Drake powered the car eastwards, anticipating making this journey frequently in the next few days and weeks. Building a picture of exactly what was going on in Dawn Piper's life meant identifying all her friends and acquaintances. Her regular gaming companions might know something to help them establish Dawn's movements in the days before her death.

Traffic was always heavy on the road towards Queensferry and Chester. It was as though the towns and cities of England and the Deeside industrial estate sucked the people and energy out of North Wales.

Drake indicated left for the junction to Flint and followed the satnav's instructions taking them onto Chester Road that linked the towns along the Dee estuary. He pressed on towards Shotton. The terraced properties of the town seemed to crowd the main road. Nothing delineated the difference between Connah's Quay and Shotton.

Drake slowed as the satnav directed him along the backstreets. Rubbish cascaded over pavements from bins tipped onto their side. The quality of housing deteriorated, windows and doors badly needed painting, weeds grew on front yards and ancient discoloured net curtains hung at rakish angles. All the properties looked like they could do with a power wash.

A left turn took them into a one-way street and two thirds of the way down Drake turned right into a cul-de-sac. They passed a garage and a tyre company on the right-hand side and Drake turned the car around and glanced over at their destination – 11 Adelaide Terrace. If zombies did exist, they probably lived in a dilapidated neighbourhood like this, Drake thought, as two scrawny looking dogs jogged along the pavement.

Drake and Sara left the car and he made certain it was locked, giving the handle a tug to reassure himself before heading over the road. The property needed a new doorbell as the one Drake reached for came off in his hand and dangled on wires. He suppressed a knee-jerk reaction to go back to his car and find a wet wipe to disinfect his fingers.

He settled for thumping on the door instead.

Moments later, a man with a tight-fitting sleeveless T-shirt appeared at the door. Tattoo-less and clean shaven he had a small dog tethered tightly on a leash wound around his left fist.

The man stared at Drake and Sara. 'Who are you?' Drake pulled out his warrant card whilst maintaining eye contact. He gave the man enough opportunity to read the card carefully, as did Sara.

'Detective Inspector Drake and this is Detective Sergeant Morgan. We need to speak to a Cynthia Holland.'

'What the fuck has that druggie done now?'

Drake took a beat. 'What's your full name, sir?'

'And what the fuck does that have to do with you?' He loosened the leash and the dog moved towards Drake: it gave his trouser leg a hungry gaze.

'She doesn't live here. She lives at number six.'

Drake and Sara paced down to the bottom of the terrace and stopped at the right house – it didn't have a number but as the next house displayed a number four, Drake assumed this was Cynthia's home. There was no doorbell again, so Drake fisted the door. Seconds later a woman in her forties opened the door.

'I'm looking for Cynthia.'

She had the worn-out complexion of a person who had allowed drugs to draw the goodness from her body. Her badly-fitting clothes were faded and misshapen.

'I'm Cynthia Holland.' She shared an inquisitive look between Drake and Sara.

'I'm investigating the murder of Dawn Piper.'

'Come in.' She gestured for them to enter, and they followed her into the small sitting room at the front of the property.

Cynthia perched on the side of a chair while Drake and Sara sat on a sofa.

'How can I help?'

'I understand you were good friends with Dawn Piper?' Drake said.

'Yeah, I suppose so.'

'What did you have in common?'

Drake hardly expected her to say drugs but she obliged by telling him about her past. 'Dawn and I both had a lot of problems over the years. I was in a support group with her because my kids were taken into care and she was in much the same position.'

'We were told you shared an interest in zombie games?'

Cynthia averted her eyes – embarrassment or amusement, Drake couldn't decide.

'She was obsessed. I enjoy playing but she had all the games and she went to as many of the conventions as she could afford to.'

'How often did you play?' Sara said.

Cynthia gave her a quizzical look as though she assumed Drake and Sara knew the answer. 'Every Friday afternoon at my place. Occasionally I'd go to hers, but she wasn't the tidiest.'

Cynthia's comment would qualify for the understatement of the century.

'So did you see her the Friday afternoon before she was killed?' Sara got a firm tone to her voice that grabbed Cynthia's attention.

She blinked. 'Of course. She came here.'

'Was there anyone else present?'

'No. But sometimes Hubert and Mattie would join us.'

'We'll need their full names and contact details,' Sara continued as Cynthia nodded. 'What time did she arrive?'

Cynthia pondered. 'She arrived about six thirty. Left at about eleven. We had Chinese before she left.'

'What was her mood like?'

'Okay, I suppose.'

'We are trying to put together a detailed picture of her movements before she was killed.' Sara moved to the edge of her seat. 'So, it's very important if you can tell us whether she said anything about her plans over the weekend.'

'She was getting excited about the new zombie attraction in the old *Duke of Lancaster* along the coast. She was dead keen on getting a job there.'

Drake listened with amazement as Cynthia outlined the plans to convert the old passenger ferry into a zombie attraction. Dawn's world was filled with films and games about zombies and she had wanted nothing more but to work at the attraction.

Sara adopted a conversational tone once Cynthia had finished. 'How long have you known Dawn?'

Cynthia paused for a second. 'It must be four or five years. We used to work in the launderette together.'

'Where was that?'

'On the High Street.'

'And how long did you work together?'

'I can't be certain, two years maybe. Then Ritchie wanted her to work in one of his pubs.'

The man's name stood out from the increasingly dull conversation and Drake cut in. 'Ritchie?'

'Ritchie O'Brien, of course – everyone knows Ritchie.' She managed a mysterious sounding chuckle. 'He owns a couple of pubs and a Chinese restaurant. He thought Dawn had good "people skills" so he got her to work in the bar and look after things.'

Drake moved forward in his seat and tried to hide the

urgency in his voice. 'How long did she work for Ritchie O'Brien? It really will help us if you can remember as much of the detail as you can.'

Chapter 9

'Why the hell didn't Olivia Knox tell us about Dawn working for Ritchie O'Brien?' Sara sounded annoyed as they walked back to Drake's Mondeo.

'And why didn't Cameron Toft mention it?'

They sat for a moment in the silence of the car.

Drake reached for the ignition. 'We'll need to speak to Knox again. She should have known that information was important.'

'Cynthia struck me as genuine enough. She was probably telling us the truth.'

Drake started the engine and pulled into traffic. 'That's more than we can say for Knox and Toft.'

Once Sara and Drake were back at headquarters, Drake fussed over brewing a coffee as Sara made an instant. Back in the Incident Room Winder began to say something until Drake raised a hand. 'Later, Gareth. I've got a meeting with Wendy Sutherland, the intelligence officer, and once I'm done, we'll do a catch-up.'

Drake set his mug onto a coaster on his desk before checking his desk was still tidy. He had one quick call to make before he could focus on the inquiry. He searched unsuccessfully for Detective Inspector John Marco's direct number. So, he called Queen Street police station in Cardiff from the internal directory. Having dealt with Marco on a previous case he guessed that if any officer would be indiscreet about Superintendent Hobbs, Marco would be top of the list.

The phone was answered after two rings. Drake was bounced from one detective to another. Nobody had seen Detective Inspector Marco, and nobody had any idea when to expect him.

'Give me your mobile number. What is it about?'

Drake composed the reply carefully. 'It's not urgent – ask him to call me when he can.'

Drake finished the call and scanned the surface of his desk before adjusting the photographs of his daughters a couple of millimetres. He moved the columns of different coloured Post-it notes to one side of his desk clearing enough space to work comfortably.

The Beltrami family featuring in the inquiry opened old wounds in Drake's mind. John Beltrami must be in his late sixties now, Drake thought as he recalled his meetings when the Beltrami family had been suspected of being involved in drug trafficking. Despite Drake's suspicions, only Jade Beltrami, John's daughter, a corrupt and dishonest solicitor, had been implicated. Her conviction for conspiracy to supply controlled drugs had been satisfying nevertheless and she was now enjoying the hospitality of HMP Rockwell.

The prison authorities had responded quickly to his request for a copy of her prison record. He read about her assisting other convicts to read and write and her contributions to the education programme, teaching prisoners computer skills. But she had developed a drug habit – perhaps the prospect of several years behind bars was daunting. As he mulled over the report, a civilian in her forties appeared in his doorway and rapped her knuckles on the door. Drake waved her in and pointed to a chair.

Wendy Sutherland had a warm face. Her blouse looked expensive and her straight hair draped her shoulders. Intelligence officers based in Northern Division now provided indispensable background support to front-line policing and having worked with Sutherland before, Drake knew he could rely on her.

'I need up-to-date intelligence about Ritchie O'Brien and the Beltrami family. Both names have cropped up in the Dawn Piper murder inquiry,' Drake said.

Sutherland nodded. 'John Beltrami senior is more or less retired now. He lives in his villa in Majorca for most of the year, occasionally making the trip back to North Wales to check on his empire. Jack, his son, looks after things now.

He's a nasty piece of goods.'

'Is there any recent suggestion they might be involved with the drug trade?' Drake said.

'It's a developing feature of their criminal profile. We class the family as an organised crime group. But being a family makes them more dangerous because there is blood loyalty. Jack Beltrami definitely wants to develop his drug trafficking activity and he's muscling into Deeside. But Ritchie O'Brien controls a lot of the action. He comes from a middle-class background – went to the local Welsh-medium school and did well apparently but he didn't go to college or university. I'll send you more details in due course. He was interviewed last year on suspicion of possession with intent to supply.'

'What happened?'

'He got lucky. The evidence wasn't strong enough and the Crown Prosecution Service decided not to proceed. But the county lines operators are on the scene too.'

'So, it could easily become a turf war?'

Sutherland sounded frustrated. 'A couple of small-time dealers linked to Beltrami have been convicted in the past two years. They've all got connections with Jack but none were prepared to implicate him in their criminality. Their loyalty to him is unwavering.'

'Any history of violence?'

'Oh, yes.'

Sutherland handed Drake a printed list of individuals connected to Jack Beltrami, all convicted of assaults of varying degrees. Drake looked over at Sutherland. 'But Jack Beltrami has never been charged?'

'It doesn't mean he isn't capable of physical violence.'

'Is he capable of killing someone?'

A tense silence followed. Sutherland adjusted her position on the chair. 'I would say so. But he's super careful, he lets the loyal foot servants take the risks. I thought there was history between you and the Beltrami family?'

Drake nodded. 'I put Jade away years ago on a conspiracy to supply charge.'

'But didn't you have an altercation with Jack Beltrami?'

'It was the old man.' Drake corrected her. 'He threatened me when he saw me in the car park of a supermarket. There were no eyewitnesses and he started raging and shouting abuse. Then he complained that we'd fabricated evidence and stolen personal items from their home. He made a complaint that was investigated by professional standards.'

Drake let the last sentence hang. Sutherland would know that such investigations inevitably cast a long shadow. 'I was exonerated but…'

'I know what it's like. Be careful, Ian. Jack Beltrami isn't the sort to forgive and forget.' Sutherland got up. 'All you have to do is get some gold-plated evidence.'

Drake didn't reply – he wished it were that easy.

Before the catch-up meeting with the rest of his team Drake texted Annie telling her when to expect him and apologising that he'd be late.

Everything OK? Don't be too late. Caru ti *x* Adding that she loved him always brought a smile to his face.

He marched into the Incident Room. It was the end of the second day of the investigation, and it was time to focus minds. Standing by the board he turned to face three sets of eyes staring at him intently.

'Based on the post-mortem we know that Dawn Piper had been dead for between thirty-six and forty-eight hours when her body was found. On the basis of the pathologist's analysis she was probably killed between midnight Saturday and early hours Sunday.'

Winder and Sara scribbled notes.

'Dawn was playing zombie games in the home of Cynthia Holland on the Friday evening before she died.'

'What games were they playing, boss?' Winder asked, a serious and interested expression on his face.

'Is it really relevant, Gareth?' Drake sounded exasperated. 'It means we can place Dawn with Cynthia at about eleven pm Friday night. She would have walked home so there's probably some CCTV along the way. Get talking to the garages, filling stations, anywhere that might have cameras. Anything to establish her movements on Friday evening.'

Luned was busy jotting details as fast as Drake dictated.

Sara piped up. 'We've got the names of two other regulars in this zombie gaming group – a Hubert Caston and Mattie Williams. We need to speak to them in due course.'

Drake turned to the board again and scanned the images of Jack Beltrami and Ritchie O'Brien. 'Dawn worked for O'Brien in one of his pubs so there's a good chance he was behind the supply of drugs she had in the house.'

'And the Beltrami family?' Winder asked.

'Sergeant Jim Finch told us she had implicated the Beltrami family in the drug trade in Deeside. So, Dawn Piper might have been killed because she was playing one dealer against another.'

'Dangerous game.' Sara sounded serious.

Drake nodded. 'And like all these drug cases it's bloody hard getting the right evidence.' Drake's attention turned to the image of Cameron Toft. 'We'd better get some more background on Toft too. All the usual details.' Drake heard the jotting of notes on pads behind him. Then he turned to face the team. 'Any progress with identifying the man in the picture Dawn met?'

'I spoke to a DI in Merseyside who identified the man as a Paul Kenny, a well-known gangster involved in county lines activity,' Winder said. 'We've spoken to most of Dawn's neighbours. A neighbour had seen her the week before she died in a black Audi – high-end car that looked out of place.'

'Typical drug dealer – flashing their money.' Luned sounded a cynical tone.

'So, get a search done on black Audis. And we need an analysis of Dawn's finances.'

Luned replied, 'I should have all the details in the morning, boss.'

'Good. I'll talk to the forensic department too. All we need to do is find out where exactly she was on Saturday evening and who she was with.'

The earnest, serious expressions on the faces in front of him told Drake they knew the task wasn't going to be easy.

Chapter 10

Since moving to live with Annie in Felinheli, overlooking the Menai Strait, Drake had a longer morning commute. It was a price worth paying for spending his evening with her and waking up by her side in the morning and feeling the warmth of her body next to his. The following morning, Drake left the house early, hoping to miss the traffic and the inevitable jams and delays caused by roadworks and contraflows along the A55. He would listen to the news alternating between Radio Wales in English and Radio Cymru in Welsh. The content could vary but the weather forecast didn't and neither did the details about the holdups.

Instead of taking the direct route off the A55 to Northern Division headquarters, Drake invariably took a slight detour to visit the newsagent near his former home for a copy of the morning's broadsheet and his first sudoku fix of the day. That morning the puzzle had been a moderately difficult one – it pleased him that he had managed to complete a row sitting in the car. Now the newspaper lay open on a shelving unit in one corner of his office with the sudoku puzzle prominently displayed.

After booting up his computer Drake scanned through the various emails clogging his inbox. He read an email from Superintendent Price confirming the time of a meeting at the end of the week for him to meet Superintendent Hobbs. Part of him knew that Price would retire – everyone did – but a new superior officer presented a challenge. Drake shook off his malaise, reminding himself he was answerable to a superintendent, who was answerable in turn to a chief superintendent and on up the chain of command to the chief constable himself.

Drake was about to make a call to Mike Foulds when his phone rang. 'DI Drake.'

'John Marco, Southern Division. What do you want?'

'I was after a bit of gossip actually, all off the record.

My new boss is joining us from Southern Division. A Superintendent Hobbs and I was wondering…'

Drake heard the stifled groan down the phone. 'I thought you might know something about him?'

'I had heard he was going back up north, but I didn't know he'd been promoted. Jesus, couldn't happen to a nicer bloke.' For a fraction of a second Drake wasn't certain he had interpreted the sarcasm correctly. The pause gave John Marco the opportunity to continue. 'He hates my guts. I worked with him when he was a DI in Queen Street. Be careful, Hobbs will look after himself before anyone else.'

Drake had expected some gossip or the occasional innuendo and indiscretion but not a full-scale attack on another officer's reputation. It didn't lessen the anxiety he already felt about Hobbs.

'Who is he replacing?' Marco asked

'Wyndham Price.'

'Good man, he's from the south. My advice would be, watch your back.'

'Thanks for your time.'

Hobbs couldn't be that bad, Drake thought. It was two days until his meeting with Price and Hobbs and being in the middle of a new inquiry was the worst possible timing. He hoped he would have something to report to both officers by then. He called Mike Foulds, knowing the crime scene manager was an early starter.

'Good morning, Mike.'

'I was about to call you. We've finished the preliminary work on Dawn Piper's possessions.'

'I'll be down now.'

Drake made his way to the forensic department wondering if the vital piece of evidence needed to crack the case wide open had been unearthed. He mulled over whether he should acquaint himself with zombie videogames. By the time he descended two flights of stairs he had made it a low priority.

Drake sat down opposite Mike Foulds. The department had a cold, antiseptic feel.

'We found her mobile.' Foulds nodded at the plastic evidence pouch sitting near a box on the table in front of him. 'All the usual activity. Texts and messages to friends. She used Facebook and Instagram. There were three texts and two calls to the same number on the Saturday night before her body was found.'

'Is it—'

'I've already checked – pay-as-you-go and untraceable.'

A handset was like a key into another person's life. Foulds continued. 'There are some videos you need to check out too. And there was no blood other than on her clothes. Which suggests that the killer either cleaned up very effectively or she was killed elsewhere.'

Drake nodded. 'The post-mortem confirmed she had been lying on her side for some time after her death and that there would have been a lot of blood, so we are working with the idea that she was killed somewhere else and then moved.'

Now it was Mike Foulds' turn to nod. 'We found some fibres on the victim's body that are compatible with mats from the footwell and boot of a car.'

'Can you trace them?'

Foulds raised an eyebrow. 'I've sent them for detailed forensic examination. Let's hope we can get an indication of the manufacturer – maybe even of the vehicle model involved.'

Drake took the box and the mobile and returned to the Incident Room where he exchanged greetings with Sara, Winder and Luned before heading to his office and dumping the box on his desk. He pulled out Dawn's mobile and began watching the videos. There were several with Dawn and other individuals – Drake recognised Cynthia Holland and Cameron Toft with a young child he assumed was Jamie. It was a video taken inside a property that took his attention. It was only a few seconds long, but the wraps of drugs laid out on a table were clearly visible. The jerky nature of the footage and its short length suggested Dawn was in a rush. The next video taken in the same room showed several bundles of cash. Drake guessed the stash amounted to several thousand pounds. One final video recorded the surroundings and for a brief second it showed the image from the window – it was a first-floor room, that much was clear.

Drake bellowed for Sara and moments later she appeared in the threshold of his room. He pointed to the mobile. 'This is Dawn's mobile – there are videos on it evidencing drug dealing activity as well as images of the street outside the property. We need to establish where the videos were taken. And make a start on the usual phone work. We need to know who she called and who rang her. Mike says she called one number twice and texted it three times on Saturday evening.'

'Okay, sir.'

She left and he rummaged through the contents of the box of Dawn's belongings which included several handbags, a purse and various items of cheap jewellery. A scuffed and damaged folder lay at the bottom, the word 'Jamie' scribbled in one corner. He pulled it out.

Inside were reams of correspondence from the social services department about the temporary placement of Jamie with foster parents and letters from solicitors working for Cameron Toft telling Dawn in strident tones that she was unfit to look after Jamie and that Toft wanted his son to live with him permanently. Why hadn't Toft mentioned this? Speaking to Toft again would be a priority and he scribbled the action needed on a Post-it note that joined the others on his desk. Mentally he reminded himself that he'd need to spend more time on the folder – it was another part of the jigsaw of Dawn's life.

Then he turned to the handbags and purses. After

discarding some loose change, two ballpoints, a pencil, lip balm and some cheap-smelling perfume, he delved through various shopping receipts. One in particular drew his attention.

It was a receipt for change from Beltrami's amusement arcade in Rhyl, but of more interest was the timing: the Friday before she died. Drake sat back in his chair and fingered the crumpled slip of paper. Perhaps the arcade had CCTV – there would be only one way to find out. He warmed to the prospect of speaking to Jack Beltrami.

It could wait, for now, Drake thought as he focused on another thread to Dawn's life: zombies.

It surprised him that zombies were so popular, and that there were games involving zombies in all walks of life and in several different historical contexts. It amused him to think what Jane Austen might think of a zombie game inspired by *Pride and Prejudice*. He recalled *Shaun of the Dead* from flicking through late night television and he had noticed the film on the shelf in Dawn's home.

A Wikipedia entry provided him with details of the steamship the *Duke of Lancaster*. It had been one of the last passenger ferries that had operated around the coast of the United Kingdom, principally from Heysham to Belfast and then on the Irish crossing from Holyhead to Dun Laoghaire. Car ferries gradually superseded passenger ferries and eventually the ship was laid up in a dock near Mostyn in 1979. Drake had passed the rusting hull on many occasions, taking the train along the North Wales coast. Some years previously an artist had been commissioned to decorate the exterior with a mixture of images including that of the ship's first captain as well as gargoyles and other decoration intended to entertain. A recent newspaper article told Drake that the vessel had now been painted black to await its new use as a zombie attraction.

Another few clicks and Drake found a website featuring zombie attractions in the United Kingdom. Drake tried to imagine what Dawn saw in these games. Perhaps it was her way of escaping her mundane life and daily routine.

He knew better than most what it was like to be obsessed with something. In the past his rituals that could drive his obsessions had forced him to work long hours, checking and rechecking facts and figures, ignoring the time, often staying in his office until late in the evening. Was her zombie fascination part of her rehabilitation? Putting the world of drug addiction and dealing behind her?

Luned hated drugs. She loathed what they were doing to young people and she couldn't understand why some senior police officers were suggesting that cannabis should be decriminalised. Couldn't they see the damage it was causing by encouraging people to become addicted?

Getting to grips with Dawn Piper's life made her realise how terribly sad it must have been for the woman. Luned glanced over at Gareth Winder and recalled how well-informed he was about zombie video games. Perhaps it was time she took more of an interest in how other people ran their lives. And if it helped solve this murder and put Dawn's killer behind bars then she would ignore her petty prejudices.

She glanced over at Gareth who was coaxing information out of an official at the DVLA. The government agency responsible for vehicle registrations could be infuriatingly incompetent, she knew from previous investigations. Finding the black Audi was the sort of detailed exercise Winder would hate. She smiled to herself, he might even ask for her help in due course, but in the meantime, she turned to the financial reports on Dawn Piper.

She had no loans, no mortgage, a credit card on which she owed £500 and a bank account with a little over £2,400. The actual balance surprised Luned. She had expected very little. Luned built a pattern of withdrawals from the account. Each would give her a date, time and a location and each might be near to a CCTV camera. This was the sort of policing she enjoyed, gathering evidence, getting nearer to a killer. Methodically she worked through the bank statements for the last four months, hoping it would give her a picture she could take to Drake and the rest of the team. After the cash withdrawals she focused on the contactless and debit card payments Dawn had made. The payment for a meal at a café in Queensferry on the Saturday she was killed caught her attention. The amount suggested she wasn't eating alone. Why would Dawn be buying food for someone when her income was limited? And who might it have been?

Luned googled the café. It didn't have a website, but the search gave her its opening hours and a Google Earth search showed the outside of the building. It looked like a typical unwholesome greasy spoon. Before she could share her discovery with Drake and Sara, she got to grips with the spending on Dawn's credit card. She'd spent money at Tesco, a local convenience store and had made several purchases from Amazon. Luned made a mental note to access Dawn's online account with the shopping giant.

Winder interrupted her. 'You won't believe how many black Audis there are out there.'

'Hundreds?' Luned offered.

'Over two thousand. Why would people want to buy a black car? It needs to be cleaned all the time.' Winder tipped his head towards Drake's empty office. 'The boss would be cleaning it every day if he had one.'

Luned smiled. Drake's tidiness hadn't gone unnoticed.

Winder continued. 'I've asked the DVLA to narrow it down to black Audis in North Wales, Cheshire, Merseyside and Manchester. And to those that have been registered in the past five years.' He stood up and put his hands to the small of his back and stretched.

Recently he had lost weight and his complexion appeared healthier. Luned hadn't met his girlfriend but guessed she was having a positive effect on his diet. 'Are you making any progress?'

Luned didn't have time to respond as Drake walked in. She caught his attention, anxious to share her discoveries without delay. 'I found something, sir.'

Drake detoured towards the board and stared over at Luned. 'What have you got?'

Chapter 11

Drake and Sara arrived in Connah's Quay by early afternoon and parked near the Jolly Friar café where Dawn had purchased a meal the Saturday before she died. But spending a little under thirty pounds in a place like this suggested she had bought more than one meal.

Cheap plastic-topped tables stood in a row against both walls and meagre lighting made the place feel miserable. A stale smell of chip fat hung in the air and a young girl chewed on a nail as she leaned against a hatch that looked into the kitchen beyond. To the left a corridor led to the back of the building. The girl straightened when Drake approached, reaching for a pad from the counter nearby, preparing herself to take an order. A few elderly customers gave Drake and Sara inquisitive glances.

'Is your boss in?' Drake said.

'Yeah, suppose.' She leaned into the hatch and shouted. 'Terry!'

Moments later a man, mid-forties, unhealthy puffy cheeks with thinning hair appeared. He looked at Drake and Sara. 'What do you want?'

Drake flashed his warrant card for a millisecond before snapping. 'A minute of your time.'

Terry wore a white faded T-shirt under a soiled butcher's style, navy apron.

'We're investigating the murder of Dawn Piper.'

'It was terrible. She was a regular here.'

'How often did she come in?'

'I didn't keep a record, but it was most weeks. Deirdre back there could probably give you a better idea.' He jerked his head down the corridor behind him.

'We'll need to talk to her.'

Terry turned on his heels and led them into a room with half a dozen tables, occupied mostly by older women chatting away and who ignored Terry, Drake and Sara as they went outside. Deirdre stood under a small smokers' awning constructed from timber and clear Perspex. She was down to the dregs of the cigarette, putting the world to rights with a similarly aged woman in her mid-fifties.

'Deirdre, the police want to speak to you about Dawn Piper.'

Deirdre ground the stub into the rough concrete surface beneath her feet as her friend returned to the café. The smell of stale cigarette smoke drifted in the air and Drake turned up his nose. 'Terry tells me that Dawn was a regular in the café. How often did you see her?'

'She always ordered a milky tea and buttered toast.' Deirdre shook her head. 'It was very sad.'

'Did you serve her last Saturday?'

'I'm not in any trouble, am I?'

Sara cut in. 'Of course not. We need to build a complete picture of Dawn Piper in the last few days of her life.'

Sara's reassurance settled Deirdre's nerves and after sharing a glance between Drake and Sara she replied, 'She sat at her usual table. And there were two young girls with her.'

'Young girls?' Drake responded too quickly and too sharply. Deirdre blinked nervously.

'I've seen her with them before. She buys them a meal – usually Terry's full breakfast, bacon, eggs, fried bread and baked beans.'

Sara adopted a softer tone. 'Can you describe the girls for us?'

'Yeah, I suppose.'

Drake left Sara and Deirdre, returning inside where he caught Terry's attention through the kitchen door. Their conversation was brief – Terry didn't remember either of the two girls and Drake got the impression he was genuine enough. The young girl in the front section of the café played intently on her smartphone and it took a sharp reprimand from Drake for her to discard it into the pocket of her apron.

'We get lots of customers in here. I don't remember faces.'

Drake doubted she was telling the truth. If the clientele in the café that afternoon was anything to go by, two young girls would have stood out. Drake found his business card and gave it to the young girl. 'This is a murder inquiry. It's important that if you recall anything you contact us immediately.' His serious tone clearly frightened her, and she blinked furiously.

Drake retraced his steps to the smokers' corner outside just as Sara was finishing jotting down the detailed descriptions.

Sara turned to Drake. 'Deirdre recalls Dawn and the two girls being in here at least three times. Their clothes smelled and they looked as though they hadn't washed for days.'

Deirdre gave Drake a confirmatory serious nod. 'Poor things, they probably come from a broken home and live with a single parent who can't manage.'

'Thanks, Deirdre,' Drake said. 'If you think of anything else or if you see either of these two girls in the future contact me without delay.' He produced another business card that Deirdre stuffed it into the back pocket of her jeans.

Drake and Sara returned to the car.

'What did you reckon about those two girls, sir?' Sara said.

'It fits the pattern of dealers using vulnerable youngsters to distribute drugs. Let's go and talk to Olivia Knox again – she might know something.'

'And we can ask her about Ritchie O'Brien.'

Half an hour later Drake and Sara sat opposite Olivia Knox. Drake hadn't noticed on the first visit that the iris of one eye was split into two colours. Now it caught his attention.

'We believe Dawn Piper met two girls and bought

meals for them in the Jolly Friar café. Do you know anything about them?' Knox's gaze darted around, a sure sign she was nervous and uncertain how to respond.

Drake continued. 'Does it have anything to do with the county lines activity in Deeside?' He kept his voice deliberately low wanting to avoid antagonising Olivia Knox. After all he wanted her cooperation, wanted to see exactly what she knew about Dawn. If Olivia Knox withheld any information, he could deal with that later.

'She didn't give me the details.' Knox bowed her head and after scooping up a ballpoint from some papers on her desk, played with it through her fingers. 'I told her to be careful.'

'What did she tell you?' Sara said.

'She was very cryptic. She had been involved with low level drug dealing in the past, but she was doing her best to get clean. But she had no idea – really no idea, how these people could operate. I was frightened for her.' Knox threw the ballpoint onto the table. 'She was going to get evidence herself. I don't know the details about those two girls, but my guess is they were trafficked into the area – modern-day slaves. If I find out who was responsible, then—'

'You'll tell us straight away.' Drake raised his voice just enough for Knox to realise how serious he was.

Knox nodded. Drake doubted she was taking him seriously. He settled back into his chair and glared at Knox. He kept his voice calm as he spoke. 'And why didn't you tell us that Dawn had worked for Ritchie O'Brien?'

More averted eye contact. 'That was a while ago.'

'But it's important. And relevant.'

'And I've told Finch countless times O'Brien is involved.'

'Avoiding my question isn't going to help.'

Knox sneered before rolling her eyes. 'Dawn knew the police couldn't do anything and…'

'And what?'

'Nothing, nothing. She was determined to do *something.*'

There was a silence before Drake added, 'I expect you to contact me if you hear anything relevant.'

Officially, Superintendent Wyndham Price wasn't due to retire until the end of September. Protocols provided for him to have a period of transition to enable him to become accustomed to civilian life.

The prospect loomed large in his mind like a stubborn piece of gristle giving him permanent and uncomfortable heartburn. He knew that a retirement party was being planned: he had overheard furtive conversations between Hannah, his secretary, and presumably other senior officers in Northern Division about the arrangements.

Until then he had Dawn Piper's inquiry to supervise. It was the first murder in Northern Division directly linked to the county lines drug activity. Policing had to keep pace with the ever-changing challenges from drug dealers who adapted their methods and pattern of activity. And when he thought about it in those terms, he realised that perhaps his retirement was well-timed. Younger officers could take over and take the battle to these dealers. How would policing look in thirty years' time? If he thought like that it was definitely time to retire. Nostalgia seemed to be a national pastime in Wales, Price often thought.

A phone conversation with Superintendent Wemyss in Western Division based near Carmarthen had given Price the distinct impression that Superintendent Hobbs, his successor, wasn't liked. Wemyss had groaned and let out a long breath when Price asked him about Hobbs. 'He was an effective back-office detective inspector, but he could rub people up the wrong way.'

Managing people had to be one of the most important parts of what he did. Getting the best out of his team was crucial, earning the loyalty of subordinates and supporting them in difficult circumstances.

Price wondered whether he was making the right decision. Perhaps there would be an opportunity to return as a civilian doing consultancy work? Anything really to keep his mind stimulated. But first he would have to endure the Caribbean cruise his wife had booked for the month of October. Four complete weeks at sea trapped on a ship filled him with foreboding.

Hobbs had still not formally confirmed when he could make a meeting with Price for him to meet Drake. The suggested date was still just that. So, in the meantime, Price would review the Dawn Piper case. Drake was expected any minute and Price reminded himself of the brief memorandum Drake had emailed over to him. It reinforced to him that the activity of drug dealers using the county lines model of supply was likely to be the greatest challenge facing Northern Division in the next few years. It appalled him how damaging drugs were to society and how unprincipled dealers in the main cities were taking advantage of vulnerable young people.

The phone on Price's desk rang and he snatched at it.

He listened to Hannah telling him that Detective Inspector Drake had arrived.

'Send him in.'

Drake wore an immaculate navy suit. The discrete red stripes on the dark blue tie complemented the powder blue shirt. His hair was neatly trimmed and everything about Drake suggested a confidence Price knew had been badly shaken in the past. It made him contemplate whether he should be sharing with Superintendent Hobbs everything he knew about Detective Inspector Drake. But he quickly dismissed the notion. Hobbs could read Drake's personnel file for himself. Price would tell the new superintendent that Drake was an effective and dedicated detective.

Drake sat down in one of the visitor chairs.

'Bring me up to date with the Dawn Piper

investigation.'

'She was a known drug user although she had been making attempts to get cleaned up. The forensic evidence suggests she wasn't killed in her home, but that she was moved.'

'It's all connected to the county lines activity, presumably?'

'Before she was killed, she had been seen with a known criminal with connections to organised crime groups in Liverpool. We've identified the man from photographs as a Paul Kenny.'

'So what was the motive for her murder?' Price asked.

Drake balanced his right foot on his left knee. 'Perhaps she knew too much, tried to bargain with her killer. Or her attempts to go clean weren't successful and she was trying to play one dealer against another.'

'A drugs turf war in Deeside, Jesus. That's all we need.'

'Intelligence suggest the Beltrami family are expanding their operation into the area.'

Price whistled under his breath. 'That's a name to conjure with.' Price continued. 'Evidence, Ian. We need evidence.'

Drake nodded and got up to leave.

'Ian, we need to arrange for you to meet Superintendent Hobbs. It's probably going to be next week, but I'll notify you well in advance.'

Drake gave him a brief nod of acknowledgement.

Price turned back to the mound of paperwork on his desk and for the first time sensed his disinclination to plough through the various reports and memos.

Chapter 12

'Are you certain?' Drake stared at Gareth Winder's monitor. The detective constable mumbled confirmation as he slurped on his morning coffee.

'I was in first thing, boss,' Winder said to confirmatory nods of approval from Luned and Sara. 'I double-checked it again. The video on Dawn Piper's mobile was taken from the pub that Ritchie O'Brien owns.'

'Play it again,' Drake said.

He and the rest of the team watched in silence as the monitor came to life. Winder explained it had been easy enlarging the footage as it passed over the window. By manipulating the software, he had identified the name of the business hoarding above the shop front on the opposite side of the street: Mal's Kebabs.

'Good job, Gareth.' Drake turned to Sara. 'Let's go and talk to Ritchie O'Brien.'

Drake returned to his office, took his suit jacket off the wooden hanger and scooped up his mobile from the desk as an email from Superintendent Price arrived. His mind sagged as he saw the request for him to attend a public meeting that evening in Deeside. Had it not been for the ongoing murder inquiry and the impending by-election, Drake doubted his presence would be necessary. Sergeant Jim Finch could have represented the Wales Police Service perfectly adequately.

He joined Sara in the Incident Room as she gathered her bag and they left headquarters.

'I've had a preliminary report from the Merseyside Police about two girls reported missing from a care home in the south of Liverpool three weeks ago. One is called Deborah, known as Debbie, and the other is Tina. Both have been disruptive, both difficult and they had been seen in the company of older men.'

Drake gave Sara a concerned look. 'Do we have photographs?'

'Yes, both with aggressive defiant stares at the camera. We'll get them circulated later.'

'And send the images of Kenny and Ritchie O'Brien to the care home. See if either man is recognised.'

Traffic on the A55 was light, allowing Drake and Sara to arrive in Connah's Quay by mid-morning. He parked on double yellow lines a few yards across from Mal's Kebabs. He found his mobile and tapped on the screen that showed the heavily pixelated image from the first-floor window of The Lamb pub across the street. There was no mistaking that Winder had been correct. Inside Mal's Kebabs staff were cleaning and preparing for the day.

An older woman emerged from the main entrance of The Lamb, which was a detached property with large windows, set back slightly from the road, its external walls covered in greying pebbledash. She set up a sign on the pavement advertising a food delivery service.

'Ritchie O'Brien must be branching out. I wonder what sort of food The Lamb provides?' Sara said.

Drake reached for the door handle. 'Only one way to find out.'

The whirring noise of a vacuum cleaner filled the entrance lobby and the smell of furniture polish tickled Drake's nostrils. Pubs, takeaway restaurants and launderettes were all cash businesses – the perfect business model for drug dealers. Drake pushed open the door that had 'Lounge Bar' screwed to a panel underneath a glass pane and Sara followed him. Behind the bar a man with a heavy beard and thick pronounced eyebrows stacked bottles of spirits onto shelves.

'We haven't opened yet.'

Drake produced his warrant card. 'I'm here to see Ritchie O'Brien.'

The man said nothing but reached for the phone on the bar. After a brief conversation he jerked his head towards the front door. 'He's upstairs in his office.'

At the top of the staircase a narrow corridor led through the centre of the first floor. Two voices in conversation emerged from a room at the end. The loudest was a man's voice – harsh and argumentative. Drake slowed his pace and glanced into the rooms along the landing. The first was filled with boxes of snacks and crisps. Some chairs had been stacked into one corner.

Drake nudged open the door to the second room with his shoe and his pulse quickened, he sensed Sara take a sharp breath as she whispered, 'This is the room, boss.'

Down the corridor the conversation had stopped, and Drake mouthed silently, 'Let's go.'

At the end of the corridor a small man in faded denims left the room and brushed past them. Ritchie O'Brien stood in the middle of the room and glared at them as they entered. He was mid-forties but the neatly trimmed hair and clean-shaven chin and his slim appearance made him look younger. He looked healthy, the exact opposite of his clientele. Crisp ironing gave his expensive-looking shirt a formal appearance, out of place in the office of a drug dealer above a pub. A Welsh Dragon was emblazoned on each cufflink. O'Brien could have been an executive in a dot.com business.

'What do you people want?'

'*Bore da*, Mr O'Brien,' Drake took a moment to study the face: it was tough and uncompromising – no reaction to the good morning greeting in Welsh. 'I'm the senior investigating officer in charge of the inquiry into Dawn Piper's murder.'

O'Brien leaned on a melamine-faced desk and crossed his arms. 'Why do you think that would have anything to do with me?'

'I understand Dawn worked for you for some time. Can you give me details of your relationship with her?'

O'Brien guffawed. 'I wasn't screwing her if that's what you mean. Jesus, what do you take me for?'

'How long did she work for you?'

'She worked in the launderette. She was useless. She wouldn't charge people properly. I was losing money. I'm no charity.'

'When did she start in your pub?'

'I took pity on her. I offered her a job as a barmaid.'

'So, what happened?'

'She was useless at that too.'

'Why did you keep her on?'

O'Brien shrugged. 'The punters liked her.'

'I'm sure you have no objection to giving us full details of her employment history with you. When she started and what she was paid. Do you have someone who does the books for you? Or somebody who does the office administration?'

'Yes, of course.'

Drake paused – revealing the existence of the video would achieve nothing. It suggested that large amounts of cash and drugs were stored in The Lamb just down the hallway from where they were standing. But did it necessarily implicate Ritchie O'Brien? The man had history and Drake decided to gauge how far he could goad him. 'I understand you've been interviewed under caution previously in relation to a suspected charge of supplying controlled drugs.'

O'Brien stood up, clenching his jaw.

Drake continued. 'And Dawn Piper had been a drug addict. Did you supply her with drugs?'

O'Brien fisted both hands and took a deep breath.

'Because, Ritchie, if I find out you've been back to your old tricks the world will come down on top of you.'

O'Brien took a step towards Drake and then laughed in his face. 'Detective Inspector Drake, you don't know fuck all.' Then aggression filled the granite tone of his voice. 'You can't come in here making these sorts of false allegations. Get the hell out of my place before I make a formal complaint.'

The Memorial Hall was typical of many built in the interwar years in towns and villages around Wales and the rest of the United Kingdom. Above the door was a commemorative plaque with the words *Lest We Forget* and the year 1924.

Sara followed Drake inside and they sat at the back of the building as conversation filled the hall as people filed in. Public meetings were a rarity for politicians who were more accustomed to soundbites for the television cameras. The age of the Internet and social media had given everyone greater access to news and current affairs.

The two candidates from the two main political parties sauntered in and glad-handed various members of the public sitting in the audience. Then candidates from the minor political parties appeared with supporters and made their way down to the tables at the bottom of the hall. Finally, Councillor Beedham joined them.

A heavily-built man with a ceremonial chain around his neck took the microphone and tapped it with his finger. 'Ladies and gentlemen, we need to get started.'

The audience fell silent.

'The by-election at the end of the month is a good time for the candidates to address their priorities for policing in Deeside.'

'No pressure then,' Drake whispered.

The Labour and Conservative party candidates began by thanking the chair for his comments and the introduction. They expressed their support and backing of the Wales Police Service in their investigation of the murder and the ongoing activity of the county lines inquiry. They expressed their support for the WPS's efforts to combat drug dealing and catch Dawn's killer.

Then Councillor Beedham stood up and fastened the buttons of his jacket, covering his ample waist. He gave Drake and Sara a contemptuous glare. 'The tragic events leading up to the murder of Dawn Piper must give everyone cause for concern.'

Sara sensed Drake moving uncomfortably in his seat.

'I think we've all had more than enough of the drug dealers in our town peddling all this crap to our youngsters and then expecting the police to do nothing about it.'

Sara wanted to believe that Beedham seriously hoped he could make a difference. Encourage local people to assist with the inquiry, offer public support for the WPS. But from the tone of his comments and the aggressive body language, Sara was convinced all Beedham wanted was for everyone to agree with him. Sara became increasingly uncomfortable as she glanced over at Drake.

'I'm amazed the Wales Police Service haven't been able to do anything further to identify the culprits involved. In this day and age of social media and CCTV cameras everywhere, it beggars belief they had been unable to make arrests. Surely as a community we are entitled to a better service.'

Clapping erupted from the audience and Beedham visibly preened. He puffed himself up and looked down at the citizens of Deeside, ready to continue his speech. This publicity wasn't doing him any harm at all, Sara guessed.

'I think we should hear from the representatives present tonight from the Wales Police Service about their progress. I'm sure everyone would expect them to keep members of the public informed. After all, making certain we can all sleep safely in our beds at night is the main purpose of the police.'

Now there were shouts of *hear, hear,* and some of the audience turned around and glared at Sara and Drake. It was like being a rabbit caught in headlights. Sara was uncertain how to react – what she should say? Should she look at Drake? She stared straight ahead unblinking, without responding.

Beedham continued. 'Inspector Drake, would you like

to say something to the meeting tonight to assure us you'll catch the killer and arrest the drug dealers taking over our town?'

Drake reluctantly got to his feet and walked to the front. Sara could see the reticence on his face. But these were ordinary people, threatened by drug dealers from the main conurbations of England. Weren't they entitled to a degree of reassurance?

Drake cleared his throat.

'The Wales Police Service is doing everything possible—'

'Do you have any suspects yet?' Beedham butted in.

'Far too early but—'

'It has been going on for months. Deaths from overdoses and all we get from the police are excuses.'

'Criminal investigations can be a complex and difficult matter. We have to be able to gather evidence that can be used to—'

'We know all that, Inspector. What we want is results – an assurance the Wales Police Service will be able to stop all this county lines activity.'

Drake wasn't being given a chance to say anything. Beedham's technique was to bluster and interrupt and Drake eventually gave up trying to say more than a single sentence.

The chair attempted to silence Beedham but the councillor ignored him and carried on a monologue decrying police incompetence. Drake returned to his seat and sat down alongside Sara. Moments later she noticed him fishing out his mobile from his jacket pocket. He read the message and he stiffened showing her the screen.

'DI Drake please attend the scene of a reported homicide.'

Chapter 13

Sara and Drake left the Memorial Hall and raced for the car. A second message reached Drake's mobile with an address and a postcode. He punched the details into the satnav as Sara fired the engine into life and accelerated towards the main road.

Three recent deaths by drug overdose; Dawn Piper's murder followed by another killing would mean a feeding frenzy for the politicians wanting to make a name for themselves.

At a junction the car screeched to a halt as Sara slammed on the brakes. The satnav told them to turn left and once safe she pulled away. Urgency meant they should get to the crime scene as soon as possible but common sense dictated that breaking the speed limit wasn't going to help.

'Sergeant Finch is at the scene with two uniformed officers from the local station,' Drake said after his mobile bleeped with a message.

A van pulled out in front of them and Sara pressed her left palm hard against the horn. The sound blared. The driver reached a hand out of his window and raised his middle finger. 'I've got his registration number.' Drake scribbled the details in his pocket.

Sara slowed as they entered a thirty mile an hour zone.

'Do we know the name of the victim, boss?'

Drake glanced at the screen of his mobile. 'There's a message here with the name somewhere.' After a few seconds Drake said. 'Hubert Caston.'

Something niggled in Drake's mind – a glimmer of recognition. 'I'm sure I've heard that name before.' Drake turned to Sara who frowned. Certainty replaced doubt as Drake recalled the name. 'He's one of the gamers who used to meet with Dawn.'

The satnav directed them to take a right turn into a cul-de-sac and Sara parked behind a marked police vehicle. A uniformed officer stood on the pavement outside the terraced property.

As they arrived Sergeant Finch emerged from the house ashen-faced.

'He's in the kitchen,' Finch said.

'Did you know him?'

'He was friends with Dawn. That's all I know.'

Drake entered the property followed by Sara and Finch. It was typical of similar properties all over Wales where ordinary people lived ordinary lives. A sitting room at the front led off from a small narrow hallway where brown leather sofas were pressed against the walls. Jewel cases of zombie video games filled the small cupboard unit underneath a television and sound system. The room behind it was less tidy, and there was a smell of day-old cannabis and dirty clothes.

Finch led Drake and Sara into the kitchen and nodded inside. Drake stood by the threshold for a moment: discarded pizza boxes littered the worktop and the top of the upright freezer. The same brand of cider bottles Drake had seen in Dawn's fridge stood half empty beside an electric kettle. Underneath a table lay the prone body of Hubert Caston. This time it was clear the body hadn't been moved. Caston had been killed exactly where he lay. Blood covered his clothes and the floor and the walls. Only the post-mortem would be definitive but Drake guessed a knife had caused the wound in Caston's abdomen.

They had become the weapon of choice in a recent spate of high-profile drug-related killings in London that had dominated the news. They were easier to acquire than guns, quieter and just as effective.

'Any sign of the murder weapon?' Drake scanned Caston's corpse. Behind him Finch replied, 'No sign, sir.'

A shout from the front door took their attention.

'That will be the CSIs,' Finch said.

Mike Foulds stood in the hallway supervising two

investigators hauling boxes and equipment.

Drake spoke first. 'The body's in the kitchen.'

'Is the death connected with Dawn Piper?'

'They knew each other apparently.'

'We better get to work then. Looks like it could be an all-night job.'

Drake and Sara left the property and stood for a moment on the pavement outside.

'Both deaths must be connected,' Sara said.

When Sara began working on Drake's team, she would have made the statement sound like a question, asking for his opinion, confirmation even, that her assessment was correct. Now she was growing in confidence, interpreting circumstances correctly and making a valuable judgement as to the direction the inquiry should take.

'Let's wait and see what evidence the CSIs uncover. But it certainly looks like both deaths are drug-related. Somebody had a motive to kill Hubert and Dawn.'

Finch joined them and Drake asked him. 'Who found the body?'

'Olivia Knox.'

Drake spluttered. 'What?!'

Finch glanced at his watch. 'She should be back in a minute. I told her you'd need to speak to her.'

At the bottom of the street a silver Fiesta parked. It made an odd knocking sound as though the exhaust pipe were loose before the engine was switched off and Olivia Knox emerged. She joined the officers.

'We need a word with you,' Drake said. 'How well did you know Caston?'

'He was friends with Dawn Piper. I met him a couple of times with her. He was a vulnerable individual. He found everyday life difficult. He had financial problems that he could never solve.'

'Was he a drug addict?'

Knox looked pensive. 'He had been in the past. He was

doing his best to… he wasn't the sharpest tool in the box and losing his mother cut him adrift in life.'

'Did he have any other family?'

Knox shook her head. 'I don't think so. His parents died a couple of years ago. It hit him badly.'

'How does he make a living?'

'He had a job in one of factories in the industrial park. He used to work for Ritchie O'Brien.' Knox paused and looked at the faces of the officers.

'Ritchie O'Brien,' Drake said slowly.

Knox jerked a finger at Jim Finch. 'Like I've told you before, O'Brien is the major supplier you should be investigating.'

Finch sounded exasperated. 'You know the practical problems of gathering evidence against drug dealers.'

Knox took a step towards Finch. 'What about covert policing? Secret recordings?'

Finch smirked. 'This isn't like some TV cop drama.'

'Well you had better do something before other people take the initiative.'

Drake responded. 'What the hell does that mean?'

Knox rolled her eyes. 'Nothing, nothing.'

'And why did you go to see Caston?'

'He rang and asked if I could call round to see him. He said he had some important information.'

'Did he tell you what about?'

Knox opened her mouth to say something, but then shook her head, making Drake snap. 'You can't run around interfering like some vigilante in a Hollywood movie. This is Connah's Quay for Christ's sake.'

Mike Foulds appeared in the doorway. 'You're in the way standing here. Can't you find somewhere more private?'

Drake folded his arms and glared at Knox before nodding at Foulds. 'You're right.'

Drake turned to look at Finch. 'Get started on house-to-house enquiries.'

'Yes, sir,' Finch said without any enthusiasm.

In the street outside a small crowd had gathered. Residents eager to know what had happened gawped at Drake and Sara as they marched down the street towards their car, Knox behind them. Drake and Sara followed Knox on the short journey to a public park. She drew up near a mobile burger van and Sara parked nearby. The smell of grease and frying onions assaulted their nostrils as they neared the counter behind Knox.

'This place is always open late,' Knox announced.

Equilibrium had returned to Drake's mind although he was still annoyed with Knox. She ordered a burger and a milky coffee. Drake settled for bottled water and he and Sara walked over to a bench, their drinks in hand, as they waited for Knox's food to be prepared. 'I hate someone who interferes,' Drake said.

The last of the summer sunshine was about to disappear. Soon the cool of the late evening would chill their skin. Drake's mind was racing with the priorities that had to be in place to commence the inquiry into Caston's death. It would mean another early start tomorrow. They found a bench and the smell of recently cut grass hung in the air.

'She probably thinks she's being very clever,' Sara said.

'Very stupid,' Drake answered sharply.

Olivia Knox had eaten half of the thin fat laden burger before she found Drake and Sara. Drake clenched his jaw as he spoke. 'You better tell us what you know. Do you know if Hubert Caston was seeing anyone this afternoon?'

Knox mumbled through a mouthful of food. 'Give me a chance.' She managed to wade through another couple of mouthfuls. 'Hubert wanted to tell me something. But I don't know what it was.' The incredulity on Drake and Sara's face must have been evident. 'Honestly. He called me and asked if I would see him.'

'Has he spoken to you about the murder of Dawn Piper?'

Knox nodded as she finished the last mouthful of her burger and scrunched up the tissue that had been holding it into a ball. 'He was really cut up about her death. I think he was frightened of somebody.'

'You're not making any sense, Olivia.' Drake used a severe tone he reserved for the most serious situations. 'Caston calls you, tells you he has important information and you go to his home without any explanation?'

'Suit yourself.'

Knox's shrug riled Drake. He counted mentally to five. 'Are you able to account for your movements tonight?'

'Jesus, you people are mad and useless. Now you think that I might have killed him? For fuck's sake. I was the one who called 999!'

'Then you'll be happy to give us the details of your exact movements and where you called the emergency services.'

In temper Knox threw the ball of tissue into the verdant grass behind the bench and spat out the details that Sara jotted into a notebook. Once she had finished Knox stormed back to her car without giving Drake or Sara a second glance. The exhaust of her dilapidated car rattled a complaint as she indicated left onto the main road.

Sara turned to Drake. 'You don't think she is involved do you?'

Drake shook his head. 'Well she had the perfect opportunity, but I don't think she was responsible… hiding something, yes. But we do need some solid evidence, and fast.'

Chapter 14

The following morning Drake sat in his Mondeo stifling a yawn, breathing in deep lungfuls of air from the open window. Attending a post-mortem was the same at any time of the year, the temperature inside the mortuary never changed.

Drake wanted to clear the smell of decaying flesh and antiseptic bleach that stuck to him from his clothes and nostrils. He doubted whether expediting the toxicology reports would hasten the results, nor did he believe they would change Kings' opinion. He had announced confidently that the catastrophic blood loss from several knife wounds to Caston's body would have been the main cause of his death.

An elderly couple sauntered past Drake's car, making for the hospital, and an ambulance rushed towards the accident and emergency entrance, its siren blaring. Drake raised his left arm to his nose and smelled his jacket sleeve. It still had the clinging odour of human decomposition. So he jumped out of the car, took off his jacket and threaded the hanging loop around the clothes hook above the inside of the rear door. Once back in the driver's seat his mobile pinged with an email. It was a brief missive from Superintendent Price confirming the time of the meeting with Superintendent Hobbs the next morning. Another Saturday in headquarters: it dismayed Drake.

He had left that morning before Annie had surfaced. She had murmured her thanks for the mug of coffee he had deposited on her bedside table. Now he thumbed a message reminding her that he had booked a table the following evening at their local bistro pub. Despite the distance from Annie's home in Felinheli to headquarters, living with her had made him feel more relaxed and he wanted more than anything to make his relationship with Annie work. Although he missed his daughters every day, their holiday at the end of the month in Disneyland Paris would give them all, including Annie, a chance to be a family. But Caston's death loomed like a large obstacle likely to ruin his plans. If needed, Superintendent Hobbs can take charge, Drake thought.

He started the engine and drove out of the hospital car park and on to the A55 before heading for headquarters. After parking he retrieved his jacket and gave it a discreet smell but the lingering odour persisted. It meant dry cleaning, of course. After checking his messages, he smiled. *I haven't forgotten. Thanks for the coffee. I'm looking forward to tomorrow X.*

Drake arrived in the Incident Room and exchanged greetings with his team as he made for the board. He stood scanning the faces looking over at him. In a few short hours, things had changed dramatically – a second death added urgency to everything.

'Nothing new from the post-mortem.' He turned to the image of Hubert Caston on the board behind him. 'Caston died of massive blood loss as a result of several knife wounds.'

Luned struck a serious tone. 'Do we assume it's the same killer?'

Drake turned to face the team. 'We keep an open mind.'

'And they were both connected to the drug scene,' Winder added.

Drake continued. 'Of course. So, we concentrate on building a detailed picture of Hubert Caston's last known movements. He must have been somewhere, and somebody might have seen him. Get started on the phone work. Sara and I are going to his place of work this morning so when I'm back I want progress on both inquiries.'

'I've requisitioned Caston's financial records.' Luned sounded pleased with herself. 'And I've asked they be expedited.'

'Good, keep me up to date.' At least the young

detective constable had used her initiative, Drake thought, happy she had anticipated what needed to be done.

'Any feedback from the care home in Liverpool?'

'Nothing yet, boss,' Winder replied.

'Chase them, find out who those two girls were.'

Back in his office Drake checked his desk reassuring himself that the Post-it notes hadn't been moved and the photograph of his daughters was in the correct position. He found Sara by her desk ready so they hurried out to the car park.

Luned decided to start with Caston's bank statements. It always amazed her how quickly financial institutions responded to a formal request for information. Her interest was heightened when she realised that Caston had various bank accounts. One was called Rent, and another was a current account. It surprised Luned that Caston had a rental property but she scolded herself for having characterised Caston as an unlikely landlord.

Luned was expecting to see regular monthly debits and credits. But there was a haphazard pattern. The personal files and papers the crime scene investigators had removed might yield more details. After squirrelling through them she noticed paperwork from the local council. Intrigued, she called the authority but the official at the relevant department was reluctant to provide the information required. A brief and brisk exchange of emails changed her mind.

'We made a payment of rent for fifteen months to Mr Hubert Caston as the tenant of his property was entitled to Universal Credit and had been in substantial arrears.'

'Why did it stop?'

Luned heard the barest whisper of a mouse being clicked and a gentle breathing down the phone.

'The tenant got a council house.'

'When did the payments stop?'

'Over six months ago.'

'Can you give me the address of the property?'

Another pause. '23 Holman Street, Connah's Quay.'

Luned scribbled the details down on a pad. Was the house empty after the last tenant vacated and if so why? She checked and ascertained that no rent had been paid into the rent account in the preceding six months. Checking more paperwork told Luned that Caston was in arrears with his mortgage on the property where he lived.

Luned turned her attention to the box of papers removed from Caston's home and combed through the documentation hoping for more details. She was rewarded with a folder with Holman Street scribbled on the outside. Inside she found correspondence from solicitors who had dealt with Caston's parents' estate, eventually establishing he had inherited the property after their death. Google Earth images confirmed it was a terrace, and the fact that a tenant had left for a council house suggested it wasn't in the best of condition.

On a plain A4 sheet of paper she jotted down the address, resolving to pin it on to the board alongside Caston's name. Before that she needed to complete the financial analysis.

The monthly income into Caston's bank account was spent before his next pay day and Luned noticed the regular cash withdrawals. The rent account had no deposits in the previous six months after the payments of benefit had stopped. Luned focused on the credit card statement where Caston owed over ten thousand pounds and realised that Caston was making payments – at least the credit card was being paid. It meant another source of income. And a cash source too, because Luned could find no trace of the money being debited from the bank account.

She sat back and pondered.

Then she found another sheet of paper and at the top wrote Caston's name in capital letters. She had seen Drake mind map this way and she hoped the process would be helpful. Underneath she wrote:

- Holman Street – tenanted but now empty – possible use as cuckoo property?
- Caston's home – mortgage arrears
- Large credit card debt – erratic payments

After a moment's hesitation she added:

- Caston – vulnerable

It all added to a picture that suggested someone was taking advantage of Caston. But who?

This was the sort of police work she enjoyed. Being thorough and methodical by nature, Luned relished the task of putting together a detailed picture of Caston's finances. Always present in the background of her mind was the fact that he had once been an addict. A person challenged by their own demons, struggling to beat his addiction. In the end, Luned guessed his involvement with the drug world had cost him his life. She recalled the words of a detective reminding her that whatever evidence existed there had to be motive. Someone had wanted to see Caston dead. But why, Luned thought?

Once the mindmap was complete Luned felt pleased with her progress. The property at Holman Street would need to be checked out. She rummaged through the box of Caston's belongings searching unsuccessfully for a spare key: it would mean a warrant to gain access lawfully. So she instigated the process, hoping Inspector Drake would approve.

Next she turned her attention to the mobile: still tacky to the touch from the chemicals the forensic team used to recover DNA and fingerprints. She concentrated on Caston's recent call history and discovered the name Peter Worsley appeared three times in the two days before Caston died. Luned checked through the inquiry's records for any reference to the name but found none. She made a mental note to call Worsley.

It took Luned a few minutes to establish that the last number to call Caston was a pay-as-you-go mobile.

Anonymous burner phones were a common feature of county line activity, Luned recalled. She sat back, realising she would have to attempt to trace where the handset had been purchased. She could hear Inspector Drake's rebuke if she didn't.

Several phone calls established that it had been sold at one of the large supermarkets in Chester. The prospect that the buyer had used a debit or credit card was remote but she picked up her phone and called the store. She became increasingly annoyed by the multiple choices announced by the tape-recorded message. The final option offered to connect her to the mobile phone shop. She jabbed a finger at the hashtag on the handset. A cheerful voice responded.

'Michelle speaking, how can I help you?'

Once Luned introduced herself Michelle's voice took on a serious tone.

'Unless the buyer used a card, we won't have any records, apart from a till receipt.'

Luned gave her voice a determined edge. 'Can you check, please.'

Luned waited as Michelle checked the record. Occasionally she heard the tap of fingers on a keyboard.

'I'm sorry all I can tell you is that that particular handset was sold on 18th June.'

It confirmed what she knew already.

Luned was about to finish the call but asked, 'Do you have CCTV in store?'

'Not in the mobile shop.'

'What about in the main store itself?'

'You'll have to ask the manager. And I can't put you through from here. You'll have to ring back.'

Luned thanked Michelle. She finished the call and redialled, finding herself becoming more and more annoyed as she listened to the multiple choices available. She almost lost her temper after choosing an option for customer services that ended with a message saying that every operative was busy suggesting she call back later. She scribbled in capitals on the notepad on her desk: call manager.

Returning to the name of Peter Worsley she decided to call him.

It rang several times before a tentative female voice answered. 'Yes.'

'I'd like to speak to Peter Worsley.'

'What do you want?'

The tone suggested the person knew Worsley. 'My name is Detective Constable Luned Thomas of the Wales Police Service and it's imperative I speak to him.' Luned mustered maximum gravitas and was rewarded with the sound of fumbling.

After a pause a voice said, 'Pete Worsley here.'

'I'm part of the team investigating the deaths of Dawn Piper and Hubert Caston. I believe you can help. I wondered when might be a good time for us to come and speak to you?'

By the end of the brief conversation Luned had jotted down the address, having insisted Worsley be at home the following morning.

Chapter 15

Drake looked out through the windscreen at the entrance of GAA Components as Sara parked. The company had a prominent site in the middle of an industrial estate on the outskirts of Deeside. Hubert Caston had no immediate relatives which meant that his work mates were the closest thing he had to family.

'I spoke to an Aaron Black, one of the managers. He's expecting us.'

'What do they make here, boss?' Sara said.

'Electrical parts apparently.'

Black paint streaked the windows of the wooden door and inside the make-do attitude extended to the ancient wooden chairs standing in front of a window beyond which two girls sat staring at monitors. Drake tapped on the glass and two surprised faces turned towards him as though visitors were unexpected and unwelcome.

'Detective Inspector Ian Drake, Wales Police Service for Mr Black,' Drake said after one of the women pulled back the glass screen.

She darted a glance towards the chairs. 'Take a seat and I'll tell him you're here.'

From behind the glass screen the word police drifted through from a muted conversation. Drake and Sara didn't have to wait long until the door from the reception area opened and a man in his early forties wearing grey trousers and a faded white shirt with no tie appeared and gestured for them to join him. They walked over and he stuck out his hand. 'Aaron Black. Come through.'

Black led them through a corridor past various offices, the sound of fingers on keyboards and paper being moved evident. A card with his name had been slotted into a small box screwed to the open door – it read 'Assistant Operations Manager'.

Two chairs of a similar vintage to the ones in reception

were pushed against the wall. Aaron Black rarely had visitors, Drake assumed.

'I'm not certain what I can do to help,' Black said sinking into his chair. 'Hubert Caston has worked on the shop floor for several years. I think he enjoyed working here and he was popular with the lads.'

'He didn't have any family so we hope that some of his work colleagues might be able to give us an insight into his personal life.'

Black shrugged half-heartedly. Then he delved into a green folder on his desk. 'I can't tell you much about his personal life. We have his next of kin as his mother, but I know that's wrong because she's dead. I never heard him talk about his family.'

'We'd like a copy of his personnel file,' Drake said. 'What did Hubert do?'

'Hubert had learning difficulties. He did fairly menial tasks around the factory moving finished parts around. It didn't require a great deal of training or aptitude.'

Black read the time on his watch. 'I've arranged for some of his work mates to talk to you as you asked. They'll be on their break.' He stood up, Drake and Sara joined him as they left the office.

A door led out onto the shop floor where the noise from machine presses and tools assaulted Drake's ears.

'What do you do here?' Sara asked.

'We make components for the electricity industry. Plugs and switches, that kind of thing.'

'How many people work here?'

'About a hundred at the moment but head office is thinking of scaling the operation down and moving a lot of the production to Romania.'

Drake and Sara followed Black into the production line, carefully threading a route along the yellow painted demarcation lines. Operatives sitting at the presses that lined the route had a labour-intensive activity, all of which suggested to Drake that the factory was on borrowed time and that the owners needed to invest in modern production techniques.

The staffroom in the middle of the shop floor had a dirty and unkempt feel. Day-old red top newspapers were scattered over a table and in a corner a kettle was boiling on a makeshift kitchen unit. Six members of staff turned to look at Drake and Sara as they entered with Black. After a cursory glance at Drake the four men gave Sara a lingering gaze. One of the women asked if they'd like tea or coffee. Sara opted for tea as Drake shook his head.

'I'm the senior investigating officer in charge of the murder of Dawn Piper and Hubert Caston.'

Drake's introduction focused everyone's attention. 'Did Hubert ever talk about his private life?' Drake scanned the employees present.

A couple shook their heads. Two others looked around the group.

'Hubert was okay.' An overweight man about the same age as Caston slurped noisily on a coffee. 'I wouldn't have thought that he had any enemies.'

'We are aware that he had a drug problem.' Drake opted for the tactic of confirming what his audience would have known, but might have been reluctant to tell him outright.

The same man replied. 'He was over that. People took advantage of him. He was vulnerable sure enough and he got into debt. That's about the only thing that he ever complained about.'

Drake shared a comment with everyone. 'Did any of you socialise with him?'

One of the older women piped up. 'I saw him in one of the cafés in town with Doreen. I sat and had a coffee with them and a piece of cake. She was friends with his mother, and she took him under her wing when she died. I don't suppose you could call it socialising really.'

'Do you know where I can get hold of Doreen?'

Sara scribbled down the contact number as Drake gave the rest of the group a hopeful glance. 'Anything else unusual that you can remember? Did he tell you where he was going on the night that he was killed?'

A youngster in his twenties with a thin wispy beard moved his position on the low seating before replying. 'I saw him a couple of weeks ago in that new letting agency in town. I was looking for a place with my girlfriend. I'm sick to death of living at home. Hubert seemed to be best mates with the boss.'

'I'll need the name of the business.'

The youngster nodded. 'Someone told me that the man who owns the business comes from Rhyl. He was dressed in this fancy suit and had a massive watch.'

Drake fixed him with a stare. Could it be Jack Beltrami or was Drake becoming obsessed with the possibility that the Beltrami family was involved? Sara jotted down the details and once the youngster produced his mobile, he read aloud the phone number.

Two other members of staff clearly encouraged by others volunteering information first shared their encounters with Caston out of the workplace with Drake. He ignored the surreptitious glance that Black gave his watch. One had passed Hubert Caston in the street in Connah's Quay. Another had seen him in the supermarket. There'd be nothing unusual that had drawn their attention.

As Drake made a move to finish, he asked for everyone's contact details. A second woman caught his attention. 'He had the afternoon off on the day he was killed. I saw him at the bus stop. He'd missed the bus he was supposed to be getting back into town and we chatted for a while. He was going to see some friends that afternoon and he told me about some games he was playing. It all sounded really weird. Anyway, I had to wait for my bus, but Hubert got a lift into town.'

'Did you know the driver who gave him a lift? Or see

his face?'

'No, but I remember the car was black.'

Drake raised his voice slightly. 'Do you remember anything else about the car? The make of it?'

She pursed her lips.

'Audi, I think.'

'And the registration number?'

Another shake of the head. 'Sorry.'

Black cleared his throat noisily. 'If there's nothing else, Inspector, we have production targets to meet.' He made for the door which he kept open for the staff who streamed out back to the shop floor.

Drake thanked Black and they retraced their steps back to the car. 'Grubby place,' Drake said wiping his hands. 'Let's get something to eat.'

Drake made for the toilet in the café they found, and Sara sat down before scanning the menu. His search for an antiseptic wipe in the car had been unsuccessful and Sara knew he'd be washing his hands thoroughly as soon as he could.

'I'll contact Doreen later,' Sara announced as Drake returned from the bathroom.

He sat down and tugged at the double cuffs before running a hand down the sleeve of his navy suit. He could be so fussy, Sara thought. A young waitress arrived, and Sara ordered a Diet Coke and a bacon sandwich. Drake ordered a cold drink but asked the waitress to give him a minute to read the menu. Sara's mobile bleeped with a message and she smiled to herself. After recently joining an online dating site, a shortlist of potential dates had narrowed itself down to a project manager working for a local authority. A flurry of messages had settled on a bistro pub in Rhyl for their first date that weekend. The other candidate was a schoolteacher but his earnest old-looking face made Sara doubt his real age, so she'd eliminated him.

'Anything interesting?' Drake said. 'New boyfriend?'

Sara looked up and thought she saw a hint of a smile on his face. It was the first time he had enquired about her private life in such direct terms. It was another example of the impact Annie was having on Drake and indirectly on Sara's relationship with him.

She gave him a mind-your-own-business smirk.

The waitress returned with Drake's Sprite and he ordered a tuna sandwich. Sara took a mouthful of her Diet Coke. 'How many black Audis are there likely to be in this area? Do you think Caston was involved with the county lines dealers?'

'We need to find out where he went the afternoon he was killed.'

'I keep thinking about those two girls,' Sara said after starting on her lunch. 'I despair of the system sometimes.'

Television documentaries often highlighted the impact of austerity on social services departments. They were the Cinderella service, unvalued and underappreciated and open to intense criticism and scrutiny when mistakes occurred. That youngsters could be trafficked from one part of the country to another challenged everything Sara valued about the society she lived in.

'We all need to pay more taxes.' Sara couldn't hide her emotion. 'Then maybe we could protect children more easily.'

'You're beginning to sound like a politician,' Drake said.

Sara sulked. Persuading any ambitious politician to campaign for an increase in taxation was as likely as turkeys voting for Christmas.

'Let's detour to the *Duke of Lancaster* on the way back to headquarters. I want to see what all this zombie fuss is about.'

It was a short drive towards the dock where the *Duke of Lancaster* had been berthed. Drake shared aloud the results of his Google search. The *Duke of Lancaster* had been a passenger car ferry in the sixties and seventies and new owners hoped to turn it a 'fun centre'. Years of delays and failed planning applications meant the vessel had been allowed to rust and decay.

Images on the Internet abounded of the graffiti and grotesque goblin-like creatures that a Latvian artist had been commissioned to adorn the hull. Now the hull was black and zombielike. Sara pulled the vehicle into a grass-lined lane that led to a gate and beyond it the quayside with the ship berthed not in water but on concrete.

'This is an odd place.' Drake got out of the car and stood by the passenger door. 'I've passed it so many times on the train you accept it as a feature of the landscape.'

Two workmen were busy on the deck and another near a Portacabin at the base of a metal staircase. She nodded in their direction. 'We should go and talk to them, boss?'

Drake nodded in acknowledgement and reached into the rear of the car for his jacket. He shrugged it on and then straightened his tie – always Mr Presentable, Sara thought.

The gates gave way as Drake pushed one end and they made their way over to the vessel. The man standing near the Portacabin had a broad chin and two, maybe, three days' worth of stubble. The yellow high visibility jacket failed to contain the paunch straining at the shrunken T-shirt.

Drake flashed his warrant card. 'Detective Inspector Drake, Wales Police Service – and this is Detective Sergeant Sara Morgan. Are you in charge?'

'John Andrews. I'm the site manager. What's this about?'

'We're investigating two murders – Dawn Piper and Hubert Caston.'

'What's that got to do with us?'

'What exactly are you doing here?'

Andrews hesitated. 'We're turning the place into a zombie attraction. It should be open next week. People pay to come on board and scare themselves shitless.'

'And they do that for fun?'

'Yeah, I know. People love all this stuff. I suppose it helps them escape from all the ordinary day-to-day drudgery in their lives.'

Sara sensed Drake's patience with Andrews' folksy take on the world wouldn't last. 'Both victims enjoyed playing zombie videogames. And we believe that one of them in particular might have called here a few days before she died.'

'We get all sorts of rubberneckers. How fucking sad is that?'

Sara scrolled through her mobile to find a photograph of Dawn Piper which she showed to Andrews. 'Do you remember seeing her round here?'

Andrews squinted at the image until recognition creased his face. 'Yeah, I remember her. She came here looking for a job as a zombie. If you can believe it?'

'Was she on her own?'

'The boss saw her when he was here one day. He told them they only employed actors.'

Drake cut across Andrews. 'When was she here?

'Last week.'

'When last week?' Now Drake was annoyed.

Andrews frowned. 'It was Friday, no come again, Saturday morning. We were doing an extra shift that day. She was here dead early with that other woman.'

Sara and Drake shared a glance knowing another piece of Dawn's timetable had slotted into place.

'Do you know the name of the person with her?' Drake said.

Andrews shook his head. 'But she had this dead weird haircut: all spiky and red and black.'

Drake raised an eyebrow as he reached for his mobile and flicked through the images on his mobile until Knox's face appeared. He pushed it in Andrews' direction on an off chance. He gave the image a quick glance. 'Yeah, that's her.'

'Is there somewhere we can sit down and take a statement?' Drake said looking over Andrews' shoulder towards the Portacabin.

'I'm very busy.'

'And this is an urgent murder inquiry.' Drake made clear it wasn't a subject for discussion.

Half an hour later Drake and Sara returned to the car. There were more statements to take, possible eyewitnesses to interview but at least they knew more about Dawn's movements. Drake's mobile rang and his face tightened as he listened to the caller.

'That was Super Price. We need to get back to headquarters. Apparently, there's some YouTube video we need to watch.'

Chapter 16

Superintendent Price pointed the remote control at the television and Drake watched as the footage of Councillor Beedham filled the screen.

'I hate these bloody do-gooders who think they have a monopoly on the truth.' Price spat out the comment. 'They have no idea about the complexities of policing.'

Beedham was walking through the streets of Connah's Quay keeping up a running commentary to the camera. Drake focused on what Beedham was saying.

'Our communities have been let down so badly in the past that it's time the people took back control. We have to get the politicians working for us, the people. We need to put Deeside first and foremost. Everybody else is so conflicted that our only real hope is having a fresh voice. Somebody to challenge the political elites in Cardiff. Someone to make certain that our voices are heard.'

Behind Beedham, Drake saw the squalid terrace of a side street in Connah's Quay. The councillor had been cynical enough to choose the back drop to his video carefully.

'Our public services are on their knees. We don't have enough teachers and doctors who understand our communities. And we certainly don't have enough police on the ground to actually catch the criminals.'

Beedham walked out of shot only to re-emerge into the footage. Drake recognised the location. It was the street where Dawn Piper had lived. Beedham then theatrically held up his mobile.

'And I've recorded a clear admission from the police that there is little they can do about the rising level of drug addiction and criminality spreading into our communities from the big cities of England.'

Drake frantically trawled through his memory recalling anything in the comments he had made in the public meeting that Beedham could have misconstrued.

'The people of Connah's Quay mustn't be ignored. The people of Deeside need to be respected.' Beedham was drawing his monologue to a conclusion. *'Now is your chance to elect a strong voice. Someone who can help make real change. Donald Trump said he wanted to drain the swamp in Washington. It's time there was a fresh face in Welsh government in Cardiff Bay. We've got to have a change. The people of Deeside deserve it.'*

Drake watched as Price pointed the remote at the television again and replayed the footage a second and then a third time. Once it had finished Price turned to face Drake, ignoring Susan Howells from public relations sitting at the table.

His voice was measured. 'Did you say anything to justify Beedham's comment.'

Drake shook his head. 'Nothing, sir, I made comments about the demands of an investigation like this requiring admissible evidence.'

Price nodded.

Drake continued. 'Councillor Beedham is taking advantage of the present publicity to bang his own drum in order to raise his profile in the community. He's an independent in the by-election so he doesn't have a chance of being elected.'

'It's not that easy,' Howells said. 'The other main political parties have picked up his comments and I've had requests for formal responses about the ongoing investigation.'

'Bloody politicians.' Price tapped a ballpoint on the table top. 'I want to see a draft of any press release. The last thing we need is a small-minded politician scratching around for publicity.'

'The recent documentaries on the television about the various deaths from drug overdoses have only added to the public disquiet,' Howells said. 'There's no way we can avoid engaging the press about this. The timing of these murders in the by-election campaign has certainly proved inconvenient.'

'Inconvenient?' Price raised his voice.

Howells looked vaguely hurt before she continued. 'What I meant is that we have to react to the present circumstances. There is no point burying our head in the sand.'

'I'll decide exactly how we deal with the press.' Price stood up, signalling that the meeting was at an end.

Howells persevered. 'You'll have to consider a press conference, Wyndham. Otherwise they could complain we weren't being transparent. The head of PR called me—'

Price raised a hand. 'I'm in charge. Not the PR department in Cardiff. We'll speak again next week. Inspector Drake and I have to review progress.'

Howells got the message, gathered up her papers and left.

Price sank back into his chair. 'Is Councillor Beedham really a self-important half-wit?'

Typical Price, Drake thought, sharing his opinion without reservation. Drake hoped that his successor would be just as forthright.

'He's not helping.'

Price guffawed. 'Bring me up to date.'

'We still need to identify the movements of both victims before they were killed and as yet we can't establish the exact crime location where Dawn Piper was killed. Phone work should give us some pointers once we've had the triangulation results. And we suspect that two teenage girls have been seen in the Deeside area pushing drugs. They may be part of the county lines activity. I'm waiting for more details from the care home in Liverpool who reported them missing recently.'

'Teenagers, Christ Almighty. Once we find the traffickers let's lock them up. Any forensics?'

'Fibres found on Piper's body suggests she was lying in

the boot of a car. She went to visit the *Duke of Lancaster* in search of work as a zombie.'

'What?'

'The ship near Mostyn docks – it's going to be converted into a zombie attraction.'

'Zombies? What the hell is the world coming to? Send me a full briefing note I can circulate to Superintendent Hobbs in advance of our meeting next week.'

Back in his office Drake sat at his desk allowing various threads in his mind to tug and pull in no apparent order. The people of Deeside deserved better than the verbal diarrhoea of Councillor Beedham. Drake googled his name. A blog entitled 'Deeside Matters' was the most prominent reference to him, and Drake read some of the posts: all full of the same rhetoric he had heard on the YouTube clip as well as angry and vindictive videos of Beedham venting his anger. Videos were now the medium for mass market communication. How long would it be before newspapers couldn't compete?

The by-election for the Welsh Assembly seat had given Beedham a stage but as an independent he had little chance of winning the seat. The publicity he generated challenged the conventional political parties. They'd have no choice but to respond and join in the debate he was creating around his blog. The media outlets loved to feature him. Little would change, Drake thought. Deeside was at the margins of the country, at the extremity of Wales and its communities conflicted. Were they Welsh or English? What did the Welsh government in Cardiff mean for them? Perhaps Beedham's outpourings were making people think. And the drug overdoses and the two recent deaths had brought the towns of Deeside to national attention. Drug dealers preyed on people at the margins.

That morning a clip on the news showed the First Minister of Wales on the campaign trail promising new initiatives to revive the local economy. No matter how often the politicians repeated the same hyperbole it was the vulnerable and disadvantaged in society who lost out.

And people like Jack Beltrami and Ritchie O'Brien took advantage of their plight.

He picked up the glossy lifestyle magazine that Sutherland had left on his desk. A text had told him an article about the Beltrami family might amuse him. He turned to the multi-page spread that had photographs of Mrs Beltrami beaming at the camera standing in the palatial kitchen of her home in the Denbighshire countryside. She boasted about the charity events she hosted and how her husband was an entrepreneur in the leisure industry. Drake choked back his disgust. The second page had images of her with her horses and then photographs of the lake and landscaped gardens of their home.

The Beltrami family had enough money and property to be unconcerned with the lives of the people who fed the slot machines in their amusement arcades or bought the drugs the family distributed. Drake relished the prospect of challenging Jack Beltrami.

He turned to his computer and started the report Price had requested – 'Briefing memorandum: Piper and Caston'. After summarising the links to the Beltrami family, Drake realised how little evidence they really had. Beltrami barely scraped over the threshold of a person of interest.

Starting a new paragraph, Drake added the name Ritchie O'Brien. Drake re-read Sutherland's intelligence report but sensed something was missing. O'Brien had been a person of interest in several inquiries. Various businesses were owned in his wife's name including The Lamb pub, a launderette and a Chinese takeaway. Laundering money would be simple, and it gave O'Brien the thinnest veneer of respectability.

Drake punched Sutherland's extension number into his office phone, and she replied almost immediately.

'I'm preparing a briefing memorandum for Superintendent Hobbs in relation to both murder inquiries.'

Drake heard the barest smirk down the phone. 'I hear he's a stickler for paperwork.'

Gossip about Superintendent Hobbs had already travelled around Northern Division headquarters faster than Drake had expected – he wondered what he might have missed.

'Ritchie O'Brien,' Drake said. 'Olivia Knox, a charity worker in Deeside who supports addicts and their families, is convinced O'Brien is involved. She thinks he could be protecting his turf against county lines operators from Liverpool.'

'It would certainly fit his profile. We've never been able to build a proper case against him.'

'Is there anything about O'Brien that you haven't included in the intelligence report?'

Sutherland paused. 'There were rumours years ago that he got hold of some cocaine from a drug bust. Allegations flew around about corrupt officers – there was a full internal investigation, but nothing was discovered, and the matter was closed. It was treated as another attempt to discredit the force.'

Drake raised an eyebrow. 'Does O'Brien have important friends?'

'His wife comes from a respectable local family apparently. Her sister is married to a local solicitor and a pillar of the local community.'

'Is there any intelligence on the *Duke of Lancaster* – you know the ship in Mostyn dock along the coast? You pass it on the train.'

'I know what you mean – odd, isn't it? It's been there for years. I'm surprised the council hasn't done something about it before now. Years ago, it was suspected that drugs were stored on board. The owners cooperated fully, and a search was done but nothing was found. Do you know how easy it would be to hide something on a ship?'

'Can you send me the details of that?'

Drake rang off. Ritchie O'Brien wouldn't be the first drug dealer to try and protect his patch from ambitious competitors. He typed up a section referring to O'Brien's status as a person of interest in several inquiries but studiously avoided any repetition of Sutherland's comments. Hobbs struck Drake as an officer who would not welcome gossip.

He turned his attention to Paul Kenny. After summarising what they knew, it was what they didn't know that Drake found puzzling – why had Dawn Piper been to see Kenny? The sound of movement in the Incident Room distracted him from his thoughts and looking up he was surprised to see Sergeant Finch appearing on the threshold of his office.

'Gareth told me you wanted me to be present this afternoon.'

Drake hesitated. 'Yes… it might be helpful.'

Finch turned on his heel. Drake gathered his papers and left his office, turning up his nose at the smell of stale cigarette smoke where Finch had been standing. He made his way into the Incident Room and over to the board. It was a maze of photographs, names, dates and interweaving connections. He cleared his throat and faced the team.

Drake turned to tap a finger on the face of Dawn Piper. 'We know that Dawn, accompanied by Knox, went to the *Duke of Lancaster* on the Saturday morning before she died, hoping to get employment in the zombie attraction. And she bought a meal in the café for two girls at lunchtime. So, we concentrate on establishing her whereabouts for the rest of Saturday into Sunday. Let's focus on CCTV cameras.'

Drake looked over as Winder and Luned scribbled furiously.

Winder made his first contribution. 'We've spoken to most of her neighbours and none of them could account for her movements before her death.'

'It was all a bit sad,' Luned said. 'They all knew about

her drug habit and tended to avoid her. Do you think she could be involved with the county lines activity?'

Finch straightened in the chair by the desk where he was sitting. 'We've tried to identify who the main dealer from Liverpool might be.' He tipped his head towards the board. 'Paul Kenny fits the right profile, but we've always been convinced Jack Beltrami was involved too. Do you have anything specific about Ritchie O'Brien?'

'Nothing that would make him a suspect. But if Kenny is intruding on his patch and Dawn gets caught up in it then O'Brien may have taken steps to protect his business interests.' Drake hated it when he sounded like he was regurgitating management jargon.

'We still need to build a picture of Caston's movements,' Sara said.

Luned piped up. 'The number that called Caston on the afternoon he died is a pay-as-you-go phone that was purchased in a supermarket. And—'

'The buyer paid cash and cannot be traced.'

Luned continued. 'Caston owns a tenanted property. He was receiving payment of rent from the council until a few months ago but since then no record of any payments, although he made cash payments against his credit card. I've organised a warrant to search the property.'

'We'll get it executed in the morning,' Drake said.

Finch cut in. 'That would tie in with a lot of the cuckooing activity that the county lines dealers favour. They find someone vulnerable and take advantage of them.'

'Any luck with the other numbers from his mobile?'

'Most were friends or work colleagues. I've traced calls that Caston made the day he died. There were three that morning to a Peter Worsley. I've spoken to him and arranged a time to interview him tomorrow.'

'Good, excellent, Luned,' Drake said.

Drake took a moment to gather his thoughts. Identifying a motive was sometimes easier than finding the evidence. If

Dawn Piper and Hubert Caston were connected to the drug dealers whose faces were pinned to the board, then all they had to do was join the dots.

He turned to face the team and after thanking Finch traipsed back to his office.

He read the time on his watch knowing that he had to leave soon, so he tapped out a message to Annie. The simple act of doing that brought a smile to his face and lightened his mood. No cooking tonight, they were eating out – he fancied steak and chips and a cheesecake.

Leaving in half an hour. See you later X

Chapter 17

The satnav took Drake and Sara off the dual carriageway in the direction of Connah's Quay, a journey of thirty-eight minutes which Sara managed in twenty-eight. The occasional disgruntled driver flashed their lights which she ignored. Grudgingly, Drake admired her determination to drive the pool car at such speeds.

Briefing memos from Sergeant Finch outlined that cuckooing was a pattern every county lines drug dealer favoured. Youngsters exploited as modern-day slaves to sell drugs were housed in the home of a sympathetic addict or a vulnerable person. The local dealers wouldn't be happy with the county lines activity encroaching on their area which meant frayed tempers and the possibility of a turf war was all the more possible.

Holman Street was very like the terrace where Caston lived. As they waited for the search team to arrive, Drake thought of his own daughters and how protective he would be if anything threatened their well-being. If there was a possibility that Caston had been letting the property to Kenny or anyone involved in the drugs trade, then he had made a bad choice. An unmarked van drew up behind them and they left the car and joined the officers on the pavement.

'Two of you go around the back while we force the front door,' Drake said.

The sergeant in charge of the team turned to the constables. 'Let's go lads.'

Drake led them towards the house and as he did so he took in his surroundings. More post-industrial terraces, the sort built for steelworkers who'd once worked in the local plant years ago. There were hundreds of these small houses, two up two down, with extensions out the back for a modern kitchen and bathroom upstairs. Assessing the decay on the exterior of the properties, Drake guessed that proud homeowners were a thing of the past. Drake took the final few yards to the house and paused until the sergeant nodded confirmation that the two officers were at the rear. It took the sergeant a few seconds to unlock the door.

Drake was the first over the threshold, Sara right behind him.

A table with three dilapidated chairs filled the downstairs kitchen. Pots and pans crowded the sink and grease-smeared plates stood to attention on the drainer. There was an overwhelming smell of stale food. Drake called out a friendly greeting – it wasn't reciprocated.

An ancient sofa had been pushed against the wall in the front room and a small television provided scant entertainment. Taking the stairs to the first floor he looked into the rear bedroom. It had a bunk-style bed against one wall with a mattress and a sleeping bag on each. A chest of drawers filled the space in front of the window. Drake moved on to the second bedroom while Sara rummaged through the cabinets in the bathroom. No bunk beds this time but two single divans. No change of clothes and no wardrobe. If anyone had been living at the property they had left in a hurry.

Drake joined Sara in the bathroom. It stank of urine and faeces.

She held up an empty syringe. 'It's an insulin syringe.' The significance clear. 'And Debbie, one of the teenage girls, is a diabetic.'

Drake nodded. 'We need to find these girls.'

Gareth Winder was looking forward to finishing work that Saturday afternoon and getting home for a takeaway pizza and a few beers before watching a film and then Liverpool playing Chelsea in the Premier League on Match of the Day. It was ample reward for his efforts that week. His girlfriend had decided to work additional overtime tomorrow so she could save for their next holiday. It suited Winder, and he planned to spend a few hours playing the zombie video game that had been a favourite of Dawn Piper's.

For the first hour after Inspector Drake and the others had left, he'd spoken to social workers, probation officers and police officers in the Merseyside and Manchester police forces. Establishing possible addresses or known contacts for the girls missing in Liverpool over the past six months would be a thankless task, but he persevered until satisfied that he had made progress.

Winder turned to look at the image of Caston on the Incident Room board. Where did he go for the last few hours of his life? Winder examined again the various statements taken from Caston's neighbours. Nobody had seen him arrive home but Winder realised not everyone had been interviewed. He made a list of the homeowners who still needed to be seen.

He returned from the kitchen with coffee mug in hand and got down to the task of watching CCTV footage. Grudgingly he admired Luned's thoroughness in building an analysis of payments from Caston's account so quickly. It certainly made his life easier.

But he had hours in front of his computer before he could leave. So he turned his attention to the CCTV footage from the garage in Connah's Quay where Hubert Caston had purchased fuel one afternoon two days before he was murdered. How had they apprehended anybody in the days before cameras?

He double-checked the time Caston had bought the fuel and fast forwarded the footage to half an hour before Caston had arrived at the filling station. He searched for Caston's car – an old Peugeot – but the only vehicle to grab his attention was a black Audi. He scribbled down the registration number of the car and peered at the driver side door waiting for someone to emerge.

Soon he was rewarded as both the driver and passenger emerged.

He hit the keyboard to freeze the footage and he gave a

brief yelp of surprise.

The image of Paul Kenny filled Winder's monitor.

'Are we sure that's Kenny?' The photograph recovered from Cameron Toft's mobile was of poor quality. Now they could pin a better-quality image from the well-lit forecourt to the Incident Room board. 'And what was Herbert Caston doing buying fuel for Kenny's car?'

Drake's questions had been asked out of frustration more than a hope anyone could offer specific answers. Whoever trafficked the young girls into Deeside was one step ahead of the investigation team. The search that morning would soon be the stuff of local gossip, only making the county lines operator more careful.

Winder added, 'The black Audi is registered to Paul Kenny.'

Drake nodded. He paused before adding, 'Hubert Caston is in difficult financial circumstances and Kenny takes advantage of him by offering him a financial lifeline if he allows two girls to stay at his property.'

Sara responded, 'But Kenny finds out Caston is going to join forces with Ritchie O'Brien for a slice of the drug action in Deeside and the red mist descends.'

'Or the other way around,' Luned said. 'This morning I spoke to a Peter Worsley who was playing computer games with Caston on the afternoon he died. Caston took a call from someone he knew, and they gave me the name of another friend of Caston's – a Mattie Williams. She's away until next week, apparently.'

Drake pondered. Sara broke the silence. 'I think we should notify every pharmacy in the Deeside area to be on the lookout for teenagers exchanging prescriptions for insulin.'

'Get that organised,' Drake said before making his way back to his office. 'And send me details of the background briefing on Kenny.'

Drake pulled the chair nearer to the desk and looked over at the photographs of Helen and Megan. He reminded himself of Sergeant Finch's original briefing that county lines operators could be clever and move their mules from one address to another to evade suspicion.

He opened Winder's email with intelligence on Paul Kenny and the name of the detective chief inspector in the Merseyside force. Drake called the officer and listened with increasing alarm to details of Kenny's connection to organised crime groups and their influence up and down Lancashire and northwards to Cumbria. 'We'll never have enough resources to see these gangsters locked up.' The chief inspector's harsh Scouse accent made the task sound even harder somehow. Drake thanked him and rang off, allowing his gaze to dwell on the smiling faces of his daughters once more.

Gathering admissible evidence against the county lines operator was laborious work. They had a direct link between Kenny and Dawn Piper and now Hubert Caston, which meant it was time to interview Paul Kenny.

He read the time, regretting most of the day had gone and reminding himself Annie expected him home at a reasonable time. A day off tomorrow would freshen his mind enabling him to refocus on interviewing Kenny on Monday. Drake was tidying his desk when Mike Foulds appeared on the threshold of his office. Drake waved him in.

Foulds sat in one of the visitor chairs and gave Drake a studious look. 'We've had the forensic results back from the fibres we recovered from Dawn Piper's clothes. Good news and bad news I'm afraid.'

'Go on.'

'We can definitely link the fibres to the manufacturer of materials used in the car industry. Apparently, the manufacturers of these boot linings and stairwell mats are fairly common to a lot of the major car companies. It's the quality of final dying which distinguishes one mat from another.'

'Is that the good news?'

Foulds nodded. 'You can get high-end mats with the specific logo and brand name of the car but those are expensive. In this case the mats were made by a company that supplies Audi vehicles. But we can't go any further. It could be for any sort of Audi vehicle within a fairly broad range of variables.'

It didn't surprise Drake. A vehicle had been used to transport Dawn Piper's body. Cleaning the boot liner wouldn't guarantee the destruction of evidence. Drake had to hope the killer wouldn't dispose of it. Criminals never expected to be caught, they took risks. And that made them vulnerable.

And knowing that Kenny owned an Audi made it even more important to interview him.

'Any other forensic results?' Drake asked.

'There was nothing further from Dawn's possessions or from her property.'

'We executed a search warrant at a property in Connah's Quay this morning. We're trying to locate two teenage girls trafficked from the Liverpool area by a county lines operator.'

Foulds raised his eyebrows. 'How old are they?'

'Sixteen and one of them is a diabetic.'

'Christ, that young. Do these bastards have no moral compass at all?'

'Not when it comes to making money from selling drugs.'

Foulds got up and paused before looking back at Drake. 'One of my kids is sixteen. I would hate to think that my daughter was dossing down somewhere. It must be terrible for the family.'

'They were in care.'

'That makes it worse. The system failed them. I hope

you find them, Ian.'

'So do I.'

Foulds left Drake reflecting on how policing was becoming more of a social service. They had to intervene in domestic disputes, protect vulnerable people and calls to the hospitals invariably meant people who had mental health issues threatening nurses and doctors. All of these people had fallen through the net. And the county lines drug operators took advantage of the vulnerable and disadvantaged and it sickened Drake. He ignored the sense of dread in his mind about the ordeal both these girls would have been put through.

He padded out to the Incident Room and told the rest of the team to leave for the evening. 'I'll see you all first thing on Monday. Relax tomorrow.' Winder, Luned and Sara gave a serious nod.

Chapter 18

It was another glorious summer morning when Drake and Annie and his two daughters arrived at his mother's smallholding overlooking Caernarfon Bay. The gravel of the driveway outside the house crunched underfoot as Helen and Megan ran over to the back door where their Nain gave them a welcoming hug. Drake gazed over the fields and countryside down towards the sea and in the distance the towers of Caernarfon Castle shimmered through the early morning sunshine.

Drake kissed his mother lightly on the cheek and Annie did the same.

'I've told the girls to go and find the plastic chairs so that we can sit outside before we have lunch.'

'That'll be lovely, Mair,' Annie said.

Drake realised as he arrived that Sunday morning, he hadn't given Annie a guided tour of the smallholding his father once tended. 'I'm going to show Annie around. We won't be long. I'm sure Helen and Megan will help you.'

Drake led Annie towards the gate into the field nearest the house. He drew back the bolt and the gate squeaked open. The earth was hard beneath their feet, grass growing abundantly. Once the gate was closed Drake turned to Annie. 'Every field has a name. This one is called *Cae Gwyn.*'

'Do you know why it's called White Field?'

Drake shook his head. As a boy he had never bothered to ask his father or his grandfather why the fields had different names. It was one of those things he'd accepted without thinking. An open gate led into a field where sheep grazed. Under a hawthorn bent by the gales stood the remains of an old horse-drawn gypsy trailer.

'How long has this been here?' Annie said peering inside.

'As long as I can remember. We went inside as kids but it's all rotten through now.'

'How romantic. An uncle of mine spent his honeymoon in a gypsy caravan in Ireland.'

'You can ask Mam when we get back. She might know more about it.'

Unlocking another gate Drake regaled Annie with a time when he'd tried to vault over it only to crash over on the other side and crack his ankle. 'I thought Dad might be angry. But he helped me home and he took me to the hospital.'

'What was your father like?'

Drake wanted to respond that his father had led a simple lifestyle, loved the outdoors and his family and treasured the community in which he lived. But memories flooded back about their recent discovery that his father had left home as a young man to live with a woman a lot older than him. Drake had only recently discovered he had a half-brother, which had made him reassess what he thought of his father. It hadn't diminished his recollection of him. It had coloured it, enhanced it even. More than anything it made him realise that seeing his parents through rose-tinted spectacles wasn't sensible.

'He was a quiet man. He loved farming. He thought there was a connection to nature. Something about maintaining an old lifestyle, maintaining a bond to an old way of life.'

'Farming isn't what it used to be. We can get too nostalgic about it.'

Drake nodded. He realised then that he hadn't shared with Annie all the details about his father and his half-brother, Huw. Drake talked, Annie listened, occasionally interrupting when she needed clarification of family connections. Reaching a small hillock of granite protruding from the field's surface, Drake scrambled to the top offering Annie a hand to join him.

'We used to stand here and watch the storms come in. They'd roll in off the sea and we could see the columns of rain falling on Caernarfon.'

Annie surveyed the scenery. 'It really is beautiful.'

From the vantage point, Drake pointed to the furthest extremity of the land his mother owned. Some of the fields were more waterlogged than others in winter, others had better pasture. Drake turned to Annie. 'We'd better get back.'

After unlocking and re-locking the same farm gates, they walked up the last field towards the house and watched as Drake's mother fussed around Helen and Megan. The girls lounged in two old deckchairs his father had bought when Drake and his sister were young.

'I've been telling Annie all about the names of the fields.'

Mair Drake smiled.

'And I peeked inside the gypsy trailer.'

'It's been there for years. I'm surprised it hasn't collapsed completely,' Mair said.

The home-made lemonade was cold and refreshing and they sat enjoying the view talking about nothing in particular until Mair Drake announced she had to finalise the arrangements for lunch. Annie volunteered to help her, and they left Drake sitting with Helen and Megan.

Spending time with both his daughters made him think of the two girls in Deeside. Where were they that morning? Nobody would be making them a roast Sunday lunch. It made him even more determined to find them. They had done nothing to deserve the way life had treated them. If the care system had failed them, Drake was resolute he wouldn't do likewise.

Soon enough a shout came from Annie and they traipsed inside. The smell of rosemary filled the kitchen from the leg of lamb resting on a plate on the worktop. A Sunday lunchtime roast had been a ritual Drake remembered as a child and his mother enjoyed continuing the tradition with Helen and Megan. The roast potatoes and buttered parsnips and carrots had soon been cleared and his daughters demolished a cream and custard laden trifle. Did he have as much of an appetite as a child?

At least his mother hadn't asked about the latest case he was investigating – she hadn't even suggested he was looking thin or that he should be eating more. Obviously having Annie in his life had satisfied his mother that he was being looked after.

His mother had accepted Annie into her life and now Drake warmed to the growing normality of his family unit. They waved enthusiastically at his mother as they drove off. That evening they would complain about how full they felt after lunch, watch television and make certain the girls knew they had to be up early in the morning so that he could drop them off with Sian on his way to headquarters.

He didn't think of the tasks facing him.

It would be another busy week.

Chapter 19

'How was your weekend?'

Drake wasn't one for small talk although recently he had shown an interest in Sara's life that she reckoned was down to Annie's influence. Drake's new girlfriend managed to smooth some of his rough edges.

The previous Friday evening Sara had been on her first date with the project manager she'd met on a dating website. They had agreed to meet at a bistro pub, and it had gone well, better than she had expected. He was engaging, discussed sports and current affairs and even enquired about her work and whether she liked being a police officer. When he had asked her if he could see her on Saturday evening, she surprised herself by agreeing readily. He had tickets to a concert in Llandudno and she enjoyed herself.

Sleeping through the alarm clock the following morning only set her mind on edge until she had finished a five-mile run in good time for lunch with her parents. She hadn't told them about the date. Early days, she had thought.

Sara glanced over at Drake as he powered along the A55 towards Deeside. 'I went to a concert on Saturday night at Venue Cymru in Llandudno.'

Drake appeared unimpressed. 'Anything good?'

'I really enjoyed it. And I had lunch with my parents on Sunday.'

Now Drake nodded his head. 'Same here, well my mother, of course. The girls enjoyed themselves – I don't know how they eat so much.'

Sara hadn't bothered with the satnav as Drake knew the directions to Cameron Toft's flat.

He pulled into the car park outside the block of flats. A young mother with a baby in a buggy and a toddler by her feet struggled to open the main door. She wore a pair of cut-off denim shorts and a crop top that displayed her navel.

'Let's hope he's home,' Drake said.

Sara and Drake made for the entrance. The strong smell persisted in the stairwell and at the top Sara paused to catch her breath. Drake did the same before making for the door of flat 312, thumping loudly but saying nothing. He stepped back, making certain Toft could see who was standing outside his door through the peephole.

The security chain fell away and Toft stood on the threshold, feet wide apart. He gave them a defiant stare. 'What do you want?'

'We need to talk to you,' Drake said.

Toft turned on his heel and Drake and Sara followed him into the room they had visited when they'd broken the news of Dawn Piper's death.

'We discovered some paperwork in Dawn's possessions concerning your application for Jamie to live with you permanently. You were in dispute with Dawn about the arrangements for your son's welfare?' Drake kept his eye contact fixed and directed at Toft. Sara had seen him do this before as though he was trying to drill down into Toft's mind and figure out exactly what was going on. Sara grasped her notebook in hand, waiting to scribble down notes from their meeting.

'It was for the best. The social services weren't going to allow Jamie to live with her. She was a smack head. He is going to be better off living with me.'

Drake continued staring at Toft. 'That's not actually true though is it? Social services were contemplating taking Jamie into long-term care. I've read some of their preliminary assessments.'

Toft shook his head. 'That was all shit. They've changed their minds now. It was Dawn they were worried about. Jamie will come and live with me.'

Drake didn't immediately reply.

Being hostile and aggressive wasn't going to help. It meant Toft was getting under Drake's skin. Drake had reminded Sara as they drove from headquarters that Toft's number had appeared as a contact in Hubert Caston's mobile.

'How well did you know Hubert Caston?' Drake said.

'What do you mean?'

Buying time to think of an answer was a sure sign a lie was coming, Sara thought.

'Exactly that, Cameron.'

Toft stared over at Drake calculating how to respond. 'I knew who he was.'

'Were you friends?' Drake kept his tone deliberately soft and conversational. Sara doubted it would work. Toft narrowed his eyes at Drake.

'I wouldn't say we were friends, but he knew Dawn of course. They liked to play those stupid zombie games together.'

'When did you last speak to Hubert?'

Toft rolled his eyes feigning a poor memory. 'I can't remember.'

'Was it last week or the week before or last month?'

Toft shrugged. 'Maybe.'

Drake barely paused before asking exactly what was on his mind. 'So, you don't recall when Hubert called you last on your mobile?'

'I don't memorise every call I make or receive.'

'Even from someone like Hubert who was killed last week?'

'I've got a lousy memory.'

Sara jotted down the last reply knowing it was likely to sap Drake's patience.

'He called you three times in the week before he died.'

Now Toft nodded. 'Yeah, I remember. Dawn called me when she was playing zombie games with him. She'd left her mobile at home. She wanted to check some details about seeing Jamie.' Toft raised an eyebrow as though he were inviting Drake to challenge him.

Drake persevered. 'Can you tell me anything about

Dawn's regular activities?'

'Apart from wasting her life playing video games and taking drugs.'

'Did she have any hobbies? Did she go to the gym?'

Toft snorted. 'Don't be absurd.'

'Are there any pubs she went to regularly? Friends that we don't know about?'

'No,' Toft replied flatly. 'Are we done?'

'We may need to speak to you again.' Drake stood up. Sara scrambled to close her notebook stuffing it back into her bag.

Drake said nothing as they retraced their steps back to the car. Once inside Drake peered through the windscreen towards the block of flats they'd just left.

'He's hiding something, boss.'

'Exactly what I thought.'

Before starting the engine, a message reached Drake's mobile and he read the email from Winder with confirmation of the results from preliminary work to triangulate Dawn's mobile on the night she died. It pointed to her being near the rugby club in Deeside. He turned to Sara.

'We've got a trip to a rugby club.'

After negotiating her way down into Deeside, Luned found a car park in the middle of Queensferry. She fumbled for the right change, fed the parking meter, extracted the ticket, and slipped it onto the dashboard of her car. She was pleased to be out of the Incident Room and getting down to some real police work. Winder had given her a jealous look before she'd left that morning. He faced all day in front of the computer monitors scanning the CCTV images.

It didn't take her long to find the shop which combined a newsagent, a takeaway sandwich and coffee outlet with a convenience store at the rear. Outside there was a layby which matched the description in the neighbour's account. Luned made her way towards the counter scanning the inside for signs of CCTV. A conscientious assistant might recall Dawn Piper and even the driver of the black Audi.

'I need to talk to the owner,' Luned said to the girl behind the counter.

'Who shall I say is asking?'

'It's official business.'

Luned didn't have to wait long. The owner bustled out and gave her offered warrant card a cursory glance.

'I'm investigating the death of Dawn Piper. She was seen in a black Audi A4 outside your premises in the week before her death.'

Luned added the correct date and time before continuing. 'Do you have a CCTV system?'

'Yes. But it's old and not always reliable.'

'We'll need all the footage from the last two weeks. Do you keep records of who was working that day?'

'Yes, of course.'

'Send the footage and details of your staff to this email address.' Luned pushed her card towards the shop owner.

Luned left the store and stopped by the layby, closed her eyes and pitched her head towards the sky letting the summer sunshine warm her face. If only it was as easy to get light onto the present inquiry. After a moment she returned her gaze to the street. Dawn had been seen in a black Audi on this very spot. It made it more urgent somehow to trace her movements and establish exactly where she had been killed.

She retraced her steps to the car and checked the directions for Mattie Williams' home.

After parking and walking up to the property, Luned peered in through the half-open door – nobody had answered the door bell – before nudging it open with a shoe. She called out a greeting but heard only the sound of crying and sobbing. She entered and raised her voice.

A tear-streaked face appeared in the doorway to a room at the front of the property. The woman was early forties, her face puffy. Walking towards Luned she wiped her cheeks. 'Do you want Mattie?'

'Yes.'

'You'd better come through.' She dropped her voice to a whisper. 'She only got back this morning. Then she heard about Bert, poor thing.' Luned wasn't certain if she meant Bert or Mattie.

Inside the sitting room three women sat on a sofa clutching a box of tissues each. The rhythmical sobbing interjected with noses being blown made them sound like professional mourners.

'Mattie Williams?' Luned said.

The woman sitting in the middle nodded her head.

Once Luned had introduced herself she glanced at the other women. 'I need to speak to Mattie alone.'

'We'll make tea,' one of them said and they both scrambled to their feet.

Luned sat next to Mattie after closing the door; it smothered the noise of a kettle being filled and the brisk conversation between Mattie's visitors.

'I need to ask you about Hubert Caston.'

Mattie's bottom lip quivered.

Luned continued. 'How well did you know him?'

Mattie reached over for more tissues. 'He was kind. He loved to play those video games and he was…' She gave Luned an edgy glance.

'We know he used drugs.' Luned sounded reassuring.

Mattie nodded briskly. 'He was always in financial trouble. Since his mum died, he went to pieces and couldn't cope. There's no help out there for people like Bert. I think it's disgusting.'

One of the women returned with mugs of milky tea, a bowl of sugar and spoons. Mattie stirred two spoonsful into her mug and clutched it tightly before taking a sip.

'Do you know anything that might help the inquiry?' Luned sipped her drink, keeping Mattie company.

Mattie drank more tea. 'I don't know… I can't think.'

'Did he mention anything odd? You know, out of the ordinary? Something unusual?'

Tears welled up in Mattie's eyes and Luned worried she had said the wrong thing. 'Things were going to change. He was going to let his parents' place to some new bloke.'

Luned moved in her chair, her interest piqued.

'What do you mean?'

'He'd been letting the place to Ritchie O'Brien for the Eastern Europeans working in his Chinese takeaway.'

Luned raised a sceptical eyebrow. This directly linked Caston to O'Brien.

Mattie blew her nose and took another large mouthful of her drink before continuing. 'I told him not to get involved with O'Brien.'

'Who was the new person he was going to start renting to?'

Mattie shrugged. 'Somebody from Liverpool who promised to do the place up.'

'Did he tell you the name?'

She shook her head briskly.

'Bert was naïve about O'Brien. I told him not to get involved and when he told me about this other bloke I…'

Luned spent another few minutes drilling down for more information that Mattie might know but she tired and sank back in her chair. Finally, Luned asked as an afterthought, 'Did he have any other friends or maybe distant relatives you know about?'

'Not really… only that woman, Olivia. Right busybody.'

Luned strangled a response. 'Do you mean Olivia Knox?'

Mattie nodded. 'She was here first thing. Asking about Bert and how I was and if there was anything she could do etc…'

Now Luned sounded surprised. 'This morning?'

Another nod, Mattie seemed oblivious to Luned's reaction. Mattie didn't move from the sofa as Luned saw herself out. She sat in the car for a moment, thinking. If the man from Liverpool is Kenny, then O'Brien was playing one violent villain against another.

Luned frowned. It wasn't a good idea.

And why had Olivia Knox called to see Mattie that morning?

Chapter 20

After Luned left the Incident Room, Winder stared over at the board. He shared his gaze between all three of their main persons of interest before returning to the various tasks Drake had prioritised the day before, namely establishing Kenny's known associates, building a picture of his movements and chasing the care home in Liverpool for a positive identification of anyone connected to the abducted girls.

Luned was interviewing Mattie Williams and he was going to be stuck in front of the computer monitor all morning. And for a brief moment he felt jealous that Luned was getting more of the face-to-face police work that he enjoyed. Was he destined to be known for watching CCTV footage? He hoped not, so he had to make progress and impress the boss.

His gaze settled on the faces of the Liverpool girls – Debbie and Tina – and he heard the urgency in Drake's voice about finding both girls. But would they help find the killer? So, he started with the care home in Liverpool. The call rang for several seconds before a voice abruptly announced the name – Hill Gate. Winder was passed from one person to another until the manager listened to him before angrily replying, 'I've told all this to them other officers. You're wasting my time. The cops here were after the same info.'

The report from the police in Liverpool was sketchy – a simple record that none of the staff could help. Winder imagined the disinterest from busy officers with other priorities. Drake would want to be satisfied that everyone had been spoken to. The staff list was open on Winder's desk.

'I'd like to check that I've got the names of all your staff.' The manager groaned as Winder ran through the names.

'Yeah, that sounds right. Hang on a minute – read them names again.'

Winder duly obliged.

'Pat and Vera aren't on that list. They work in the kitchen.'

'Do you have mobile numbers for them?'

Another groan. A few seconds passed before Winder could jot down the details. He finished the call and dialled the first number – it rang out, as did the second. He scribbled a reminder to try again on a Post-it note, just as Drake favoured, and pinned it to his monitor.

He turned his attention to Paul Kenny. Merseyside Police's file gave Winder enough material to build a detailed picture of Kenny's associates and inner circle. One of the men involved even owned a pub in one of the resort villages on Anglesey. After a hurried lunch he got back to his desk and started on tracking Kenny's Audi. The automatic number plate recognition software soon enabled him to establish that Kenny's vehicle had made several trips to Deeside in the past month. Winder requisitioned the footage for every time the ANPR system had recorded the vehicle, hoping there'd be images they could enhance to give them the face of the driver or passengers.

He relaxed, knowing that he had some progress to report when Drake returned.

Winder sauntered over to the board, stretching his back as he did so. His gaze settled on the images of Hubert Caston and he recalled Drake's summary from his meeting with Caston's work colleague about seeing him in a lettings agency in Deeside. The previous Saturday, Winder had spent time building a picture of where Caston had been on the day he'd died, and it had niggled that the timeline was incomplete. Now there was another piece of Caston's life he needed to check. Was Caston looking for a new tenant?

He dialled the agency's number.

'Deeside Lettings.' The voice was cheery, too cheery

for Deeside.

Once Winder had identified himself the voice became serious. 'I don't think I can help you.'

'But surely you can tell me if Mr Caston was a client? We know that he owned a rented property.'

'You'll have to talk to the boss.'

'Can you put me through?'

'I can give you Mr Beltrami's number.'

Winder paused and then spoke slowly. 'Mr Beltrami?'

'Yes, he owns the agency. Do you want his number?'

Winder wanted to say that he knew exactly where to contact Mr Beltrami, but settled instead for thanking the girl for her help and jotting down the number she read out.

He urgently searched for the name and number of Caston's work-mate who had seen him in the lettings agency. Eventually Winder found his name – Jack Grundy.

A hesitant voice answered Winder's call. 'Hello.'

'This is Detective Constable Gareth Winder. I need your help.'

'What's this about?' Jack sounded less nervous now.

'I'm going to send you a photograph of a man and I'd like you to confirm whether it's the same person you saw meeting Hubert Caston.' Winder fumbled with his phone as he spoke attaching Beltrami's image to a message. Winder could hear the phone being handled as he kept Jack on the line.

Seconds later Jack announced, 'Yep, that's the man.'

Winder finished the call, content with his progress. Reading the time, he calculated that he'd do some more digging into Beltrami's letting business before Inspector Drake returned.

Drake toured around the area surrounding the rugby club. The triangulation reports would only give them an approximation of where the mobiles had been used. Fortunately, a phone mast was nearby, making it likely the results were reasonably reliable.

Drake pulled up alongside the pavement and fumbled with a map of the area, convincing himself that he'd get a better understanding of the geography if he could see it on paper. Somewhere among the streets and houses and pubs was a murder scene. A killer had taken a knife to Dawn Piper. The phone calls and texts meant she had been alive during the early part of Saturday evening. If they could find the murder scene, they could garner evidence, extract DNA and build a case. He found a coloured highlighter in the storage compartment of the door by his feet and circled the street where Dawn Piper lived and then he did the same for Caston's home.

He turned his attention to the main street of Connah's Quay and the café where she had purchased meals for the two girls. Dawn had been somewhere for the rest of that Saturday afternoon and early evening. He kept thinking that Cameron Toft or Olivia Knox must have known where she had been. Neither had been truthful, neither had been cooperative. But there was nothing to suggest that either was involved with Dawn's death.

'Do any of Dawn Piper's friends live nearby?' Drake said staring at the map trying to make sense of the coloured sections.

'I'll pin the map to the board in the Incident Room when we get back to headquarters.'

Drake nodded. It might focus their attention on establishing where exactly Dawn Piper had been killed. Drake sensed they were inching closer to finding the crime scene. He tipped a plastic bottle to his mouth and drank some water. A jogger ran past them and then two girls in cut-off jeans and thin summer tops pushing prams strolled past the car.

Drake started the engine. 'Let's go down to the rugby club.'

He followed Sara's directions as they made their way

through a housing estate that had once been exclusively owned by the local council. Swanky porches and glistening UPVC doors and windows and well-maintained gardens suggested that most were now in private hands. He drove along the perimeter of the rugby club. The grass badly needed cutting and the posts deserved a lick of paint, but it was at least a month until the start of the season. He pulled into the car park in front of the flat-roofed building. The main entrance door into the club was open and once Drake and Sara had left the car, they could hear the sound of crates of bottles being shifted and casks moved.

There was no other pub in the immediate vicinity so Drake hoped it had been the last place visited by Dawn Piper. Walking through the entrance hall, the sound of cleaning emerged from the toilets and after pushing open the door into the main bar area 'The Summer of 69' blasted out from the PA system. Drake wondered what Bryan Adams would make of the place – it certainly didn't conjure up the romance of his song.

Several members of staff were busy setting out the tables in a room at the far end of the bar area. A man in an open-necked white shirt and black jeans by the bar gave them a quizzical frown. 'You're early.'

'Are you the manager?'

'What do you want?'

Drake flashed his warrant card. 'We are investigating the murder of Dawn Piper. And we have reason to believe that she might have been here on the Saturday evening before she died.' Sara pushed her mobile towards the man with an image of Dawn on the screen dictating the date simultaneously.

'I've never seen her before. Although I read about it on Facebook.' His tone was neutral as though the death of another human being was irrelevant. 'And we were really busy that Saturday. There was a wedding that went on late. And even if she was here, I doubt we'd remember.'

'Do you have any CCTV cameras?'

'Of course not. We can't afford anything like that.'

His indifference angered Drake. 'We'll need to talk to all the members of staff.'

The man darted a glance towards the staff working before giving Drake a weak smile. 'We've got this big charity do this afternoon. Perhaps some other time?'

'Get them all here, now. It won't take a minute.'

The smile turned into a pout in a second, then he glared at Drake before marching to the room where the staff were working. One by one they examined the photograph of Dawn on Sara's mobile, each shaking a head in turn. Sara jotted the name of each into her notebook. Then she turned to the manager. 'Is there anybody who was working that Saturday who's not here today?'

The manager ran his gaze over his employees, then he nodded. 'I think Howie and Becky were working that Saturday night.' He dipped a hand into his pocket and thumbed through his mobile until he had the contact details which he sent to Sara's mobile.

Behind them guests were arriving. The manager's demeanour changed. He smiled broadly, paced over to the entrance, exchanging warm greetings with the visitors. Drake and Sara left and watched as taxis arrived and departed. Drake stood for a moment watching a white Mercedes with the livery of AAA Taxis on the bonnet and the doors. Taxi drivers and the companies who employed them would make a reasonable living from delivering and collecting people to and from the rugby club.

He stood for a moment recalling the manager's words that the rugby club had been busy the Saturday Dawn had last been seen alive. Perhaps a taxi driver had seen her, perhaps one of the guests had seen her. It meant more people had to be interviewed. Then he stared at the windscreen of the taxi. Something looked out of place. A black lump hung down from the rear-view mirror – a dashcam.

He turned to Sara. 'Look at that taxi.' She gave him a quizzical look. 'There's a dashcam.' Other taxis arrived: most were the same. A small black box that would record everything going on in front of the vehicle.

'If there were taxis here on the Saturday night Dawn was around, they might have recorded her.'

Sara nodded her understanding.

'Let's get back to headquarters. We've got taxi companies to contact.'

Chapter 21

Winder jumped to his feet as Drake and Sara entered the Incident Room. Drake stalked over to the board ready to dictate instructions, but Winder's enthusiasm got the better of him.

'I've tracked down the owner of that letting agency.' Winder paused for dramatic effect. 'It's owned by Jack Beltrami. Apparently, he's been buying up properties cheaply in Deeside. The letting agency is a new development as part of his property business.'

'And the rest,' Sara added, failing to disguise the disdain in her voice.

Drake took a moment to ponder the significance of Winder's discovery. Was it coincidence that Hubert Caston had been seen with him? Or was something more sinister going on? And had Dawn Piper travelled to Rhyl simply to play the slot machines in the Beltrami amusement arcades… it seemed unlikely.

'It's time we had a chat with Jack Beltrami.'

Sara nodded. Luned's frown was a mixture of worry and severity. 'I spoke to Mattie Williams. Apparently Caston had allowed Ritchie O'Brien to use his property for Eastern Europeans working in his takeaway restaurants. But then he had decided to terminate that arrangement and let the property to someone new. No name, just that he was a Scouser.'

Winder whistled. 'That's not the recipe for a long and happy life.'

Drake chortled, as did Sara. Luned looked sombre.

'Did she know if the Scouser was Paul Kenny?'

'She couldn't say, boss.'

Drake turned to face the board, moving his gaze from Paul Kenny to Ritchie O'Brien and then Jack Beltrami. If Caston had been playing O'Brien against Kenny, it would have been remarkably foolish.

Luned cleared her throat to gain Drake's attention. He turned to face her. 'And Olivia Knox had been to see Mattie Williams before I arrived.'

'What! That bloody woman gets everywhere. She keeps poking her nose into everything associated with this inquiry.'

'I also checked to see if there were any phone numbers in common between Caston and Dawn Piper.' Winder sounded pleased with himself. 'Caston had the same number on his mobile that Dawn called the night she was killed.'

Drake sounded encouraged. 'Good, excellent. Get some triangulation work done on that number as well. But before that we've got some work to do on the taxi companies of Deeside.' Drake rattled through his instructions as the rest of his team jotted down the action needed.

They watched as Winder googled 'taxi companies in Deeside'. 'There are six listed here, sir.'

'That's three each,' Drake said sharing a glance between Winder and Luned. 'Sara, you're with me. Let's go and talk to Beltrami.'

The Beltrami family appeared to have the same arch-enemy status for Drake as Moriarty had for Sherlock Holmes. And Drake's determination to implicate Jack Beltrami worried Sara. She knew nothing about the previous case involving the Beltramis other than gossip Winder had shared with her one lunchtime.

Criminals rarely forgave, Sara thought, and if their inquiry into the deaths of Piper and Caston was getting near to the Beltrami empire, they would want to protect their interests. It worried her whether Drake's judgement was being impaired.

Drake said little as he drove from Colwyn Bay to Rhyl gripping the steering wheel tightly.

'How are you going to deal with Jack Beltrami?' Sara decided her general open-ended question might be the best way to release the tension.

'We'll caution him then ask him politely if he killed Piper and Caston. And when he confesses, we'll arrest him and take him to the area custody suite.'

For a split-second Sara thought Drake might be serious.

He continued. 'But in the real world we'll ask him how he knew Dawn Piper and Hubert Caston.'

Drake indicated left for the junction to Rhyl. Funfairs and leisure parks filled with static caravans lined the route. It was hard to believe the town had once been a popular Victorian resort from its present-day reputation earned from the high levels of deprivation and poverty. Nearing the centre, box-like bungalows with neat drives stood sentry-like along the road. The place had become a mecca for retirees from Liverpool and the other cities of northern England.

Drake pressed on and parked near the promenade. The beach was wide and flat and on that summer's afternoon it appeared attractive. What wasn't so attractive were the amusement arcades and pubs and takeaway food outlets lining the main road.

Drake paused and gazed over at an amusement arcade owned by the Beltrami family.

'Let's hope he's working,' Sara said.

Drake nodded. 'He'll be there alright. The summer is their busiest time when Scousers flock to this place for the weekend, drink a skinful of cheap lager and pour money into slot machines.'

'I think we need to be careful, boss,' Sara said. 'It might sound like you're acting out of personal malice.'

Drake turned towards her and narrowed his eyes. For a moment she regretted her over-confidence. Drake might rebuke her, but she felt it prudent to sound a warning.

Drake let out a long breath. 'You're right.'

It pleased her he agreed.

Drake added, 'You take the lead.'

Sara did a double take. She hadn't expected that reaction. 'Yes, sir,' she said after a brief hesitation.

Sara followed Drake over a pedestrian crossing and into the amusement arcade. A girl with shocking scarlet hair pulled up into a Mohican style occupied a booth near the door. Sara slipped her warrant card through the opening in the glass screen as though she were paying for a cinema ticket. 'We want to speak to Mr Jack Beltrami.'

The girl increased the intensity of her gum-chewing. She blinked lazily and scooped up the phone, turning away from Sara who couldn't hear what she said above the din.

The girl tipped her head towards a door and Sara led the way up the staircase to the first-floor landing. Walking down the corridor Sara peeked into various rooms. Staff tapped on keyboards while staring at computer monitors. At the end Jack Beltrami emerged from his office.

'It must be important if the Wales Police Service want to see me.'

Sara didn't reply, neither did Drake.

Beltrami turned on his heel and led them into his room where he waved at two visitor chairs. The modern art hanging on the walls had an expensive feel. One of the works reminded her of Piet Mondrian and two others were striking Cubist watercolours.

Drake sat down. Beltrami adopted an uncompromising look that Sara hoped wouldn't morph into something more hostile. She let out a silent breath of relief when she noticed Drake scanning the framed photographs on a wall discreetly lit by a downlighter.

'We're investigating the death of Dawn Piper and Hubert Caston,' Sara said.

Beltrami frowned.

'I understand that Dawn worked for you some time ago.'

Beltrami drew a hand over his mouth. 'And your question?'

Sara took another slow breath. 'What was your relationship with her?'

Beltrami guffawed. ‘Relationship? Did you really say that? Look, love. I employ a lot of people and—’

‘It’s Detective Sergeant.’

Beltrami ignored her. ‘My business employs a lot of people and I haven’t got time to get to know everyone.’ He gave a regal dismissive wave with his right hand.

‘Dawn was in the arcade downstairs on the afternoon before she was killed.’

‘So what?’

‘We’ll need the CCTV footage you have for that afternoon.’

‘Go to hell.’

The matter-of-fact tone caught Sara off guard. She squinted over at Beltrami and saw the deep vein of malice in his eyes that were almost entirely one colour – black.

‘Do you know a Hubert Caston?’ Drake said.

‘Are you playing good cop now, Ian, to your oppo’s bad cop routine. Surely you’re better than that.’ Beltrami turned to Sara ‘You see, *Detective Sergeant*, the Inspector and I go back a long way.’

‘Well do you?’ Sara said evenly.

‘I have no fucking idea who you’re talking about.’

‘You were seen with him in the lettings agency you own in Connah’s Quay.’

‘And that’s all you’ve got?’

‘Mr Beltrami—’

‘Please call me Jack, dear, because you’re not going anywhere with this.’

‘What did you and Hubert Caston discuss?’

Beltrami stood up. Then he snarled. ‘I’ve got history with Inspector Drake here. He’s a slimy piece of shit that stitched my family up good and proper and when I complained, guess what happened. Fuck all. Now don’t you come in here asking if I have any connection with two dead druggies in Deeside. Because I don’t give a shit. Now get out.’

Drake and Sara got up and stood for a moment giving Beltrami a defiant glare.

Then they headed downstairs and left.

Drake spoke first as they sat in Drake's Mondeo. 'Charming, isn't he?'

'He really likes you, sir.'

Drake chuckled.

Sara added, 'How did he know Dawn and Hubert were druggies?'

'I thought the same.' Drake started the car engine. 'Let's get back to headquarters.'

Chapter 22

Superintendent Wyndham Price checked his watch for the fifth time in the last half an hour. Superintendent David Hobbs wasn't due for thirty minutes and he really should prepare for the press conference organised by Susan Howells from the PR department. Recent media coverage of the county lines activity around the United Kingdom had highlighted the challenge faced by police forces. Some of the statistics about drug addiction and the scale of organised crime groups were appalling and Price deplored the inability of politicians to address the issues in society causing such problems. His career-long battle for more resources was only a small part of a bigger picture. Hobbs could face the task of persuading senior management that more money was an imperative.

A few minutes before eleven o'clock the phone rang and Hannah announced Hobbs' arrival. He wasted no time asking his secretary to show Hobbs into his office. It would soon be Hobbs' office in any event.

'Wyndham,' Hobbs said stretching out a hand as Price walked over to the door. 'Good afternoon.'

'David,' Price said. 'Good to see you again.'

Hobbs' grey suit looked expensive and silver links kept the double cuffs of his white shirt firmly in place. His thin, bloodless lips and small, dark eyes gave him an expressionless appearance. Price went back to the desk and sat down. 'Perhaps you should be sitting here.'

Hobbs gave him a weak smile.

'Did you travel up this morning?'

'Stayed overnight with my mother. She lives near Bangor.'

The vowels were rounded. There was warmth and a singsong lilt to his voice which surprised Price who expected a Cardiff accent: after all Hobbs' entire career had been in Southern Division based in Cardiff.

'Are you a native of North Wales?'

Hobbs nodded. 'My parents were teachers and after I went to university in Cardiff, I joined the WPS.'

Price could hear the warm rural tones of a Gwynedd accent the more Hobbs spoke.

'Congratulations by the way on your promotion. Is Mrs Hobbs looking forward to moving to Northern Division?'

Price made it sound like a posting to a distant Gulag.

'She's from Anglesey, so she's pleased to be coming home to where she was raised.'

Hannah bustled in with coffee and biscuits and Price formally introduced her. 'Hannah has been my secretary for many years. She will be a great help when you're settling in.'

Hannah nodded appreciatively. Hobbs didn't respond.

Price spent an hour outlining the basic structure of the team Hobbs would be taking over. He included the occasional light-hearted comment, but Hobbs barely responded. He would need a little more humour to survive Northern Division as a superintendent, Price thought. Being serious all the time wouldn't endear Hobbs to his subordinates.

'Are you looking forward to retirement, Wyndham?' Hobbs managed during a lull in the conversation.

'No, I'm not, if truth be told,' Price observed. No point pretending with anyone.

'Do you have children and grandchildren? You'll have more time to spend with the family.'

Price wasn't going to share that he couldn't abide his son-in-law who was a swimming pool engineer in Florida with little interest in anything apart from baseball and beer. It amazed him what his daughter found attractive about the man. Their only son was an overweight, loud youngster Price saw once a year.

'I shall be playing golf of course. And my wife is expecting to see me more often around the house I daresay.

Do you have family?'

Hobbs rolled his eyes. 'Teenagers.'

Price nodded before glancing at his watch. Drake was expected any minute and his meeting with Hobbs had reached the stage where the natural rhythm slowly dissipated. He would need to concentrate on the nuts and bolts of his role as a superintendent with Hobbs in due course, so mixing small talk about family and retirement felt awkward. The phone on Price's desk rang and he snatched at it.

Hannah told him Drake was waiting.

'Send him in.'

Once the introductions had been completed, Drake sat down alongside Hobbs.

'Superintendent Hobbs will be taking over once I finally retire.' Price managed to say the dreaded 'R' word out loud.

Drake gave Hobbs a friendly glance of acknowledgement. It was barely reciprocated.

'Detective Inspector Drake leads the serious crime team. He is the SIO on the recent deaths in Deeside.'

'We believe both deaths – Dawn Piper and Hubert Caston – are linked to drug dealers. And organised crime groups running county lines operations may be involved.'

'The county lines activity is a scourge.' Hobbs sounded angry.

Drake continued. 'Apparently Dawn Piper was trying to turn over a new leaf: clean herself up. And she wanted to prevent these drug dealers from ruining people's lives.'

Hobbs again. 'A one-woman campaign? That's very dangerous.'

Drake balanced his right foot over his left knee. 'She was seen with a Paul Kenny in Liverpool a few days before she was killed. He is known for his connections to organised crime groups. Ritchie O'Brien, one of the home-grown drug dealers in Deeside, is also a person of interest. She may have been a victim of a turf war between the competing factions. And intelligence also links Dawn to Jack Beltrami.'

Price turned to Hobbs. 'The Beltramis are a well-known family outfit of gangsters.' Price continued. 'We need evidence linking back to their activity.'

Hobbs brought their conversation to a natural conclusion. 'Perhaps we can schedule another briefing.'

Drake nodded and got up to leave.

'And don't forget the press conference later,' Price said. 'Have you read the press release from Susan Howells?'

'Yes, sir.'

Once Drake had left, Hobbs turned to Price. 'So, what can you tell me about Drake?'

Drake filed into the conference room behind Superintendent Price and Susan Howells. Journalists filled the several rows of chairs in front of the table and Drake sat at the end. He squinted towards the back of the room as the lights from three television crews blazed.

Susan Howells was the first to her feet. She made a general introduction referring to the press release already circulated. Drake recognised a few faces from the television evening news. He wasn't convinced that press conferences were particularly useful. The nature of a police inquiry meant they couldn't really share with the public exactly what was going on. It was no more than a public relations exercise. The impending by-election and the noise created by the politicians added a new dimension to the inquiry and to the attention the press had given it.

Once Susan Howells had finished, she sat down and nodded towards Superintendent Price. He cleared his throat and outlined more details about Piper and Caston's circumstances. He ended by looking towards the cameras and appealing for anyone with information about their whereabouts in the hours before they were killed to come forward. Finally, Price read out the number of a dedicated confidential phone line before Susan Howells announced they would take questions. Drake guessed she already knew most of them in advance, had even participated in their drafting. Eager hands darted into the air and she pointed at a journalist from the BBC.

'Is it true both deaths are linked to the ongoing county lines activity of organised crime groups from the major cities of England?'

Price responded. 'The involvement of organised crime groups in the distribution of heroin and crack cocaine is something we are monitoring very carefully, as are all police forces. We are following several lines of inquiry in relation to both these deaths.'

The journalist persisted. 'The details we've had about the cause of death are sketchy. Can you confirm both victims were stabbed?'

'That's correct and—'

'It's true to say that county lines operators favour knives as their weapon of choice.'

Price paused: he wouldn't have liked the interruption.

The journalist continued. 'Are you aware that seventy-five per cent of police forces are reporting that county lines criminals have been using guns as well? Are they a feature of this inquiry?'

'Guns were not involved in the deaths of either Piper and Caston,' Price snapped.

Susan Howells jerked a hand at another journalist calling his name a little louder than necessary. He piped up.

'Have you asked for assistance from the National Crime Agency?'

Drake didn't recognise him but from the tone of his accent he was probably from one of the London-based broadsheets.

'We are liaising with all relevant government bodies,' Price replied sharply.

Drake had switched his mobile to silent before the press

conference began but it vibrated silently in his jacket pocket as another reporter asked a question.

Drake finished out his handset – an unfamiliar number. He dropped it back into his pocket.

Price had narrowed his eyes. Drake guessed the superintendent was thinking – *this is our inquiry and we will handle it as we damn well please.* Instead he sounded emollient.

'As I've said we are liaising with all relevant government bodies.'

Susan Howells jabbed a finger towards a journalist in the second row.

This time the accent was from Cardiff. Drake could almost sense Price relaxing. 'Are these county lines operators based in the cities of England?'

Simple enough question might justify a simple reply. As Drake watched his superior officer calculating how to reply, his mobile rang again. It was the same number again. Why the hell had he not turned the thing off completely? He hit the decline button. Moments later the phone bleeped confirmation that a voicemail had been left.

'It would compromise the confidentiality of our inquiry if I were to confirm our lines of interest.'

Drake mentally congratulated Price. The journalist had clearly been searching for a Wales versus England storyline.

Howells stood up now and called out the name of a journalist sitting right at the back.

'As you know one of the major features of county lines activity is the use of children. I understand one of your active lines of inquiry is a search for two teenage girls. Can you confirm that?'

Price drummed the fingers of his right hand on the desk. Howells gave the superintendent a worried look. The journalist could have gathered his information from any source – not necessarily the police. Much to Drake's annoyance his phone vibrated again, and he discreetly checked the number. It was the same caller for a third time.

Price hid any anger effectively. 'As I've said before, I can't comment on the day-to-day activity of the inquiry.' Then he stood up, pushed the chair away from the table and breezed out. Howells followed him, Drake bringing up the rear as he retrieved the voicemail.

He was outside the conference room when he pressed the mobile to his ear.

'This is Dr Williams of the accident and emergency department. Dr Sian Drake has been involved in a road traffic collision. I think you should make your way to the hospital.'

Chapter 23

Drake ran to his car and fumbled with the key after unlocking the Mondeo. He cursed when he missed the ignition the first time, ramming it into the slot at the second attempt. A dark, stiff curtain dragged itself through his mind. He fired the engine into life and accelerated out of the car park. He braked hard at the junction as he indicated left. He wasn't on police business, but he didn't care so he flashed his lights and sounded his horn at cars dawdling in front of him as he drove. Moments later he was in the outside lane accelerating up to seventy miles an hour even though it was a fifty mile an hour speed restriction area.

He glanced at the speedometer knowing he would have pushed on faster had it not been for the traffic. After his brief conversation with the doctor before leaving headquarters he realised he should have asked what he meant when he said rammed. Despite reassurance that Helen and Megan were well, a sick feeling almost overwhelmed him. He would instigate a full inquiry, demand to know exactly what had happened. He would call in favours with traffic officers he knew.

It wasn't an accident – the doctor had said Sian's car had been rammed. The word kept repeating itself in his mind over and over like one of his rituals. Somebody must have attended at the scene. As he raced past the long straight stretch of road that skirted the beach before Abergele, he agonised if an ambulance had been called? Had Sian been taken to the hospital in the back of police car?

After leaving the A55 for the hospital the traffic slowed but his impatience rose until he swore and cursed at the vehicles searching for a place to park. Hospitals never had enough parking spaces. It amazed him that a multi-storey car park hadn't been built years ago.

He pulled the car slowly onto a grass verge, remembering the *On Police Business/Heddlu Swyddogol* sign in the glove compartment of his car. He found it and thrust it onto the dashboard.

He jogged and then broke into a run until he reached the entrance of the emergency department and breathlessly spoke to a woman at reception. 'Sian Drake,' he said between deep lungful's of breath. 'There's been a car accident.'

The woman turned her attention to the computer screen on her desk and started clicking through the records. 'Ah, yes, I see.' Drake wanted to yell at this woman. What the hell did *ah, yes, I see* mean?

'I'll ask a doctor to come and speak to you. Please take a seat.'

Drake cast a glance at the packed waiting room area to his left. The word 'rammed' spiked again in his mind. 'What's the doctor's name?'

'Dr Williams. He won't be a moment.'

'I'm not going to wait.' Drake spotted the double doors leading from the emergency department waiting area into what he assumed was the clinical area. He heard the woman at reception telling him again to sit and wait but he had already reached the doors and managed to slide through after a nurse before the swipe card locks engaged again.

Inside the place teemed with people. Nurses milled around in blue scrubs adorned with the logo 'GIG | NHS'. Stethoscopes hung around the necks of individuals Drake guessed were the doctors although they looked barely out of university. Studious faces stared at computer screens around a collection of desks and Drake marched over. 'I'm looking for Dr Williams. He's treating Dr Sian Drake.' Drake raised his voice against the ongoing activity and the sound of muffled conversations from the cubicles.

A man with a long face and powerful eyes under a tall forehead topped with a tower of black hair looked up at Drake. 'What did you say the patient's name was again?'

'Dr… I mean Sian Drake. She's a GP.'

'Are you a relative?'

Drake struggled to keep his impatience in check. He found his warrant card and flashed it at the doctor whose name badge said Nigel Wall. 'Detective Inspector Drake. Tell me where I can find Dr Drake.'

'Your wife was taken to Dolbadarn Ward a while back; your children are with her.'

Drake hurried down the corridor towards Dolbadarn Ward, but all he could think about was whether Sian and the girls were injured.

The corridors were too busy for Drake to break into a jog. At the entrance door he took a moment to cover his palm in an alcohol foam before barging inside. He checked the cubicles and bays but he couldn't see Sian or the girls anywhere in sight. He reached a workstation where nurses and doctors barely looked up from their paperwork. In the far corner he spotted a uniformed officer and hurried over.

'DI Drake. I'm looking for Dr Drake and her children,' Drake said.

'Your wife's in a private room; the children are with her,' the officer replied.

'Wait until I've talked to them. I want to know what happened.' Drake turned on his heel and marched towards the room as a doctor emerged. He gave Drake an inquisitive look. 'Inspector Drake? I'm Mr Williams the orthopaedic registrar. I've been looking after your wife.'

'We are not… how is she?' An explanation of his domestic life could wait. He wanted to know how Sian was and to speak to the girls.

'They're all shaken up. Your wife has a nasty break to her wrist so she has a temporary cast on but will need to go to theatre tomorrow, if we have space on the trauma list, to get it fixed operatively. The A&E doctors are happy for your daughters to go home, they have a few minor bruises.'

Drake entered the private room where Sian sat on a bed as a nurse took her blood pressure. She looked pale and drawn, her plastered forearm held in a sling.

'I'm so glad to see you, Ian,' Sian said. 'Helen and Megan were in the back of the car.'

Sian shooed the nurse away which made Drake feel relieved she was back to her bossy self. 'They're being entertained in the relatives' room, someone's found them an iPad.'

In the adjacent room Helen and Megan smiled when he entered. He hugged them both gently and was reassured from the smile the nurse gave him that they were well looked after. 'They're only here because we have nowhere else to put them. Don't worry, they've had the all-clear from A&E.'

'I'm going to talk to Mam again.' Drake smiled at his girls, the relief they were unharmed making him tearful.

Back in Sian's room he sat on a rigid plastic chair by the window.

'Do you remember what happened?'

'I was driving home and…' Sian faltered. She wiped away a tear and forced herself to continue. 'There was a jolt and a car rammed me from behind. I lost control of the car.'

Drake nodded. 'Did you see the other car?'

Sian shook her head. 'It all happened so quickly and I…'

Reliving the events sapped what energy she had left. Mr Williams returned with the nurse Drake had seen earlier. 'We're going to try to get this arm sorted for you in theatre as soon as possible today as I'm worried about the tingling in your right hand. You'll likely be in overnight.'

Sian gave him a plaintive look. 'I'll be fine.' She sounded unconvincing. Mr Williams gave her a faint patronising smile. Sian curled up her mouth and sighed. 'What about Helen and Megan?'

'They can stay with me,' Drake replied. 'I'll go and tell them now.'

He left the doctor and the nurse with Sian and found his daughters eating chocolate and quaffing a soft drink. He sat down on one of the stiff plastic chairs. 'Mam needs to stay in hospital overnight.' Helen reacted with her usual matter-of-factness. 'Are we going to stay with you, Dad?'

'Yes.'

Megan had avoided his eye contact. 'Is Mam okay?' She sounded anxious. He stood up and pulled her close. 'Of course, she is. The doctors want to make certain she gets the best possible care. I need to go and talk to one of them again and then we'll get your things from the house.'

Drake made for the door, intent on speaking with the traffic officer before he left. He found him pouring granules and two sachets of sugar into a plastic beaker before filling it with water from the urn on a trolley. 'What are the details?'

'It was lucky I was so close. I arrived at the scene within five minutes.'

'What happened?'

The traffic officer grimaced as he took the first mouthful of his drink. 'Your wife's BMW had been shunted off the road near a junction. She went through a bollard and ploughed into the crash barrier. No other car was involved.'

'Were there any witnesses?'

'Yes, sir. I took a brief statement. She makes it clear that the other car deliberately forced your wife off the road.' He plonked the drink down on the trolley. 'She was scared. And quite shaken up.'

'Do we have any details of the car that rammed Sian?'

'Just that it was a black Audi.'

The sound of activity around Drake dulled. The officer appeared to reach out for his drink in slow motion. Drake wanted to blot out the possibility that Sian and his daughters had been targeted by someone involved in the deaths of Dawn and Caston. A black Audi featured in the case and it sickened him that his work had brought his family to this.

'Did the eyewitness get a registration number?'

He shook his head. 'No, it all happened too quickly.'

Slowly Drake's training kicked in. 'Are there any

forensics at the scene from the other car.' There had to be a possibility that a paint fragment or piece of glass had been left behind.

'The traffic forensic team is there now.'

The tension building in Drake's chest made him feel sick and an ache developed over his shoulder. His mobile buzzed in his jacket and he fumbled to find the handset. He read the three messages from Annie and two missed calls and remembered she was expecting him home.

Drake found a quiet corner and dialled her number.

'What's wrong, Ian?'

'It's Sian – there's been an accident. Her car was rammed off the road.'

'That's awful. Is she all right? Were Helen and Megan with her?'

'They're keeping her in overnight. The girls will have to stay with us tonight.'

'Of course. Are they okay?'

'Yes. And I'm sorry I didn't call… it's been…'

'I understand. I'll see you and the girls later.'

He rang off and stood quite still as the hurly burly of activity in the ward took place around him. Out there someone was sending him a warning – that was clear enough. He must have been getting close with his inquiries, close enough for someone to pull a stunt involving his family. Did they really think it was going to stop him? Sian and Annie would need to be told the black Audi might be linked to his ongoing inquiry. But his daughters didn't need to know.

For now, his priority would be to see that Helen and Megan were safe.

He read the time on his watch. He'd call Sara later and he'd brief Hobbs in the morning. Before he had time to make other priorities, Robin Miles entered, Sian's new boyfriend or partner, he wasn't sure how to describe him.

'Ian, I've just heard. What the hell has happened?'

Chapter 24

Images of a black Audi following Drake along the A55 and then turning away as he approached headquarters interrupted his sleep. He woke in a sweat and padded to the kitchen, surprised he didn't feel more tired. Annie had fussed over Helen and Megan when they arrived at her home the previous evening. They had been unusually quiet, only picking at the food she had prepared. Drake hoped they would be more rested that morning. A brief call to the hospital ward sister told him Sian was still asleep after a comfortable night.

Annie joined him in the combined kitchen and sitting room on the second floor of the house they shared in Felinheli. Drake steeled himself to tell her all the details.

Coffee mug in hand she sat by the table with Drake.

'There's something you should know,' Drake began. 'The traffic officer who attended the scene yesterday told me that Sian had been deliberately rammed off the road by a black Audi.'

Annie tightened her grip on the mug.

'A black Audi features in the present inquiry.'

'You don't think they could be linked?'

Drake nodded. Annie thrust a hand to her mouth and mumbled, 'That's awful.'

This morning he'd pondered the implications he hadn't wanted to address the evening before. Sian would need to know; he couldn't avoid telling her.

'I think it would be best if Helen and Megan stayed here for a few days.'

Annie nodded as she frowned and then she reached over a hand and gave his a reassuring squeeze. He continued. 'And you and Sian will need to be careful.'

'Are these people dangerous?'

An image of Dawn Piper and Hubert Caston filled his mind and he lied. 'Someone was sending me a message.'

He left Annie sitting by the table and, after he'd showered and dressed, he eased open the door to the bedroom where his daughters were sleeping and took a moment to listen to the gentle rhythm of their breathing. He closed the door softly and after giving Annie a lingering hug and kissing her on the lips he went downstairs. The reflection he saw in the mirror by the front door looked haggard and drawn. He tightened the tie up to his collar and narrowed his eyes as he squinted at himself. It was Beltrami, he thought – he has an axe to grind, a large one at that, with his sister languishing in jail. Or maybe Paul Kenny from Liverpool or O'Brien from Deeside. Whoever it was would regret threatening his family. Police work and its demands on his time had caused the breakup of his marriage. Now he wasn't going to let anyone threaten them without facing the consequences.

He pulled the door closed behind him and drove off towards headquarters. On the A55 he regularly checked his rear-view mirror, monitoring the cars behind him, checking for a black Audi. He slowed and detoured through Llanfairfechan hoping it would flush out anybody tailing him. He rejoined the dual carriageway without spotting anyone driving suspiciously, and he dismissed his fears as being irrational and obsessive.

He parked the Mondeo away from other vehicles in the car park at headquarters, wanting to avoid unnecessary bumps and scratches. Speaking to Hobbs would be unavoidable but first he'd speak to Sara. His calls to her mobile the previous evening had all gone to voicemail which was unusual.

It was another hot, balmy summer's day and a bead of sweat broke out on his forehead as he reached the top of the staircase regretting his decision not to use the lift. Sara was alone in the Incident Room when he entered, and she gave him an energetic smile and a cheerful 'good morning'.

'I need to talk to you,' Drake said making for his office.

Sara followed him and he waved her to one of the visitor chairs. 'I tried to get hold of you last night.'

'I was out.'

'Your mobile was switched off?'

Sara paused. 'I was at the cinema. By the time I was home the battery was flat and I didn't check for any calls. We do have—'

'I know. I'm sorry. Someone in a black Audi rammed Sian off the road yesterday and caused her to crash.'

Sara's eyes widened. 'Was she hurt?'

'A broken wrist and the hospital kept her in overnight. The girls stayed with me last night.'

'They were in the car as well?'

Drake nodded.

'Did you say it was a black Audi?' Sara's tone underlined the implications.

The sound of Winder and Luned arriving for work drifted from the Incident Room. Drake bellowed for them to join him and he shared the events of the previous evening before both officers retreated open mouthed to their desks.

Sara joined them when Drake announced he had to brief Superintendent Price.

He made his way to the senior management suite and spoke to Hannah. He always thought of her as Price's secretary so it would be difficult changing his mind set. 'Is the super available?'

'Superintendent Hobbs is here. Wyndham… I mean Superintendent Price is away in Cardiff today.'

Drake was daunted by having to speak to Hobbs about his family. It made him wonder how much Hobbs already knew about him. He sat and waited. Hobbs emerged from his office and waved at Drake. Inside Drake started in Welsh, knowing Hobbs spoke the language and wondering if he was comfortable using it in informal briefings. '*Bore da.*'

Hobbs gave him a startled look. 'What's this about, Ian? I'm deputising for Superintendent Price at a local community forum meeting and I can't afford to be late.'

English it is then decided Drake, even informally, and Drake recounted the events of the previous evening. Hobbs looked at him unblinkingly which intimidated Drake. Price would have reacted with defiance and anger at the unknown perpetrator.

Once Drake had finished Hobbs sat back in his chair. 'I hope your family will be okay. I'll make certain forensics expedite the results from her car and for now we keep an open mind about the circumstances.'

Hobbs got up signalling the meeting was at an end.

Drake threaded his way back to the Incident Room. Superintendent Hobbs had appeared indifferent, almost dismissive. Drake smothered his apprehension – he was too accustomed to Price's personality. It would take time for him to get to know Hobbs. Somebody had seen the black Audi. Somebody would remember its registration number. Somebody might even be able to describe the driver. He had to prioritise and by the time he reached the Incident Room door he was ready to allocate tasks. He pushed the door open too briskly and it crashed against the wall behind it. It drew the attention of the rest of his team as their gaze followed him over to the board.

'I don't believe in coincidences,' Drake announced. 'We have to urgently establish who was driving the black Audi yesterday. And discover if it's linked to any of the persons of interest in our current inquiry.'

He paused and savoured the moment, as he realised he had their complete attention.

'Gareth, I want progress on identifying all the owners of black Audis in the North Wales area. Today.'

Winder nodded.

'We need to get yesterday's footage from every CCTV camera in the Colwyn Bay area so we can try and identify where the black Audi might have been.'

'Whoever it was probably did everything possible to

avoid the cameras,' Sara added.

'And they could have had false plates,' Luned commented.

'Don't give me obstacles,' Drake responded sharply. 'I want this work done this morning. Now. I'm going to talk to the traffic officers coordinating the investigation.' Drake turned to the board behind him. He moved his gaze from Kenny to O'Brien and finally Jack Beltrami, determined he'd find out who was responsible. One of the mug shots staring out at him belonged to a man that had threatened his family yesterday.

Drake stalked back to his office and sat down. He warmed to the smiling faces of his daughters in the photograph next to the phone and he reached for the handset and called Annie. 'They're still sleeping, Ian. What time will you be back?'

Drake wanted to give Annie a specific time, reassure her that things would be okay and dispel the uncertainty he could hear in her voice. The sound of activity from the Incident Room reminded him he had no idea when he'd be home. 'I don't know, I really don't know at the moment.'

'Call me, Ian.'

'Of course.'

Once the call was finished Drake punched in the number for the officer he'd met the previous afternoon. A brief conversation told him the incident was being handled by a Sergeant Harris in the road traffic division covering Colwyn Bay. It took Drake five minutes to track the officer down.

'Bring me up to date with the investigation into the collision yesterday involving Dr Drake, my ex-wife.'

'We've got forensics working on the rear bumper of Dr Drake's BMW. There were some paint scrapings that hopefully we can match to a particular manufacturer.'

'Have you got any officers doing house-to-house inquiries near the scene of the collision?'

Drake could hear Harris take a deep breath. 'We've made a public appeal for any eyewitnesses. There aren't many houses immediately adjacent to the scene.'

Drake sensed his patience straining. 'This was an attempt on Sian's life and my daughters were in the car. Other vehicles could have been involved and somebody might have been killed.'

'Our protocols don't normally provide for house-to-house inquiries in these circumstances.'

'Then I'll do it myself.' Drake slammed the phone back onto its cradle. He yelled for Sara. She appeared in the threshold of his office moments later. 'Get your coat. We're going to look at the crash scene.'

Drake led Sara downstairs and out of reception to the car park without saying a word. As they walked over to the Mondeo, Sara asked, 'How are your daughters, boss?'

'They were still sleeping when I spoke to Annie.' Drake unlocked the car and they jumped in.

'I need to know where the accident happened.' Drake turned to Sara, his hand on the key in the ignition. Sara nodded.

Retracing Sian's route was straightforward. The roads were familiar, Drake had driven them many times. But Colwyn Bay wasn't like the centre of a major city with CCTV cameras screwed to every lamppost. They passed a petrol filling station and Sara scribbled down the name of the business. By the time he reached the junction where the collision had happened, he realised the difficulty they faced in tracking the black Audi. Drake understood why Sergeant Harris hadn't embarked on house-to-house inquiries. The owner of the black Audi had chosen his spot carefully enough. Drake parked a little way from the junction and walked with Sara towards the buckled remains of the traffic barrier Sian's BMW had crashed into.

They crossed over two junctions and Drake could imagine the black Audi idling in a side road waiting for an opportunity to slip in behind Sian's vehicle. He recalled the officer's comments yesterday confirming that traffic had been light. Drake contemplated that more than one car was involved. A second vehicle could have delayed other cars allowing the Audi enough time to ram Sian. They had wanted her injured, they had wanted Megan and Helen hurt. A thick claw of tension scratched at his chest.

At the junction he passed the sign asking for eyewitnesses to come forward and contact the Wales Police Service. He swept his gaze around the area. Trees lined one side, houses were set back neatly from the road. A dog walker or a woman pushing a pram or a jogger or a cyclist could have seen something.

'We should do some house-to-house,' Drake said.

Sara kept her voice low. 'Shouldn't the traffic officers do that?'

Drake stared over at the houses knowing she was right but the urge to knock on every door, interrogate every householder was overwhelming. As he decided what exactly was the right thing to do, his mobile rang.

It was Gareth Winder. 'I turned up something.' Winder raised his voice a fraction too much to gain Drake's attention. 'The DVLA sent me details of people who own black Audis in North Wales. Jack Beltrami has two – a small hatchback and an A4 saloon.'

And Kenny owning a black Audi made him and Beltrami persons of real interest in the inquiry. 'Good, progress.'

Drake conjured up Beltrami's image in his mind. He would be bold enough to threaten Sian and the girls. Drake salivated at the prospect of arresting Beltrami and dragging him to the area custody suite to be interviewed.

Chapter 25

Drake stood before the Incident Room board staring over at the rest of his team, clenching his jaw. Since the beginning of the investigation when Jim Finch had referred to Jack Beltrami's possible involvement, the gangster from Rhyl had never been far from Drake's mind. He was unprincipled enough, aggressive enough and hated Drake enough to have organised the ramming of Sian's car. How did Beltrami think he would react, Drake thought? Driving back to headquarters he had smothered every instinct that suggested he should go to Beltrami's amusement arcade in Rhyl, arrest him on suspicion of murder and seize the two black Audi vehicles he owned.

He couldn't afford to lose his objectivity but involving his family had crossed a line. 'Do we know where Beltrami's Audis are actually located?'

Luned gave a puzzled frown. Winder gave Sara a worried glance.

'We haven't got any basis for suspecting that either vehicle owned by Beltrami was involved,' Sara announced slowly.

She was right, of course, Drake gave her a brief nod of acknowledgement and continued. 'Have you been able to check any of the CCTV around Colwyn Bay?'

Winder replied, 'We found snippets of footage with Dr Drake's BMW, but we couldn't find a black Audi and nothing to establish she had been followed.'

Luned added, 'We did look at footage on the A55 for an hour either side of the accident but again, there was no sign of a black Audi.'

Drake nodded. 'The car could have kept to the side streets. It might take us days to track it down.'

'How much more time do you want to spend on it, sir?' Sara said, although Drake guessed the same question was uppermost in the mind of the other two officers. Without evidence that his inquiry was linked to the incident, it was nothing more than a road traffic collision – hardly a priority for any police force these days.

'We leave it for now.' Drake saw the tension ebb away as face muscles relaxed. 'I need progress on Beltrami's known associates and…' Drake recalled the shopkeeper and the unreliable CCTV system. 'Chase up the footage from the Queensferry convenience store. And chase the care home in Liverpool again – someone must have seen those girls in the company of a person they could describe.' He raised his voice. 'Go there if you have to.'

Drake paced over to his office and reached the threshold where he turned and marched back to the board. 'And chase the taxi companies for details of the drivers near the rugby club.' He sounded angry, he felt angry. He stalked back to his office.

He had to focus on unpicking the threads, but he kept returning to Jack Beltrami. He had to be involved, it was the only conclusion and there was evidence, somewhere.

All they had to do was find it.

He chided himself when he contemplated the possibility that he was obsessed with the Beltrami family. But they were an organised crime group that deserved to be prosecuted. As was Paul Kenny and O'Brien and any one of them would be capable of ramming Sian's car and threatening his children. His chest tightened at the thought.

A prominent Post-it note reminded him that Hubert Caston's work colleagues had recommended he talk to Doreen – he found her number in his notebook and she answered after two rings. She was available that afternoon and Drake welcomed the opportunity of leaving his office, fearing that if he stayed tied to his desk he would start to obsess about Jack Beltrami. He bellowed Sara's name. She appeared in the doorway of his office moments later. 'Let's go and see Doreen. She was friendly with Hubert Caston.'

The inside of the Mondeo was clammy and warm. He

opened the window as he sped away from headquarters. Once they were outside the fifty-mph speed restriction zone, Sara cleared her throat and glanced at Drake. 'The team are doing the best they can, boss.'

Drake gave her a sharp glance. Had he been unnecessarily abrupt with Luned and Winder? Making progress was essential. That was all he had wanted.

'We all want a result, and Gareth and Luned were both shaken up over what happened to Sian and your daughters,' Sara added.

Drake grunted a reply. 'Okay, thanks.'

Sara persisted. 'You need to be careful with the Beltrami family. We need evidence.'

Significantly less direct than telling Drake he was losing his objectivity but just as meaningful. Drake nodded. 'I know. You're right.'

'As soon as we've got evidence from Sian's accident implicating Beltrami or any of the other persons of interest we will proceed accordingly.'

'We're getting too close to Beltrami.'

'Or one of the others.'

'And they want to rattle my cage.'

'Let's build a case we can prosecute.'

Drake indicated off the dual carriageway and drove down into Connah's Quay. The satnav announced the directions for Drake to find Doreen Smith's home. The semi-detached property had a slightly elevated position and after parking, Drake and Sara took the half a dozen steps up to the front door. A healthy-looking woman in her early sixties opened the door. She gave Drake and Sara a warm smile tinged with uncertainty.

'Come in.'

She led them into a sitting room that had a stale, second-hand feeling as though it was rarely used, kept for Sunday best. Doreen sat at the edge of a chair, Drake and Sara on the sofa opposite.

'I understand you were friends with Hubert Caston's mother,' Drake said.

Doreen nodded. 'I was with her in school. I'd been friends with her for years. She never came to terms with Hubert… being a bit slow…'

'When did she die?' Sara asked, her voice soft.

Doreen looked into the middle distance through the window. 'It was over a year. Seems like only yesterday.'

'We're trying to build a picture of Hubert's background, his friends and acquaintances so that we can identify anyone who might have a motive to kill him.'

Doreen's face turned a shade sadder. 'He wouldn't hurt a fly.'

Drake continued. 'We've interviewed a Mattie Williams who tells us that Hubert had been letting the property he inherited from his parents to Ritchie O'Brien but that recently he decided to bring that arrangement to an end and let the property to someone else. Do you know anything about that?'

Doreen's face turned a little ashen. 'I used to go and visit Hubert regularly. I would take him something to eat and check up on him. Sometimes he wouldn't look after himself properly. I arrived one evening and…' Doreen threaded the fingers of her hands together, 'the rear gate was open. I went into the rear yard as usual, but I could hear an argument in the house. They were arguing about the property Hubert was letting – and it was all very one-sided. And I could see that it was Ritchie O'Brien taking it out on Hubert.'

'Can you be certain that it was Ritchie O'Brien?'

Doreen nodded. 'I've seen him in The Lamb. He struts around that place like a peacock thinking he's so important.'

'Did you hear the exact words Richie said to Hubert?'

Doreen blinked rapidly. 'He said things like – *you'll live to regret this,* and *nobody crosses me*. I was quite upset, and I left soon afterwards. I came back to see Hubert later that night and I told him that I'd heard the argument, but he said everything had been sorted out.'

'Did you believe him?'

Doreen gave Drake and Sara a helpless look.

After they had established the precise date and whether Doreen had heard other arguments between O'Brien and Caston and whether Caston had complained before about O'Brien, Drake and Sara left. They sat in the car as Drake switched on his mobile. Sara had her notebook in hand. 'O'Brien threatened Caston. That's direct evidence.'

'I agree.' Drake read the message from Winder asking him to call. 'Something we can ask O'Brien in due course.' He dialled the number and waited.

'Superintendent Price has told us that there is a public meeting outside the old police station in Shotton,' Winder said. 'Apparently the press have been in touch asking if we have any comments to make.'

'And he wants us to attend?'

'Yes, sir.'

A few minutes later after parking on double yellow lines and sticking his *On Police Business/ Heddlu Swyddogol* sign onto the dashboard, Drake and Sara made their way over to a crowd gathered outside the old police station where a decaying 'for sale' board had been screwed to one of the boarded-up windows. Councillor Beedham stood on a plinth constructed from three breeze blocks and several large pieces of timber, strong enough to hold his weight. He stood near another man with a gold chain draped around his neck, a megaphone to his mouth. The majority of the crowd were elderly members of the community as well as an aggressive-looking group of younger people. Two uniformed officers were keeping a discreet distance from the group.

After listening to a preliminary introduction from the man wearing a chain of office who praised Councillor Beedham's efforts to protect local services and offering to make his voice heard in Cardiff, he passed the megaphone to

Beedham. Drake listened to Beedham's rant about cutbacks in local policing, education and the health service.

> *Just look at this police station behind us. The town hasn't got a police presence any longer. This is a sad indictment of what our politicians think is best. Things have got to change. If we're going to make our community safer, offer the best chance for youngsters, then we have to keep our streets safe. And the only way is to have police officers on the beat. I would reopen closed police stations.*

He gestured to the building behind him as the crowd shouted their agreement.

'Is he going to offer to increase taxes?' Sara whispered.

'Fat chance of that happening,' Drake replied.

> *And we've seen the damage that drugs coming into the town has caused. The recent spate of overdoses and avoidable deaths are an indictment on our society and on our ability to police and keep our community safe. There's no point talking about human rights for these criminals. Where are the human rights for our youngsters when they get trapped into drug dependency?*

More cheers and applause.

Drake searched for the sign of any television crew and couldn't see any. Their absence would disappoint Councillor Beedham – a little less exposure for the likes of Beedham. They stood listening to more of the populist jargon being pumped out by Beedham who sounded increasingly desperate, as though he realised that as an independent in a by-election he had little prospect of success. He kept repeating the same phrases, the same words until the response from the audience waned.

'I've had enough, let's go back to headquarters,' Drake said.

Winder needed little encouragement to leave headquarters

and make the journey to Liverpool. Before leaving he had called one of the names the care home had given him – Patricia Walsh. She had sounded helpful but disappointed that she would have to give up part of her day off to be interviewed by him. His call to Vera, the second employee that Merseyside Police hadn't spoken to, rang out. At least he had one of the employees to interview and he decided to contact Vera again once he had spoken to Patricia.

Knowing he had the rest of the day to interview both women meant he could take a detour to Liverpool One, the main shopping area of the city, to visit the Liverpool Football Club outlet. Clothes and accessories branded with the name of the club were ridiculously expensive and his girlfriend would criticise any expenditure as a frivolous waste of money especially as they were saving for their next holiday. But he didn't care. If you were going to support a football team then you needed all the kit.

After a McDonald's washed down with a large milkshake, Winder spent an hour in the store and left after adding £60 to his credit card bill. He held the plastic bag containing two fashion polo shirts tightly, placing them safely in the boot of his car under a blanket. He tapped into the satnav the postcode for Patricia's home and waited whilst the system calculated the route. Winder's knowledge of the city only extended to driving from the Mersey Tunnel to the car parks for the Anfield ground where Liverpool played their home matches. While he waited, he dialled Vera's number, again with no luck.

Once the satnav had finished, Winder stared at the screen getting his bearings. The directions took him north for Fazakerley and he passed Goodison Park, home of Everton football club, the main rivals to Liverpool, and then Anfield itself before the satnav took him past HMP Altcourse.

The street where Patricia Walsh lived was a post-war development of terraces with small front gardens. Cars parked up and down the street meant Winder had to find a slot in an adjacent road. He locked the car, tugging at the handle to make certain.

Patricia Walsh's doorbell rang out with a modern sing-song tone and Winder heard movement inside seconds later.

A bottleblonde opened the door and gave him a warm smile – somewhere in her fifties, Winder thought.

'Come in, pet.'

Winder pushed the door closed behind him and followed her into a sitting room where another woman of the same age sat. She wore a short-sleeved summer blouse, a fraction too tight. It matched Patricia's that stretched around her waist when she sat down.

'This is Vera. She works in the Hill Gate too.'

Vera smiled an acknowledgement.

'I've been trying to contact you.'

'Sorry, hun, must have had a low battery or sommat.'

Pat butted in. 'What's this about?'

'She's going on holiday next week. Doesn't want nothing interfering with her plans.'

Pat sounded exasperated. 'It's not that.' She turned to Winder. 'Don't pay her any attention.'

'We're investigating two murders in North Wales and we believe they may be linked to the disappearance of two girls from Hill Gate – Debbie and Tina.'

'They were a right pair,' Pat replied. 'Rough as old boots.'

Vera nodded her head solemnly in agreement.

'I need to establish if you ever saw them in the company of older men.'

Pat glanced at Vera who encouraged her to reply. 'We told Rick, he's the manager of Hill Gate, that we'd seen them out at all times and that he should be careful. After all he was in charge—'

'He had a duty of care. That's what we told him, didn't we, Pat?'

'That's right, Vera.'

Winder cut across the mutual appreciation. 'Where did you see them?'

Pat replied. 'All over – in the shops and the cafés near Hill Gate. Even in the launderette. God knows what they were doing in there.'

Winder got in before Vera could hijack the conversation again. 'Did you ever see them as passengers in a car with strangers.'

'Once.' Both women in unison now.

Pat continued. 'But they were back in Hill Gate the following morning.'

'I've got some photographs with me and I was wondering if you could look at them and tell me if you recognise any of the faces.'

From the folder on his lap Winder produced images of Kenny and several of his known associates, as well as O'Brien and Beltrami.

Both women scanned and discarded the images of Beltrami and O'Brien but paused and stared at the photographs of Kenny. One of his henchmen in particular drew their attention.

'That's him.' Pat looked up at Winder, an angry look on her face.

'He even looks like a scally,' Vera interjected as Winder reached over for the photograph.

Vera nodded when Pat pointed at the image of Paul Kenny.

'I've seen him with Debbie and Tina too.'

Winder reached for his legal pad, excited that he had made progress. 'I'll need to take a statement from both of you. Just so that I've got all the details recorded correctly.'

'Would you like some tea, hun?'

Winder nodded.

Chapter 26

Drake detoured to the hospital on the way back to headquarters. He left Sara in the car and paced down the corridors to Sian's ward and through to her private room. A doctor stood to one side of the bed, Robin Miles on the other. Sian was listening intently to the surgeon's instructions.

'Good afternoon, Inspector Drake,' the doctor said.

Drake nodded a greeting in reply which he shared with Miles. He smiled at Sian. 'How are you?'

The doctor replied, 'Dr Drake is fit enough to be released later. Provided she takes it easy for a few days then I'm sure there will be no long-lasting damage.'

Miles chipped in. 'Sian is coming to stay at my place for the next week or so until she improves.'

'That sounds sensible,' the doctor added as he made to leave.

Once he had left Miles continued. 'Have you had any success in tracing the driver?'

'No, not at present but it's still early days. We've requisitioned a lot of the local CCTV footage and there has been a public appeal for eyewitnesses. So, it shouldn't be too long.'

'Do we get to know what's happening in the inquiry?' Miles said.

Drake gave him a weak smile. 'Of course.' Drake couldn't delay sharing his suspicions with them about the link to the Deeside cases. 'And you need to be aware that I suspect a link to my present case. A black Audi features in the investigation.'

'Jesus, Ian. Are we going to be targeted by some criminal because of you?' Miles sounded livid.

Drake's heart ached as he looked at Sian's frightened face. 'We can't be certain. Just be careful.'

Drake left Sian's room and returned to Sara who was

listening to some classical music on the radio in the car. She turned the volume to low as he sat in the driver seat. 'How's Dr Drake?'

'They're discharging her today. She's going to stay with her partner for a few days.'

Sara nodded. 'I hope she'll be okay.'

Arriving back in the office, he slumped into his chair. Realising he would think more clearly in the morning he decided to leave, but first he called Annie. 'How are the girls?'

'They're fine… I've been expecting to hear from you.'

Drake sensed the criticism in her voice. A spasm of guilt struck home – he should have been with his daughters, but police work was never that simple. 'We've been working on finding a link between what happened to Sian and our inquiry.'

'When will you be home?'

'I'm leaving now.'

'The girls are looking forward to seeing you. I think they are still quite upset from yesterday.'

Traffic delays extended his journey by thirty minutes. Cars pulling caravans and coaches filled with sightseers dawdled in the outside lane much to his annoyance. Unsuccessfully, he tried to banish the images of Jack Beltrami to the outer edges of his mind, but his sneer and cold eyes returned to haunt Drake. The Beltrami family were more than capable of a double murder, but Drake worried how much of his focus on the family was coloured by gossip and by his association with Jade Beltrami from a previous case. He couldn't simply dismiss the link to Paul Kenny. As soon as they found the two girls Olivia Knox was convinced had been trafficked into the area, they'd have a link to their abductors.

But it still wouldn't give them evidence relating to the murder of Dawn Piper or Hubert Caston. The prospect that the killer would escape justice made him shiver.

He indicated left off the dual carriageway for Felinheli.

His mood lightened. It was still a bright summer's evening.

Annie met Drake at the door. She kissed him and held him close. 'You look tired.'

'It's been a long day.'

Annie whispered, 'Both Helen and Megan have been quiet today. It's been difficult to get them to talk.'

'I spoke to Sian earlier.'

Annie looked surprised, taken aback. 'You went to the hospital?' There was an underlying tone of reproach, she would have known it was out of his way.

'I called on my way back from an interview in Deeside.'

Annie smiled but her eyes didn't light up as they normally did.

'I'm going to talk to the girls.'

Drake found his daughters propped up on the bed they were sharing in one of Annie's bedrooms playing computer games. 'Have you seen Mam today?' Helen asked. At ten years of age she was always the one that took the lead. Megan was three years younger and deferred to her older sister.

'I called at the hospital.'

That simple confirmation that their mother was alive and well was reassurance enough and their faces lit up.

'She's going to stay with Robin for a few days until she feels better.'

Helen must have contemplated that she and her sister could do the same, but she deferred her eye contact and the moment passed.

'When can we go home?' Megan asked.

Drake didn't have an easy answer. The simple certainties of childhood weren't something he could solve with a date. 'Once she's better you can go back home.'

It struck him then that his home with Annie wasn't a

home for his daughters. It was where he lived. 'And remember we're going on holiday in a few weeks' time. So perhaps tonight or tomorrow we can have a look at things to do when we get to Disneyland Paris.'

Helen and Megan nodded enthusiastically.

After their meal the girls settled down to one of their favourite films on television and Drake sat outside in the small garden, sharing a bottle of wine with Annie and enjoying the last of the spectacular sunset over Anglesey.

As Annie cleared the dishes Drake rang Robin Miles' home.

'How is Sian tonight?' Drake said when Miles answered. 'Can I talk to her?'

Miles sounded irritated. 'I'll go and see if she is awake.'

Drake heard movement and guessed Miles was walking through into the master bedroom at his property. He had only ever been into the ground floor for boozy dinner parties in the past and he tried to imagine Sian sitting up in bed with Miles standing over her offering her the handset.

'How are you?' Drake said when he heard Sian's weary voice.

'I'm going to take something to help me sleep tonight.'

'I haven't told Helen and Megan anything about the possible link to my inquiry.'

'I understand. Can I speak to them?'

Now Drake traipsed downstairs and handed the phone to his daughters. He rejoined Annie sitting in the kitchen.

'I've spoken to Sian.'

Annie nodded.

'Robin said she was still tired.'

Another nod of the head.

'He's worried about her and she's going to stay with him for a few days. And—'

'Ian, there's no need to obsess about Sian. She's got Robin and… I know she had the accident and that the girls were involved… but don't you think… I'm frightened too?'

The realisation struck Drake.

Annie wiped away a tear. 'You haven't asked once how I'm feeling since this thing started.'

Drake scrambled to his feet and sat by her side holding her tightly as he tried to forget how insensitive he had been. Allowing his focus to concentrate on Sian without realising he had neglected Annie came crashing into his mind. He had allowed the inquiry to invade his personal life again, something he hoped would never happen.

Chapter 27

The following morning Drake breakfasted with Annie on the balcony. They kept their voices low so as not to wake the girls. Being so preoccupied with the inquiry he had failed to see how the person he loved was hurting too. Annie deserved better and he determined to remember that she and his daughters were his priority.

'I need to get to work,' Drake said eventually.

Annie smiled. 'Of course.'

She drew a hand down over his cheek as he kissed her before leaving.

Driving to headquarters gave him time to think.

The exact scene where Dawn Piper had been killed needed to be found and then forensically analysed. Results of the phone work so far had led them to the rugby club but triangulation reports could be unreliable. Olivia Knox kept reappearing in the investigation which convinced Drake she was hiding something.

Winder was already at his desk when Drake arrived. Sara and Luned crowded around him.

'I've found an eyewitness who saw Kenny and one of his oppos with Debbie and Tina the day they went missing.' Winder fell over his words in the rush to share the details with Drake.

'Good.' Drake made for the board and tapped the image of Kenny. 'I think it's time we spoke to Mr Kenny. Send me all the details.' He remained by the board peering at the image of Dawn Piper.

'She and Olivia Knox and possibly even Hubert Caston were up to something. We've got to focus on finding where Dawn was killed. So today, concentrate everything on the phone work. I want her mobile cross-referenced with the phone numbers in Caston's mobile. There's a pattern there somewhere – we need to find it.'

The team around the desks nodded their agreement.

'I've started with the taxi companies as well,' Luned said. 'There are dozens of part-time drivers mostly working for themselves.'

'Contact them all. I want to know if they were near the rugby club the night she was killed and establish if any of them had a dashcam.'

Drake's mind turned to another thread that needed their attention. 'Have we had any feedback from the pharmacies in Deeside about the insulin prescription?'

Luned piped up. 'I've spoken with a couple of the managers, but they were reluctant to disclose personal information. They're going to refer the request to their head office.'

Drake took a deep breath. 'Bloody paperwork. We may have to go and see them. But for now,' he turned to Sara, 'let's go and visit Merseyside.'

Drake threw the right coins for the Mersey Tunnel toll into the receptacle and seconds later the security barrier lifted out of the way. On the journey from Deeside, Sara had been reminding Drake about Paul Kenny's background. Substantial resources spent by Merseyside Police on surveillance had proved to be inconclusive. Kenny's name was linked with two unsolved murders, several severe beatings and money laundering on an industrial scale. Kenny sounded like a bigger version of the Beltrami family.

Drake threaded his way through the streets of Liverpool towards an address in Aintree. The satnav punctuated the interior with its disembodied directions and within half an hour Drake parked outside an imposing pub. It gave Kenny a legitimate business, a front from which to trade, launder money effectively and act as a central hub for drug distribution.

He switched off the engine and they sat for a moment looking over at The Dublin Castle pub.

Sara pointed towards a side street. 'That's where Dawn

must have been standing when she was photographed speaking to Kenny.'

Drake glanced over to the opposite pavement. 'Cameron Toft must have been sitting in a car over there.' He jerked a hand in the direction of where he'd been looking.

'It still doesn't make sense that Toft would have been following Dawn.'

'I don't think we've learnt everything about Cameron Toft.'

'Surely you don't think he's involved?'

'We keep an open mind about everybody. It's difficult to believe that a man would kill the mother of his child.'

Before Sara could reply, the bulky figure of Paul Kenny emerged from the pub. 'Here's our man,' Drake said. They watched as Kenny spoke with two other men both as smartly dressed in grey suits and tieless open-necked shirts as him. Kenny pointed a hand towards the BMW 6 Series coupe and the headlights bleeped as the car unlocked. 'Where's he going?'

'We could follow him, boss?'

Drake started the engine as Kenny got into the car. At the junction near the pub Kenny indicated left and Drake pulled out and followed him. 'Let's see where he's going.'

Sara scrambled through the rest of the documentation in the folder on her lap. 'I'll see if he's got any other businesses he might be visiting.'

Drake enjoyed following Paul Kenny through the streets of Liverpool. It was like something out of a television crime drama. He'd relish even more, however, having enough direct evidence against Kenny to arrest him, take him to the custody suite of Northern Division and then charge him with murder.

Traffic circulating avoided any possibility that Paul Kenny would notice a grey Mondeo behind him. His BMW 6 Series coupe was large enough and smart enough to stand out amongst the grey cars and white vans, making it easy to tail.

Kenny pulled into the car park of a hotel. Drake parked up alongside the pavement nearby.

'Got it.' Sara sounded pleased with herself. 'The Aintree Forest Hotel is a small part of Paul Kenny's empire.'

'Let's see if he'll stretch to a coffee.'

Drake drove into the hotel car park and slotted the Mondeo in alongside Kenny's coupe. They left the car and strode over to the entrance. Cleaning staff milled around the main reception area as raised voices directed activity. A thin man in his early twenties gave Drake a harassed look. He spoke with a strong East European accent. 'How can I help you?'

'We need to speak to Mr Paul Kenny.'

'He's not here.'

Drake found his warrant card and flashed it into the face of the receptionist. 'Don't give me any of that bullshit. I've just seen him park.'

The man flushed, turned on his heel and moments later Paul Kenny appeared, frowning.

'What do you lads want? What nick are you from?' His accent was exactly as Drake expected – thick and Scouse and hostile.

'Detective Inspector Ian Drake, Wales Police Service. And this is Detective Sergeant Sara Morgan.'

Kenny relaxed. 'For fuck's sake – the bizzies from Wales – Keystone Cops or what? I didn't think you had time to spare from catching all them sheep shaggers.'

Drake didn't respond. He had had more than his fair share of derogatory and insulting comments by English crooks who thought they could get away with crime in Wales.

'We need a word in private.'

Kenny raised his eyebrows in mock surprise. Drake waited.

Then a puzzled look crossed Kenny's face. 'How the fuck did you know I was here?'

'Like I said,' Drake said, 'we need a word in private. Unless you'd like to discuss matters out here so everyone can listen.'

Kenny relented. 'As you please.' He joined Drake and Sara and motioned for them to follow him down the corridor. 'There's a private room down here.'

Kenny fumbled with the key and unlocked the door to a space that barely qualified as a room. A small table had been pushed against a wall underneath a narrow oblong window high up near the ceiling. Kenny leaned against the table. There weren't any chairs.

'I'm a very busy man, so you'd better get on with it.'

'We're investigating the murder of Dawn Piper. Her body was found a week last Monday at her home in Deeside.'

'What the fuck has that got to do with me?'

Drake drew out the photograph of Dawn Piper from Sara's folder. He pushed it over at Kenny. 'Have you ever seen Dawn Piper before?'

The barest hint of recognition filtered across Kenny's eyes. It was there for a second, Drake was certain.

'I don't know who you're talking about. I've never seen this bird before.'

'Take a good look. Are you sure?'

Kenny scanned the image. 'Nope, sorry.'

'You were seen with her a few days before her death.'

Kenny guffawed out loud. 'You really are off your trolley, mate.'

'It's Detective Inspector.'

'Yeah, whatever.'

Drake fumbled for the second photograph. It wasn't the best likeness. The lighting was poor, the camera struggling to focus but Kenny was clear enough, as was Dawn.

'This was taken the Thursday night before she was

killed. That's you, isn't it?'

Kenny grabbed it and glared at it. Was it incredulity or surprise that crossed his face? Drake was uncertain. If he had read Kenny's previous reaction correctly then he had recognised Dawn, never contemplating someone had taken a photograph of them both talking together.

'What did you talk about?'

Kenny gave him a pained confused expression. 'I remember her now. She was some daft woman who kept ranting about drug dealers. I told her it had nothing to do with me.'

Kenny managed to surprise Drake by sounding genuine. 'We're also investigating the disappearance of two girls from a care home here in Liverpool known as Hill Gate. Are you familiar with it?' Drake announced the exact date the girls had been seen with Kenny.

Kenny wrinkled his brow as he squinted at Drake. 'What do you take me for? Some sort of sad paedo?'

Drake dug out the images of Debbie and Tina from a folder and pushed them over at Kenny. 'These are the two girls. Have you seen them before?'

Kenny gave them a brief glance.

'Take your time, Mr Kenny. This is a murder inquiry that we believe is somehow linked to the abduction of these two young girls.'

'Nope.'

'I'm sure you realise that at this stage we hope you'll cooperate fully with our investigation. We have an eyewitness that confirms you were seen with the girls.'

'Well they're fucking lying.' Kenny stood up and adopted a threatening cross-armed posture.

'When did you last go to Deeside?'

'I wouldn't know how to get there. I go to Ibiza or Minorca or somewhere in the sun for my holidays. I don't go to bloody Wales where it pisses down with rain all the time.'

'Connah's Quay and Shotton and Queensferry are the

three towns that make up the Deeside area. They've got quite a lot of history and Flint further to the north has a famous castle. Take your time to think about it carefully.' Drake paused. 'So, have you ever been to that area?'

Kenny shook his head with mock seriousness. 'Sorry, *Detective Inspector*.'

Drake reached over for the folder and took his time searching through its contents before extracting with a certain theatricality the image of Kenny and Hubert Caston.

Drake looked over at Kenny. 'I believe you own a black Audi A4.' Drake read aloud the registration number. Kenny nodded.

'It was seen in a garage in Deeside last week.'

A heavy expression settled over Kenny's face.

'We have an image from a petrol filling station. It shows you with a Hubert Caston.' Drake handed the photograph to Kenny. 'I'm also investigating Caston's murder. Why did you lie to me, Mr Kenny?'

Kenny stepped towards Drake and snarled. 'Not even the local bizzies have the cheek to come in here and start accusing me of being some sort of pervert.' He jabbed a finger at Drake. 'People like you need to be careful. Bad things happen. Shit happens.'

'Are you threatening me?' Drake kept his voice low.

Kenny smirked and leaned forward slightly invading Drake's personal space.

'Let's just say that our local constabulary take a more… cooperative approach. Talk to my brief if you need to speak to me again.' Kenny continued with a quiet tone. 'Now you fuck off back to them caves you crawled out of this morning and leave us city folk alone.'

Chapter 28

Drake arrived at the Incident Room early the following morning. Sara was already at her desk and Winder and Luned trooped in soon after he had hung his jacket on the wooden hanger on the coat stand in his room. He bustled over to the board and listened to Sara sharing the details of the interview with Kenny.

'I hate these toerags from Liverpool who think we're rural simpletons,' Winder said.

'He denied anything to do with the girls,' Sara said. 'And he threatened the boss.'

Luned and Winder looked at Drake for a reaction. He shrugged off the incident even though it had affected him more than he wanted to admit – waking early that morning, his dreams dominated by Kenny, wasn't to be shared with the others.

'We need to find these girls. And we'll talk to Kenny again if we have to.'

He spent half an hour getting up to date with the rest of his team. Winder and Luned had been working their way through dozens of taxi drivers in the Deeside area. Of the ten spoken to so far, only three had dashcams and none had been in the vicinity of the rugby club on the Saturday evening in question.

'Keep at it. Let me know as soon as you establish which taxi drivers were outside the rugby club that Saturday night.'

Back in his room Drake carefully moved some of the columns of Post-it notes to one corner of his desk and drew out from a drawer a sheet of paper. Mind mapping always had a calming and constructive effect on his ability to order priorities. The impact on Sian and his daughters and Annie sharpened his resolve that nobody would threaten his family. He dismissed any notion he was becoming paranoid. Sian's collision hadn't been an accident. One of the men whose mugshots were pinned to the board was sending him a message – a message intended to complicate and confuse, and he was having none of it.

He started with the triangulation reports from Dawn Piper's number. He focused on her calls and texts on the Saturday evening she was killed. In the centre he wrote Dawn Piper's name and underneath it her mobile number. He drew a circle around it and then on the top right-hand side he added the number she had contacted repeatedly on the Saturday, the day she was last seen.

Who are you, he wondered?

The pattern of usage was sporadic – it wasn't in daily use. It was clearly a second mobile for somebody who wanted to retain a degree of anonymity.

Drake found the details of Hubert Caston's mobile. He followed a similar routine of adding the number underneath Caston's name in the top left corner. Working through Caston's numbers methodically confirmed that the same number on the top right-hand side had also been called by Caston.

Fortunately, Caston had been a light user of his mobile handset. Most of the contacts were work colleagues or friends. A Chinese takeaway was also on the list and Drake spotted the numbers for Doreen and Mattie Williams. He scrolled through the names and found Olivia Knox. He cross-referenced the date of Caston's last call to her and when Drake established it had been three weeks before his death he paused. A loose knot of suspicion gathered in his belly as he recalled Knox telling him that Caston had called her. He dredged his memory – *He said he had some important information.*

Why had Knox been evasive when questioned? Now Drake had something else to ask her – how did Caston call her? It was time that he had another conversation with Olivia Knox.

Mid-morning, he organised a coffee from the kitchen. The grounds were an Italian espresso brand that he had found on the Internet. It was certainly rich and he enjoyed the caffeine hit. By lunchtime he had finished the phone work linking Dawn Piper to Hubert Caston and the mysterious third party. He wondered if Olivia Knox was the owner.

Drake got to his feet, grabbed his jacket, walked into the Incident Room and nodded at Sara. 'Let's go and talk to Knox again. And we can visit some of those pharmacies at the same time.'

After the case began, Luned had binged on catch-up television, watching all the recently screened documentaries about county lines activities, listening carefully to the comments made by the senior police officers. It disheartened her to realise the county lines drug operators were the greatest threats policing in North Wales faced. None of her friends had taken drugs and she didn't know anyone who did. Until she had joined the Wales Police Service after university, she had felt comfortable in the certainties of her way of life and the communities in which she lived. It unsettled her to feel that her family and the lifestyle she valued might be threatened by these people. But she knew modern policing meant adapting and changing to the demands of criminals.

She couldn't help but think that Dawn Piper and Hubert Caston had known their killer. Very few murders were actually random, and she focused on assuming the killer was the same person.

If the pathologist was correct, then Dawn had been killed late Saturday–early Sunday. They had spent all of the morning calling taxi companies and their drivers searching for anyone who might have seen Dawn in the vicinity of the rugby club. She had spoken to two drivers with dashcams but one had been on a fare to Manchester airport and another had a pickup in Chester.

They still had no certainty where Dawn had been and

Luned wondered if Dawn had visited another pub or club. Everyone is a creature of habit, Luned reminded herself. There were things she did regularly, and it was likely Dawn Piper was the same. Inspector Drake had already reported that Toft knew little about her regular habits which Luned found unlikely. So she decided to call him.

'I'm trying to establish the details of Dawn's movements for the Saturday evening she died. And I hope you might be able to help.'

'It is going to take long?' Toft put Luned on edge. 'I've told the other cops everything I know.'

'Did she do anything regularly on a Saturday evening?'

'Such as?'

'Did she have a favourite pub?'

'I know she listened to country and western occasionally in that barn of an old pub on the outskirts of town. But she didn't mention anything else. Are we done now? Only I've got things to do.'

'What's the place called?'

'The Bluebell.'

'Thank you.'

Luned rang off. A Google search gave her the address and contact phone number. A website looked about twenty years old with ancient, poor-quality photographs of the lounge and function rooms. She didn't imagine it was the sort of place to have CCTV cameras. A woman with a strong Birmingham accent answered the phone.

'How can I help you, love?'

'Do you have country and western evenings?'

'It's one of our favourites. We get one of them Welsh bands from Wrexham quite often and next weekend we've got a local band.'

'When was the last time a gig was organised?'

'Let me think, it must have been last Saturday night, pet. I wasn't working but the boss told me the place was packed.'

'Do you have CCTV cameras inside?'

'The boss installed them a month or so ago. He thinks it's going to stop the hooligans.'

By now Luned was sitting up straight on her chair. 'Can you send me the footage for last Saturday night?'

The woman chortled. 'Don't be daft. I wouldn't know how to work it. And anyway, you need to talk to the boss.'

It irked Luned that it needed ten minutes of cajoling and threats to persuade the owner of the Bluebell that her request was a priority.

Then she waited.

Winder had been unusually taciturn after Drake and Sara had left. Watching CCTV footage had a soporific effect on him and although she had heard him make the occasional groan and express his irritation – he had even scribbled some notes – he had generally been undemonstrative. She offered to make coffee. He nodded his agreement and she trooped off to the kitchen. Reminding herself of his preference from a sheet pinned to the inside of the door she let the kettle boil before adding two teaspoons of sugar to his drink. Drake's small cafetière and his tin of ground beans had pride of place in the cupboard. Luned had never seen anyone fuss so much about making coffee.

She returned to the Incident Room. Winder grunted an acknowledgement when she placed his mug on a coaster.

'I've been trying to spot Kenny's black Audi on the CCTV footage.' Winder stretched his arms high above his head and then rested them on the back of his neck.

'I thought you were tracking down the taxi drivers?'

'Give me a break – we need some variation, or my brain will get addled. It could take us hours maybe even days to work through it all.'

'The boss won't be happy with that,' Luned added before she settled back to work and opened the emails filling her inbox. She clicked onto the email from the manager of the Bluebell and downloaded the footage she had requested.

Two cameras had been installed. One covering the main entrance and a second the main bar area which included most of the tables but, after visiting the Bluebell's website, Luned could see that the footage didn't include the hall or stage.

She scrolled on to early Saturday evening and set the speed to race ahead. If Dawn Piper had actually been in the Bluebell, she could always watch the footage in real time.

When she saw Dawn's recognisable scrawny image appear in the main entrance she paused the screen. It was eight-thirty pm. She blanked out the activity in the Incident Room and her pulse throbbed.

Progress. Luned moved to the coverage of the bar area and fast forwarded the footage until she recognised Dawn standing by the bar. She was alone, passing the time of day with the bar staff and a couple of the other customers.

Luned had hours of work ahead of her.

She called over to Winder. 'I think I found where Dawn Piper was on the Saturday evening before she died.'

Winder gave her a noncommittal reply. 'Good.'

Luned let the footage run on and moments later, after Dawn had moved away, another person she recognised entered the bar area. She frowned. She hadn't expected to see Councillor Beedham. Maybe he was taking some time off from canvassing. But it made Luned decide that the staff at the Bluebell would need to be interviewed.

Exactly who was Dawn Piper meeting, Luned thought?

Chapter 29

An hour later Drake and Sara were sitting in Olivia Knox's office. Sara opted for a mug of tea while Drake satisfied himself with a glass of water. Knox kept shifting her position in her chair, crossing and uncrossing her arms, clearly ill at ease.

'What can I do to help?' Knox squinted at Drake.

'We're still trying to track down Dawn's movements on the Saturday night she was killed. It's proving very difficult to identify the exact crime scene.'

Knox picked at the cuticles of the fingers on her right hand. Drake gave Sara an imperceptible nod. She reached down for her bag, fumbling for her mobile while fingering a tissue at the same time. The number Drake had given her before they left headquarters had already been punched into the handset – all she needed to do was press dial. She kept her bag on her knees and drew out a tissue she blew into needlessly.

The muffled sound of a mobile behind Drake and Sara startled Knox. She glared at the fleece crumpled on a cupboard in one corner of the room. Drake beamed at her while reaching for his glass of water. 'Do you want to get that?'

She turned back to give Drake an unfocused gaze. A brief false smile followed.

Sara picked up the conversation. 'Olivia, I think it's time that you were more honest with us.'

The direct in-your-face approach worked – Knox's eyes opened wide. 'What do you mean?'

'We think you know something about Dawn's whereabouts that you're not telling us. After all Hubert Caston had something important he wanted to share with you. You do realise that withholding information is a criminal offence.' Sara paused and Drake reached into his jacket pocket and pretended to check the messages on his phone. Instead he pressed dial – it was linked to the same number that Sara had just called. He replaced the handset in his pocket. He didn't look at Sara. He gazed straight at Knox. The mobile in Knox's thin fleece rang again – more persistently this time as though it were demanding to be answered.

'That's your mobile again,' Drake said.

'It's nothing,' Knox snapped.

Drake reached for his mobile and pushed the screen of the handset towards Knox. 'We know it was you, Olivia. Dawn called you on this number the Saturday night she was killed, and she texted you. Now I want to know the truth. Because if you don't cooperate this instant, I'll arrest you for perverting the course of justice and take you back to the area custody suite.' Colour evaporated quickly from Knox's face. Then she grabbed her coffee mug with both shaking hands and took a mouthful. 'What will your boss think of that?'

Olivia managed a stilted reply. 'You're right.' She shared a despairing look between Drake and Sara. 'Dawn did call me and told me that she wanted to see me urgently. I honestly don't know what it was about. You have to believe me. And when she didn't arrive, I assumed she had changed her mind. I didn't think for a moment that…'

'Did it involve Hubert Caston?'

Knox shook her head. 'No, no. Dawn had been helping Councillor Beedham.'

Drake planted his elbows on the desk. 'What the hell do you mean, helping Councillor Beedham?'

'She knew where drugs had been hidden on the *Duke of Lancaster*. Councillor Beedham persuaded her to get evidence he could use to show that you lot are incompetent.'

Beedham was stupid enough to believe he could grandstand his way into winning a seat in the Welsh Assembly. It amazed Drake that anyone could be so foolish.

Knox continued, the words coming out in a rush. 'He had some grand plans about being able to get the television crews to accompany him when he showed to the world he had discovered the haul of drugs.'

'And how the hell did she know where these drugs could be?'

'She had some friends from Rhyl. People she knew when she worked in the town. Really, seriously. She was convinced.'

By the time Drake and Sara had finished questioning Knox, she had finished her drink. Her hands had stopped shaking but she had thinned before their eyes. Drake and Sara made to leave. 'Don't hide anything else from us.'

Knox nodded weakly.

Walking over to the car, Sara turned to Drake. 'Shouldn't we be talking to Councillor Beedham?'

'And what do we ask him?' Drake stopped by the vehicle. 'We don't go anywhere near Beedham until we have more information.'

'At least we know where Dawn was going that Saturday evening.'

'But we still need to find where she was killed.' Drake started the engine. 'Let's go and talk to those pharmacies.'

Sara watched as Drake fiddled with his phone. Then the cabin filled with rock music.

'Trying to relive your youth, sir?' Sara smiled

'It's 'Gwenwyn' by Alffa – the first Welsh language song to have been played over a million times on Spotify.'

Sara curled up her mouth, acknowledging the achievement.

Drake drove out of the car park and, following Sara's directions, found the first of the pharmacies in Flint. Although the town was some distance from Deeside, Drake decided that they needed to be thorough.

Drake and Sara asked for the pharmacist in charge of each shop and flashed their warrant cards that they accompanied with a serious whispered request for a private discussion. The three pharmacy shops in Flint cooperated fully and it encouraged Drake to think that it was going to be easier than he had anticipated. Each checked their records, none of them had issued a prescription for a girl of Debbie's age and every member of staff were shown images of both girls. They met with polite shakes of the head.

Once they had finished in Flint, Drake drove down towards Connah's Quay along Chester Road. Sara had a list of another dozen pharmacies.

The pharmacy manager at a large supermarket shook his head and refused to allow any other staff member to speak to Drake, citing confidentiality in preventing him from accessing patient records. Drake urged him to reconsider, jotted down his full name and requested details of his immediate superior in the hope that a threat of contacting his line manager might help. It didn't.

'Text Gareth,' Drake said angrily stalking back to his car. 'Get him to request a warrant so we can access their data.'

Sara nodded and did as she was told.

The next two pharmacies were more cooperative and the staff's willingness to examine the photographs and check their records improved Drake's mood. He contemplated that perhaps the teenage girls had brought their own medication with them. Or else he would have to extend the search to the other surrounding towns. And that would mean a much larger exercise.

The next pharmacy was in another supermarket chain. Drake repeated his request to speak to the pharmacy manager who appeared from behind a small counter area. 'One of my colleagues is using the consultation room.' Howard was printed on his name badge. 'We'll have to talk here.'

Luckily the pharmacy wasn't busy and apart from three young assistants milling around, Drake's conversation wasn't overheard. 'We are trying to trace two teenage girls, one of them is an insulin dependent diabetic and we need to trace her. Can you check your records?'

Howard frowned. 'I'm not certain I can help you. Patient records are confidential after all.'

'It is important.' Drake began the first stage of his charm offensive. 'They are teenagers and it's part of an important ongoing inquiry.' Howard's non-cooperation now would lead to the threat of reporting it to his superiors.

Howard gave a pained expression. 'I really don't think I can breach our standard protocols. Don't you need a warrant or something?'

Drake gave him a kindly smile. 'I was hoping you might be able to provide information without me having to get too formal.'

It didn't have the effect Drake hoped.

'I think that might be best.'

Drake found a business card and pushed it over towards Howard. 'If you reconsider, please get back to me.'

A voice shouted Howard's name from the depths of the pharmacy, and he discarded the business card on the countertop. He turned to Drake. 'I'm sorry I can't be more help. I've got to go.'

Drake threaded his way through the customers pushing trolleys between the aisles as he hurried towards the car park, Sara following in his slipstream. He slowed his pace as Sara went in search of bottles of water, but it didn't lessen his annoyance towards Howard. Sara joined him outside the main entrance.

'I really had hoped they might be more cooperative,' Drake announced after a couple of mouthfuls from the bottle he cracked open.

'Confidentiality of personal data and information has gone too far sometimes,' Sara said.

Drake led the way back to the car. 'You sound like one of those politically correct politicians.'

Sara didn't respond and as Drake reached his Mondeo

his mobile rang.

He didn't recognise the number. 'Detective Inspector Drake.'

The voice whispered, 'You've been to the pharmacy where I work. I think I can help you.'

Chapter 30

Drake entered the café and surveyed the customers, hoping he might recognise the assistant from the supermarket pharmacy. Sara joined him, making them an incongruous pair standing by the door checking out every customer. A continuous loop of boring acoustic guitar music played repeatedly. The walls were painted black and staff all dressed in black stood behind the counter at the rear.

A figure at the very end table next to a wood burner slotted into the corner turned her head and looked over at Drake. She gave him a nod and a brief wave. Drake and Sara sauntered over and sat opposite the young girl. She had thin unkempt hair and a long chin, small eyes and sunken cheeks. She sipped on a latte in a tall glass. 'I saw you with the pharmacy manager. I saw them two girls.'

A waitress appeared before Drake could reply and he and Sara ordered.

'What's your name?'

'Stephanie… Jones.'

'How long have you worked in the pharmacy?' Sara asked.

'Two years next month.'

'Stephanie, when did you see both girls?' Drake reached for the smartphone in his pocket. He scrolled through the photographs waiting for Stephanie to reply. He glanced up at her as she sipped her drink. He slid his smartphone over the table towards Stephanie.

She nodded slowly. 'That's them. I saw them earlier this week. We see some pretty rough people coming into the pharmacy, but they stank, and they looked so young. And the manager he … Well, he ignored them, he didn't say anything to them. I tried to tell him that something wasn't right, but he just told me to get the prescription organised.'

She ran out of steam and took another long mouthful of her drink. A latte arrived for Sara and an Americano for

Drake.

'Did you talk to them?'

Stephanie shook her head. 'I thought there was something wrong. They had bags under their eyes, and I don't think they'd eaten a square meal for days.'

'Do you remember the medication that was prescribed?'

'We're supposed to keep everything confidential.' Stephanie gave Drake a pleading look, searching for reassurance that whatever she told him would never be disclosed to anyone.

'We suspect both girls may have been taken against their will. It's imperative we find them.'

Stephanie's eyes opened wide. Drake reassured her. 'Anything you can tell us about them is going to help us protect them.'

Stephanie reached into a pocket of her thin fleece and took out a folded piece of paper. 'I jotted down the address and the details of the prescription they were given.'

Drake read the information, delighted that they were one step closer to finding both girls.

'I'll lose my job if my boss ever finds out I helped you.'

Drake leaned over and lowered his voice. 'You've done the right thing. I'm sure with your help we can trace both girls.' His smile didn't eliminate the anxious look on her face. 'We'll need your contact details.'

Sara paid for the coffees and once they had Stephanie's address, they returned to Drake's car.

'Should we get backup?' Sara said.

Drake pointed the remote at the car and it unlocked with a heavy thud. 'No time.'

Sara punched the postcode into the satnav as Drake started the engine. The disembodied voice dictated instructions and they found themselves nearing Shotton.

'It's disgusting that a man would take advantage of young girls like that.' Revulsion filled Sara's voice. Drake nodded – it disgusted him too that teenage girls could be trafficked around the United Kingdom.

'It's hard to believe it happens these days.'

Drake glanced at the satnav – they were within three hundred metres so he slowed and parked alongside the pavement. The street they wanted, a little way ahead, was another terrace of properties built for the steelworkers whose jobs had long since disappeared. Disrepair indicated that well-paid employment was a thing of the past. It meant ideal fertile ground for a man like Paul Kenny, Drake thought. And Ritchie O'Brien and Jack Beltrami, both of them would have wanted to protect their own interests against an interloper from Liverpool.

'Let's drive past and see if there is any sign of anybody in the property. We go to the end of the road and then walk back.'

Sara nodded and craned out of the windscreen. 'There might be a lane at the back. All these terraces seem to have backyards that lead onto alleys.'

Drake engaged first gear and pulled away from the pavement before indicating right. There was little traffic although he was reduced to a crawling speed by the various vehicles parked at the pavement. A group of youngsters kicking a football at the end gave the Mondeo a lingering look. They both glanced to the right at number fourteen as they passed along the terrace.

'At least the curtains on the windows weren't drawn,' Sara said.

'I didn't see any sign of life.'

At a T-junction at the end, Drake indicated left and parked. A woman pushing a pram emerged from a lane that stretched behind the properties. 'I'll take the back lane.'

Sara nodded and they left the car.

It surprised Drake that the tarmac surface was reasonably clean and tidy. From one backyard he heard the shouts of children and a mother's remonstration. School holidays were the hardest, and it reminded him again that if he was going to be much later getting home, he would have to call Annie. She had already taken a couple of days off work to look after the girls and Sian's collision had disrupted all the carefully planned childcare arrangements for the summer holidays.

He reached the gate that was ajar, pushed it with his left shoe and peeked in. A gravelled area led to the back door. Two striped plastic chairs sat on a small paved area. Somebody had been enjoying the sunshine, Drake thought. He walked in and, reaching the door, gazed into the house. Newspapers and flyers and correspondence were piled on a cheap table under the window.

He turned to the back door as his mobile bleeped. It was Sara. 'No one answering the front door, sir.'

'I'm by the back door,' Drake whispered. 'I'll call you back.'

He rapped a knuckle on the door. It gave way slightly under his contact. He shouted. 'Hello, is anyone home?'

Silence.

Inside air smelled warm and muggy as though someone had been cooking recently. He glanced into the hallway and called out again. There was no sign of movement. He found his mobile and dialled Sara. 'Get round the back. The place is open.'

As he waited, he looked around the kitchen. Was this unlawful entry? He wasn't going to debate with himself the niceties of the legal position when the well-being of two teenage girls was at stake. He didn't have latex gloves so as a precaution he took a fork from the draining board and gently eased opened the cupboards. Their contents were unremarkable – noodles, bags of crisps and soft drinks.

'Nobody home?' Sara said. 'Should we be here? After all we haven't got a warrant and…'

Drake's tone was defiant. 'Let's see if there is any evidence of these girls having lived here.'

Both downstairs rooms had sign of recent activity. A

thin crumpled duvet covered the sofa and a newspaper and celebrity magazines littered the floor. Upstairs the bedrooms were similar to the rooms Drake had seen in Caston's late-parents' property – a simple mattress thrown onto a floor and sleeping bags. A highly patterned pair of pyjama bottoms in a garish red colour had been discarded in one corner.

'They must have left in a hurry,' Sara said.

Drake nodded.

They retraced their steps to the kitchen and then out to the yard at the rear. Drake dragged the door closed behind him.

'Let's get back to the car,' Drake said.

He felt less conspicuous sitting inside the Mondeo. It gave him time to think. 'It feels as though we are one step behind them all the time.'

Sara nodded. 'I really thought Stephanie's information would give us a break.'

Drake reached for his mobile. 'I'll organise surveillance. We need to get some officers here. I want to know who goes into that house.' It took twenty minutes for Drake to follow all the correct protocols to get authorisation. He became increasingly annoyed with every obstacle put in his place. There had to be an easier way of making progress with a murder inquiry surely, Drake thought.

Once he had finished, he let out a long breath. Then his mobile rang. He was expecting another irritating call from operational support, but he recognised Annie's number.

'Ian, where are you?' Her voice trembled.

'I won't be long. What's wrong?'

'There was someone at the door earlier on. He said he was doing a survey. But I'm… Perhaps I am being paranoid.'

Drake blotted out the dread creeping into his mind.

'Did you ask the neighbours if…'

'Yes – nobody had called with them. This man kept asking how many people lived at the house.'

‘Annie, are the girls with you?’

‘Yes, of course.’

Drake managed the next reply through gritted teeth. ‘Keep the front door locked – I’m on my way back.’

Chapter 31

Drake rang operational support as soon as he was on the A55, demanding a marked police car call at his home. Then he called Annie who sounded relieved when he told her officers were on their way. The nearer he was to Felinheli the less stressed he felt. Sara spoke to him as he indicated off the dual carriageway in Bangor confirming that the surveillance team was in place. With luck they would have something to report by the morning.

Drake made good time and he pulled up into the drive of Annie's home. A marked police car was parked nearby. He let himself into the property and shouted a greeting. Annie joined him by the front door and kissed him warmly on the lips.

She grabbed his arm and took him back outside. 'I don't want the girls to hear.' She pulled the door towards her but didn't close it. 'They're watching television upstairs. I hope you don't think I'm paranoid.'

'Of course not. Tell me what happened.'

'This man came to the door. I've never seen him before. He was wearing a lanyard that had an official-looking sign and he said he was conducting a survey for the Welsh government on second homes.'

'Did he speak Welsh?'

'No… But I didn't ask him. He didn't look right somehow.'

It could be another attempt by someone he was investigating trying to frighten him. Perhaps they thought he'd be reassigned, that another officer would be allocated. That he could be intimidated. No matter what happened he would protect his family.

'And he didn't visit any of the other properties?'

'I've spoken with some of the neighbours and he didn't call to anybody else's house.'

Drake paused and then he looked around as though he

had expected some mysterious person with a clipboard to appear. 'Can you describe him?'

Annie nodded.

'I'll get someone from headquarters to check out whether a government survey is being undertaken at the moment.'

She smiled her reassurance.

He leaned down and kissed her on the cheek. 'Don't worry, you're safe.'

'Have you eaten?'

Drake shook his head.

'There's a bottle of Pinot Gris in the fridge, I'll pour us both a glass and I'll make you something.'

Drake thanked the two officers who left soon afterwards and joined Annie as soon as he'd made a call to operational support. The person on duty that evening sounded disinterested, reminding Drake it might take some time to find the information he needed. Helen and Megan had already eaten but they sat with Drake and Annie as they made good headway through the wine. Both girls had been browsing the Disneyland Paris website and were focused on the activities and rides available. Drake relaxed as he listened to them, although the chilled alcohol helped.

After his daughters had gone to bed, exhaustion dragged at his bones. His head sagged and he yawned. Annie reached over and kissed him and then she found the remote and silenced the television. 'I'm sorry if I overreacted earlier. I missed you today.'

'I'm sorry I was late back.'

Annie stood up held out both hands for his and he got up. 'Well you can make up for it now.' She ran a hand over his cheek and along his mouth. Despite his tiredness he sensed his desire. Annie led him to the bedroom and slowly closed the door behind them.

Silvery shards of moonlight filled the room and as Annie drew close his hands circled her slender waist and they kissed hungrily. She unbuttoned his shirt and having her run her fingers over his chest dispelled any lingering fatigue. They embraced passionately and he opened her blouse and then the strap of her bra which fell to the floor. Their tongues intertwined and Drake pulled her tightly into his body sensing her breasts against his flesh. Annie fumbled with his belt as he unzipped his trousers. Soon they were both naked, warmed by the summer heat and a simple desire to consume each other.

Drake tossed back the duvet and they fell onto the bed.

Once they were finished, he drew her close pulling a hand over her thigh down her leg and kissing a nipple and she responded to meet his passion. Annie hummed. 'I hope we didn't make too much noise.'

Drake didn't care. He wanted moments like this to last forever.

A noise outside caught Drake's attention. There was always some activity from the nearby marina and the sound of yachts creaking under the swell of the Menai Strait could have a mesmerising effect. This was mechanical, an outboard motor maybe. He glanced at the clock on the bedside table. It was a little after midnight. Then a muffled conversation caught his attention and intrigued, he got out of bed and stepped over to the window. No one could see his nakedness and he heard Annie moving in the bed. 'What's wrong?'

The sound of something crashing against the window and his daughters' bedroom window on the first floor answered her question.

Drake snapped. 'Stay inside.'

Quickly he scampered around the room recovering his clothes and then he dragged on his trousers and shirt before opening the French windows to the small garden area.

He heard a scream from upstairs. He sensed movement behind him and saw Annie fumbling with her dressing gown. He glanced up at the glass of his daughters' window and saw the splash of red all over it. Then he spotted the paint pots on the garden area by his feet.

He darted to the bottom of the garden.

In the distance he saw a RIB powering away down the Menai Strait, two men sitting in the stern.

Chapter 32

A uniformed police officer arrived promptly the following morning after Drake had spoken to a sergeant at the local station. Annie and his daughters would get personal protection until he got back that evening. Silently he doubted whoever staged the stunt would try again. They had sent their message – they knew where he lived and wanted to frighten him. But it wouldn't work.

Before leaving, he arranged for a contractor to clean the windows and dispose of the cans of paint. He didn't disturb Helen and Megan who had been awake until the early hours after the commotion. He held Annie in a long embrace and told her she would be safe. He longed to tell her the inquiry would be over soon, but she would have known he was exaggerating had he done so.

He ignored the speed restrictions on his journey to headquarters. He travelled in silence, letting his anger settle into a determination to identify the culprits who had threatened his family.

Sara, Winder and Luned were sitting at their desks as he stalked over to the board. 'I need to tell you about an incident that happened last night.'

Three troubled faces looked over at him as he explained the circumstances.

'It could be Kenny,' Winder said. 'His sort is mad enough to do something like that. And one of his known associates has a pub on Anglesey.'

'Don't go there, Gareth. There's no way we can trace the culprits.' Although Drake had briefly contemplated getting any vehicles owned by Kenny checked through ANPR from the previous evening travelling through the Conwy tunnel into North Wales. But it would prove nothing, and he quashed his anger.

'Are your daughters all right, boss?' Sara asked.

'Shaken up of course, but they were sleeping when I

left.' Drake paused and turned to the board. 'We need to make progress. If we discover where Dawn was killed, then we've got a crime scene. And that means possible forensic evidence.'

Luned interrupted. 'We've established Dawn visited the Bluebell pub on the Saturday night before she died. And we spotted Councillor Beedham on the footage too.'

'Bloody hell. Councillor Beedham. We are overdue a chat with him.'

Winder continued. 'We've arranged to take statements from the staff later this morning.'

The door to the Incident Room opened and Wendy Sutherland the intelligence officer entered, nodding at Drake.

'Keep me informed. Sara and I will finish the work on the taxi drivers this morning.'

He stalked over to his room gesticulating for Sutherland to follow him.

Intelligence officers were indispensable for every modern police force and whenever senior officers provided soundbites for reporters inevitably 'intelligence led policing' became the common mantra.

'Morning, Ian.' Wendy sat in one of the visitor chairs in his room. 'It has come to my attention that Dawn Piper had been an authorised informant.'

Drake let his face show his surprise.

'I know, it surprised me too.'

'Why the hell wasn't I told?'

'Apparently she hasn't been active for several years. We don't have any recorded meeting between Dawn and the intelligence team for some time.'

'Who was the officer that handled her?'

Standard practice provided for authorised informants to be handled by a specific team and always seen by two officers. Procedures were one thing, but the actual reality was something quite different.

'Sergeant Finch.'

Drake paused, allowing the name to sink in. 'But he's leading the county lines inquiry.'

'I don't think he's involved with the intelligence side of things at the moment.'

'Then who was her most recent handler?'

'It's a Constable Simon Olney.'

'I'll need to speak to him.'

Sutherland got to her feet. 'How is the inquiry going?'

'Slowly.'

Sutherland gave him a nod that told him she understood his difficulties. Drake kept in check the rising annoyance at Jim Finch and Simon Olney. He should have been notified that Dawn Piper had been a registered informant. He wanted to know exactly what intelligence she had shared with them – did it have any bearing on their current inquiry? How the hell did they justify withholding the information?

Drake dialled Finch's number and it rang twice before voicemail announced he wasn't available and inviting the caller to leave a message. Drake didn't bother. After discovering Olney was working on secondment to the economic crime unit, he decided to speak to him in person. He left his office and threaded his way through headquarters.

Simon Olney gave him a quizzical look when he entered his office. Drake stood over him at his desk. 'I'm the SIO on the Dawn Piper inquiry.'

Olney swallowed uncomfortably.

Drake continued. 'I understand she was a registered informant and that you were her handler.'

Olney nodded. 'That was two years ago.'

'Why the hell didn't you think to tell me or my team? Didn't it occur to you that it might be important, relevant to our inquiry?' Drake's voice rose as he tried to curb his irritation.

'It was such a long time ago… and Jim said that he would tell you.'

'What do you mean?'

'He's got all the details about Dawn.'

His eyes darted around while Drake trawled his memory for recollection of exactly what Jim Finch had told them. There had never been any mention of Dawn being a registered informant. There were rules to be followed, procedures to be discharged. Jim Finch should have known that.

'I need you to tell me everything you can remember about the information Dawn provided.'

Olney nodded his agreement. 'A lot of stuff she shared with us was worthless. Nothing more than gossip. We struggled to get authorisation to pay her regular sums. At first she gave us details about Jack Beltrami's money-laundering activities.'

'Jack Beltrami?' Drake's voice squeaked.

'We passed everything onto the economic crime unit. They were going to action it. It was when her boyfriend got involved that we doubted her value as an informant.'

Drake sounded puzzled now. 'What do you mean "got involved"?'

'She got her boyfriend signed up to be an informant too.'

'And did he provide useful intelligence?'

Olney dipped his head. 'I never met him.'

Drake cut in using his sharpest tone. 'I thought two officers were needed to interview intelligence sources?'

Olney kept his gaze on the fingers of both hands he was threading together tightly. 'You know how it is, sir.' Olney glanced at Drake before averting his gaze. 'It's not always possible to… Jim saw him a couple of times.'

Olney and Finch breaking standard protocols annoyed Drake. He constructed a reprimand for Jim Finch. Then he glanced at his watch and realised he was late for a briefing with Superintendent Price.

Drake returned to the Incident Room feeling uneasy. During

their meeting, Superintendent Hobbs appeared aloof and detached – becoming accustomed to a new superior officer would be difficult. Wyndham Price had glanced over at his successor occasionally and Drake was certain he had seen hesitancy in his eyes.

Winder and Luned weren't at their desks and Sara answered his question before he could ask it. 'They've gone to the Bluebell pub.'

Drake sat at Winder's desk. 'Wendy Sutherland told me that Dawn Piper had been a registered informant.'

Sara raised her eyebrows.

'Jim Finch was her handler.'

Now Sara's eyes widened.

'I was surprised too. And I've spoken to a Simon Olney who was her last handler. Finch told him he was going to tell us all about Dawn.'

Sara flopped back in her chair.

Drake drummed the fingers of his right hand on the desk. 'We need an explanation from Finch.'

Drake called Finch again and this time left a message for him to call him back. Another call to operational support told Drake Finch was on leave until the beginning of the week so he had to hope he'd return his call soon.

Sara added, 'Maybe he's become so involved in the county lines inquiry the lines have become blurred.'

'Blurred? Protocols are there for a good reason. Although I know how difficult it can be when there's an ongoing inquiry. We need to talk to him again. He's not sharing all the details with us. And we have to establish if the taxi drivers can help us. And we need to find those two girls.'

Sara nodded. 'I'll call the café where they were seen with Dawn.'

'And extend the search to include all the cafés in that same area. And the convenience stores. Gareth and Luned can help you when they get back.'

'Do you think they might be involved?'

Drake shook his head but an ugly possibility crawled into his mind that in the world of drug dealers where life was cheap and cash plentiful, nothing might surprise him. He gave Sara a plaintive frown. 'They are teenagers, no more than kids. We should be protecting them, keeping them from harm's way.'

Sara's brow furrowed and after a moment's silence she added, 'You're right, boss.'

Once he was alone, Drake called Annie.

'How are you feeling now?'

'I spoke to Rhian and Mark from next door and they were surprised and shocked. Helen and Megan are very quiet. Do you think it'll happen again?'

'No, of course not.' Drake hid the uncertainty he was feeling. 'I won't be late home.'

'Try and call later if you get a chance.'

'Of course.' He paused. 'Love you, Annie.' He didn't want it to sound feigned – he really meant it and he regretted not being there to tell her in person.

'And me you, Ian. Don't be late tonight. I miss you.'

Drake continued smiling to himself after the call ended.

Then he turned his attention to the taxi companies of Deeside.

The first name on the list that Winder hadn't contacted was a Jamie Bale. He dialled the number, relieved when it was answered after a couple of rings.

'Jamie Bale?'

'What's this about?' the accent was Deeside – a mellowed-out version of Scouse laced with softer Welsh tones.

Drake explained what he needed and after he finished, Jamie cut across him. 'I wasn't anywhere near the rugby club that evening. Have you spoken to Spike? He does the club regularly and he has a dashcam.'

Drake matched up the nickname to a Michael Pritchard

with Jamie's help and then ended the call. He called Spike but an answering service clicked on and Drake left a message.

He broke off and traipsed through into the kitchen to make coffee, pondering whether it was too early to call Annie again. Back in his office he waited for the coffee to brew, setting the timer on his smartphone for exactly a minute and a half. Sipping from the mug of coffee he checked the emails cluttering the inbox on his computer. When he saw the message from the shopkeeper in Connah's Quay, he clicked open the email and soon navigated to the attached footage.

Normally he would have delegated the activity of spending hours watching CCTV footage to Winder or Luned. It would have been late morning when Dawn visited the store so Drake started the coverage at ten am. After five minutes he fiddled with the controls and increased the speed of the replay. Fortunately, the camera was at the front of the store and comparatively low down so people on the pavement and cars passing in the street were all recorded.

By eleven am, Drake's concentration lapsed. Dozens of customers visited the shop and none resembled Dawn Piper. Memories could be unreliable and people seeking attention often made statements to the police that turned out to be a fantasy. He got up, stretched his back, rubbed his hands over his face and stared out the window. Landscape contractors were busy cutting the grass on the parkland surrounding headquarters. He sat down again and got back to work.

At three minutes to midday he saw Dawn Piper standing outside the shop and he paused the footage. At last, he thought. He restarted the recording and watched as she glanced up and down the road as though she were looking for somebody, waiting for someone to give her a lift perhaps. After a minute she went into the shop, emerging moments later munching a chocolate bar.

She stood outside concentrating on eating her snack

when an Audi pulled up. Drake's chest tightened and his pulse gained an extra beat. He squinted down at the image as she exchanged a few words with the driver. Moments later she moved round to the passenger side.

It gave Drake a clear view of the driver – Jack Beltrami.

Chapter 33

Gareth Winder talked of little else on the journey to the Bluebell pub. 'I can't believe it – his ex-wife's car is rammed. And now someone attacks him in his own home.'

Luned said little during the drive although she had checked her smartphone on several occasions. 'I'd hardly call it being attacked,' Luned said.

'Two pots of paint were thrown at the property from the garden. It was the middle of the night, for Christ's sake. What else would you call it?'

'Nobody was hurt, if that's what you mean.'

Winder settled into a brief period of silence as they drew into the car park of the Bluebell. A brewery delivery van was reversing towards the rear door, its warning alarms beeping loudly. Winder parked a safe distance away and he and Luned marched over to the entrance. A woman mopping the floor gave them a frustrated look as they walked over the damp floor. Voices drifted from inside and they followed the sounds to the bar area where a man with a ten-pint-a-night habit, judging from the size of his girth, engaged the delivery man in a loud voice with explicit instructions. The place looked familiar from the footage Winder had already viewed. A small stage dominated one end of the room.

'Danny Pocock?' Winder said.

'Yeah. Are you the cops I spoke to yesterday?'

'Detective Constables Gareth Winder and Luned Thomas.'

Pocock gave their warrant cards a disinterested glance.

'Follow me.' Pocock hauled the belt of his trousers up to his waist and led them out of the bar area.

A large flat-screen monitor dominated the wall of the room Pocock called an office. A computer hummed quietly on the desk. Stacks of paper covered the available surfaces.

'Bit stuffy in here, sorry.' Pocock yanked open a window. 'The barmaids should be in soon. After we chatted yesterday, I texted them both.' Pocock found a handkerchief and mopped his brow.

He cleared an area on the desk and fiddled with the mouse until the monitor came to life. He moved back and dragged over two chairs, waving a hand as an invitation for Winder and Luned to sit. Pocock left them and Winder got to work.

'We need to see if the footage has any record of Dawn talking to anyone,' Luned said.

'And interview the staff,' Winder reminded her.

An hour later Winder and Luned had watched several hours of speeded up footage, clicking open the images of Dawn Piper whenever they appeared. Winder dictated the times that Luned jotted down on her notepad. The CCTV cameras recorded the bar area and the front entrance, but there was no footage of Dawn leaving the Bluebell. Speaking to the staff might provide more details. It confirmed where Dawn had been the last few hours of her life.

Pocock returned, announcing that the two barmaids had arrived.

'I'll need to make a backup of all the footage from Saturday,' Winder said.

'Of course,' Pocock said.

'And don't destroy any of the previous footage.'

Pocock nodded.

Leaving the claustrophobic room for the bar was a relief. Two women sat on stools near a small table. Pocock introduced them. 'This is Donna and Marie. They were working that Saturday night you're asking about.'

Neither woman made any attempt to introduce themselves or stand up and offer a hand.

'We understand Dawn was a regular here. Do both of you remember her?'

The older of the two barmaids had thin blonde hair and tattoos over her shoulders and upper arms. 'I'm Donna. I knew Dawn. She came in regularly for the country and western evenings.'

'Did she have friends?'

Donna and Marie shared a glance Winder couldn't make out.

Luned jumped in before Winder could say anything – she had obviously seen the same glance. 'If there's anything you think might be important, you should tell us.'

Marie replied, 'She and some other friends were dead keen on zombie games. They wanted to organise a zombie night here. It was all strange. I told them to talk to the boss.' She jerked her head at Pocock. 'They wanted to dress up as zombies and have a band play music from zombie films.'

'News to me,' Pocock said.

Marie persevered. 'And they kept talking about that ship, you know the *Duke of Lancaster*, that was going to be converted into a fun palace or something. It promised to create jobs and, God knows, we all need that around here.'

Winder decided they could colour in more of Dawn's background later. For now, he wanted to find out what had happened on the Saturday evening before she died. 'The CCTV footage has a record of Dawn arriving in the bar at about eight-thirty. Did either of you serve her?'

Donna and Marie nodded in unison although Donna replied first. 'She was drinking rum most of the night.'

'Do you remember how much she drank?'

Winder watched two heads shaking.

Luned asked, 'Was she drunk?'

'I didn't pay much attention,' Marie said. 'I just get on with doing my job.'

'Did you see her with anyone in particular?' Winder asked.

Luned took his question as a prompt to search her mobile for the photograph of Councillor Beedham. 'Did you see her with this man?' She pushed the handset at both girls who scrutinised it before nodding.

Progress, Winder thought; Inspector Drake will be pleased. It would give them an opportunity to speak to Councillor Beedham, although from seeing the man perform on the YouTube videos, Winder doubted Drake would make much progress.

Luned leaned over and gave both girls a serious and intense stare. 'It is very important if you can remember whether she was with anybody else that night. It was the night that she was probably killed, so the killer might have been here, might have been with her, or waiting outside.'

The *waiting outside* was a little over the top, but Winder shared Luned's attempt to get both girls to think seriously.

Donna blinked furiously. 'I've seen her with that Ritchie O'Brien bloke a couple of times.'

Luned kept staring at her. 'Was he here that Saturday night?'

Donna looked away. 'I can't remember.'

Marie blurted out, 'I saw him here. He argued with Councillor Beedham. And I've heard all sorts about him. He's always up to no good. Dawn was sitting over there.' She nodded towards a section of the bar area well away from the narrow angle covered by the CCTV camera.

'Did O'Brien speak to Dawn?'

Before Marie replied, Winder's phone rang and he recognised Drake's number. He stood up, made to move outside. He answered the phone as soon as he was in the outside hallway.

'There's another body,' Drake said. The coldness in Drake's voice rooted Winder to the spot for a moment. 'You and Luned are the nearest officers. I'll send you the postcode. Get there immediately.'

Winder rushed inside. Marie was nodding as she gazed at the screen of Luned's mobile.

'We've got to go. Now.'

Chapter 34

Ornamental railings lined the park boundary. A marked police car stood in the entrance, a crowd of onlookers had gathered nearby, exchanging worried looks and muffled conversations. Drake and Sara flashed their warrant cards at the uniformed officer standing by the car as he ventured to challenge them. The constable waved them through, telling them to follow the path through to the far end. Box hedges lined the drive and shrubs and trees flourished in the beds. To his left, Drake passed a bowling green mowed to a snooker-table finish. In the distance Drake saw the fluttering crime scene perimeter tape and the sound of activity. He recognised Gareth Winder's voice.

It was the sort of park that could be found in any town in Wales. A small war memorial stood nestled in an opening of trees as Drake and Sara neared the centre. As they approached, Winder called out to Luned. They joined Drake and Sara before the yellow crime scene tape. Behind Winder, three CSIs hauled boxes of equipment out of the rear of the scientific support vehicle.

'Is Mike Foulds here yet?' Drake said.

Winder didn't need to reply as a white-suited Mike Foulds emerged from behind the CSI van and walked over to Drake. 'Good morning, Mike.'

'Ian,' Foulds said. 'We haven't been here long. We're going to wait until the pathologist has arrived before we do any substantial work. The body is concealed in overgrown shrubbery.' Foulds tipped his head towards the thick undergrowth nearby.

'Who found the body?' Drake said.

'An old bloke who was walking his dog this morning. Apparently, the animal went ballistic. Barking and generally creating a din, so he thought something was wrong.'

Instinctively Drake cast his gaze around to see if there was a civilian inside the cordon. Winder continued. 'He didn't look too well when we arrived, so we sent him home, boss,'

Drake nodded. It made sense.

'We need to get an outer extended perimeter formed in due course,' Foulds added.

The crime scene manager always made operational decisions, so Drake decided not to interfere. The railings paid for by the good citizens of Connah's Quay in a more prosperous era would provide the natural boundary. If there was going to be any evidence it would be in the immediate vicinity of the corpse, Drake thought. He turned and searched the area for CCTV cameras. It was his default position these days, hoping their job would be made easier by CCTV footage. It was a fruitless task, but he saw Dr Lee Kings, the pathologist, talking with the uniformed officer standing by the gate.

Kings followed the same route as Drake and Sara had done and joined the four officers. Once pleasantries had been exchanged Kings turned to Drake. 'Where is the body?'

'In the middle of that thicket behind the scientific support vehicle.'

Kings looked over in the direction where Drake was pointing. He nodded. 'Let's get on with this.'

The pathologist struggled with the white one-piece forensic overall the CSIs provided but eventually zipped it closed to his neck. Drake looked over into the thick shrubbery of rhododendrons and trees. Erecting a tent would be impossible, Drake realised, so it meant the crime scene investigators had to work quickly. The body would need to be moved, evidence preserved to ensure that any trace of the killer would be documented and recorded for the investigation team.

Drake watched as the pathologist strolled towards the location of the corpse. Initially Kings had been able to stay reasonably upright, brushing away the occasional stray branch but after a few yards it became increasingly difficult and he had to crouch. He almost stumbled before regaining his foothold and persevering until he joined two of the investigators kneeling on the ground.

Drake and the three officers in his team stood watching.

'We spoke to the park manager,' Luned said. 'He told us that one of the gardeners started quite early this morning. I got a name and a contact phone number, sir. I was wondering if you wanted me to speak to him?'

Typical of Luned to get on with things promptly, Drake concluded.

'Yes.' Drake regretted sounding curt. 'Of course, Luned. There could be regular walkers or runners, anybody who noticed something out of the ordinary.'

'Yes, sir,' Luned replied.

'A lot depends on the time of death,' Sara said. 'If it was last night, we need to focus on who used the park and discover if the gates were locked. There could be kids coming in here late at night having a barbecue or parties.'

'I agree, and we should…' Drake's developing thought process was interrupted by Kings emerging onto the gravelled path.

He dusted himself down and hauled himself out of the protective clothing. 'Blunt force trauma. Time of death is difficult to say exactly until I've done the post-mortem, but death would have been almost instantaneous from a quick look at the way the skull was bashed in.'

'Thanks, Lee,' Foulds said. 'I assume we can move the body?'

Kings kicked off the last of the overall and nodded his agreement.

Drake turned to Sara. 'Let's take a look.'

She nodded apprehensively.

The prospect of his shoes being scuffed and his trousers ripped or torn by the branches and trees wriggled its way into his mind but he dismissed them into a corner. A life had been cut short – he could buy another pair of shoes.

He tried to imagine how the killer had dragged the body through the undergrowth. Clothes must have been ripped, torn, shards caught on twigs and branches, and it meant the CSIs had fertile territory to gather evidence. If it was Dawn and Caston's killer, there was a chance he or she had been careless.

There was every likelihood that he would have to return to the scene at some point. He hoped that by then the overhanging trees and branches would have been hacked away. He was almost crouching by the time he reached the investigators both sitting on their haunches next to bags of equipment. They nodded at Drake and Sara.

The body was lying curled up as though it had been discarded like a piece of rubbish. Staining on the jeans suggested the corpse had been dragged through the undergrowth. Deep gashes in the blouse exposed the pink flesh underneath. He neared the body sinking to his knees and shuffling awkwardly under the low canopy of branches and twigs.

Then he stopped and looked down at the bloodied, bruised and lifeless face of Olivia Knox.

Chapter 35

Olivia Knox's bungalow was set back behind a road of semi-detached properties. On the journey from the park, Sara had spoken to one of Knox's colleagues who had confirmed that Knox's relatives lived in the Midlands where she had been brought up. Sara had spoken to the local force and arranged for a family liaison officer to speak to them. Drake pulled up into the drive of the property and they left the car. He fingered the keys the crime scene investigators had recovered.

Drake reached for the handle and unlocked the door, pleased that breaking bad news was something they would avoid. Inside the furniture was anonymous, as though a team of removers had recently visited and arranged the bungalow for viewing by a prospective tenant. Newspapers and magazines filling a stand by the side of a sofa and a pile of CDs alongside a music system in the sitting room were the only suggestion someone lived there.

'Doesn't feel very homely,' Sara said.

A single upturned cereal bowl occupied the draining board. Drake opened the fridge door while Sara rummaged through some of the cupboards. The prepacked lettuces and tomatoes and cold meats and cheese pointed to Knox having a healthy, if simple, taste in food.

'It feels like a holiday cottage,' Sara said. 'Functional but characterless.'

'She must have had some personal possessions.'

He left the kitchen and at the end of the hallway he pushed open a door. What he had already seen of the property hadn't prepared him for what faced them in the bedroom. A brash red curtain draped the window, its bottom dragging on the floor. The television, a fifty-inch screen at least, screwed to a wall looked down at a fourposter with extravagant lace cloth twisted around each pillar.

'Bloody hell,' Sara said. 'It looks like a brothel.'

Sara pulled out a drawer from a chest and let out an exclamation. 'You should look at this, boss.' Sara ran a hand through the flimsy underwear and lingerie. 'There are dozens here.'

Sara examined the contents of the rest of the drawers while Drake turned his attention to a bedside cabinet. Various toys and implements strained his imagination. What would Knox's parents make of all the paraphernalia?

Everyone is entitled to a private life, Drake thought. She could do whatever she wanted in the privacy of her own home.

'There's a laptop here,' Sara said lifting out the computer.

Sara opened the lid. The screen popped into life.

'This is interesting,' Sara said.

'Let's take it through to the kitchen.' Sara followed Drake and they sat by the small kitchen table. Sara placed the laptop down and opened the lid once again.

The image of Knox's front door appeared on the screen.

'She must have a camera setup,' Drake said.

'Why the hell would she have that?' Sara sounded intrigued. Then she hit enter on the keyboard as an image of a man reaching up to press the doorbell filled the monitor. Drake and Sara watched wordlessly as he stood waiting to be let in. The time on the recording read nine pm the previous evening.

The door opened. Drake assumed the person in the doorway to be Knox. He didn't have to make an assumption about the identity of the man. He recognised Jack Beltrami immediately.

An hour later, Drake sat at one of the tables in the Incident Room scanning the faces of his team. In front of them was the laptop removed from Knox's property. A preliminary examination had established that Knox used adult dating websites. Several threads of conversations made clear her interest in frequent casual sex. And the camera installed under the eaves of the property had been a sensible precaution but the link to dating websites unnerved Sara. Everyone used them these days, she reassured herself.

'Gareth, Luned,' Drake began. 'Establish the name of every man recently in touch with Knox. Go through the CCTV footage and trawl through the websites she visited. If needs be, get warrants for all the information to be disclosed. And go through her mobile. We need to know everyone she contacted in the hours before she died.'

Winder and Luned nodded their understanding.

A picture of Olivia Knox had already been pinned to the board alongside the images of Dawn Piper and Hubert Caston. 'We assume the deaths are connected.'

'It was a different MO,' Winder said.

'Just because a knife wasn't used, doesn't mean it was a second killer.' Sara added.

'But she could have been killed by a jilted lover.'

Luned sounded disgusted when she made her first contribution. 'You don't know what sort of people are on these Internet dating sites.'

Sara felt her cheeks flushing and hoped no one noticed.

Drake continued. 'We know about one – Jack Beltrami. He is now a significant person of interest and I am looking forward to hearing exactly what he has to say.'

'We have a report in from the surveillance team,' Winder said. 'Nobody returned to the address listed on the prescription the girls used.'

'Damn. Where are these girls?'

'Perhaps Knox was killed because she found out where they are living.' Luned again, sounding serious.

Drake stood up and motioned for Sara to join him in his office. 'Before we plan the Beltrami interview, let's talk to Jim Finch. He should have told us about Dawn being a registered informant – all he suggested originally was that she had given him intel informally.'

Sara followed Drake through the corridors of headquarters. A reorganisation had seen the name 'drug squad' disappear, but its functions still persisted. And it was even more important now with county lines dealers dominating the headlines. Three other officers sat around, all busy with paperwork, clicking on their mice.

Finch sat at a desk scanning the monitor. 'Can we have a word?' Drake said.

Finch hesitated. 'I've got a lot of—'

'There's been another death. Olivia Knox's body was found this morning. Her head was bashed in.'

'Jesus, that's awful.'

Finch nodded to a door on the opposite side of the room. 'We can use the conference suite.'

The smell of furniture polish drifted in the air and Sara watched as Drake drew a finger along the surface of the table: another of his foibles. After the meeting first thing with the rest of the team, Sara felt unsettled. That evening she had another date with Mark, who she had met on a dating website and she scrutinised everything she knew about him. What was he really like? Did he have any weird habits? Sara wanted to dismiss Luned's comments as a prudish over-reaction, but a lingering reservation filled her mind. Maybe she would take things a little more slowly. Get to know him better. But she persuaded herself that everybody used dating website these days. They were the new norm.

Drake glared at Finch. 'I understand Dawn Piper was a registered informant.'

Finch nodded. 'That was years ago.'

'Why didn't you tell us?'

'It wasn't relevant. She was just in it for the attention. She never gave us any useful intelligence.'

'It's hardly irrelevant is it?' Drake raised his voice a notch. 'She's a murder victim. Surely we should have been told.'

If Finch was intimidated, he wasn't showing it. 'As I said, sir, I can't even remember when I last spoke to her officially.'

'Is there anything else you haven't told us?'

It was a good tactic from Drake, Sara thought, inviting Finch to volunteer the information that Drake knew already.

He fell into the trap, shaking his head noncommittally.

'And what about Cameron Toft?'

Finch squinted at Drake.

'He was a registered informant too. Did you see him?'

'Ah, yes, of course.' Finch feigned ignorance. 'Again, that was years ago. He was ex-services. And he thought he was some sort of secret agent. He kept bragging that he'd seen action with special forces and that he was a hot shot with rifles. He was completely unreliable.'

'Did you minute all the meetings you had with him?'

'Yeah, of course.' Finch sounded unconvincing.

'I bloody well hope so. Is there anything else that you haven't told us?'

Finch shook his head slowly.

Once they had finished, Sara walked back to the Incident Room with Drake. 'What did you make of that, boss?'

'I don't like it when officers are evasive. Makes me feel uncomfortable.'

Drake didn't need to say more. Sara knew him well enough to realise he was contemplating whether Finch was involved in some way.

Drake continued. 'Whoever is moving those missing girls around seems to be one step ahead of us. I hope they're not getting information from the inside.' Drake gave her the sort of look that suggested his comment wasn't to be repeated under any circumstances. Perhaps he was right to be suspicious of Finch, Sara thought. But suspecting a police officer was a prospect too serious to contemplate.

Drake texted Annie as soon as he left headquarters. He was already later than he had hoped when they spoke briefly that afternoon. Trepidation had been evident in her voice when Drake shared the news about Knox's death.

He drove home through the tunnels under the Conwy estuary and mountains near Penmaenmawr and Llanfairfechan on autopilot without registering the traffic. His thoughts dominated by the prospect of interviewing Jack Beltrami in the morning, Drake's anger towards the man made him feel tense. Sara had sounded words of caution when they discussed the interview plan, but Drake wasn't going to be circumspect with Beltrami anymore. He knew he had to be objective, but it wasn't easy when Sian and Helen and Megan were involved.

And Annie of course. He had hoped that she wouldn't have to endure the excess of his working life as a detective. Criminals had a habit of ruining plans for a normal nine-to-five life. She had accepted his long days and disrupted weekends with good grace but feeling threatened in her home was different, very different.

He parked and let himself into the house.

A television was playing in the living room upstairs. Drake saw Annie sitting in the garden, so he walked through their bedroom and out into the evening sunshine.

'I thought I heard the car.' Annie beamed but she appeared drawn. They embraced and Drake sat down by her side.

'How are the girls?'

'Your mother called today. She's really good with them. And Robin rang earlier asking if they could collect the girls tomorrow.'

Annie sounded relieved and Drake realised the additional responsibility he had expected Annie to assume. Helen and Megan weren't her children, but she had cared for them while Sian was recovering, and he was committed to the inquiry.

Annie added, 'I suppose you'll be working tomorrow.'

He gave her a thin smile. 'I'm sorry. But…'

'Don't worry.' She reached over and squeezed his arm. 'Will you be finished before our holiday?'

By tomorrow he might have a better idea. 'I really hope so.'

Chapter 36

Drake parked across from the amusement arcade owned by the Beltrami family. The promenade was quiet, still too early for the crowds that Sunday morning, even if the summer sunshine made the seafront look attractive. After locking the car, he and Sara crossed the road. If the girl behind the cash desk recognised them, she didn't show it. Even repeating the process of pushing their warrant card at the window of the booth had little effect.

She made a brief phone call and the door to one side unlocked with a loud click, allowing Drake and Sara to take the stairs to the first floor. At the end of the corridor he pushed open the door into Beltrami's office.

A familiar face scowled up at him.

'What do you want?'

'We want to interview you in relation to our inquiry into the deaths of Dawn Piper, Hubert Caston and Olivia Knox.'

'You must be off your fucking trolley, Inspector. Do you realise the trouble you're in? You won't get away with this harassment so easily. You waltz in here on a Sunday morning in the middle of the season disrupting my business and expect me to drop everything.'

'I'm giving you the chance to cooperate and attend an interview voluntarily.'

Beltrami stood up and puffed out his chest.

Drake continued. 'If you prefer, I could arrest you. Handcuff you and escort you to the police station. I'm trying to avoid any unnecessary embarrassment.'

'Very fucking considerate.'

Beltrami grabbed the phone on his desk. He punched in a number.

'Eric, I've got the cops here. Get over to the police station. They want to interview me.'

He slammed the phone down and glared at Drake. 'My

solicitor is on his way.'

Once Beltrami and his solicitor were sitting in an interview room, Drake called Winder with instructions to execute the search warrant at Beltrami's premises – soon the black Audis would be seized by the crime scene investigation team.

Drake completed the necessary formalities for the tapes before he and Sara shared a cautious glance. Interrogating a suspect created conflicting emotions – nerves mixed with adrenaline in anticipation that they were getting closer to an arrest. Two bottles of expensive carbonated spring water stood on the table in front of Beltrami and Tomkins. Both men oozed confidence as though being interviewed by detectives undertaking a murder inquiry was an everyday occurrence. Beltrami had draped the jacket of his suit on the back of the chair behind him.

Eric Tomkins held out a hand. 'Detective Inspector Ian Drake, it's been some time.'

Not long enough, Drake thought. Tomkins had small, brown, shifty eyes and a manner that instantly created distrust. Drake had come across the lawyer many times. He always took every opportunity to expose any weakness and press home his advantage.

'Eric, good to see you,' Drake lied.

He turned to face Beltrami. 'Mr Beltrami, we want to interview you in relation to an ongoing murder inquiry. You do not have to say anything. But it may harm your defence if you do not mention when questioned something which you later rely on in court. Anything you do say may be given in evidence.'

Tomkins sighed. 'Is it really necessary to caution my client? He is here voluntarily, after all.'

Drake ignored the lawyer and slotted the tapes into the machine sitting on the table and screwed to the wall. He nodded at both men opposite, who acknowledged they were ready to start. Drake got down to his first question.

'Did you know Dawn Piper?'

'I read about her death in the newspapers and it has been on television, of course.'

'Did you know her personally?' Drake persevered.

'Like I told you before, Inspector Drake, I meet a lot of people in my line of business. But she wasn't known to me *personally*.'

It was the 'to the best of my recollection' sort of an answer a politician might give – justifying a lie that concealed an inconvenient truth. Beltrami sounded almost plausible.

'Dawn Piper was found dead at her home from a knife wound to her stomach.' Drake sorted through the photographs in the file in front of him and pushed the sample taken by the forensic photographer over the table towards Beltrami and Tomkins. Both men turned up their noses.

'It was quite a vicious and brutal attack.'

'And your question, Inspector Drake?' Tomkins said. 'I know my client is assisting you with this inquiry but unless you ask some direct questions it's going to be very difficult.'

Drake ignored Tomkins. This was his interview and he would conduct it as he chose. Even so, he could feel the lawyer's arrogance seeping under his skin, annoying him.

'Dawn was worried about the impact of the drugs from Liverpool coming into the area. Perhaps you've heard of the county lines dealers?'

Beltrami shrugged. 'Hasn't there been something on the telly?'

'Dawn hoped she could stop the drug trade in the Deeside area getting any worse.'

Beltrami gave a world-weary sigh. 'Like I said I don't recall ever having met her.'

Drake took a moment to gather his thoughts. Jack Beltrami had a finger in drug dealing – it was easy money, taking advantage of the disadvantaged and vulnerable in society and the cash could flow through his legal businesses without a hitch. Beltrami disgusted Drake and he sensed his anger rising.

'Can you confirm your whereabouts the Saturday before last?' Drake turned to Sara who was ready with the date.

Beltrami pretended to ponder his reply. 'Saturday you say? This is our busiest time of the year. I would have been working until late then I'd have gone home and watched Netflix like everyone else.'

'Could someone account for your movements that evening?'

'Of course, talk to my staff and my wife.'

All independent witnesses, Drake thought pointedly.

'I understand that you have a black Audi A4.'

'I own a lot of vehicles.'

He was answering a question – progress at least.

'CCTV footage places Dawn Piper inside your black Audi A4 a few days before her death. Why did you give her a lift?'

Beltrami shook his head in a patronising pathetic gesture.

'Did anybody else in your organisation have use of this car?'

'I employ a number of people and quite a few of them would probably have driven the car.'

'I'll need the names of those people.'

Sara jotted down the details of Beltrami's employees.

He found the image of Beltrami and Dawn Piper he had printed from the CCTV footage recorded in the convenience store and he pushed it over the table. As he did so he studied Beltrami's face looking for a tell-tale sign of weakness. But all he saw were blank expressionless eyes. What are you thinking, Drake thought? Calculating how exactly to explain this?

'Is this Dawn Piper?' Tomkins asked.

Drake looked straight at Beltrami. 'This is you meeting Dawn Piper a few days before she was killed. Can you tell us what you discussed?'

Beltrami didn't reply but settled his expression into a heavy glare.

'Jack.' Drake sounded almost friendly. 'You've denied having met Dawn Piper, but this photograph clearly confirms you did – quite recently. Would you like to reconsider your previous answer?'

Drake kept his eye contact direct. It was always good to second-guess the mind of an interviewee. No matter how sick.

After a few seconds Drake announced, 'For the purposes of the tape-recording Mr Beltrami does not reply.'

'I shall need full details of where the photograph was taken and how it was recovered in order that we can make a complete forensic analysis.' Tomkins made it sound as though he was in charge of the evidence.

'Dawn wasn't killed in her own home.' Drake thought he detected a shadow crossing Beltrami's face. 'We believe she had been lying on her side for several hours before she was moved. Forensic examination of material recovered from her clothing suggests she was kept in the boot of a car.'

Beltrami's charmless eyes convinced Drake that this was the man, either by himself or through one of his cronies and associates, who had been responsible for forcing Sian off the road. His daughters had been in that car and his stomach churned at the memory.

'I don't see what this has to do with my client?' Tomkins said.

'We believe Dawn was kept in the boot of an Audi. The same type of car Mr Beltrami owns.'

'Well you'll have to check mine, won't you?' Beltrami raised his voice.

Drake contemplated telling him they were doing just that.

'I think Dawn Piper had evidence incriminating you in drug dealing activity in Deeside. You couldn't take that risk, could you? So you had her killed.'

Beltrami guffawed. Tomkins interjected. 'Don't be absurd. Anyone can see you're jumping to conclusions. Where's your evidence?'

Drake paused and pulled from the folder on the table a photograph of Hubert Caston. He pushed it at Beltrami. 'Do you know Hubert Caston?'

Beltrami shoved it back at Drake after a hasty glance. 'No.'

'Look again.' As Drake waited, he read the statement from one of Caston's work colleagues.

When Drake looked over at him, Beltrami spat out a reply. 'Like I said. I didn't know him.'

'An eyewitness confirms that you met him in your letting agency.' Drake read out the correct date.

Beltrami glowered. 'I meet a lot of people in my agency. I can't remember them all.'

'What did you talk about with Hubert Caston?'

Beltrami threw his hands in the air and slapped them down on the table. 'How can you possibly expect me to remember?'

A message reached his mobile switched to silent near his papers and Drake read Winder's confirmation that two black Audis had been recovered from Beltrami's premises. His mind suddenly focused on the accident involving Sian and his daughters.

He couldn't avoid asking the question any longer.

'Did you think that trying to run my ex-wife off the road would deter this investigation?'

'What the hell are you talking about?' Tomkins spluttered.

Beltrami beamed.

Drake's pulse hammered in his neck. 'Dr Drake was injured when her car was rammed off the road. And my daughters were inside at the time,' Drake said through gritted teeth.

'This is absurd,' Tomkins continued.

Beltrami said nothing. He grinned at Drake who sensed his anger reaching the point where he knew he'd say something he shouldn't, do something he would regret.

He counted to five mentally whilst searching through some of the papers on his desk pretending to look for something, until he finally resolved to ask Beltrami about Olivia Knox.

'Did you know Olivia Knox?'

Another shadow crossed Beltrami's face. It was something in the eyes, an uncertainty, a flicker of worry.

Drake continued, directing his words directly at Beltrami. 'Olivia Knox was a charity worker who supports drug addicts and those in rehabilitation in the Deeside area. Her body was found badly beaten yesterday morning.' Drake recited the full details while staring at Beltrami, gratified when he turned away, unable to maintain his eye contact.

'Do you know her?'

An invisible corset tightened itself around Drake's chest each second drawing its strings tighter and tighter. 'Are you going to answer the question, Mr Beltrami?'

Would he lie? Would he gamble that they hadn't made the connection?

'I don't know who you're talking about?'

The tension in his chest subsided slowly. Beltrami had stepped over into the abyss, taken the chance, lied. As criminals often did.

Drake took a moment to find the photograph of Beltrami standing outside Knox's front door. He pushed it over towards Beltrami. 'I think this is you.'

Recognition was clear on Tomkins' face.

Blood drained from Beltrami's cheeks. He kept gaping at the image.

'Where was this taken?' Tomkins asked.

'It was taken outside the home of Olivia Knox on the evening she was brutally murdered. Jack, perhaps you would like to reconsider your earlier answer denying you knew her.'

Chapter 37

Drake shook his head as Tomkins complained bitterly that he and his client had been ambushed by Drake.

'I've never seen anything like this in twenty years of legal practice,' Tomkins snorted as he stood up. 'I demand an opportunity to speak to my client.'

Drake was happy to oblige. He gathered up his papers and left.

After an hour, Beltrami's demeanour had changed completely as Tomkins announced when Sara and Drake returned to the interview that Mr Beltrami wanted to cooperate.

Yes, of course he knew Olivia Knox.

Yes, they had met on an Internet dating site designed for couples who wanted casual, commitment-less relationships.

Yes, he had visited her home on the evening shown in the CCTV coverage. He could do little else, Drake thought.

No, he hadn't killed Knox. He had left her drinking a foul-smelling herbal tea concoction and scrolling through her mobile.

Beltrami surrendered his handset, an enormous top-of-the-range iPhone, that weighed a ton. Grudgingly he gave Sara the passcodes.

Beltrami and Tomkins were left festering whilst Drake and Sara discussed their options with the custody sergeant. Charging Beltrami was out of the question – they simply didn't have the evidence, yet. Drake hoped the forensic teams busy on the black Audis would provide them with something, but it meant waiting. The custody time limits would be against them.

'We can only hold him overnight,' Sara said.

The custody sergeant nodded.

A night in a cell next to a drunk or drug addict would suit Beltrami perfectly, Drake thought. Once the decision had been made that Beltrami would enjoy the hospitality of the Wales Police Service overnight, Drake returned to headquarters.

Drake poured the freshly made coffee from his usual cafetière into a mug sitting on the coaster on his desk and admired the thin sheen of crema on the top. Jack Beltrami's computer had been seized by officers led by Winder. Luned had supervised a search of the Beltrami home, a palatial estate with a substantial house and stables, in the Denbighshire countryside. Mrs Beltrami had said very little as they rummaged through her husband's possessions, recovering a laptop and a computer.

In the Incident Room, Winder was analysing Beltrami's browsing history. Luned stood by the threshold to Drake's office clutching her notebook carefully. Sara leaned against a table in a corner of his room.

'Tell me again exactly what Mrs Beltrami said,' Drake said.

'She was adamant that Jack had returned by about eleven thirty the night he'd been with Olivia Knox. He complained about being tired.'

Drake chuckled. Luned continued in a serious vein. 'He told her he had been working late. She had been watching television and she was certain about the time.'

'That could give him an alibi,' Sara said.

It was the last thing he wanted to hear. He wanted to believe that Beltrami had murdered Olivia Knox and that he was involved in the deaths of Dawn Piper and Hubert Caston, all as part of his desire to build a drug dealing empire in Deeside. He probably wanted to extend all over North Wales. And more than anything Drake wanted to blame Beltrami for ramming Sian and endangering his daughters.

Winder joined Luned in the doorway of Drake's office.

'I've been through Olivia Knox's computer, boss. There are at least a dozen men we need to contact. And that's only in the past three months. There are messages to all of them about meeting up and discussing their sexual preferences. She was dead keen to know… I mean… how can I put this… How—'

It was unusual to see Winder being prudish. 'Spit it out,' Drake said.

'How big they were.'

'You mean how tall they were, Gareth?' Sara said adding a light touch to her voice.

'No, I mean, how—'

Drake raised a hand. 'Spare us the details. Make a list of the men involved and contact them.'

Luned added, 'It could take us hours to go through all of Jack Beltrami's devices and identify his movements for the night Knox was killed. A triangulation report on his mobile should confirm where he was.'

'All of which justifies holding Beltrami in custody for twenty-four hours. Minimum,' Drake said gleefully.

Drake finished his coffee and called the senior management suite, knowing he couldn't avoid briefing Superintendent Hobbs. Their conversation was brief – Hobbs confirming he wasn't leaving headquarters any time soon. Drake found his new boss settling into the room he had visited so many times in the past. The desk had been moved, the conference table repositioned, and new paintings hung on the wall – watercolours of well-known Welsh scenes. It was the final stage of exorcising Wyndham Price.

Hobbs jerked a ballpoint clutched in his right hand towards a chair in front of his desk. Drake sat down and gave the superintendent a summary of the day's activity. Hobbs frowned, pursed his lips, occasionally scribbled a note on a pad. Price would have interrupted Drake, sought clarification of something inadequately explained and Drake felt unsettled that Hobbs hadn't done the same.

'We should have the result from the forensic examination of Beltrami's Audis tomorrow.'

'I wouldn't hold your breath, Detective Inspector. Keep me up to date with everything. I expect regular briefing notes.'

Hobbs turned his attention back to the files in front of him and Drake left the room dragging the door closed behind him. He regretted losing the certainties of his relationship with Wyndham Price. He knew where he stood. Price understood him, knew his background, had been supportive when the pressures of the job had been too much. Would he be able to rely on Hobbs for such support in the future?

Back in his office Drake's unease with Hobbs' criticism of the inquiry developed into a murky shadow in his mind. Then he focused on the paperwork on his desk aiming to reassess everything again.

He clicked open his computer and found an image of Dawn Piper and then began rereading all the statements. There was something they had missed. He wanted to believe Jack Beltrami was connected to her murder. If only he could find the link. He ignored the time and the only sound were the cleaners gossiping as they hoovered.

He pored over the Dawn Piper timeline. Assembling the details had been painstaking work. At least they knew she had been in the Bluebell on the night she was killed. He scribbled a reminder to himself that in the morning he'd speak to Councillor Beedham and find out exactly what he was doing with Dawn. Then he wrote Ritchie O'Brien's name at the top of his notepad. He had been seen with Dawn on the night she died – another person to talk to.

Drake found the image of Paul Kenny. All three victims were killed to protect the county lines operations in Deeside and the turf war it was creating of that he was convinced.

Proving it would be a different matter.

He was going to turn his attention again to the world of Jack Beltrami when his mobile rang. 'Ian, where are you?' Annie said.

He glanced at the clock on the monitor, shocked that it

was so late. He scrambled to his feet, embarrassed. 'I'm still at headquarters.'

'Come home, Ian. Come home.'

Chapter 38

Drake woke in the middle of the night, his shoulders damp with sweat, the vivid dream still fresh in his thoughts. It involved a car chase. He wasn't attempting to apprehend a suspect, now he was being chased. By a black Audi. It jolted into him when his car was stationary on the entry to a roundabout. Drake turned and jerked his hand making his anger clear. But he couldn't see anyone through the blacked-out windows. After the roundabout, the black Audi kept close, ridiculously close, close enough to connect to Drake's rear bumper so he had pressed on, hoping he could shake off the driver. Reaching a hundred miles an hour he feared for his own safety. Then he had woken up.

He threw off the duvet and got out of bed. He drew back the curtain a few inches and saw the first of the morning sunshine light up the opposite bank of the Menai Strait. He left Annie sleeping soundly and padded out into the bathroom where he doused his face with water before staring at himself in the mirror.

The previous evening had been a throwback to the bad old days, when his rituals and obsessions of making certain every piece of paperwork was in its place kept him chained to his desk, working long hours. It had cost him his marriage and only time would tell how it affected his daughters. He didn't want the same thing to happen to his relationship with Annie.

He put it all down to Jack Beltrami, of course. And to his history with the Beltrami family. He towelled himself down and went back to bed.

He woke with the alarm clock at the usual time and turned over, giving Annie a tight hug as she murmured good morning. Having only the two of them for breakfast suited Annie, Drake could tell from the way she was more relaxed and brighter. Colleagues with new wives or husbands with children from previous relationships complained about the difficulty in getting step-children to slot in with their new lovers. So, it didn't surprise Drake that domestic arrangements with Annie might be difficult to start with. He hoped their imminent holiday would help improve the position.

He called Sara before he left Felinheli.

'Morning, boss.'

'I want to track down that taxi driver – Spike – and then speak to Beedham before the time limits for keeping Beltrami run out.'

'Have you heard from forensics?'

'Not yet.'

Drake rang off after agreeing to collect her at headquarters. The journey was uneventful, he listened to the news – complaints about long waiting lists in the hospitals and school budgets being stretched – and hummed along to a few tracks of a Ward Thomas album Annie had given him. Less rock these days, more country music. Arriving in the car park he spotted Wyndham Price's Jaguar parked next to a swanky Range Rover Evoque. It was a striking red colour with a contrasting black roof. Its personalised number plate had the letters ADH and Drake realised Superintendent Hobbs obviously wanted to flaunt his status.

'Good morning, sir.' Sara got into the car.

'Morning.'

He powered the car onto the A55 and then eastwards.

Michael Pritchard lived in the end property of a terrace of three houses all of which needed just as much attention as number six, the taxi driver's home. Chunks of masonry were missing from the walls that marked the boundary with its neighbour. Calling the area at the front a garden would be complimentary, Drake thought. Grass had given up a long time ago, now it was thick with weeds and moss. Two recycling bins had been discarded in one corner.

Drake rang the doorbell. No response. He pressed again and followed it up with a fist thumping the door. Moments later, a woman in her fifties with a cigarette at her lips opened the door and quickly scanned the cul-de-sac before giving Drake and Sara an intense inquisitive glare.

'I'm looking for Michael Pritchard.'

'Why do you want him? You the cops?'

'Where can I find him?'

'What's he done?'

'Are you his wife?' Drake stuck his warrant card into the woman's face. 'I don't have time for this. I need to speak to him now. Where is he?'

She made a double take and blinked rapidly. 'He went out dead early. He goes to take photographs. He's in this group that go out first thing in the morning or last thing at night. He's got all these bloody gizmos and cameras. Doesn't spend any money on me.'

The last sentence was true enough, Drake thought unkindly.

'When will he be back?'

She shrugged. 'How would I know?'

Drake pushed a business card towards her. 'Get him to call me as soon as he's back.'

Drake and Sara walked back to the car once the woman had closed the door.

Drake's mobile rang as he reached his Mondeo. It was Mike Foulds. 'Morning, Mike, I hope you've got good news for me.'

'Sorry, Ian. There weren't any traces of blood in the boot of either black Audi we recovered from Beltrami's place. I guess it's not what you were hoping for.'

Mike Foulds rang off and Drake looked over at Sara shaking his head. 'Forensics drew a blank.'

'We'll have to release Beltrami on bail.'

It was the last thing Drake wanted to contemplate but he knew that without evidence they couldn't charge him. But it didn't mean that the case against Beltrami was finished. He would return to the police station to answer bail in a month –

enough time to triangulate his phone, hopefully placing him near the various crime scenes. And they still had to finish analysing Beltrami's computer.

Drake read the time on his watch. The custody time limits ran out in a few hours. Until then, Beltrami could enjoy the hospitality of the Wales Police Service.

Every window pane at Councillor Beedham's home had been decorated with a poster adorned with his image and a campaign slogan 'Better with Beedham' printed in red letters. The councillor's smiling face featured on an estate agent-type placard nailed to a post screwed to the gatepost.

It amazed Sara that a by-election was being held in the summer. A lot of people would be on holiday, making it difficult to engage people in the political process. And judging by the disinterest in Mrs Beedham's manner when she opened the door, Sara doubted her husband had much chance of succeeding. 'I don't know where he is today.' Starting to close the door in Drake's face was bound to rile him, especially after their visit to Spike's home earlier.

'This is a murder inquiry,' Drake said forcibly. 'We need to speak to your husband.'

It had the desired effect when Mrs Beedham blinked vigorously.

'He must have told you where he was going today. He's in the middle of an election campaign. Surely you have some idea?'

'He's got this office... I mean... it's a room in the Cheerful Spaniard.'

'Cheerful Spaniard?' Drake growled.

'It's a restaurant in town.' She forced the door closed.

Drake unlocked the car with the remote. 'What a stupid name for a restaurant.'

Drake left the street of semi-detached properties behind and Sara noticed far more Labour and Conservative party posters in windows than any supporting Mr Beedham. From the little Sara knew of politics, it seemed unlikely an independent was going to be successful, even one with as big a mouth as Councillor Beedham.

Paint peeled off the sign above the door of the Cheerful Spaniard and a thick white blob of bird excrement needed to be cleaned from one corner of the window near Beedham's poster sellotaped to the inside. Drake had to give the door a heave before it opened, and the decor and ambience suggested the owners and the clientele were thoroughly miserable. A specials board next to the serving counter had a title but nothing underneath.

It was difficult to decide the age of the woman who looked over at them from behind the counter. The lines and wrinkles on her face might have made her a fifty-year-old who had enjoyed far too many hours under a sunbed, or a seventy-year-old with lots of stories to share.

Drake flashed his warrant card at her. 'We understand Councillor Beedham has an *office* here.'

She looked vaguely disappointed as though the opportunity to take an order was something she had longed for. 'Out the back.'

Sara followed Drake down a small passageway that led towards the rear. The sound of conversation drifted from a room at the bottom and they entered to find Councillor Beedham sitting behind a desk. Leaning against a filing cabinet nearby was a thin man, cadaverous cheeks, long strands of white hair combed back over his skull that brushed the worn collar of his shirt. A woman perched on a chair opposite Beedham stopped mid-sentence and turned to look at Drake and Sara.

'We're finalising our strategy for the last week of the campaign,' Beedham announced.

Neither of the other two present reacted, although Sara had the distinct impression they appeared tired of Beedham. Did he really believe his own hyperbole, Sara thought?

'We need a word in private,' Drake said.

Beedham waved for the other two to leave and they bustled their way past Drake and Sara. Beedham fiddled with his mobile and tidied the papers on his desk.

'Always more than happy to assist the Wales Police Service.' Beedham pointed to two hard-backed plastic chairs.

Before they sat down Drake asked, 'Are you recording this conversation?'

Beedham pretended to look offended. 'What do you take me for, Inspector?'

'I'm sure you appreciate that obstructing our inquiry could be a criminal offence. Any recordings of private discussions and interviews might well be considered by the Crown Prosecution Service to be a serious matter.'

Beedham nodded. 'I understand, of course, how difficult it is for you to complete an inquiry like this.' He sounded utterly unconvincing as though he'd prefer to shout and bang the table at Drake.

Drake kept his voice determined. It was the sort of approach Beedham would understand. 'When did you last meet with Dawn Piper?'

'I don't recall…' Beedham glanced at the mobile on his desk. Sara guessed he had started to record the conversation and was regretting it. Beedham waved a hand limply in the air. 'I may have met her at one of my surgeries.'

Covering his back, Sara thought, wondering how Drake would deal with it.

'How often do you hold your surgeries?' Drake's voice was more cooperative now. Sara could see he was trying to gain Beedham's trust.

'Usually every month. I try and provide a good service to the people in my community. They know they can trust me. They know I look after their interests.'

Drake adjusted his position on the chair, crossing his right foot over his left knee. Beads of sweat glistened on Beedham's forehead.

'What did Dawn Piper discuss with you when she came to your surgery?'

'Normally, Inspector, my discussions with constituents are private. They have to rely on my discretion and confidentiality.'

Drake gave him an ingratiating smile. 'But I'm sure you can make an exception, as this is a murder inquiry.'

'Well... as far as I can remember, it was about her campaign regarding the drug dealers in the town.'

'Do you keep a record of the discussions with your constituents?'

'Ah... I'd need to check.'

'And are there any other occasions when you met Dawn Piper?' Drake sounded casual as though he was expecting a negative reply.

'No, I don't think so. It wasn't as though I saw her socially or anything.'

Beedham couldn't help himself, Sara concluded. There was something inherently dishonest and dysfunctional about the man. Hubris made him vulnerable.

Drake stiffened in the chair alongside Sara as he prepared for the final few questions. 'You never met Dawn Piper socially?'

Beedham shook his head. 'No.'

'Then how do you account for the fact that we have CCTV footage of you meeting her on the evening of her death in the Bluebell pub?'

Like a fish gasping for water, Beedham's mouth opened and closed while his eyes fixed Drake with a blank look. 'There must be some mistake, I mean... Where do you say that was?' There was a contented smile on Drake's face as he reached for his mobile. Once the screen came to life, he pushed it over at Beedham. 'This was taken inside the Bluebell – you can see the time in one corner.'

Beedham's already pasty complexion turned a sickly colour.

'Yes, of course, I remember.' Beedham pulled his senses together. 'She rabbited on about what I was going to do about the drugs coming into Deeside. She could be like a dog with a bone. She kept insisting I had to do something to be able to put pressure on the Wales Police Service to get things done. I've been talking to Sergeant Finch and he can be pretty useless.'

Beedham grew in confidence and leaned forward over the over the desk. 'Is it too much to ask the Wales Police Service to actually do something? After all, everyone knows that Ritchie O'Brien is involved directly in the drugs swamping the town. He flaunts his money, all over the place.'

Drake replied slowly. 'You're lying, Councillor Beedham. We have a statement from Olivia Knox before she died telling us all about your relationship with Dawn Piper.' He settled back into his chair. 'Unless you tell us everything now, I shall have to arrest you for perverting the course of justice and obstructing a police inquiry. We'll take you back to the custody suite and interview you under caution.'

Beedham's lower lip quivered and his double chin gave a nervous wobble.

'And while everything is confidential, I can't guarantee that news of your arrest might not leak. You know how people talk.'

Panic gripped Beedham who flushed as he overheated.

'Did you have any engagements this morning?' Drake sounded conversational as he tipped his head at the phone on the desk. 'You might like to cancel them.'

'All right, all right.' Beads of sweat broke out all over Beedham's forehead. 'Dawn told me she knew where the drugs had been hidden on the *Duke of Lancaster*. And she had videos implicating Richie O'Brien and Jack Beltrami in drug dealing – or so she said.'

'Why the hell didn't you contact the police?'

Beedham spluttered a reply. 'I told Finch, who laughed

and said that Dawn was a druggie who couldn't be trusted.'

'You were going to embarrass the police. When were you going to pull that stunt?'

Beedham sifted his gaze quickly between Drake and Sara. His nostrils flared and he shook his head vigorously. He wasn't in charge any longer and no amount of bluster could save him now.

'You planned to take the credit for announcing a discovery of drugs. It was a cynical political ploy as part of your election campaign. Can't you see how dangerous that could be? It was your civic duty to tell us about your discussion with Dawn.'

'Civic duty – don't give me that crap. I don't think the Wales Police Service knows anything about civic duty or else you'd have locked up these drug dealers a long time ago.'

'You must know we need admissible evidence—'

Beedham chortled. 'You're running around like headless chickens.'

Beedham was back to his usual form – argumentative and confrontational.

Sara decided to intervene. 'How long were you in the Bluebell that Saturday evening?'.

He turned to look at Sara. 'How can I possibly remember?'

'Did you see Dawn with anybody else that evening?'

Beedham paused before replying. 'I caught a glimpse of Ritchie O'Brien.' Beedham managed to sound satisfied.

Sara continued. 'Where exactly are the videos that Dawn mentioned?'

Beedham ran a tongue over his lips. 'I don't know. In her place I suppose.'

Drake stood up and glared down at the politician. 'Don't do or say anything that might prejudice my inquiry.'

Beedham nodded.

Sara followed Drake out to the car. He was already on

his mobile dictating instructions for Winder and Luned to get a search team organised at Dawn's property. When he finished the conversation, the handset rang again.

'DI Drake.'

Sara watched the recognition on his face. 'Stay where you are.'

He turned to Sara. 'That was Spike, the taxi driver. He's back home.'

Chapter 39

A three-year-old Mercedes C-Class looked out of place on the driveway next to the decrepit piece of garden. It displayed prominently the livery of Benji's taxis on the bonnet and door panels.

A short man in his fifties with a symmetrical paunch clearly nurtured by hours sitting in a taxi appeared, once Drake had rung the front door bell.

'Are you Michael Pritchard?'

'Yeah. What's this about? This is my day off.'

'I'm in charge of investigating the murder of Dawn Piper. We believe she was in the vicinity of the rugby club on the evening she was killed. I understand you regularly pick up fares from the rugby club.'

Pritchard nodded. 'I work most Saturdays.'

'Can you remember if you were at the rugby club?'

He frowned before nodding. 'Most likely. I usually get a good couple of fares from the club on Saturday evenings.'

'I understand you've got a dashcam installed.'

Pritchard responded warmly. 'Yeah, that's right, I love photography. It's one of my hobbies. Gets me out of the house.'

'We'd like to see the footage from that Saturday night if that's possible.'

'Can you come back later when I've got more time?'

'Mr Pritchard, we need it now.'

Pritchard led Drake and Sara into the property. Despite the untidy front garden and the less than salubrious neighbourhood, the inside was immaculate. Drake admired the neat and tidy sofas and the spotless surfaces. Upstairs in a small back bedroom, Pritchard sat by a computer and fiddled with the dashcam, recovering the necessary footage. A digital SLR, various lenses, filters and a high-end tripod sat on a cupboard in one corner.

After a few minutes Pritchard announced, 'This is the

footage from Saturday night. My first visits to the rugby club were drop-offs.'

The image showed the front of the club and, moments later, the vehicle pulled out of the car park, onto the road and drove away.

'What time is that?' Drake said.

'It was about half past eight. Do you want me to fast forward until I was back at the club?'

'No,' Drake replied curtly. 'But you can speed up the footage. We're looking for a woman in the rugby club area.'

Pritchard did as he was told and Drake and Sara stared at the screen willing it to show images of Dawn striding down the pavement. But they were disappointed and Pritchard fast forwarded to exclude time on fares at the other end of town.

He nodded vigorously as he watched one section. 'I remember now. I went back at half ten to pick up a couple. The wife had drunk too much and she was puking in the toilet. I didn't want her being sick in my car. So, I had to wait.'

The vehicle pulled into the car park and reversed until its nose pointed out towards the road. The footage continued playing. After ten minutes, a figure darting across the street a little way up from the car caught Drake's attention. 'That's her. It's Dawn.'

Pritchard paused the footage.

Sara squinted at the monitor. 'Certainly looks like her, even with her hood up.'

'Let's see the rest of it,' Drake said.

Pritchard clicked to restart and a man with a dog on a leash passed on the opposite pavement. He paid the hooded figure no attention. Dawn hurried down to the left of the car and out of sight of the dashcam.

'Where is she going?' Sara said.

'There's a path that goes down round the side of the club.'

Drake kept his voice even, despite knowing another piece of evidence had fallen into place. 'We'll need that original footage.'

Pritchard nodded his understanding. Seconds later he detached the USB from the computer and handed it to Drake who gestured at Sara. 'Let's find out where that footpath goes.'

Drake bought the Mondeo to a halt in the dusty car park at the club. He glanced to his right and saw the tarmacked surface of the footpath leading around the rugby field. Leaving the car, Sara following in his slipstream as he made his way along the path.

They stopped when the path turned sharply right onto a small bridge over a stream. Dawn must have taken this route, hurried over the bridge, Drake thought. So he did the same and after passing through a narrow gate found himself at the bottom of a long strip of tarmac leading over a field towards more properties in the distance.

He turned to Sara. 'Let's get to the top of this footpath.'

Either side of them the grass was thick and lush. It looked untended. Drake's father would have been appalled and his grandfather disgusted at the lack of attention the farmer paid to it. There was valuable silage here.

Drake pressed on but the gradient increased. It was another hot day and perspiration gathered under his armpits as he reached a stile. On the other side he stood for a moment gathering his breath in a gravel area that led into the street some distance away. Thick gorse and rhododendron bushes crowded them.

Dawn Piper had crossed the field too, passing through the same gate, arriving at this spot. Had she stopped to get her breath? Something looked familiar about the street of houses. 'What's the name of this road?'

As Sara googled the answer, Drake checked out the surroundings: it was secluded enough to have given any killer the perfect opportunity.

'Cleveland Avenue,' Sara said.

'Dammit, I thought I recognised the street. Olivia Knox's bungalow is at the end.'

Sara responded slowly. 'So, if Dawn reached the top of the path and stood where we're talking now, she was either killed here or abducted and killed elsewhere. Because she never made it to Olivia's property.'

Drake was already on his mobile. He barked an order. 'I want a full CSI team. Now.'

Mike Foulds was the first to arrive in a scientific support vehicle.

'Is this it?' Foulds said.

Drake drew a hand to include the entirety of the area where they were standing before Cleveland Avenue began properly. 'I want a full search done of this. I suspect that this is where Dawn Piper was killed. '

'What's the basis—'

'Just get on with this, Mike. It's top priority. I'm going to start house-to-house inquiries.'

Having worked with him for many years, Mike Foulds would accept unquestioningly Drake's judgement. Two more crime scene vehicles joined Foulds and after establishing a perimeter they got to work.

Drake and Sara took one side of the street each.

An elderly couple opened the front door of the first property. They looked shocked when Drake explained the nature of his visit. They lived very quietly, they went to the supermarket once a week and both played bridge on a Friday night. Sometimes on Sunday they went out for lunch but otherwise they rarely socialised. They shook their heads mournfully when Drake asked if they could remember anything about the Saturday evening Dawn had been killed.

'There have been lots of youngsters causing trouble in the street in the past year or so. We keep our door locked and chained overnight,' the husband announced solemnly.

The second and third properties were empty – Drake assumed their occupants busy at work. He glanced over at Sara, she shook her head.

Music drifted out of the next property and a man in his thirties wearing over-sized round glasses opened the door. The guitar chords and psychedelic edge to the music and acrid smell in the air suggested the occupiers adopted the lifestyle the drug dealing suspects in the inquiry might approve of.

'I've not seen anything, man.' The voice drawled disinterest.

'Can you be certain. Please think very carefully.'

The man frowned, long and hard as though he were constipated. 'No, sorry. Did you say a Saturday night? I'd be staying with my girlfriend.'

Drake thanked him and left.

Two more empty houses frustrated Drake. Where were the occupiers? He cast a glance down the road and saw the CSI team busy at work. A man with a dog approached him. 'I want to go down the path. What's up over there?'

Drake raised his voice. 'It's a routine police matter. No entry I'm afraid.'

The man pouted and left. Drake turned his attention to the next property. Its owner had a military bearing. Clean white shirt, navy trousers and well-polished black shoes. The haircut was straight off a parade ground, as was his slim figure.

'I'm investigating the murder of Dawn Piper.' As Drake showed the man his warrant card, he shared with him the correct date.

'Is she the drug user who was killed recently?'

'We believe she may have been on your street on the evening of her death.'

'The place is going to the dogs if you ask me. I blame Brexit. We've got kids running around all the time making a nuisance of themselves. Two of my neighbours have had their car windows smashed in the past six months. And I've had paint thrown at my front door.'

'I'm sorry to hear that.'

'I've complained of course. Fat lot of good it will do me though. Nothing ever happens. And what is worse is that nobody tells me that nothing is happening.'

Drake moved away from the door wanting to avoid a discussion with a man in full rant mode. 'If you remember anything about that Saturday evening, contact me.'

'You can watch the CCTV if you want.'

For a moment Drake wasn't certain he had heard correctly. 'I'm sorry?'

The householder took a step over the threshold and pointed to the first-floor window. 'I put the camera in a couple of years ago. I wanted to catch those little buggers in the act. So far, they've been clever enough not to do anything that has ever been recorded.'

Drake's mouth dried. 'Yes, I want to see the footage. Thank you.'

He glanced over at Sara who was emerging from an adjacent property. He waved and she hurried over to join him.

'He's got CCTV,' Drake whispered.

Sara raised an eyebrow.

A small desk had been pushed against the wall of a downstairs room and William Fleming, who had introduced himself with a crisp handshake to Drake and then Sara, sat in front of the monitor clicking until he accessed the right footage. Drake could barely contain his impatience, smothering the urge to tell Fleming to get a move on.

Eventually Fleming found the coverage from Saturday evening.

'You can fast forward the footage to at least ten thirty.' Drake hoped he didn't sound too abrupt.

They watched as the timer clicked on. The waiting was

unbearable. Drake glanced at his watch. 'Can you speed up slightly.' Fleming gave him a hurt look but did as he was told. They kept looking for a pedestrian, a hooded woman, walking or running or jogging. But there was little activity apart from vehicles passing. It would have taken Dawn no more than a few minutes to walk from the rugby club up the path towards Cleveland Avenue. But there was no sign of her.

'Go back, go back.' Drake raised his voice, realising he had missed something. 'Start again at ten.'

Fleming restarted the footage and now Drake focused on the cars and not the pedestrians. At ten forty-two he was rewarded as an Audi drove sedately past the property.

'Stop it right there,' Drake blurted out. 'I need the number plate of that car.'

Chapter 40

Luned sat at her desk staring at the photographs of the three victims pinned to the Incident Room board before turning her gaze to the mugshots of the persons of interest. The looming deadline for a decision to be made about releasing Jack Beltrami had dominated the comments Drake and Sara had made the previous evening. The inspector had resigned himself to the inevitability that Jack Beltrami would be released on bail. Knowing about the history between Drake and the Beltrami family underlined for Luned the necessity of being objective. Arriving early that morning, she started working on the mobile data on Beltrami's handset while Gareth analysed the laptop and computer removed from his home. Several hours of work lay ahead of them.

It worried her whether, in the middle of the activity focused on Jack Beltrami, other threads had been overlooked. Her gaze drifted over to the images of Debbie and Tina, the young girls reported missing from the care home in Liverpool.

She found their personal details and their early childhood made for harrowing reading. Tina's mother had left an abusive partner and Debbie's single mother had been a drug addict unable to cope with the demands of raising a child. Drake had commented in team briefings about the importance of tracing the girls and Luned agreed. Protecting children in society was so paramount. So where were they now?

The surveillance of the property where the girls had last been staying proved inconclusive. She searched in vain for details of any inquiries undertaken in the adjacent properties. Drake had been convinced that the abduction of both girls was linked to the persons of interest in their inquiry. She decided to leave the work on Beltrami, at least for now. She requested details of the ownership of the property where they believed the girls had been staying. The land registry surprised Luned by returning confirmation quickly – the owner was a Christopher Ireland. The name was unfamiliar. Protocol demanded she check out the name, so she searched the police national computer. There were several individuals with the same surname but no Christophers with a criminal record. So she turned to the intelligence database of the Wales Police Service hoping for more information. The monitor on her desk soon filled with details about the background of Christopher Ireland and it reassured Luned that she wasn't wasting time.

Christopher Ireland's known associates and his 'suspected criminal activities' made for interesting reading. Organised crime groups spread their tentacles wide and, like a spider's web, once a person was caught it was impossible to escape.

When she read that Ireland was linked to Ritchie O'Brien, she did a double take, her alertness sharpened. Another search of the electoral roll quickly told her that Christopher Ireland lived in Shotton, a journey of ten minutes from the address where the girls had been staying. Had they been taken there?

Establishing the whereabouts of both girls wasn't part of the murder inquiries. But Inspector Drake had made it a priority finding them. Where were they? It niggled in Luned's mind.

She stood up, grabbed her bag and the light fleece draped over her chair and left the Incident Room. Normally she would never have done anything impulsive, normally she wouldn't have defied Detective Inspector Drake, but having two teenagers trafficked into Deeside as modern-day slaves wasn't normal.

She journeyed eastwards, a grain of regret working its way into her mind like a stone in a shoe. But she pressed on and soon she drove down the street of terraced properties where both girls had been living. Before leaving the car, she called Winder for an update.

'I can't talk. The full search team here are taking Dawn Piper's place apart. And the boss is on his way.'

'What are you looking for?'

'There's some DVDs with videos apparently.'

Luned rang off and left the car.

The occupiers of the first two properties had never heard of Christopher Ireland nor had they ever seen him. Luned pressed on despite the initial disappointments. Two empty houses followed. She jotted down into her notebook the numbers in case a return visit might be needed. Her disappointment turned to despondency as she reached the end and the reactions from householders were shaking heads and blank faces.

She turned into a side street and passing a lane to her left that backed onto the property where the girls had been staying, she faced another terrace. Benidorm was the name of the first and as Luned neared up to the door, she glimpsed a framed holiday poster in the front room advertising the virtue of holidays in the Spanish resort. Spain was a long way from Deeside even on a warm summer's morning, Luned thought wistfully.

Preliminary introductions concluded and her warrant card back in her purse, Luned spoke to the householder, a cheery-looking woman in her fifties with tangerine-coloured hair and leathery skin. 'We believe that two young girls may have been living at one of the properties in the adjacent street. We need to trace them.'

Behind her Luned could see two trolley cases with miniature locks attached to the zips.

'Are you going on holiday?' Luned smiled hoping to put the woman at ease.

'Benidorm, love.' Listening to the thick Lancashire twang made a change from the commonplace Scouse accent. 'They were a scrawny looking pair.'

Luned stiffened imperceptibly. 'What can you tell me?'

'They looked shifty to me. But then again, I'm a bit

suspicious. We've fitted new locks on all the windows and doors. Takes me an hour to lock up before I go on holiday. We always rent this little apartment in Benidorm. We'll be there until October and then over Christmas.'

'Do you remember when you saw them last?'

'I always take the dog for a walk last thing. I don't like him making a mess in the house. He was my mother's, poor thing.' Luned smiled sympathetically hoping she meant the pet. 'I was coming home one night – now let me remember when it was. It was Monday, must have been. I'd finished watching a film with Tom Hanks on Netflix. Then I took Bernie for a walk. That's when I saw the girls being bundled into his car, just as I turned into the road.'

Luned scribbled the details in her notebook.

'Did you recognise who it was?'

'It was Christopher. He gave me a sort of nervous twitch of a laugh.'

'Was there anybody else with him?'

The woman frowned as she dipped into her memory. She shook her head. 'I don't think so. But it was difficult to see inside the car. It had tinted glass.'

'And did you notice the make of the car by any chance?' Luned said slowly.

Another moment's contemplation before the woman looked down at Luned. 'I think it was an Audi.'

Winder stood in the kitchen of Dawn Piper's property as the search team pulled everything apart. Cupboards were dismantled and unscrewed from the wall. Other officers were upstairs searching every drawer in every cupboard, opening the wardrobes and taking bedding apart. Electric saws made quick work of the floorboards and torches illuminated between the joists. So far nothing had been found. Winder speculated whether Drake's information was reliable.

The team paused when Drake and Sara arrived before aiming to start downstairs.

'Nothing, yet, boss,' Winder said.

'How much has been done?'

Winder dipped his head upwards. 'They've finished upstairs.'

Drake took the stairs to the first floor. Sara and Winder followed him. Organised carnage was the best way to describe the scene in the first bedroom, Winder thought. A shredded mattress along with the divan were pushed against one wall alongside a wardrobe and chest of drawers. A narrow film of dust hung in the air. It tickled Winder's nostrils, Drake turned up his nose.

'What a way to live,' Drake announced.

Winder stood in the corridor as Drake and Sara examined the rear bedroom. A similar scene awaited them, and they quickly retreated, crowding the landing. Drake made for the bathroom at the end and scanned the inside. Black and green streaks stained the grouting in the shower cubicle and a sickly smell of human excrement clung to the air. The toilet had been screwed against the external wall underneath the sill of a small window. Drake tapped on the discreet wooden panelling behind the toilet that stretched along the wall towards the nearby basin and pedestal. He turned to Winder, a frown creasing his forehead. 'Have they taken this off? It sounds hollow.'

'I don't know, boss.'

'Let's find out.'

Winder yelled for the search team supervisor who quickly ran up the stairs. He listened intently as Drake explained exactly what he needed to have done. He returned moments later with a box of tools and quickly got to work.

As the last of the upright timbers came away, a plastic bag from a well-known supermarket appeared hanging on a nail protruding from the wall. The officer reached over and handed it to Drake.

It looked tacky. Drake handled it gingerly and after peering inside he turned to Winder and Sara. 'There are some DVDs in here. We need to get these examined without delay.'

Before leaving the property, Drake turned to the search team supervisor. 'When we need a full search, that's precisely what I expect.'

The officer gave Drake a sheepish nod. 'Of course, sir.'

Stepping out into the street, Winder squinted against the summer sunshine and noticed Luned's car pulling up behind his own. She jumped out and ran over to them. 'I've found someone who saw one of Ritchie O'Brien's associates taking the girls from that house where the pharmacy assistant thought they lived.'

'Excellent, Luned,' Drake said. 'Back to headquarters, now.'

Chapter 41

Drake stood staring over Winder's shoulder as he booted up his computer. On the journey back to headquarters an image of Jack Beltrami's face had haunted Drake's thoughts. He had authorised Beltrami's release earlier, but Councillor Beedham's reference to Beltrami made him hope that the DVDs they were about to watch might implicate Beltrami sufficiently to enable him to be charged.

The camera angle recording the footage in Fleming's home made it impossible to identify the registration number of the Audi that had passed his house on the evening Dawn was killed. The darkened windows prevented them from seeing an outline of the driver or any of the passengers, which only exacerbated Drake's frustration.

Once the monitor flickered into life, Winder found the DVDs and inserted the first into the machine. Drake took a deep breath and fixed the screen with an intense concentration, as did Sara and Luned.

Despite the elevated position of the camera angle, Drake recognised the location where Dawn Piper's footage had been recorded.

'That's taken inside The Lamb, Ritchie O'Brien's place,' Drake said.

Sara nodded.

'She must have concealed it. Clever,' Winder said.

'It probably cost her life,' Luned announced, sharing with the team what was on everyone's mind.

They stood watching the footage, waiting. Soon they were rewarded with an image of Ritchie O'Brien entering the room with three other men.

'Stop it there,' Drake snapped. 'Who are these men?'

Luned squinted at the screen. 'I'm sure one of those is Christopher Ireland. I've seen his image when I searched the intel database.'

Winder nodded. 'I can get some facial recognition done

on the other two.'

'Get it done,' Drake retorted. 'Restart the footage.'

Winder clicked on his mouse and the activity restarted. Drake and his team watched in silence as they listened to Ritchie O'Brien organising the activities of his drug dealing business. The three men produced, in turn, thick wads of cash that were counted carefully around the table. Ritchie O'Brien got up and from a cupboard behind the door he drew out a plastic box and from it distributed various sachets and wraps of drugs. It was a simple commercial activity. The employees of O'Brien's business were being given stock to distribute, help them build relationships, create regular customers all longing for their next fix.

'There's enough to arrest O'Brien for supplying, surely?' Luned said her voice edged with desperation.

'Do we know his mobile number?' Drake said.

The likelihood was that Ritchie O'Brien changed his handset every month, maybe even more frequently. Three heads shook a reply.

'Talk to Jim Finch. I need to know if there is any information on Ritchie O'Brien's recent number. There must be something we could triangulate.'

Winder slotted the second DVD into the computer compartment and they waited whilst the machine hummed as it read the desk. It was dusk on the footage, a street light illuminated a car park.

'I know that place.' Now it was Sara who recognised the location. 'It's where we spoke to Knox after Caston had been discovered.'

At first it seemed that Dawn was sitting on one of the park benches, but the camera was unnaturally still. 'She's got it propped up against something again,' Winder said.

A black Audi turned into the car park and a figure got out. There was no mistaking Jack Beltrami and his familiar swagger. Moments later a Range Rover swept in and parked right in the middle. When Paul Kenny jumped out Drake's mouth dried. So much for never visiting Deeside.

Both men spoke for a few seconds and got back into their cars. Kenny followed Beltrami and then the footage stopped. It restarted, only this time it was jerky, obviously the phone was being hand held. Drake could make out the clear outline of the *Duke of Lancaster* concreted into its berth. The sound of clothes against shrubbery was clear as though Dawn was hunched up against the brambles near the ship. There was the sound of indistinct chatter but making out a conversation wasn't possible.

The sight of Beltrami walking next to Paul Kenny made Drake feel breathless. 'Stop there, stop it there.' Winder did as he was told. 'Can you zoom in on the faces of Beltrami and Kenny.' Winder fiddled with the mouse. Soon the image of both men filled the screen. It energised Drake, refocused his mind on the possibility that Beltrami really was involved.

After Winder restarted the footage the team sat watching both men passing the time of day as though they were old friends. Occasionally Beltrami jerked a hand up towards the old passenger ferry and Kenny nodded.

The second piece of footage on the DVD displayed Dawn's whispering face. 'I'm in the engine room of the Duke.' She looked around nervously before reversing the angle of the camera and walking down a metal stairway into the bowels of the ship. Even from the poor quality of the footage illuminated by a powerful torch Dawn was holding, Drake could understand Sutherland's comments about the difficulty of searching the vessel.

Dawn announced that she had discovered the whereabouts of drugs hidden in the *Duke of Lancaster* and that she wanted to record the location. After five minutes of negotiating her way around the inside of the engine room, she finally got to her knees and slid on her back, the camera close to her face. Seconds later Dawn pushed herself into a narrow recess and lifted out with one hand a small package shrouded in thick black tape.

'Knox said that she was going to produce the stash of drugs so that Beedham could take the credit for finding them and give himself some publicity,' Sara said.

'He's an unprincipled dishonest scumbag.' The disgust in Drake's voice surprised the other officers.

Winder contributed. 'Little wonder nobody trusts politicians. Most of them are in it for themselves. Get their noses into the trough and away they go.'

Once all the DVDs had been viewed, Drake almost fell into one of the chairs by the desks in the Incident Room, blowing out a mouthful of air. Winder and Luned organised coffee and returned with Drake's cafetière, his usual mug and instant for the rest of the team. A plate of stale digestives provided the fuel their bodies needed.

'We should have forensics from Cleveland Avenue first thing in the morning as well as the results from the park where Olivia Knox was found. If I'm right and we've got a crime scene for Dawn Piper's murder, there'll be DNA, forensic evidence, something to help us. And in the meantime, we've still got two teenagers to find.'

Luned added. 'I was going to suggest, sir, that we request a detailed triangulation report on the other mobile number common to Dawn Piper and Caston. We might be able to link it to Olivia Knox.'

Drake nodded.

Winder picked up the thread. 'Especially if we can place that number near the park where she was killed.'

Drake nodded again. 'And get full details of properties owned by Christopher Ireland and Ritchie O'Brien. If they are holding these two girls, it must be in a property in Deeside.'

Drake finished his coffee. 'Get some sleep tonight. A long day tomorrow.'

Back in his room he reached for the jacket on the wooden hanger on the coat stand and draped it carefully on his left arm before heading back through the Incident Room and out into the car park. The A55 was quiet, a stream of lorries from the port at Holyhead trundled eastwards. He arrived back in Felinheli his eyes heavy, his body fatigued. Annie would ask about his day, but he wouldn't be able to tell her what had happened or what was likely to happen tomorrow. He sat in the car for a few seconds looking up at the light seeping around the blind on the kitchen window. He was glad to be home.

Chapter 42

Drake pulled into the car park at headquarters a little before seven-thirty the following morning after a journey uninterrupted by heavy traffic. A call from his car to Mike Foulds had confirmed that the crime scene manager was already at his desk. The normal hub of activity at Northern Division hadn't got started as Drake threaded his way through the corridors to the forensic department where he greeted Foulds.

'Morning, Mike.'

'You're up early. Couldn't sleep?'

'Early bird and all that. I need your preliminary report on the possible crime scene at Cleveland Avenue.'

Foulds nodded. 'Good news. We did find traces of blood. And it matches Dawn Piper.'

It vindicated everything Drake and the team had been working for. He wanted to punch the air.

'And we found a watch in the undergrowth. It had a small engraving on the back – "To Dawn from Mum and Dad".'

Drake settled back in his chair. It was progress, real progress. 'Now we know the crime scene.'

Foulds added, 'I've got a photograph of the watch.' He clicked into his computer. A couple of seconds later an image appeared on the monitor. 'It's not a very valuable piece.'

Someone would need to contact Jane, Dawn's sister, and get confirmation it had belonged to Dawn. 'Can you print me a copy?'

Foulds clicked his mouse and behind them a printer purred into life.

'And we took lots of samples of the gravel and soil and dust so we'll try and make a match to evidence we recovered from Dawn's clothes. We also removed a cigarette butt. They are always a good source of DNA.'

'And anything from the scene of Olivia Knox's murder or Caston's home?'

'We drew a blank at Caston's home. There was a ton of soil samples and shrubbery and twigs from the park where Knox was found. There was no sign of any weapon and from the pathologist's report there's nothing to suggest any fragments left on her body. But it is early days. You need to give us time.'

Time is what Drake did not have.

The inquiry needed to be finished. He sensed he was within touching distance of something, a conclusion, finding the girls, establishing guilt. But how much of that was his desire to see Beltrami prosecuted?

'Send me your preliminary report,' Drake said standing up. Then he left the forensic department clutching the printed image of Dawn's watch.

Sara, Winder and Luned were already busy at their desks, the first coffees and teas of the day in steaming mugs on coasters, a bag of pastries placed strategically in front of Gareth Winder. At the board Drake pinned up the A4 sheet of paper announcing over his shoulder.

'Forensics found samples of Dawn Piper's blood in Cleveland Avenue.' He turned to see three smug gratified faces looking over at him.

'You were right then, boss,' Sara said.

'One of you contact Jane Piper and ask her to confirm that the watch belonged to her sister.'

'I'll call her,' Sara said.

'We'll do a full review later this morning.' Drake paced over to his office.

Luned turned her attention to assembling all the details of what they knew about Ritchie O'Brien. He had several bank accounts, three credit card accounts and business accounts all interconnected with the businesses he ran. Putting together a summary would take some time so she got to work. It was painstaking stuff but rewarding, knowing there would be hours of toil ahead to plough their way through the statements.

Luned flicked through the bank statements scanning entries, knowing Inspector Drake would want to hear about progress later. There were payments for visits to a cinema in Chester, meals at restaurants, petrol filling stations and she noticed the regular debits at a supermarket – the same supermarket that had sold the mobile used to call Caston on the afternoon he died. They knew it wasn't Knox's but whose was it? Luned revisited her notes from her brief conversation with the shop at the supermarket in Chester. None of the staff could describe the buyer – hardly surprising when they told Luned they could sell between thirty and fifty new mobiles every day.

It reminded her she had still not viewed the CCTV footage the supermarket had sent her. Justifying her inactivity because the footage was of the main entrance to the store and not the mobile shop wasn't good enough, she chided herself. As soon as she established when the purchase had been completed, she scrolled back an hour and clicked play. The screen filled with the grainy images of customers pushing trolleys as they entered the store, others leaving, their trolleys packed with groceries.

She concentrated intently on scanning for familiar faces. After half an hour she clicked pause and sat back in her chair stretching her back. After a brief sojourn to the kitchen where she made coffee for herself and Winder, she decided to watch for another thirty minutes. Her concentration waned and she was about to finish when a figure walking out of the store struck her as familiar.

She paused the footage again, enlarged the image and glanced over at the Incident Room board for reassurance. She whistled under her breath. 'Ritchie O'Brien has got something to explain.'

Establishing the crime scene settled things in Sara's mind. Hopefully it would give Jane Piper a degree of closure, if only to learn where her sister had been killed. Sara composed how she would start the conversation. Dealing with grief was challenging and complex. The suffering of relatives of individuals murdered in cold blood was often underappreciated, Sara thought. She scooped up the handset of her phone. After finding Jane Piper's number she punched in the details.

'Have there been any developments?' Jane sounded nervous. She hadn't replied to Sara's initial greeting.

'I was calling to inform you we have now established the location where we believe Dawn was killed.'

Sara heard Jane catching her breath.

'Where?' Jane's voice trembled.

Sara gave Jane the barest outline. There was no recognition, no confirmation she knew Cleveland Avenue. 'Why was she there?'

'We think she was on her way to see a friend. The crime scene investigators did discover a watch at the scene.' Before Sara could continue Jane butted in. 'Did it have "To Dawn from Mum and Dad" engraved on the rear?'

'Yes,' Sara confirmed simply.

'They gave it to Dawn on her 18th birthday. She rarely took it off. What'll happen to it?'

'It will be returned to you once the case is complete.'

Sara couldn't answer Jane's questions asking about progress and identifying the killer or how long a prosecution might take. She promised to keep in touch and after finishing she hoped she had played a small part in Jane Piper's closure.

Sara spent the rest of the morning assisting Winder watching footage from the CCTV cameras in and around Cleveland Avenue area, hoping automatic number plate recognition would provide them with details of the Audi that had passed Fleming's property. It was a frustrating exercise and she left Winder staring at the screen.

Then she focused on the triangulation reports of the number common to Dawn Piper and Hubert Caston that they hadn't been able to trace. It had also called Olivia Knox on a couple of occasions. It confirmed the handset had been near to the park the evening Olivia Knox had been killed. It reminded Sara she needed to contact Jim Finch.

'Do you have information on the mobile number used by Ritchie O'Brien?'

Finch sounded wary. 'Why do you ask?'

'We are trying to triangulate his movements at the time of Olivia Knox's death.'

'I'm sure I've sent Inspector Drake everything I've got on Ritchie O'Brien's mobiles. But I'll double check. How is the investigation going?'

'We've recovered some DVDs from Dawn's property. She'd discovered where a stash of drugs had been stored on the *Duke of Lancaster*. And there was an interesting video of Ritchie O'Brien.'

'So you're making progress?'

Winder squealing in delight interrupted Sara. 'I have to go.'

She walked over towards his desk and watched as he enlarged the image of the number plates of the black Audi they had been searching for.

Intelligence from Jim Finch suggested Beltrami was involved in developing his drug dealing business into Deeside, but there was no evidence to implicate him in the deaths of Dawn Piper and Hubert Caston. The recent disclosures that Finch had been secretive had sown a seed of apprehension in Drake's mind. Was he being unfair? Drake hated the prospect that another police officer could not be trusted.

He tapped the ballpoint in his right hand on the notepad

on his desk. Beltrami was on bail and his passport surrendered so if evidence did emerge, he could be charged and interrogated. Drake allowed his imagination to run away with itself. Beltrami would confess to the murder of Olivia Knox followed by confessions to the other two murders. He sat back for a moment realising how absurd his thinking had become.

He moved the paperwork relating to Beltrami into a neat pile on the cupboard in a corner of his room. Only then could he focus on Ritchie O'Brien.

Drake pulled out a blank sheet of A4 paper from a drawer. It always helped to plot things out in a simple mind map format. He wrote the name Ritchie O'Brien in the centre and a circle around it. Above it to the right he jotted down the name Olivia Knox and drew an arrow towards O'Brien's name. She had been the first person to refer to O'Brien.

Underneath her name Drake added the name Dawn Piper and added an arrow to O'Brien's name. They knew from the CCTV footage from the Bluebell pub that O'Brien had been seen with Piper the night she died.

Drake paused for a moment. Innuendo, gossip and hearsay wouldn't get the inquiry very far. Drake needed evidence, the sort he could take to Superintendent Hobbs and then to a senior Crown prosecution lawyer with a recommendation that a murder charge stood a reasonable prospect of success.

He added Hubert Caston to the left-hand side, together with several exclamation marks. Then below Caston he scribbled 'zombie games' and underlined the words three times. He drew an arrow from Caston to the ring encircling O'Brien's name – Hubert had been threatened by O'Brien after all. Finally, he added the name Beedham with an arrow to Dawn's name.

At the bottom he wrote EVIDENCE and added 'videos x2', 'ANPR black Audi', 'watch' and 'Dawn's blood'. A pang of anger jolted his mind that he had spent too much time focusing on Jack Beltrami and not enough on Ritchie O'Brien. Another conversation with Finch would be needed to explain what he knew about Ritchie O'Brien. Hobbs would insist on having every scrap of information.

He sat back for a moment realising the exercise had been constructive and much like his past rituals it soothed the lingering anxiety. So, he got started on Ritchie O'Brien's background.

Standard financial checks had produced details of his bank accounts – all of which had healthy balances. A holiday in Antigua the previous Christmas had cost £10,000, substantially more than Drake was spending on his holiday in Disneyland Paris. The launderette O'Brien owned showed a decent profit as did the fish and chip café and the snooker club. Ritchie O'Brien avoided any of his drug dealing activity tainting his otherwise seemingly legitimate businesses. The runners lower down in the business had occasionally been prosecuted for supplying drugs but they pleaded guilty quickly and accepted the inevitable custodial sentence with the resignation of a hardened criminal. Most would return to Ritchie O'Brien's business activities on release and be suitably rewarded for their silence and loyalty.

Drake's attention was taken by an entry – property repairs and maintenance. It made him think of the two girls moved from one house to another in the Deeside towns. He took more of an interest in the accounts and tried unsuccessfully to find the property addresses. He paced to the threshold to the Incident Room and looked over at Luned.

'Have you got details of any residential property owned by O'Brien?'

'No, sir. It was next on my list.'

'I'm on to it.'

Back in his room, Drake scooped up the phone on his desk and followed standard protocol with the land registry demanding they provide full details of every property in Ritchie O'Brien's name. When the person at the other end explained he should expect a delay Drake snapped. 'I want it in the next hour. People's lives are at stake. Three people have been killed already.'

Drake slammed down the handset and waited. He chewed a nail sensing he might be criticised for not having done this exercise sooner.

Half an hour later an email reached his inbox. He drew his tongue over drying lips as he clicked it open and read the details of the three properties owned by Ritchie O'Brien. Then he did a Google search, opening a separate page for each but found that only one had a street view.

The other two were in isolated locations.

He bellowed for the team to join him. Sara sat down on one of the visitor chairs as did Luned. Winder adopted a wide-legged posture on the threshold.

'Updates, please,' Drake said.

Sara responded first. 'The number that called Dawn and Caston also called Olivia and it's near the park on the night she died.' Drake made to ask something, but Sara continued. 'And before you ask, being near the park isn't part of its normal pattern of activity.'

Drake looked at Winder who shared his discovery. 'The Audi outside Fleming's house is registered to an Alpha Motors of Warrington which is linked to Ritchie O'Brien.'

Luned added, 'And Ritchie O'Brien was seen on CCTV in the supermarket the same day that the mobile was bought.'

Drake turned to the three officers in front of him. 'Ritchie O'Brien owns two properties in the countryside near the Deeside towns. I'm going to see the super and request a search warrant for each and we'll divide up into two teams. If he's there, we arrest him. If not, we find him.'

Chapter 43

Drake ignored Superintendent Hobbs' gesture inviting him to sit down. He grasped in one hand the A4 sheet of paper with his scribbled mind map as he addressed his senior officer. His right leg twitched, the unfamiliarity of dealing with Hobbs making him edgy, especially when discussing his decision to arrest a suspect.

Once Drake had finished, Hobbs slowly crossed his arms and pulled them tight to his chest. 'And what is O'Brien's motive?'

'Knox and Dawn Piper had evidence that threatened to expose O'Brien as a major drug dealer. Perhaps she was prepared to give evidence, or she knew someone else who was prepared to give evidence, but the video Piper had would have rattled him.'

Hobbs looked unconvinced. 'And what about Caston's death?' Hobbs paused. Drake was uncertain whether he was expecting a reply. The superintendent continued. 'You're suggesting he was killed by O'Brien because he had decided to let a property to Kenny?' Hobbs shook his head.

Drake interjected. 'There are two teenage girls involved. They were last seen in a house owned by one of O'Brien's known associates. If there is any chance they are in either of O'Brien's properties, we have a duty to protect them.'

Hobbs stared at Drake for a few long seconds. Drake simply couldn't make out what was going on in his mind. He had been used to facial expressions, the occasional tapping of impatient fingers, a profanity or two, but trying to anticipate how Hobbs would react was challenging.

Slowly Hobbs announced, 'Have you contacted the appropriate team from social services?'

'I'm waiting for a phone call.' A lump developed in Drake's throat as he thought Hobbs would prevaricate.

'Good. I'll arrange a magistrate to issue the search

warrants you've requested. And find and arrest O'Brien.'

Drake stood for a moment allowing the realisation Hobbs had acceded to his request sink in.

Hobbs added, 'Anything else, Inspector?'

As Drake made the door he turned to Hobbs. 'I'll report progress in due course, sir.'

Back in the Incident Room Drake marched over to the board. He turned to face the team. 'Search warrants are being requested for both of O'Brien's properties and the address for Christopher Ireland in Shotton.' Now he saw determination in their eyes.

'We've got search teams ready,' Sara said.

'Good. We'll divide up. Gareth and Luned both of you lead the search in one of the properties and Sara and I will do the other. Have social services called whilst I was with the super?'

Shaking heads now.

Drake pulled his mobile from a trouser pocket and stalked over to his room. Every local authority in North Wales had a specialist team ready around the clock to protect the interests of young children. After apologising for not getting back to him, the duty officer confirmed a team could be at either of the properties within fifteen minutes of a phone call. Drake jotted down the contact details of the social worker in charge and rang off.

It was late afternoon now and they only had a few hours of daylight left. Drake paused and gazed out over the lush parkland surrounding Northern Division headquarters. If he was right about the girls, he wondered what their living conditions were like. If they were as squalid as the others they had seen, then O'Brien deserved to be locked up for a long time.

Drake walked over to the coat stand and dragged on his suit jacket. He joined his team in the Incident Room. 'Tell the search teams we're ready. I don't want any flashing lights or sirens. Are there stab jackets and tasers in the cars?'

Winder nodded. 'I checked earlier, boss.'

'Good. Let's go.'

Drake hurried down to the car park, Sara alongside. Winder and Luned headed for the second pool car allocated by operational support. Drake pointed the remote at the other vehicle and he and Sara got in.

'Was Superintendent Hobbs okay with authorising searches?' Sara said without a hint of criticism. Getting accustomed to the new senior officer would be challenging. Drake knew Sara and the rest of the team would want to know that the superintendent was supportive.

'Yes, he double-checked that we had contacted the social services department.'

Drake kept his opinions about Superintendent Hobbs to himself. He drove down towards the A55 heading east for the Deeside towns. Winder and Luned followed, the search team vehicles a discreet distance behind.

Soon a message reached Drake's mobile that the warrants had been authorised. 'We're good to go then,' he said and pressed the accelerator to the floor.

Drake indicated left off the dual carriageway for the junction signposting Flint Mountain but he swung right taking the bridge over the A55 and down into the village of Northop. At a set of traffic lights, he caught sight of Winder several cars behind but there was no sign of the search teams. Drake drummed his fingers over the top of the steering wheel as he urged the lights to change. When they did, he almost stalled the car as he turned left. It led him to another bridge that crossed the A55 and immediately afterwards he noticed Winder signalling right to take a minor road towards Ewloe Castle.

Sara studied the satnav and warned Drake they were nearing their destination. He slowed and pulled into the verge by a field gate allowing the search team vehicle to pull up behind.

'It's only another three hundred metres,' Sara said.

Drake called Winder although Luned answered. 'How near are you?'

'We're about to park and the satnav says we are two hundred and thirty metres away.'

'Good. Let's get this done.' Drake finished the call without waiting for Luned to reply. He turned to Sara. 'Let's hope those girls are there.'

He pulled out into the main road and silence and apprehension filled the car as they made the short journey down Mold Road. Haulfryn was an uncommon name for a property in this mostly anglicised area of North Wales. It was a dilapidated, detached house set back from the road. A path led up to the front door from a gate in the stone wall topped with a line of dwarf railings. Small patches of overgrown grass badly needed cutting. Drake pulled into the gravelled drive, the search team vehicle following behind him.

The place felt empty. A clump of weeds bristled from one end of the gutter and underneath it discoloured render from cascading rain water. The two officers from the search team headed for the front door as Drake and Sara made for a gate in a rear wall. It was an old-fashioned latch that Drake undid easily enough but the door squeaked open. To his right were several outbuildings. The glass in the windows of one was cracked and in another gaping holes replaced frames.

Drake turned his attention back to the main property and walked over to the rear door, hammering on it. All he heard was an empty echo. Sara cupped her hands to the filthy glass of the kitchen window nearby. 'Doesn't look like anybody's been living here.'

Both search team officers now joined Drake. The taller one, who had a shaven head and five-day stubble asked Drake, 'Which door do you want us to break down, sir?' It sounded as though he relished the opportunity.

Drake stood back to one side and tipped his head at the

door. 'Get this one done.'

The smaller and stockier officer laboured towards the door with a mini battering ram quaintly called the big key. The sound of wood splintering filled the air after a couple of sharp taps. The officer stood to one side and Drake and Sara moved quickly into the property, searching each room on the ground floor.

They found no one. The kitchen was surprisingly tidy. Plates and mugs and crockery had been stored away, as had various cutlery. A tall fridge had the barest essentials – milk and tubs of margarine. Newspapers and magazines littered the surface of a table in one of the rooms downstairs, alongside a large flat-screen television.

'Let's go upstairs,' Drake said, and shouted a warning, 'police, is there anybody there?'

He didn't wait for a reply.

None came.

He took the stairs to the first floor with Sara and inspected each of the bedrooms. The sleeping bags crumpled from recent use, sets of pyjamas discarded on pillows. Sara called out from the bathroom, 'They've been staying here, boss.'

Drake joined her and she produced the same prescription medicine they discovered at the last property.

Drake despaired – always one step behind O'Brien. Did he know they would be executing this search warrant? And if he did, how?

'Dammit. Where the bloody hell are they?'

Drake reached for his mobile and dialled Winder's number who answered after a couple of rings. 'I hope you've got some good news,' Drake said.

'Sorry, boss.' Drake's heart sagged. 'There's nobody here.'

'We're almost finished here – get over to us as soon as you can.'

The search team at the Shotton property had a similar

report.

Back outside, Drake stood in the cooling summer evening air, relieved to be out of the stale air inside the house but worried that two teenage girls were still unaccounted for.

He turned to Sara. 'Let's search the outbuildings just in case.'

Drake and Sara took the set of low buildings to the left. The two other officers made for the semi-derelict sheds to the right. A slatted wooden door gave way to Drake's hefty kick and the smell of manure and horse feed assaulted their nostrils. He glanced around but could see no doorway into another property.

Sara emerged from the adjacent doorway shaking her head. Drake walked over to her as did the two uniformed officers. They gazed out over fields and pastures.

Drake stared down into a thicket of trees a hundred yards or so from where they stood. He could see the ridge of a low-lying building. He raised a hand and pointed down towards it. 'What's that?'

Drake didn't wait for the others to answer – he jogged down the field. His newly cleaned brogues squelched through the droppings of cattle dung and he cursed himself as he worried that the hem of his trousers would be filthy. But he had two girls to worry about. They were his priority.

He pushed on and his jog turned into a run as his own momentum propelled him to the bottom. He hadn't sprinted like this for years – his chest tightened as his lungs wanted to explode.

They reached the small cottage that looked like something out of a Lord of the Rings film. Small windows were sealed shut and white paint peeled off the wooden slatted door. Sara put a face to the window and shouted, 'There's someone inside.'

Drake nodded at both search team officers who had joined them. 'Break it down, now, but be careful.'

Sara shouted, 'Stand back from the door.'

The big key smashed the door that careered open. Drake and Sara were the first over the threshold.

The two teenage girls cowered in one corner. Even in the poor lighting, Drake saw the resemblance to the photographs of Debbie and Tina on the board back in the Incident Room.

Both girls looked terrified.

'We're not going to harm you. We're the police. We've come to take you to somewhere safe.'

Ten minutes later Drake had made two phone calls. The duty officer from the social services department confirmed their emergency response team would be with them very quickly. Sara helped both Debbie and Tina out of the cottage and escorted them up the field back to Haulfryn.

Winder and Luned were waiting for Drake and Sara. Winder was sipping on a can of soft drink and Luned was halfway through a supermarket sandwich. Winder offered Sara and Drake a can each. 'I thought you'd like something to drink, boss,' Winder said.

'You've all done well. At least we've been able to find Debbie and Tina.'

'And they've both confirmed Ritchie O'Brien was responsible for imprisoning them,' Sara added.

'Any sign of him?' Luned said.

Drake shook his head. 'We'd better ask them if they have any idea where he might be.' He scooped up a sandwich and drink Luned had bought and walked over to his car with Sara, where both girls were sitting in the rear seat. He smiled at them and handed them the sandwich and his drink. 'You must be hungry.'

They took the food and ate ravenously.

Drake continued once they'd finished. 'We've got social workers arriving in a minute and they'll look after you from now on. When did you last see Ritchie O'Brien?'

Debbie spoke with a strong Liverpool accent. 'This

afternoon. He was here and got really angry talking to somebody on the phone. That's why he locked us up in the cottage. He got really worked up.'

Tina nodded.

'Do you have any idea where he could be going?'

'He was meeting someone.'

'Did you hear a name?'

Both girls shook their heads. Then Debbie continued. 'He said something like "we'll have to move it tonight" and then said about zombies getting in the way.'

Chapter 44

'It can only mean one thing. The drugs are still in the *Duke of Lancaster* and that he's going there tonight.' Drake straightened, buttoned his jacket, adjusted his tie. 'We need to find Ritchie O'Brien. Sara you're with me, let's visit the *Duke of Lancaster*. Gareth and Luned you get over to The Lamb and see if he is there. And then try the takeaway and the other addresses we have for him. And if you find him, arrest him.'

Winder and Luned said in unison. 'Yes, sir.'

Drake dragged a hand over his shirt sleeve and read the time. The social services team were late. Before he could call the duty officer, he saw a car approaching, signalling to stop. He handed over responsibility for Debbie and Tina to the social workers and joined Sara in his car as she punched the postcode into the satnav. 'It's twenty-seven minutes.'

'Let's make it in twenty,' Drake said starting the car engine and accelerating away from Haulfryn.

The satnav took them down onto the main Chester Road that led up to Mostyn docks. They passed the Connah's Quay power station on the right and Drake ignored the speed limits as he flashed at the occasional dawdling motorist and accelerated to overtake slowing traffic.

The journey took them near the park where they had spoken to Olivia as she munched on her burger the evening Caston's body had been discovered. The location was at the other end of the park where Olivia had been killed. She had been a regular at the van, Drake recalled from her friendly conversation with the owner. A possible link germinated in his mind.

He slowed as he reached the entrance.

'What's up, boss?'

'We need to check out one more thing.' Drake drove onto the dusty surface of the car park.

The burger van was quiet but the smell of fried onions

and bacon fat hung in the air. He hurried over and looked up at the owner, making certain she could see his warrant card.

'I'm investigating the death of Olivia Knox. I believe she was a regular customer.'

The woman sighed heavily. 'That's right. Terrible what happened to her.'

'Did you see her the night she was killed?'

The woman frowned and nodded. 'Only from a distance. We had finished and were getting ready to leave. She was talking to someone in her car.'

'Did you see who it was?'

'I can't be certain, love, but he was smoking and the window was wound down.'

Once Drake had her contact details they jogged back to the car.

'Does O'Brien smoke, boss?'

'Only one way to find out,' Drake said powering out of the car park. 'We'll ask him.'

Lights flickered from the villages and towns on the Wirral, across the Dee estuary as the sun weakened. Drake paid no attention to the thirty mile an hour speed limit as he powered through Flint and then on towards Bagillt and Greenfield. He caught sight of the outline of the old passenger ferry against the skyline. He took the same road for the vessel he had done the first time and the surface was still uneven and full of potholes.

A small stream of people chattering energetically streamed past Drake and Sara as they made for the makeshift entrance.

'Sounds like they had a good time,' Sara said.

The woman sitting behind the reception desk had black hair, black eye make-up, and heavy eyelashes that seemed to wave at Drake as he spoke to her. 'Have you seen this man here tonight?' He pushed over the image of Ritchie O'Brien displayed on his mobile screen.

She peered at it.

Drake lost patience. 'Come on. Can you remember him?'

'Yeah, come to think of it suppose I do. He was in a hell of a rush.'

'Have you seen him leave?'

The woman pondered.

'For Christ's sake.' Drake made for the entrance door towards the zombie complex experience, listening to her plaintive yell.

'You can't go in there, you haven't paid.'

A few yards away was a metal staircase leading up to the main deck of the vessel. Drake and Sara sprinted over and brushed aside an inquiry by a member of staff for their tickets with a jab of their warrant cards into his face. Their shoes clattered against the superstructure and Drake felt his lungs aching again as he reached the top and entered the vessel.

He stood for a moment gathering his breath. He looked around. A dusty smell filled the air. The carpets were threadbare and the dimmed lighting made it difficult to make out exactly where they were. Drake heard the crackle of a radio before he saw a man approaching. 'What do you want? We've finished for the day.'

'Detective Inspector Ian Drake of the Wales Police Service. And this is Detective Sergeant Sara Morgan. Can you get some lights switched on? I mean *proper* lights.'

'I'm not sure I can do that.'

Meanwhile Sara was fiddling with her phone and found the torch function. An intense bright light lit up a tall thin man with black streaks over his cheeks, black mascara around his eyes and a black-and-white T-shirt with the outlines of a skeleton. Sara pushed her warrant card at him illuminating it at the same time. Drake followed suit.

'I want this place lit up now.'

The man scurried off to a cupboard a few yards away where he used a small torch and he fiddled with the bank of switches. Eventually fluorescent tubes in glass domed lights flickered into life. Drake trooped over towards a board displaying an outline of the decks of the ship.

'We only use deck A for the zombie attraction,' the staff member said.

The plans showed the first-class lounge, dozens of numbered cabins including several called deluxe, a first-class restaurant and the quaintly titled 'First-class Smoke Room'. Second-class passengers enjoyed a lounge and a cafeteria. It was difficult to imagine now that this vessel had been considered the height of luxury in the 1960s and '70s.

'Who else is on board?' Drake said.

'Nobody much, I was finishing up.'

Drake glared at the man. 'Stay here and don't let anybody off the ship until I tell you.'

His vigorous blinking created a comic impression as the whites of his eyes alternated with the black mascara. 'I'll try and fiddle with these controls to get the lights on in the corridor.'

Drake studied the outline of the decks on the vessel carefully. At one end of the lobby was a corridor leading down past numerous first-class cabins. He raised a hand towards a glazed door to his left and turned to Sara. 'You take that corridor and I'll take the opposite. Keep your mobile at hand.'

Drake found his own mobile and fumbled for the torch setting. Soon both Drake and Sara had mobiles in hand with lights burning intensely. Drake pushed open the door and made his way down the first-class cabin corridor pushing open each door as he did so. In the first cabin, Drake recoiled when he saw an enormous tall zombielike creature that held a cutlass in its hand.

Drake retreated and moved to the next. Two dummies lay on the bed inside the cabin both with javelins protruding from their chest and head. By now Drake got into the swing of things, realising the extras the company paid for presumably stood in the cabin frightening the paying public. Why anyone would pay money for this sort of experience dumbfounded Drake.

Back in the corridor, music blared out of speakers. He heard a muffled apology from the man in the hallway. It was like the music in a cheap amusement arcade horror show and not a scary zombielike tune.

Each cabin had a variation on a scene intended to frighten. The darkness would probably do that by itself, Drake thought, as he imagined hordes of actors and extras stalking the first-class deck of the vessel doing their best to make people think they were getting value for money. There was no sign of Ritchie O'Brien or anyone else for that matter.

Drake stopped and called Sara. It was a poor signal and he could barely make out what she was saying, but he got the gist – she had seen nothing.

By the end of the corridor he noticed a light bobbing up and down from a link corridor and assumed it was Sara. He hadn't realised how spooky it could actually be standing in the corridor of a vessel used as a zombie attraction.

She turned to look in his direction as she reached the corridor and they walked together towards the stern. 'He could be anywhere.'

Drake made no reply and carried on until they faced a bulkhead door. He pushed it open. The cool evening air chilled his face as he walked onto a flat area that covered the original poop deck of the vessel.

From the starboard side he heard the sound of footsteps and muffled conversation. He nodded briskly to Sara and then ran over to the starboard railing. Ahead of them were five lifeboats held in place on tall gantries and near the last was a figure.

Drake set off in pursuit yelling at the same time. 'Police, stop!'

The figure paused, glanced over at Drake and at the end

he left the shadow of the vessel's bridge that jutted over the deck. The dying sunshine illuminated the man's face – Drake recognised O'Brien.

'There's nowhere you can run,' Drake gasped as he reached the final lifeboat gantry. Sara was close behind him, her breathing heavy. 'You've got nowhere to hide and we've got Debbie and Tina. It's over Ritchie.'

O'Brien leaned on the handrail behind him. 'You've got no fucking idea. No idea at all who is involved.'

'What the hell do you mean?'

'Just that.'

'You're under arrest Ritchie O'Brien for the murder of Olivia Knox and—'

'You can go fuck yourself.'

'Stay exactly where you are.'

Drake heard Sara fiddling with a pair of handcuffs.

He started towards O'Brien.

Then a gun shot rang out and O'Brien's head snapped backwards. His grip on the handrail loosened and his arm trailed over the edge of the boat, followed in slow motion by the rest of his body.

Drake ran over. He looked down and saw the crumpled remains of Ritchie O'Brien on the concrete below.

Chapter 45

Drake and Sara ran round the deck and heard the crash of a door closing into place. Drake yanked at the handle, but it was stuck fast. He tugged and heaved and cursed until finally it gave way. Drake almost fell against Sara. They peered into the murky surroundings of the stairwell. Descending would take them back to the lobby they had reached when they first entered the vessel. He gestured to Sara and they hurried down the stairs.

In the far corner of the lobby where they had spoken to a member of staff, they now saw his body slumped into a doorway. It took Drake a few short urgent strides to reach the man. He knelt and put two fingers to the man's throat, elated when he felt a pulse.

'He's alive,' Drake shouted.

'I'll call for an ambulance.' Sara reached for her mobile.

'And get an armed response unit here urgently.'

Drake stood and made for the staircase leading off the ship and looked out over the surrounding countryside. No sign of life other than the lights from the reception building on the quayside. He shouted for Sara to join him. The metal staircase rattled and complained as he and Sara sprinted down. The reception was empty, but Drake could see a doorway into a rear office. Inside, the same woman Drake had seen earlier sat in front of the monitor screen, a set of wireless headphones clamped firmly to her head which bobbed up and down rhythmically. The other member of staff emerged from a kitchen area. The woman yanked off the headphones when she saw Drake.

Evacuating the civilians from a scene where a gunman was present was the only priority.

Drake yelled, 'Police.' He held aloft his warrant card. 'We need to evacuate everyone here. Now.'

She blinked her surprise, the shock rendering her

speechless. Her mouth fell open, her eyes stretched wide in disbelief. 'What…?'

'Now. Both of you.'

Drake and Sara ushered them out into the chill of the evening gloom, the last of the summer sunshine having disappeared over the horizon. Drake turned to the startled employees. 'Follow us, quickly.'

He led them to his car. In the distance they heard the sirens of an ambulance and a police car approaching. The armed response vehicle was the first to arrive. As Drake explained the details to two armed officers, an ambulance pulled up behind the armed response vehicle. One of the armed officers made for the metal staircase and bounded up towards the entrance to the vessel securing the entrance. Another accompanied a paramedic to the crumpled body of Ritchie O'Brien.

Winder and Luned soon joined Drake and Sara.

'What happened, boss?' Winder asked.

Drake tipped his head towards the paramedic kneeling by O'Brien. 'Ritchie O'Brien was shot and then he fell off the deck.'

'Were you there?' Worry laced Luned's voice.

Drake nodded. 'There is somebody else involved. Somebody wanted Ritchie O'Brien dead. Let's get back to headquarters. We've got to go through everything again.'

Drake ran back to his car, Sara following behind. He flicked a switch and the blue flashing lights illuminated the night sky. Winder was close behind as both cars hammered along the A55 back to headquarters. Speed limits could go to hell, Drake thought as he swept cars from the outside lane with a flash of his lights and a blast of the car horn.

Back at headquarters, all four officers ran up the steps of reception and then through the building to the Incident Room where Drake paced towards the board. As he peered at the face of Dawn Piper he listened as his team settled into their chairs. His gaze drifted over towards Cameron Toft.

'Why did Toft follow Dawn?'

Drake turned to face the team. Sara replied, 'He gave us our first direct evidence linking Dawn to Paul Kenny.'

'And Toft knew of Kenny's background in organised crime and his links with county lines dealers,' Luned continued. 'And the photograph gave us our first line of inquiry.'

'It made us think that Paul Kenny was involved,' Drake said. 'And it distracts us from Ritchie O'Brien.'

Winder frowned. 'So you do think that Toft is involved with O'Brien?'

Sara again. 'It might make sense of the photograph.'

Luned had been searching through the paperwork on her desk before she looked up, excitement evident in her face. 'Toft was in the army. We have evidence he boasted about being a good shot.'

'Of course,' Drake exclaimed. 'And Finch and Knox suggested he was involved in small-scale cannabis dealing. Perhaps he wants to develop his own business.'

'And he's consistently lied to us about Dawn and social services,' Sara said.

Luned's contribution silenced the rest of the team. 'It's difficult to see Toft being complicit in the murder of the woman who mothered his child.'

Drake had been mulling over another thread worming its way into his mind. It had been there from the early stages of the inquiry and Drake hated the consequences. He turned to face the board, hoping he could find a reason to definitively exclude Jim Finch from his suspicions.

He failed.

Drake kept his voice low and purposeful. 'It was Jim Finch that first implicated Beltrami.' He turned back to face his team. Now he could see incredulity in their eyes.

'Surely you're not suggesting…?' Luned said.

Winder stretched in his chair. 'He was ex-services as well.'

Drake sat down heavily into a chair by the desk. 'He took me to Dawn's body that first morning and he was the first officer on the scene at Caston's house. And he didn't tell us about Dawn and Toft being informants. It didn't suit his agenda for them. And he admitted that she hadn't given him any useful intelligence when I spoke to him.'

Sara made to say something, but Drake raised his hand to prevent her from continuing. 'There's something else that's been niggling on my mind. We went to see him after Olivia Knox's death and his reaction wasn't right. He knew she was dead.'

Sara cleared her throat. 'There's something else, boss. When I spoke to him earlier about O'Brien's mobile numbers he asked about the inquiry. I told him about the video of Dawn finding the drugs in the *Duke of Lancaster*.'

An embarrassed silence gripped the room. She had done nothing wrong. Finch was a fellow officer involved in the case. Drake was on his feet now. 'If he is involved, he must have known about the stash and he and O'Brien panicked thinking we were going to discover it. I've got a call to make. In the meantime, find Jim Finch's home address.'

Back in his office it took Drake a few minutes to find the phone number he needed. It rang a couple of times before Wendy Sutherland answered. 'Do you realise the time?'

'I'm sorry to call so late. I need some background details. You mentioned there had been a drug raid a few years ago, where police officers were implicated in drugs that went missing.'

'What about it?'

'I need more details – who were the officers involved?'

'It's a while back.' Sutherland reeled off the names of an inspector whose career had been shortened by involvement with organised crime groups and two other officers who had left the force.

'Do you remember the names of any of the other

officers?'

'Can't you check the files?'

'It's urgent, Wendy.'

'Jim Finch will know. I'm sure he was one of the officers involved. If you speak to him, I'm sure he can give you more details.'

Drake barely managed a thank you as a cold spasm ran up his back.

Drake jumped to his feet and rushed out into the Incident Room. 'It's time we visited Jim Finch.'

Chapter 46

An hour later, Drake sat in an unmarked vehicle in the car park of a supermarket on the outskirts of Rhuddlan, a small town inland from Rhyl. Conflicting emotions battled for dominance in his mind. A police officer couldn't possibly be involved in the murder of four people although Drake's own experience knew police officers, when pushed, could plumb the depths of human depravity.

A brief conversation with Superintendent Hobbs had sought the authorisation for Finch's personnel file that he had read on the short journey from headquarters. Sara had said little as she drove. It was clear she shared Drake's reservation that a colleague, someone trusted with upholding the law, should have been involved with such heinous crimes. Behind them an unmarked police car waited, its occupants two burly police officers well accustomed to cracking heads in Rhyl on a Saturday night.

Winder's journey to Cameron Toft's flat was longer, which meant Drake and Sara had to wait. Drake powered down the window, allowing the cool evening air to bathe his face. Chatter from the supermarket night duty staff taking a smoking break under a canopy drifted over the car park.

'If Finch is involved, the press are going to have a field day,' Sara said.

She was right. The murders of Piper, Caston and Knox had generated a substantial amount of press interest. Drake read the time. 'Where the hell are Gareth and Luned? They should be there by now.'

Drake tapped on the screen of his mobile and read again the details in Finch's personnel file. He was divorced, no children and lived alone in a bungalow. Failing the inspector's exams on two occasions had meant he was destined to remain a sergeant for the rest of his career. Reading between the lines of the evaluations made by his senior officers, Drake got the impression Finch was difficult to manage.

His mobile rang and he recognised Winder's number. 'We've just parked outside the block of flats, sir.'

Drake glanced over at Sara. 'They've arrived.'

Sara started the engine, switched on the lights and noticed the police car behind her do the same.

They drove off, skirting around the castle, a timid version of the great castles of Edward I along the western coast of Wales, but a reminder of bloody Welsh history, nevertheless. The detached property sat on a corner plot surrounded by older bungalows all running a little shabby. None of the curtains had been drawn and the absence of any lights in any of the rooms made Drake regret not acting sooner. Had Finch already bolted? Sara parked across the entranceway. 'Doesn't look as though anyone is home, sir.'

The police car passed them and pulled up a short distance ahead.

Once Drake and Sara left the car the other two officers joined them.

Drake led the way as they skirted round the garage and gazed in through a window. The vehicle inside had its boot lid open and Drake could see jackets piled on the rear seat. 'It looks like he is planning a journey.'

Sara raised an eyebrow.

At the rear, light seeped through the vertical blinds hanging at a window which Drake guessed was the kitchen from the waste pipes protruding from the wall. He jerked his head for both officers to go round the front. He went up to the rear door and thumped it with his right fist. Sara stood behind him monitoring signs of movement. When he turned to face her, she shook her head.

Gently he pressed the handle. But it was locked.

They returned to the front of the building re-joining the two officers and stood surveying the surrounding properties. A man walking a golden Labrador neared on the opposite side of the street. Knocking on front doors was out of the question but speaking to a possible neighbour late at night was entirely different. Drake strolled over.

'Excuse me, I hope you can help.' Drake smiled before showing his warrant card. 'I'm Detective Inspector Drake and I'm trying to contact Sergeant Finch. We were told he'd be in this evening. He might have slipped out. I don't suppose you have any idea where he might be?'

The man glanced over at Sara and the two officers. Drake hoped his explanation would be enough to satisfy the man's curiosity. 'I can't say I know him that well. He keeps himself to himself.' There was a pause and Drake contemplated seriously the option of hammering on every door in the street demanding to know if anyone had seen Jim Finch that evening. But the man continued. 'Is it something hush-hush?'

Drake nodded conspiratorially.

'Have you tried his allotment? It's a bit late for that though.'

Drake's tried to sound casual. 'Well, we could try it, I suppose, on the off chance. Do you know where it is?'

Once he finished giving directions Drake jogged over to his car yelling at the uniformed officers to follow him. En route Winder called.

'We've spoken to Toft. He's been with Jamie all day and this evening he's been with his girlfriend. We've spoken to the social worker as well. His alibi for tonight checks out.'

Drake turned to Sara. 'Toft has an alibi.' It removed the last vestiges of doubt about Finch.

Parking near the entrance of the allotment gardens would make the marked police car utterly conspicuous, so Drake called the uniformed officers, telling the driver to find somewhere less obvious to park. Drake and Sara left the car and pushed open a small gate that opened onto a gravelled path. The soles of his shoes crunched against the fine stones as he searched urgently for any sign of activity.

The allotment gardens were divided into higgledy-piggledy lots. Potato plants pushed their way through earth banked against their early growth and courgette leaves tumbled over the edges of raised banks constructed from railway sleepers. Through the window of a shiplapped shed all Drake could see were tools. Sara took a path to his right that doubled back and rejoined Drake after a few yards. Another makeshift building had a wooden patio area constructed outside, where a round metal table and two rusty chairs had centre stage. But it was empty too.

Drake paused for a moment and looked around, hoping he might see some sign of activity and worried this was a complete waste of time. He heard the sound of wood splintering from the far corner and he nodded at Sara. They jogged down the path and were rewarded by seeing a light streaming out of the window of a shed.

Somebody was walking around inside. He could hear footsteps on floorboards.

Drake put a finger to his mouth in a gesture that he and Sara be quiet. He tiptoed round the edges of the path avoiding any sound of his footsteps on the gravel. The surface became grass as he neared the shed and within a few more steps he yanked open the door and burst inside followed by Sara.

Jim Finch turned to face him.

'What the fuck…?'

Behind Finch on a table was a stash of a dozen, maybe more, equal sized packages in brown paper carefully duct-taped together.

'How the hell did you find me?'

Underneath the table were lengths of timber that had been removed from the floor. Finch had a convenient hiding place for the stash piled on the table.

'James Finch, I am arresting you on suspicion of murder and of possession with intent to supply of controlled drugs. You do not have to say anything…'

Finch didn't reply. He reached a hand over behind the

packages on the table and produced a handgun that he pointed at Drake. 'Shut up. Don't say a fucking thing.'

He gestured with the pistol for Sara to sit on a plastic chair in one corner. Drake calculated how quickly he could reach Finch. Sara did as she was told and it took Finch's attention as he pointed the gun in her direction. A second later there was a loud tapping on the window to Finch's right and he jerked the gun towards it firing as he did so. The sound of glass smashing filled the shed and Drake took his chance. He threw himself at Finch like a rugby player heading for the try line. He smashed into Finch throwing both their bodies against the side panel of the shed that groaned under their weight. Finch fumbled to regain the upper hand, lashing out at Drake with his left hand. It connected with Drake's face and he winced in pain. He sensed a figure alongside them. One of the uniformed police officers fell on Finch's right arm knocking the gun out of his hand before directing a punch that knocked Finch unconscious.

Chapter 47

In the early hours of the following morning, Drake arrived home and slipped into the warm bed alongside Annie. She mumbled an acknowledgement. He had considered staying in a hotel overnight, knowing that the next day would bring a frantic round of activity. Driving along the coast he had yawned vigorously and briefly contemplated parking and sleeping for a few minutes, but he wound down the window and found a playlist on iTunes of rock music that filled the car with noise.

After five hours' sleep, he heard Annie's alarm and the sound of her moving in the bed. She silenced the clock and Drake slid back into a doze. He could hear movement around the house, a boiling kettle, a running tap but he was also asleep somehow. Annie returned with coffee and sat on the edge of the bed.

'What time did you get back last night?'

'Late.'

'What happened?'

'It's finished.' Drake reached over and sipped a mouthful of hot coffee. 'The inquiry is over.' Despite only a few hours' sleep he felt refreshed: certain in the knowledge that Jim Finch was behind bars enjoying the hospitality of the Wales Police Service.

'I'm glad.' Annie leaned down and kissed him on the lips.

'It's going to be a busy couple of days.'

Annie nodded and smiled. 'At least you'll be finished by the time we go on holiday. Helen and Megan were worried.'

'You didn't tell me.'

'There was nothing you could have done, and I didn't want to worry you.'

Annie left, announcing she would make breakfast.

Drake's mobile bleeped with messages as soon as he

switched it on. Search teams in Jim Finch's property had discovered his packed suitcases and the tickets booked using a fake passport on the ferry from Hull to Rotterdam. Drake didn't need the result of a preliminary field test to tell them that the packages they recovered from Finch's allotment were substantial amounts of Class A controlled drugs – heroin and crack cocaine.

Once fuelled with a cooked breakfast, a rare luxury, Drake hugged Annie and promised to be back promptly that evening: knowing he'd be able to keep the promise. He switched the phone off as he drove to headquarters, enjoying the silence and the opportunity to plan the interview with Jim Finch.

Perhaps Finch would decide to make a 'no comment' interview, challenging the police to do their worst, build the evidence hoping there'd be a chance he hadn't left enough forensics to tie him incontrovertibly to the murder of Ritchie O'Brien. Finch's travel arrangements all suggested he believed he could make good his escape.

Sara and Winder and Luned had been building a picture of Jim Finch. They had cajoled and demanded information from financial institutions and by mid-morning Drake sat in the Incident Room listening to Sara.

'Finch has a major gambling habit. He maxed out his credit cards, is up to the limit of his overdraft and has re-mortgaged the house three times. And we found evidence that he bought property in Bulgaria, in the same area where Ritchie O'Brien owns a block of flats. We haven't been able to trace the deposits into Finch's bank account.'

'O'Brien?'

'It will take some time. And a lot of the deposits were in cash.'

'Impossible to trace.'

Sara nodded.

Winder sounded jubilant. 'The possible eyewitness from the burger van made a positive video identification of

Finch this morning.'

Drake smiled. 'Excellent. You've done really well to get that organised so quickly.'

Winder preened himself. 'It was a team effort, boss.'

Luned gave a bashful smile, adding, 'And one of the mobiles we recovered from his house and the allotments is the mystery number we thought belonged to O'Brien.'

Drake nodded at Sara. 'Let's go and talk to forensics.'

They left the Incident Room and threaded their way through the corridors to Mike Foulds' lab.

'I still can't believe it's Jim Finch.' Foulds shook his head in disbelief.

'Were you able to match Finch's gun to the bullet that killed Ritchie O'Brien?' Drake said.

Now Foulds nodded. 'Oh, yes. The pistol is SIG Sauer P226 which is standard issue in the British Army. They were purchased as an interim measure when the army was engaged in Afghanistan. I've heard before that quite a few went missing. My guess is that Jim Finch probably did a tour in Afghanistan. We matched the bullet that killed Finch to the pistol.'

'We have an eyewitness who places him in the park with Knox on the night she was killed.'

'I've got the results of DNA from the cigarette stub this morning and I've run an analysis against Finch's DNA taken last night and it's a match.'

Drake drew a slow smile while Sara covered her mouth with a hand and gasped.

Foulds continued. 'He was there, at the scene, when Dawn was killed.'

It meant enough evidence to charge for two murders.

By late morning Drake had spoken with Superintendent Hobbs after preparing the detailed briefing memorandum his superior officer expected. Wyndham Price called him to express exasperation and disgust in equal measure that one of their own had been responsible for the death of Ritchie

O'Brien. Price barely skipped a beat when he added, 'And the world will be a better place without the bastard.'

Drake arrived at the area custody suite and found an empty office where he spread out on a table the summaries, notes and paper work. Had Finch ever visited the Incident Room late in the evening? Taking the opportunity to scan the board, rummage through the desks.

Sara joined him with a chilled bottle of water each. They settled down to prepare for the interview.

Drake entered the small airless room. Jim Finch was dressed in a one-piece white paper suit – all his clothes now in the possession of Mike Foulds and his team. Tony Peters, a solicitor from one of the specialist criminal firms Drake crossed swords with regularly, sat next to his client. His double cuffed white shirt had been ironed to within an inch of its life, a pristine silk tie knotted precisely to the collar.

Drake addressed Peters. 'Good afternoon, Tony. How are you?'

'Fair to middling.'

'Let's get started then.'

Once the tapes had been securely fitted into the recorder sitting on the table but screwed to the wall, Drake began.

'Do you know why you're here?'

'Of course I do.' Finch sounded even tempered, calm.

It caught Drake initially off guard. He had anticipated Finch would be stubborn, awkward.

'I'm investigating the murders of Dawn Piper, Hubert Caston and Olivia Knox.'

'Yes, I know, I know. You can cut out all that preliminary introductory stuff.'

Drake frowned, glanced at Sara. She had a troubled look on her face as he cleared his throat. He never asked a suspect right at the beginning of an interview whether they had killed this or that victim. He enjoyed the task of building an interview using all the evidence until the suspect had no choice but to confess.

Drake leaned back in his chair. 'Did you kill Dawn Piper?'

'Of course not. Ritchie O'Brien did. She had a video that implicated him in the drug dealing activities in Deeside and she threatened to go to the police. But she was an addict and he fed her addiction. Every time she tried to shake him off, he played her like a fish on a fly – allowing her a little bit of freedom and then reeling her back in. She was a sad case.'

'Spare us the sanctimonious bullshit.'

The last comment earned Drake a reproachful glare from Peters. 'Let's move on, Inspector.'

Drake smiled at Peters. 'Let's move on to the murder of Ritchie O'Brien.'

Drake produced the image of the gun used to kill O'Brien and slid it over the table.

'We recovered this pistol from your allotment. It is the weapon used to kill O'Brien. Why did you kill him?'

'It was time.'

'What the hell do you mean, *time*?'

'Time for him to move on. He'd been around too long.'

Drake consulted the notes on his desk. 'You were involved in the raid on a premises two years ago when it is believed an amount of Class A controlled drugs went missing?'

Finch nodded his head before Drake finished asking the question. 'It was too good an opportunity to miss. When I was in the army, I saw my mates at home getting high. And they spent all their money on coke or heroin. I needed some extra cash.'

'You were gambling heavily,' Drake added.

Finch nodded, clearly assuming they'd accessed his full financial records. 'Some of the drugs saw their way onto the streets of Deeside courtesy of Mr Ritchie O'Brien and I did very well out of it, thank you very much.'

Sara butted in. 'Don't you know how much misery is caused by drugs? Six people have overdosed in the last six months alone.'

'Not my problem. If your average Joe wants to inject stuff into his veins or sniff it up his nose, that's his choice.'

'How did Ritchie O'Brien fit into all this?' Drake asked.

'He was expendable.'

'Expendable?'

'Yeah, I couldn't see any future to our business relationship. He had killed Piper and Caston and Knox. He was… dangerous.'

Drake sat back in his chair for a moment. How the hell did someone like this end up as a police officer? The prisons were full of drug dealers who took the risks associated with their lifestyle as an occupational hazard. Finch was taking this approach to a new level of depravity. His life inside would be protected as a vulnerable prisoner, shielded from the day-to-day assaults and hostility from ordinary prisoners. But he'd still be in jail, for at least fifteen years, maybe longer.

'Was it your idea to ram Sian off the road?'

Finch shook his head. 'O'Brien told me he'd organised that after it happened. It was a stupid thing to do. You were getting too close and he thought he could get you transferred off the case.'

Finch even managed a sympathetic look. If he asked after Sian and the girls, Drake might reach over the table and throttle Finch. Luckily for Drake and Finch he didn't.

Finch was playing the system. Betting that he'd only face a single murder charge and that cooperating early in the process would give him a credit when he was sentenced. At least he was being practical, Drake thought. How practical would he be once he had seen the rest of their evidence?

'Let's turn to the death of Dawn Piper. Where were you on the night she was killed?'

'That's easy. I was in the IMAX cinema in Chester. I was watching the latest Star Wars film. You should check out their CCTV.'

'What time was the showing?'

'It was after eleven. I'd been working a late shift.'

Finch had his alibi all ready and neatly packaged. Drake nodded at Sara. She scribbled on her notepad.

'And Hubert Caston took a phone call from somebody he knew on the afternoon he was killed.'

'I know, you told me.' Finch managed a smile – or was it a smirk? – that riled Drake. Finch continued. 'And before you ask, it wasn't me who phoned him. It was Ritchie O'Brien. Surely you realise that O'Brien was responsible for all the deaths.'

Drake crossed his arms pulled tight towards his chest. He wasn't listening to a confession it was more of a conversation.

'Can you account for your movements on the evening Hubert Caston was killed?' Drake dictated the correct date.

'I was at home.' Finch made it sound the most reasonable, normal thing in the world. 'Ritchie had been to see him that afternoon. Apparently, Hubert had thrown in his lot with Paul Kenny. That Scouser promised to pay the arrears of his mortgage and fifty per cent more than what Ritchie was paying him.'

'So what happened?'

'Hubert was a bit simple. It was unwise to try and get more money out of Ritchie. He didn't like that. Not one single bit.'

'Did Ritchie O'Brien tell you what he intended to do?'

'Not a chance, Ian. There's not a chance I'm going to give you the evidence that I was involved in some joint venture with Ritchie O'Brien to kill three people. I knew nothing about that.' Now Finch's voice was hard. He had seen Drake's question coming. Finch would know that a person involved in a joint venture to kill three people could just as easily face a murder charge as the person who held the knife or pulled the trigger. At least it had the effect of stopping Finch's pretence of charm and good-natured civility.

'Let's go back to Dawn Piper. When did you see her last?'

'I can't remember.'

'And have you ever been to Olivia Knox's home?'

'No. I've no idea where she lived.'

'And when did you see her last?'

'Ages ago. I cannot remember.'

Drake sat back – three lies in a row. The interview couldn't have gone more smoothly. Finch thought they were completely incompetent.

Drake let out a brief sigh. 'Let's see if you can help us with these details. We recovered a mobile from your property.' Drake glanced at Sara who read out the number and showed a photograph of the handset. 'Does it belong to you?'

'Don't know.'

For the first time uncertainty.

'Simple question, Jim. Is it yours?'

'Yeah, suppose.'

Finch's control of the situation slipped out of his grasp.

Several more pieces of paper were shuffled over the desk. 'These are the logs of calls made on the mobile recovered from your property. It shows various calls to the numbers of Dawn Piper, Hubert Caston and Olivia Knox.'

'Don't know anything about that.' Finch paused, gathering his thoughts then feigning forgetfulness. 'I remember, Ritchie borrowed it a while back.'

'Really.'

Sara took over as agreed. 'I'd like you to look at this exhibit.' She pushed across the table a photograph of the cigarette stub. 'This was found in the gravel at the end of Cleveland Avenue. Traces of your DNA were found on it.

Cleveland Avenue is where Olivia Knox lived. How do you account for it being there?'

Drake looked for the tell-tale signs that Finch was frightened but he didn't spot any rapid blinking or tightening of the shoulders. He had launched a lie and was keeping fast to it.

Peters responded, 'It was found in the gravel, you say. In the street. Where is that taking you?'

'At the same location a watch belonging to Dawn was recovered. It has positively been identified as hers by a family member.'

Finch shook his head and Peters stared at Sara who continued. 'At the scene we discovered traces of blood that match the DNA of Dawn Piper. We believe that she was on her way to see Olivia Knox and that she was murdered near her home at the top of the path that leads onto Cleveland Avenue. Your DNA on the cigarette places you at the scene. Why did you kill Dawn Piper?'

Finch leaned over and whispered something to Peters. Moments later the solicitor announced, 'We shall need to see the entire evidence chain before we can respond. The possibility of contamination cannot be ruled out.'

'And you put on a right performance when you took me to see her body. You even made yourself sick – fingers down the throat was it?'

Drake glanced at Sara and nodded for her to continue.

'You've lied to us consistently today, Jim. You were present when Dawn was killed, and you were with Olivia Knox on the night she was murdered too. An eyewitness confirms seeing you with her earlier in the evening in her car in the parking ground at the other end of the park where she was killed.'

Finch crossed his arms, a tightness evident on his jaw and neck.

Drake cut in. 'You've lied throughout this interview hoping to put the blame for the murders of Dawn Piper and

Olivia Knox entirely on Ritchie O'Brien. Instead the opposite is true. You were jointly responsible for their deaths. Do you have anything you wish to say?'

Finch pushed up his shoulder and jutted out his chest. 'No fucking comment.'

Chapter 48

Two days after Drake had finished the last of the interviews with Finch, he entered Superintendent Hobbs' office and was met by Wyndham Price who got up from his chair and stretched out a hand shaking Drake's warmly. Superintendent Hobbs appeared wrongfooted by the display of emotion. Drake stared for a moment at Price's short-sleeved patterned shirt: a strong check of yellows and blues. Drake couldn't recall ever having seen his superior officer dressed casually before. It made Hobbs' grey suit and matching grey tie seem greyer somehow. Hobbs hadn't taken off his jacket, despite the warm August temperatures.

'Well done, all of your team did exceptionally well. They all deserve congratulations,' Price said.

'Thank you, sir.'

Drake pulled out a chair and sat alongside Wyndham Price and across from Superintendent Hobbs around the well-polished table in Hobbs's office. Its position was unfamiliar – Hobbs had made a statement by moving the furniture around. Drake would have to get accustomed to the new layout and, hopefully, working with a new superintendent.

Hannah appeared with a cafetière of coffee and a set of china cups and saucers the senior management of Northern Division kept for important meetings. They didn't have to wait long until Andy Thorsen, the Senior Crown Prosecutor, joined them. The lawyer would get on just fine with Hobbs, Drake thought, knowing Thorsen was a man of few words and even less personality.

No matter what decisions were made in the meeting, Drake was leaving after lunch. He had promised Annie that he wouldn't be late home. A colleague of Annie's had arranged to take them for a ride in his RIB on the Menai Strait before returning for an evening meal in the pub near her home.

Thorsen registered no surprise seeing Wyndham Price. He simply nodded an acknowledgement adding a single 'good morning'.

Wyndham Price poured coffee for everyone unselfconsciously as though he was still in charge. Drake reached over for his cup and saucer. The coffee was good, strong and clean tasting.

Hobbs cleared his throat. 'Let's get on, shall we?'

Reviewing the evidence in a multiple murder case was always a multi-layered activity involving lawyers, senior police officers and occasionally specialist barristers from outside the force.

Hobbs continued. 'The evidence is clear that Finch was at the scene of Dawn Piper's death and his alibi was deliberately evasive.'

CCTV had placed Finch at the IMAX, as he alleged, but careful analysis of the time and distance made it feasible for him to travel to the cinema and be present with O'Brien when they killed Dawn.

Thorsen made his first comment. 'The DNA evidence in the cigarette stub and the pattern of his mobile usage makes a compelling case for him to be charged with her murder.'

Thorsen fiddled with the papers open on the table in front of him before turning to Drake. 'You believed from your initial inquiries that Jack Beltrami was a clear suspect for the murder of Olivia Knox because he had been with her that night. Is there anything to suggest that Jim Finch was one of her… *friends*?'

Drake took a mouthful of coffee before replying. 'We've searched through all the contacts Knox had on her mobile and through the Internet dating site she used and we didn't get any link to Jim Finch.'

Thorsen again. 'And did you get the same result from Jim Finch's social media activity?'

Drake nodded. 'The eyewitness is the most compelling evidence we have that Finch met Olivia on the night she was killed.'

'And the mobile usage,' Hobbs added.

Thorsen now. 'All the evidence clearly points to Finch and O'Brien being involved in a conspiracy to protect their drug dealing empire. Dawn and Knox had become a threat to that. The videos are clear evidence as are the efforts of both women to curtail their activity. Finch's involvement cost them their lives.'

The officers in the room relaxed collectively as the Crown Prosecution lawyer summarised their thoughts. The CPS had to approve every charge. Drake held his breath as he waited for Thorsen to continue.

'Finch's risible attempt to confess to O'Brien's murder, presumably hoping for maximum credit before the sentencing judge only exposes the depth of his evil nature.'

Serious nods around the room now.

Thorsen carried on. 'We charge him with the conspiracy to murder Dawn Piper and Olivia Knox and Hubert Caston.' Thorsen glanced from one face to another. 'All three. Finch needs to be locked up for a long time.'

Chapter 49

Drake had replaced the photograph of his daughters on the desk with a new one taken in Disneyland Paris. All four of them beamed at the camera and every day since his return from their holiday he had lingered for a few precious seconds as he recalled the pleasure of relaxing with his children and Annie.

A week had elapsed since Finch had appeared at the Crown Court in Mold. Finch had ignored Drake when he entered the dock and when he left, after being sentenced to four life sentences with a minimum tariff of twenty-four years. It probably meant he'd spend at least thirty behind bars. If he ever was released, he'd be a very old man.

That morning a report from the Merseyside Police had reached his desk. In due course it would be filed away with the rest of the papers involving Jim Finch. Drake read the details from the officer who handled the prosecution of Paul Kenny for modern-day slavery. Debbie and Tina's evidence that he had initially trafficked them into Deeside made the case against him compelling. O'Brien had been responsible for abducting them from Caston's home once he had realised Kenny posed a threat to his business. Now he was starting a ten-year sentence. The hotel business was being sold and a specialist unit involved in recovering the profits from criminal activity were trying to identify all his assets. Although the drug supply network would be damaged, others would take it over. It meant a constant battle to identify the main players and build evidence against them.

Reading the details of Debbie and Tina brought a smile to his face. They had been placed into a long-term fostering family who had experience of dealing with damaged youngsters. It reminded him that Jane Piper had applied to adopt Jamie. It would be a long and slow process, but the child deserved to be part of a loving family.

Mid-morning, Sara offered to make coffee and Drake

accepted. He joined her in the Incident Room – quiet now, the board had been dismantled. Winder and Luned were on a course in Wrexham.

Drake plunged the cafetière and sipped on his drink. Sara was mastering making coffee as he liked it.

'Did I tell you about Mrs Beltrami?'

Drake raised a quizzical eyebrow. 'No?'

'She's divorcing Jack, and she's hired a firm of aggressive family lawyers. She's going to take him to the cleaners.'

'Couldn't happen to a nicer guy.'

Sara asked if Annie was looking forward to the party that evening. Drake enquired about her training for the Bangor 10k and Half Marathon run at the beginning of October. They finished their coffee, killing time, making small talk.

Back in his office he gave the papers on his desk the briefest of guilty glances and decided that everything could wait until Monday. That evening he'd be attending Wyndham Price's retirement party, so he had to leave promptly to change and collect Annie. He grabbed the morning's newspaper, open at the sudoku puzzle – some things need not change after all.

In reception, a crowd of dignitaries, including the new Assembly Member of the seat Councillor Beedham had contested, milled around. They paid him no attention and Drake wondered if Beedham had been invited. Losing his deposit, having failed to get five per cent of the vote, had been humiliating. Somehow Drake doubted it would shut him up for long.

Drake curled his arm around Annie's waist as she stood by the hall mirror checking her hair and make-up one last time. 'You look fabulous.'

She turned and drew a hand over his cheek before kissing him on his lips. 'Thanks.'

Her short cocktail dress was a warm pearl pink and the scalloped-edged neckline and the cap sleeves let the tan on her arms glow. There was nothing modest about her heels, making her legs look shapely. Her dark auburn hair glistened – she looked healthy and the warmth and intensity he had seen when he first met her filled her eyes.

She reached up and adjusted the tie he had carefully knotted against the collar of the new white shirt. The navy suit he had chosen for Wyndham Price's retirement party hadn't been worn for some time. 'We need to leave – we don't want to be late.'

During the journey from Felinheli to Llandudno they shared reminiscences of the holiday in Disneyland Paris. Watching Helen and Megan enjoy themselves helped Drake believe that they had been able to put behind them the recent events. After the first couple of days, both his daughters appeared more relaxed with Annie, and she with them. They shared a joke, listened to her when she made suggestions about what they could or couldn't do. At the end of the holiday Drake felt that he and Annie had turned a corner in their relationship with his daughters.

He indicated off the A55 and drove through Deganwy and then on into the centre of Llandudno. He parked not far from the five-star hotel where Wyndham Price's retirement do was being held. Annie threaded her hand through Drake's arm as they strolled over to the hotel. They followed the signs to the ballroom on the first floor. At the entrance, Drake scanned the tables set out along the perimeter of the room. To one side a bar was busy and Wyndham Price stood with his wife talking with Superintendent Wemyss from Western Division. When Price saw Drake, he walked over bringing his wife in tow.

'Good to see you, Ian.'

'And you, sir.'

'You can stop all that, sir, business.' Price pushed out a hand. 'We can drop the formality now. Call me Wyndham.'

Price gave Annie a discreet all over scan. 'You must be Annie.' Price smiled. Annie offered him a hand.

Calling Price Wyndham would feel strange, unfamiliar. It would be something Drake had to get used to. Perhaps the superintendent, retired superintendent, would call in at headquarters occasionally, catch up with former colleagues.

'This is my wife,' Price said. 'Elizabeth.'

Once introductions had been completed, Price turned to Annie. 'I'm sure this recent case must have been a cause of worry. It wasn't easy. Ian and his team had a great result.'

Price and his wife drifted over to talk to an assistant chief constable from Cardiff who Drake knew from a previous investigation. She gave him a brief nod of acknowledgement. Drake organised glasses of wine for himself and Annie and they mingled. She managed small talk effortlessly and Drake basked in the reflected attention she received. Sara was the first to complement her: 'I love your dress.'

Annie responded warmly to Sara's interest and luckily the seating plan had provided for them to be at the same table. Sara rearranging the name cards ensured that both women sat together. The hotel staff quickly served a three-course meal and speeches followed. Assistant Chief Constable Neary from Cardiff made complimentary comments about Wyndham Price's career with the Wales Police Service wishing him every happiness and success in his retirement. She was followed by Superintendent Wemyss from Western Division who shared jokes and nostalgic recollections about their antics as young trainee officers.

Finally, Price got to his feet and his voice trembled as he thanked the senior officers of the Wales Police Service. He also had a special thanks to all the junior officers in Northern Division who had worked with him. Drake warmed to this vulnerable side to Wyndham Price.

After a resounding round of applause, the guests adjourned back to the bar as the alcohol loosened their tongues, lessened inhibitions. Superintendent Hobbs made his way over towards Drake, a small, dumpy woman in a cheap-looking dress following behind him. Drake was convinced he was wearing the same grey suit that he usually wore to work.

'Inspector,' Hobbs said, 'we're just leaving.' He gave a brief nod of acknowledgement to Annie after Drake introduced her. 'Don't forget our meeting on Monday morning to review the latest statistics.'

'Of course, sir.'

Hobbs replied with a weak smile before leaving, his wife trailing behind him.

'Is that your new boss?' Annie whispered.

'Yes.'

'He's not very nice, is he?'

Drake took Annie's hand. Working with Superintendent David Hobbs meant facing new challenges. He had become so accustomed to Wyndham Price that having a new superior officer might be daunting. But with Annie by his side he was ready to face anything.

Made in the USA
Coppell, TX
05 June 2020

26953619R00177